KEN K

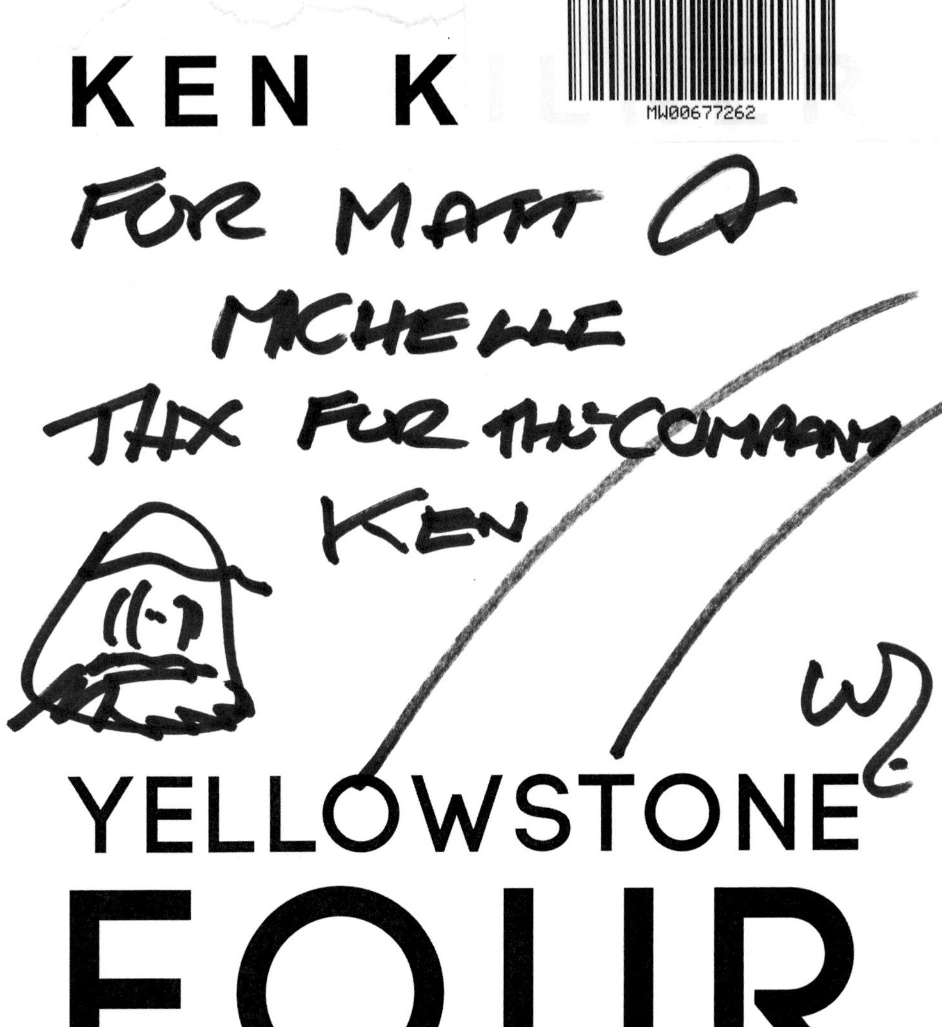

FOR MATT &
MICHELLE
THX FOR THE COMPANY
KEN

MW00677262

YELLOWSTONE FOUR

Horrifying and Hilarious
A disrespectful novel about
The end of all life as we know it

Publisher: Expert Subjects, LLC
4775 Collins Avenue, suite 3206
Miami Beach, FL 33140

Disclaimer: This is a work of fiction. Names, characters, places, and incidents, either are the product of the author's imagination, or are used fictitiously, and any resemblance to actual persons, living or dead, business establishments, events or locales, is entirely coincidental. The publisher does not have any control over and does not assume any responsibility for author or third party websites or their content.

Yellowstone Four

An Expert Subjects' book, published by
agreement with the author

Copyright © 2014 by
Ken Kilner.

All rights reserved.
No part of this book may be reproduced, scanned or distrubuted in any printed or electronic form without permission.

ISBN 978-0-9886765-4-1

Printed in the United States of America
Cover Design by Jason Alexander

Expert Subjects, LLC

Among the many and various doomsday scenarios we fret about, perhaps the most imminent, and certainly the most horrifying to contemplate, is the forthcoming eruption of Yellowstone National Park. Three previous eruptions have taken place at intervals of six hundred thousand years. Number three happened 640,000 years ago. So you might say number four is overdue. There is widespread agreement among those in the know that Yellowstone Four (Y4, if you must) will be an extinction event of global proportions. Few living things will survive.

For all of us

CHAPTER 1

Visitation

Saturday June 20, 2026

God came to Jesús Maria Martinez around midday on his thirty-third birthday. This was two months or so before humankind woke up to some really bad news, namely the imminent eruption of the mega volcano commonly known as Yellowstone National Park. God had the neat, decisive demeanor of a retired NASA administrator (not surprisingly as it turned out). As is often the case, the appearance of the Almighty did not bode well for his chosen one.

Jesús had just finished a forty-mile bike ride along Seattle's Burke-Gilman and Sammamish River trails. The temperature hovered in the mid eighties. Relative humidity was miniscule. A cooling breeze wafted in from Puget Sound. Above, the sky was a picture-perfect blue, with contented little patches of cumulus scattered here and there. All about were the quiet murmurs and forest scents of late spring. He was happily strapping his bike—a twelve pound marvel made entirely from ultra-compacted Styrofoam—to the back of his compressed air drive Toyota Homelander/GM, and thoroughly immersed in the surrounding pleasantness, when God tapped him on the shoulder.

Jesús was startled by the sudden appearance of the other man. Seconds ago the trail had been empty in both directions. "Can I help you?" he asked warily, no longer hearing the forest murmurs—as if someone had thrown a switch.

"Well, yes, actually you can," said God. "May we sit in your vehicle while we talk, though? It's nice enough out here, but I don't tolerate the heat so well these days."

God's handshake was firm. His hand wasn't the least bit clammy, and he flashed a smile that reminded Jesús of a past president. The face was there, but he couldn't quite recall the name. Then it came to him: the old man looked like Jimmy Carter. In fact, he could have sworn he *was* Jimmy Carter.

Jesús glanced at the man's pockets, looking for some sign of a weapon. Then he chided himself for being over cautious. What could go wrong? He had to be less than half the age of his visitor, twice as strong, and four times as fast on his feet. "Sure," he said, "let me finish strapping on the bike and I'll be right there. I don't have conventional air conditioning, though, just a solar powered sensor and micro-cooling fan, so it might not be as cold as you're used to."

"I should have known," murmured God.

"I'm sorry," said Jesús, who had turned back to the bike, "I didn't quite catch that."

"Don't mind me," replied God in a brisk voice. "It's just that at my age it's sometimes hard to keep track of new trends."

As soon as they were settled, God opened the conversation. "I approached you, so it's my nickel. You were surprised to see me here, weren't you? You didn't think there was anyone else around."

"Well, no, I didn't," Jesús said. "As a matter of fact, I'm glad you mentioned that, because I'm still wondering."

The passenger gazed thoughtfully out of the window for several moments before speaking. When he turned, he was grave—Joyful Jimmy no more. "There's no easy way to say this, Jesús, so I'll come right out with it. I am the being you would normally refer to as God."

Never having dealt with a mad person before, Jesús told himself to be calm, conciliatory, and above all very, very alert. "No shit!" he remarked casually. "Listen, why don't I just start the car and we can talk while I drive. Just let me know where you live and I'll be happy to drop you off." He couldn't look the other man in the eye. He wasn't so much afraid as embarrassed this could be happening to *him—on his birthday*. Some old frigging lunatic climbing into his Toyota, claiming to be the Almighty, and using his name for Chrissake! And now he is having trouble getting the key in the ignition, because that part of his brain responsible for muscle memory really is afraid and is suddenly screaming at his nervous system, "Get Out! Get Out! Now!"

"I'll prove it. Watch this," God said, flashing his Jimmy Carter smile. Then he disappeared. Ten seconds later he was back.

While God was gone, Jesús knocked his head against the steering wheel four times in slow succession. After each encounter with the wheel, he stared uncomprehendingly at the empty passenger seat. God showed up just as he was about to bump his head for the fifth time.

"So," God said, "now do you believe me?"

Jesús froze in mid bump, his mind struggling to decide which was scarier: God vanishing, or God showing up out of nowhere; either way, he was definitely convinced. Clearly, he was in the presence of a superior being. His mouth was suddenly dry, wanting to choke on words, but he managed to croak what he hoped was an acceptable response. "Okay, now I believe you, but why me, er, Lord?"

"It's a bit complicated," God said, "and I will definitely explain later. In case you're wondering, though, it has nothing to do with you being called Jesús. That part is pure coincidence. By the way, do I remind you of someone?"

"Yes," Jesús said, "as a matter of fact you're the spitting image of Jimmy Carter."

God was clearly relieved. "Thank heaven for that," he said. "I never really know who I'm going to be, so it can be a bit unnerving at times."

Then Jesús listened in astonished silence as God explained in measured tones that Yellowstone National Park was about to erupt for the fourth time: an event that would make Mount Saint Helens seem like a puff on a cheap cigar.

"Six months from now? Are you sure?"

God nodded soberly. "I'm God—sure I'm sure. Well, give-or-take a month or two anyway. I wasn't here the last time something like this happened, so I can't be a hundred percent certain how much warning we might get. Also, language hadn't really gotten started back then, so they could hardly have written down the details."

Jesús squeezed the steering wheel so hard, sweat from his palms trickled down the rim. "Why not stop it? And why wait until we've got just six months before telling anyone, for God's sake!" He couldn't help the sacrilege; it just came out.

If God noticed, he didn't show it. Instead, he let out a faint sigh of exasperation. "Listen, Jesús, there are some laws even I must obey, chief among them being the laws of the Universe."

Jesús didn't respond; he was still trying to absorb the news. His first reaction to the vanishing trick had been a creeping mental numbness. Now, the numbness was wearing off and his brain was desperately seeking denial.

"The fact is," God continued, "we have better sensors and forecasting techniques, so we can see a little farther down the road than you guys. But we can't control nature. When that magma decides to blow nothing will stop it, and it certainly won't consult with me first. I *can* tell you this, though: it will defintely be the end of all life as you know it."

"So what the hell do you expect me to do about it?" Jesús was almost relieved at his sudden burst of anger. Except that it wasn't anger, it was the first wave of a gathering tide of terror rising up from somewhere beneath his knees.

God gave him a kindly look. "During this difficult time I will want you to act as my representative here on Earth."

"What?" Jesús protested. "You mean like the second son of God or something?"

"In a word, yes, although had things worked out differently you would be number three."

By now, Jesús was grappling with more than he could reasonably be expected to handle. But he pressed on, hoping this might turn out to be one of those lucid dreams, where you know you're dreaming but can't quite figure out how to wake up.

"What do you mean, number three? What happened to number two?"

"He did quite well for himself, as a matter of fact, but I made a serious miscalculation. I said he could have free will and, boy, did he take me at my word. In the end, we went our separate ways. I didn't acknowledge him and he certainly never acknowledged me."

"Anyone I might know, like somebody famous?"

"Oh, yes," God muttered, looking uncomfortable. "Ever hear of Genghis Khan?"

"Excuse me," Jesús said, "but I have to say something. Just don't hold it against me, will you?"

God reached across and patted Jesús on the knee. "That's okay my boy," he said in a fatherly voice. "Whatever it is, just get it off your chest."

"*Holy-mother-of-Christ!*" Jesús screamed, and immediately felt better.

God, on the other hand, was clearly displeased. "You know," he said, "technically, I am not allowed to regard that sort of thing as blasphemy, but that doesn't mean I have to like it."

"I'm sorry, I just had to let go. All of this is just too much. I almost feel like I want to cry."

"Listen, if it will help, before we get down to the nitty-gritty, so to speak, I'll be more than happy to arrange for you to talk with number one son." Then God was Jimmy Carter again, beaming with the joyful enthusiasm of a recently beatified saint. "You know what? I am *really* taken with that idea. How about it? You want to meet Jesus?"

"No!" Jesús answered emphatically. "I already know what he thinks. Get me Genghis Khan."

"No problem," God said, "we'll be in touch." Then he was gone.

CHAPTER 2

Genghis Khan and Jesus One

For a thirty-three-year-old single male with close to zero time off from his job, yard work is not an attractive proposition. Nor are housework, remodeling, roof repair, home decor, and anything else remotely associated with ladders, vacuum cleaners, and power tools. Thus, in common with many of his urban fellows, Jesús Maria Martinez lived a life of Spartan simplicity and maximum convenience. His apartment was no bigger than it needed to be: one bedroom; one bathroom; one living room; one kitchen; and one sort of work area—cum dining nook—extending off the living room—which, incidentally is where he kept the refrigerator. Furnishings were likewise minimal: one massively upholstered brown fabric recliner squatting in front of the TV, a stylish Scandinavian futon bought for the overnight guests he never had, a green leather settee across from the futon, a dinette table and four chairs, a computer workstation, and an anonymous chest of drawers opposite the bed.

Jesús had expected the Khan to materialize out of thin air, rather like God. Instead, an hour after he returned from his bike ride, the doorbell rang. When he opened the door, the two of them were standing there like Mormon missionaries: all guiltless smiles and suspiciously firm handshakes. Ominously, they were carrying overnight bags.

He had generously offered the recliner to Genghis Khan. Jesus One, who had opted to come along for the ride, was relaxing on the futon sipping from a glass of Mike's Super Hard lemonade.

One thing seemed fairly odd.

"So, how come you have a Scottish accent?" Jesús asked the Khan.

The Khan pointed to Jesus One. "That would be his fault. You ever see the movie, *Braveheart?*"

"I don't think so. It was probably before my time."

"No matter. The point is, *Braveheart* was about a Scotsman called William Wallace who sacrificed himself for the clans. He was a wild-eyed bastard too—right up my alley."

The Khan drank generously from a coffee mug filled with Columbia Vineyards Merlot, spilling a goodly portion down the front of his robe. "So, Mister Sensitivity here kept going on about how bad it was being martyred and how would I like it? Anyway, it got to where I was tired of hearing it, so I persuaded God—against his better judgment, I might add—to give me a second chance and send me back down as the savior of Scotland. Round about that time the English were kicking the shit out of the clans; giving them a really good rogering, they were."

"Excuse me," Jesús interjected, "what does rogering mean exactly? I can guess, but it's not an American expression is it?"

You've heard the term screwing, no doubt?"

"Yes, I'm very familiar with it."

"Well, rogering is another term for screwing, although it usually has more of a same-sex connotation. There's a verse from an English rugby song, about the *Good Ship Venus*, that gets it across really well. I can sing it if you like."

He cast a sly look at Jesus One, who rolled his eyes. The Khan grinned and gulped down more Merlot.

"I was just asking," said, Jesús. "It's not a big deal."

"No problemo," the Khan answered, setting down the coffee mug with a flourish and clearing his throat. "I'll just give you the verse in question."

Jesus One sighed and carefully placed his glass on the coffee table.

The Khan, it turned out, had a good singing voice. It was deep and mellow—not a full baritone, but close.

"On the trip to Buenos Aires,
We rogered all the fairies,
We got the syph. at Tenerife
and a dose of clap in the Canaries."

"You two don't get out much, do you?" Jesús observed.

The Khan winked confidentially and nodded in the direction of Jesus One. "He knows all twenty four verses."

"Can we move on?" Jesús said.

"Where was I?" queried the Khan.

"You were saving Scotland."

"Yes, well, first I sorted out the *Sassenachs*—that's what the clans called the English—then I had to go get betrayed and martyred. They dragged me naked behind a horse through the streets of London. Then they suspended me by the neck for a while. Then they opened me up and ripped out my intestines. Then …"

"That's enough," interrupted Jesús, "I think I get the idea. But I didn't ask you to come all this way to hear about sibling rivalry. I'm dealing with some serious shit here, and I could use a little advice."

Unlike the Khan, who was dressed in his traditional robe and sandals, and still sporting a drooping Mongol moustache and beard, Jesus One preferred a more modern look. His hair and beard were close-cropped and his clothes were one hundred percent Gap: a loose fitting, coarse weave gray sweater topped nicely tailored pre-worn jeans. Open toed composite-fiber sandals completed the ensemble. "Don't mind him," he said with a captivating smile. "He's just trying to fit in. Before we came down, he boned up on American males. He seems to have the idea all you do in your spare time is drink and tell dirty jokes."

"Actually," Jesús said, "that's pretty close."

"Not so different from when I was your age," the Khan broke in, "except the wine had more body to it. We also had young virgins coming out the ying-yang." He smiled knowingly. "Boy! Has that changed, or what!"

"Not necessarily," Jesús countered, looking peeved. "It all depends on which college you go to. Some are known for it. Mine wasn't, unfortunately," he added ruefully.

Jesus One, who had been intently observing this interchange, gently clapped his hands. "Very good, now that we've established our manly credentials can we please get down to business?"

"You've got my attention," Jesús said.

"No, it's the other way round," Jesus One pointed out. "You have ours. That's what we're here for: to listen to you."

Jesús shot a sarcastic look at the Khan.

"You could have fooled me," he said.

"Easily done," shot back the Khan.

"Look," Jesus One said, getting to his feet and stretching, "the fact is you asked for the Khan, not me. So I think you'd better tell him what you need to know."

"Fair enough," Jesús said, "but since you're here, feel free to join in anytime."

Jesus One nodded and sat down again.

"First of all," Jesús said, "I need to get one thing straight. Why didn't God send down one of you guys to sort this out?"

The Khan nodded to Jesus One. "You explain. My head hurts just thinking about it."

Jesus One sat back with his arms folded and glanced briefly at the ceiling. "Well, to tell the truth, we did volunteer. For me, it was more a matter of showing I was still willing, and in any case, I *am* expected back one of these days, you know. The Khan, however, thought the job was tailor-made for him, and I thought he was right, so I stepped aside."

"I explained to God," said the Khan, "that this whole thing would probably end up sooner or later in Outer Mongolia. And who better qualified than me? My only stipulation was I wasn't about to get martyred a second time. But after the William Wallace thing there was no way he would agree to another try."

Jesus One got to his feet and started to pace. "A flip chart would really help right now, but I'll do my best. What you call heaven is really a bunch of alien beings in space ships. God is sort of the chief executive. They're not all tentacles and multiple rows of dripping green teeth; they're humanoids like us, so they can actually observe and infiltrate pretty much at will."

Jesús put his head in hands. He let out a long sigh then gazed woefully at the Khan." "Now I see why your head hurts."

"I'm almost done, so please be patient," admonished Jesus One. "The thing to understand is why they're here. Their basic mission is to help planets develop to the point where they can be admitted to some sort of intergalactic confederation. They do this in three ways: they observe; infiltrate; and intervene when necessary. The rule is, however, if they decide to intervene, they can only do so by using a human, and a first-timer at that. Apparently, if they use one of their own or a previously chosen one like me, it's considered cheating, and believe me, they *are* audited. Your reward for being a chosen one is you get the option living forever on the mother ship. Now do you understand?"

"What about Genghis here going back as William Wallace?"

"It was a judgment call," said Jesus One. "In the event, God got away with it. Because it worked out so well for the Scots, the Confederation let him off with a warning. His point was that nobody in the Highlands was likely to recognize a barbarian emperor who had died forty-five years before Wallace was born, let alone admit to it."

"Listen," Jesús said. "This is all very interesting, and I'd love to sit up all night listening to you two reminisce, but I'm getting hungry. Anybody mind if I call out for pizza?"

CHAPTER 3

Noahu

The biggest downside to Noahu was the community of saltwater crocodiles living on the western edge of the lagoon. Otherwise, the island was a South Sea paradise. When they first sailed in, Chamberlain was all set to bypass the locals and make for the beautiful but entirely deserted beach he had spotted off to starboard. It was early evening and he wanted the anchor down before dark.

"Frank!" his wife, Marge, cautioned, "there's probably a good reason that beach is empty."

"Bullshit!" he answered. "Recreational beach use is something the natives can't grasp, Marge. On their time off, they'd rather be indoors knocking back fermented tree roots."

"All the same," she said, "the least we can do is ask someone."

So he asked. He anchored close to the village, dropped the dinghy, attached the outboard, and headed in. He did this without further argument because deep down he knew Marge was right. Marge was always right. For example, right now he was heading for the village on his own, when his instinct would be for them to go together, or at least have him take the dog. Marge didn't see it that way. "What if they're not friendly, Frank, or there's some kind of trouble?" she had said on more than one occasion. "Take the radio with you. Then if there's a problem you can let me know. Hilda needs to stay with me for protection."

Frank Chamberlain never went more than one round with Marge. If he scored a knockout, he would count his blessings. If not he would throw in the towel then-and-there.

He beached the dinghy close to a scattered collection of fishing canoes. Nearby, three men were sitting on folding lawn chairs at a plastic table, complete with beach umbrella, drinking something that looked like mud from hollowed out coconut shells. Chamberlain walked over and introduced himself.

"Me, Frank. Me *belongim* white man *kanu*," he said, pointing to his boat, the *Mary Rose.*

"Yeah, we can bloody well see that, mate," said the youngest of the three, with a grin. He stuck out his hand. "Pull up a chair and sit yourself down. I'm George, this is Norman, and the old bloke is our chief, *Noahureake*. Everybody calls him, Barry."

Norman shook hands, but the chief, whose head was painted blue on one side and red on the other, just nodded. He was unable to shake hands because he had only one arm and that was holding his coconut shell. Chamberlain grabbed a chair from a nearby stack and sat down next to the chief.

"What are you lads drinking?" he asked, ever eager to sample the local beverage of choice.

"This is two-day kava, mate," George said. He emptied his coconut shell with one swallow. Then his eyes bulged and he coughed as though he had just taken a swig of drain cleaner. Chamberlain watched with fascination as George turned to spit a mouthful of mucous gray liquid onto the sand.

"It's bloody good stuff, too," croaked George. "You want some?"

"I thought you'd never ask," replied Chamberlain, licking his lips.

Norman reached under the table and came up with a green plastic cup. "That's all we have left, mate. We don't have any more glasses, sorry."

"That's okay, I'm American. If you didn't put my booze in a plastic cup I'd be insulted."

George poured a small amount of the mud-like kava from a jumbo Mountain Dew bottle. "You got to drink it down fast, mate," he said, with a cautionary grin, "otherwise, you'll spit it all out. It tastes like shit. It's best to close your eyes too."

Ever the man for a challenge, Chamberlain closed his eyes and tossed back the kava. He was unimpressed. "Tastes more like two day-old dirt. Is that why it's called two-day kava?"

"No," George said. "Believe me, you put down four of em, you'll sleep for two days solid."

Chamberlain held out his cup for more. "I'll try another one then. So, why am I closing my eyes?"

George pointed to the horizon. "Sun's not quite down yet. When it gets dark, you'll be all right. Kava makes your eyes sensitive. If this were during the day, we'd all be drinking in Barry's shed."

Chamberlain downed his second kava and kept his eyes wide open. "What the wife and I were wondering," he said, "is would it be okay for us to drop anchor by that beach over there? We'd be happy to stay where we are, but we don't want to be in the way."

George threw back another kava. This time he didn't cough and he didn't spit. He shook his head emphatically. "You put your boat over there," he said grimly, "it'll be the last time you drop anchor anywhere." He nodded to the chief. "Tell him about your arm, Barry."

Barry held up his stump. The arm had been severed just above the right elbow. "*Mi yet hukim pis. Mi yet wokum pis-pis insait kanu. Dispela taim, tru nogut bikpela fukin pukpuk brokim dispela ya.*" He pointed with his good hand to what was left of his right arm. "*Fukin tru nogut bagarap it was.*"

Chamberlain scrutinized the bottom of his plastic cup. "Yeah, well. I didn't really get much of that," he confessed.

"What he said was," George, was grinning again, "is that he was out there catching fish and taking a piss from the canoe when a fucking big crocodile came out of the water and bit his arm off."

"What was that he said at the end about a *bagarap*?" inquired Chamberlain.

"Well, a *bagarap* is what you'd call a right bloody mess. It comes from *bugger up*. It's pommy swearing our ancestors picked up from the old Presbyterian missionaries. Barry gets English all right, Frank, but he speaks it just about as good as you speak Pidgin."

George indicated the distant beach. "Nobody goes over there because it's where the crocs hang out, mate."

Just then, a fearful scream came from the huts. Moments later, a woman ran towards the beach carrying a small child. In hot pursuit were three men brandishing long sticks covered with thorns. The men were dressed in sacking remnants tied with string and decorated here and there with banana leaves.

"What the heck is that?" Chamberlain cried, knocking over his chair in his haste to stand."

George chuckled. "Sit yourself down, Frank. It's just the mid-year hurters having a go."

Chamberlain sat down and topped up his kava without bothering to ask permission. By this time, the men had caught up with the woman and were prodding her enthusiastically with the sticks. The child sat in the sand, wailing, but mercifully untouched. Chamberlain threw back the kava and watched as the men whooped and dashed back to the huts.

"We're not the only island that does this," explained George. "It's a Melanesian custom from way back when. They do it once a fortnight between April and August to celebrate the yam harvest. They dress up like that and run up and down hurting people."

"How come they're not hurting us?" inquired Chamberlain.

George stretched his arms and belched. "Give me a break, mate. They come anywhere near us, they'll get their fucking teeth knocked in."

Chamberlain unclipped his radio. "Just checking in with the wife," he said. "You don't mind do you? Only, we like to keep in touch so she knows there's nothing to worry about."

CHAPTER 4

Phewhw!

In the event of an imminent threat to the security of the nation and/or the well being of the president, all was provided for. Located in a bombproof cavern directly beneath the White House lawn was the Protective Haven Eastern White House facility, code named *PHEWH*. This was the principal refuge for the president in times of national calamity, but it wasn't the only one; a backup facility had been constructed at a secret location south of downtown Seattle. This alternate facility was known as the Protective Haven Extended White House West, or *PHEWHW*. Jesús Maria Martinez worked there; he just didn't know it.

On February 28, 2001, a large earthquake (6.8 on the Moment Magnitude Scale) rocked the state of Washington. Apart from one stress related heart attack, no one was seriously hurt, but buildings suffered. Among the casualties was the air traffic control tower at Sea-Tac International Airport. Three years later a new, 235-foot tower rose from the rubble. Designers promised a structure that would reflect the natural wonder of its surroundings. The tower would blend elegantly with the great outdoors of the Pacific Northwest: it would mirror the skies, and the rain forests, and the colors, and the pioneering spirit of the region. As it turned out, when finished, the tower was pretty much a giant assembly of pre-cast concrete slabs, but it could withstand a category nine earthquake, and that's what really counted.

Jesús was an air traffic controller, one of twenty-four assigned to the Sea-Tac tower—coincidentally, the same number employed there in 2007. Despite a fourfold increase in traffic since then and sporadic surges in recruitment, the number twenty-four seemed to be a fundamental constant, like *Pi,* or the speed of light. As a result, Jesús, like the rest of his colleagues, was chronically overworked.

His principal complaint was having to work alone in the wee small hours of the morning. This didn't happen very often, but when it did he was terrified of falling asleep on the job, or even more frightening, suffering a temporary attack of insanity. What made it worse was that something like this had happened before; his fears were far from groundless.

In 2006 a Boeing 747-400 inbound from Taiwan radioed Sea-Tac tower for permission to land. No one answered. Shortly thereafter, a Delta jet asked permission to take off. No one answered. The tower was silent for twenty-five minutes until someone went over to the guard shack and had the guard rouse the solitary air traffic controller. Naturally, the results of the subsequent FAA inquiry were not publicized. Admittedly, it was three-o'-clock in the morning when this happened, but someone really should have answered the phone.

Jesús found about the *PHEWHW* when he put his second question to Genghis Khan. "Okay," he said, "so now I understand why you guys didn't get the job, but why me?"

"You have access to Sea-Tac Tower don't you?" asked the Khan.

"Sure I do, I work there."

"Well then, tell me this. When you come in through the main doors on your way to the elevators, have you ever noticed those big double doors off to your right?"

"Er, yes, well, maybe."

"You ever tried going in there?"

"Why should I?"

"Exactly, why should you? That's what they all think, and even if you did try, your little chip wouldn't help."

Jesús nervously stroked his left forearm where a tiny RFID identity chip was implanted. "How come you know about that?" he asked.

"The same way we know about the double doors," Jesus One answered. "Remember what I said about observing and infiltrating?"

"Sure," Jesús said. "So you're telling me God has someone on the inside."

"He did have. Twenty-five years or so ago, when the tower was being rebuilt, one of our observation sensors for Seattle showed unusual underground activity. God sent down an infiltrator and he found out the government was putting in a secret bunker beneath the tower. That's what the double doors are for."

"Jeez!" Jesús said.

Jesus One frowned.

"I'm sorry," Jesús, said. "No offence intended."

"None taken," Jesus One said with a forgiving smile. "Anyway, it's the perfect cover. Air-Force-One can fly in and be towed to a hangar; the presidential party disembarks, and five minutes later they're home free. No motorcades, no questions asked, champagne already on ice, and all the beds turned down."

"Good Lord!" Jesús said without thinking.

Jesus One ignored that and helped himself to a small slice of pizza. Jesús had ordered an extra large triple bacon pepperoni for himself and the Khan. Jesus One had asked for the individual Hawaiian Pineapple.

"In a nutshell," explained the Khan, "when the time comes, God wants you to seize the tower and the shelter. Then wait until the ash settles so you can rebuild civilization"

"Oh really. And how long might that take?"

The Khan raised an eyebrow, "What, waiting for the ash to settle or rebuilding civilization?"

"I was thinking about the ash."

"Who knows? The last time this happened, no one was left to write anything down, not to mention writing hadn't even been invented. It might be a year. It might be ten years. Best estimates put it at three to five."

Jesús put his head in his hands again. "Three to five frigging years, stuck in that control tower all by myself. I'll go crazy."

"Think of the alterative," interposed Jesus One.

"Also, added the Khan, "I have a couple of ideas."

Jesús looked up. "Be my guest. That's why you're here, and believe me, I'm all ears."

"First off, you'll need to put your hands on forty or so young virgins. I say young, because they'll be in there for a long time, not to mention they'll have some serious child rearing to do."

"I've often thought about that," Jesús mused, "putting my hands on forty virgins. So far, I've only managed one. Anyway, how the hell am I going to handle forty?"

The Khan raised his other eyebrow. Jesus One smirked.

"Listen," the Khan said, "not only did I have twenty wives, I always kept at least forty virgins in the harem, and I never had a problem—nothing to it." He stroked his beard thoughtfully. "You know, given the circumstances, God might be agreeable to me helping you out, strictly as an advisor, of course."

"So that's how we get to repopulate the earth," Jesús observed, it being his turn to raise an eyebrow, "everybody's going to be descended from me?"

"Not if I can help it," said the Khan.

CHAPTER 5

Muriel Banks

Two days after meeting Jesus One and Genghis Khan, Jesús Maria Martinez was, understandably, a changed man. His heart thumped as he passed under the sweeping glass canopy of the control tower's south entrance. Behind a tiny aperture centered over the blast-proof doors, a radio frequency scanner sensed his approach, verified his chip ID, and the doors opened. As nervous as he was, Jesús couldn't resist walking over to the heavy double metal doors just inside the elevator lobby. The doors were nondescript—no signs, no obvious security—but he did notice the same tiny aperture that was above the main doors.

"Just a matter of lifting the code and reprogramming my chip," he murmured. "God, if you're listening, would you run that down please. I'm sure it's well within your capabilities."

"Jesús Martinez! You're talking to yourself. One word from me and you'll be talking to the shrink, mister, and don't you think I won't turn you in."

Jesús froze. If there was one thing he feared more than being left alone in the tower at night, it was being left alone in the tower at night with Muriel Banks. He turned slowly. "As a matter of fact, Muriel, I wasn't talking to myself, I was talking to God. And he's already arranged counseling, thank you very much."

Muriel Banks was the most beautiful black woman Jesús had ever met. Scratch that—she was the most beautiful woman he had *ever* met, period. The downside was Muriel could be a holy terror.

"Jesús," she countered, "one of these days you're going down the pipes. You're going to lose it big time and I'm going to be there when you do, and I am going to nail you." She stared at him with deep and deadly brown eyes. "You think your dumb insolence crap is clever, don't you? You think being smart with me gets you brownie points with those other losers up there, don't you?"

"Yes."

"Well, think again, fool. What Muriel wants, Muriel gets, and you're at the top of Muriel's list. Now drag your sorry ass over to this elevator and let's get to work. And by the way, happy birthday!"

This was typical of Muriel. Just when he was getting comfortable with her being on the warpath, she would say or do something nice and burst his bubble.

The elevator lifted them past the two floors of the base building, up through the core of the tower and into the wineglass: a two story reinforced fiberglass bulb sitting atop the concrete tower stem. The entire west wall of the wineglass was an inset panel of luminous glass. Fluttering outside were the flags of the United States, Washington State, and Canada. It was a breathtaking design concept and the view was stunning. Jesús barely noticed. He was in a trance-like state induced by Muriel's rotating rear end.

Above the pneumatically supported concrete roof of the wineglass was the control cab. Because the designers wanted an uninterrupted 360° view for the controllers, the elevator shaft ended at the top of the concrete stem. To get to the cab they took a flat top hoist for the final two stories.

Covering three shifts with twenty-four controllers meant a lot of short shifting. Even the graveyard shift, with a two controller compulsory minimum wasn't immune. If someone called in sick at the last minute, you were on your own, whatever the FAA had to say about it.

Today was a good day. There were only three empty seats. Muriel snatched the shift supervisor's headset the instant it was offered. The departing supervisor snarled. Muriel ignored him.

"Muriel's on the job, children," she announced. "Martinez gets the busy seat. Move your fat asses. Anybody drops equipment on downtown Seattle gets his parking permit revoked, and don't think I don't mean it!"

Muriel always assigned Jesús the busy seat. He wasn't sure whether this was because she trusted him or because she despised him, and he wasn't about to ask. His relationship with Muriel had not been a happy one thus far.

Entranced by her evident attractions, Jesús had asked Muriel out shortly after arriving at the tower, and she had totally shocked him by saying yes. Not that he thought of himself as unattractive or dork like in any way. He had a good-enough build—a shade under six feet—and was blessed with the lustrous dark hair and high cheekbones of his Aztec forebears. He had also inherited the innocent countenance and calm country-green eyes of a more recent ancestor (but that's another story, for another time). No, his surprise was engendered by Muriel's willingness to take him, a newbie, to her bosom—so to speak—while openly spurning everyone else. He had toyed with the idea that maybe, underneath it all, she was merely a shy person, yearning for attention; that somehow his charm and good looks had broken through.

Boy, was he wrong.

Over the meal, his jubilation at reaching first base quickly turned to disenchantment when he realized he had walked into a trap. Muriel, it seemed, hated trade unions. She wanted him on her side before *they* got to him. Dinner was a diatribe. But it was too late: *they* had made damn sure to sign him up on the very first minute of his very first day.

Ever since that one and only date, Muriel had been on his case, as if he were a known wife-beater and scallywag. He just didn't get it, but he didn't hold a grudge. As far as he was concerned, she was entitled to her opinions; he just wanted not to be in the line of fire.

"You'll never nail me, Banks, I'm just too damn good," he mumbled, grabbing a headset and checking the congested screen over the shoulder of the incumbent.

"You talking to yourself again, Fly-Boy?" chuckled the other controller. Everybody had a nickname, Jesús being so called because of his penchant for flying the simulators at Boeing Field. The controllers didn't get many freebies, but they did have access to the Boeing flight simulators. Not only was this a low-cost way of saying thank you, since Jesús was one of the very few to take advantage of the offer, but Boeing also recognized a good PR opportunity when they saw one. As a result, Jesús was one of a handful of people who could claim takeoff and land in all weather ratings on every Boeing aircraft still in service. Of course, he had never actually left the ground during these excursions, but he did have a bunch of proficiency certificates no one ever looked at.

The man in the busy seat was known as *Teeth*, and it wasn't hard to figure out why. His real name was Dennis Floyd. He had three years to go before mandatory retirement. Unlike Jesús, Dennis refused to give Muriel the benefit of the doubt. He was convinced she had it in for him. "The bitch is after my retirement," he confided on Jesús' first day. "I'm not kidding. She's an FAA plant. You ever see that old movie, *The Great Escape* with Steve McQueen? It's like we're POWs and she's a Nazi spy. Either way, she's a fucking Nazi."

Jesús had just met Muriel and had fallen instantly and innocently in love. "You're being paranoid, man," he retorted. "She's just doing her job."

"Oh, yeah," Teeth replied. "Get this: she's already had two guys canned. The first one told the doc he'd caught a tone in his headset and couldn't hear a fucking thing, so he copped two weeks off. The bitch had one of her girlfriends call him up a day later. So the fucking dimwit answers the phone and tries for a date and she tapes it."

Jesús had pretty much ignored Teeth then, and he ignored him now. The reason being that as he was sitting down, the conflict alert sounded.

"What the heck?" inquired Jesús mildly as he scrutinized the display. Two approaching China Airlines flights had just been handed off by in route controllers and the lower jet was suddenly gaining altitude.

"China Flight 2837, this is Sea-Tac Tower, conflict alert."

There was no answer. Jesús tried again."China Flight 2837, this is Sea-Tac Tower, conflict alert."

He could feel Muriel breathing down his neck. Most controllers hated the alarm sounding while they tried to resolve an alert. Jesús, on the other hand, got a kick out of remaining dead calm in the midst of the cacophony.

The jet continued to gain altitude and still didn't respond. Jesús went to the upper aircraft. "China Flight 839, Sea-Tac Tower, conflict alert."

"Sea-Tac Tower, this is China Flight 839. I have the TCAS alert."

"China 839, this is Sea-Tac Tower. Fly heading two-seven-zero. Climb and maintain seven thousand feet immediately. You have traffic beneath you and climbing."

Before China 839 could reply, China 2837 burst in. "I sorry Sea-Tac, I got wrong field. I want to go Portland. Oh, sorry, I also want to say this Flight China 2837."

"Roger, good morning, China 2837. This is Sea-Tac Tower. Descend to three thousand feet immediately. Fly heading one-eight-zero and expect vectors to Portland from in-route control."

"This China Flight 2837, I am copy Sea-Tac."

"Roger, China 2837, have a nice day."

The shrieking alarm turned itself off and Muriel slapped Jesús on the back of the head. "I want an incident report right now, Martinez, and don't you go blaming the pilot like you always do."

Jesús turned to look up at her. "Muriel, every day, we're getting fifty planeloads of Chinese coming and going. Swear to God, they're so short of pilots they're asking for volunteers from coach. This one just woke up and realized he was dropping in at the wrong airport."

"Don't you snow me. I want that report and I want it now. I also heard you using forbidden pleasantries. You are not permitted to say 'good morning' or 'have a nice day' and you damn well know that."

Jesús grinned.

"You're not getting a report. There was no incident, so you write it up. If you have a problem, talk to my union rep. I'm in the clear on this one. By the way, go screw yourself. How's that for a forbidden pleasantry?"

Without waiting for a reply, he turned back to the screen.

Someone tapped him on the shoulder. He ducked and turned, expecting another dope slap from Muriel. Instead, he found Debbie Crank wringing her hands. By her side were two stocky maintenance men.

"I'm sorry, Jesús," she whispered. Debbie was Director of Occupational Safety and Health for the airport, and a nicer person you would never meet.

"What have I done now, Debbie? Did I flush something unclean down the john?"

"No, it's nothing like that. We need your chair, Jesús, we're collecting all the chairs."

He glanced at the other seats. Six more maintenance men were grappling with the occupants. Morris Cox, two seats down and otherwise known as Sucker, was threatening to hurl hot coffee—and winning.

"What's going on?" Jesús asked politely.

"It's a new FAA directive, effective immediately," she answered with a wan smile. "OSHA just ruled that all government-issue task chairs no longer meet safe standards. The FAA doesn't want the liability, so they're confiscating our chairs."

"Well, if my chair is a threat to my well being, the least you can do is explain why," he said, with a dangerous smile.

"As I said, it's because of the new OSHA standards. More than eighty percent of Americans are seriously overweight, and of those, seventy percent are morbidly obese. So the minimum mandatory seat width has just been increased from twenty-four inches to thirty-two to prevent repetitive motion disorders. That's people constantly shifting position because they don't fit into their chairs properly. Your chair just isn't wide enough. It also seems the average American male now weighs two hundred and eighty eight pounds, so the old chairs no longer have enough load bearing capacity. I'm sorry, Jesús, I know you guys have to stay in shape, but there are no exceptions."

"Not a problem," Jesús said, graciously rising to his feet. "Just wheel in the new chairs and we'll all get back to work. You do have new chairs, don't you, Debbie?"

"Yes," she said, "but they're still in the warehouse. I just found out I have to send them all back. I've been authorized to lease some temporary chairs in the meantime, but my request didn't get signed off until an hour ago, and it will take all day to get a purchase order. The old chairs absolutely must be removed today, though, so I'm afraid everyone will just have to be on their feet until tomorrow morning."

"So, how come the new chairs are going back?"

"There was a problem."

"Which was?"

"They called it chronic involuntary gastric emissions."

"You mean frequent farting."

"Well, yes."

"How, pray, could a harmless squeeze now and then disable a chair?"

"They weren't disabled, they were hazardous."

Jesús rubbed his forehead in mock agitation. "I'm about to go postal, and we wouldn't want that, now would we. So please tell me as succinctly as you can why I will now be required to do my job standing up."

Debbie tried to hold back a smile. "It's really not funny, and I'm sorry to be the bearer of bad news, but all the new chairs were made in China. It seems the upholstery is held together with formaldehyde-based glue. When the seats are warm and moist all the time, they out-gas formaldehyde. People were getting seizures and passing out at their desks. Not to mention falling off their chairs."

"How many chairs, Debbie? How many of these Chinese screw ups did they buy?

Debbie couldn't hold back the smile anymore. "Well, I suppose it is funny when you think about it. The government bought six million. The Mexicans offered to buy them cheap, but the World Trade Organization objected. They say it contravenes international tariff agreements. Apparently, chair futures could collapse and trigger a worldwide recession. All the government can do is negotiate a buy-back with the supplier."

Jesús saw Muriel then. She was standing on the observation deck wearing the biggest self-satisfied grin he had ever seen. Standing didn't bother Muriel one bit. She was always on her feet. Even in the break room, she wouldn't sit. Instead, she would pace back and forth denouncing trade unions. For Jesús, this was tantamount to Adolph Hitler bad-mouthing Stalin, but he knew better than to voice his opinion.

"I'll tell you what, Debbie," he said, loudly enough for Muriel to hear. "You want me to do this job standing up, I'll do it standing up. You want me to do the job standing on my head, I'll do it standing on my head. You know why? Because I can, because I'm that good, that's why!"

Without waiting for an answer, he turned to check his screen and gaze out the tinted window. At over two-hundred-feet the panorama was spectacular. A snow-capped Mount Rainier stood majestically to the south. A glistening Puget Sound extended all the way to the far ocean. The view was vibrant with color and life and light. He had savored this scene almost every day for three years. Today, though, was different. Today, there was a sense of urgency, as if the mountain and the ocean were reaching out to him, pleading to be frozen in time. He couldn't get enough of it and he didn't know how to respond. He stared up at the flawless blue sky. "God," he implored, "if you can hear me, would you beam me up? Like, right now please. I'm all yours!"

"I heard that, Martinez," Muriel yelled from the back of the room. "You keep talking with God, you're toast, mister."

CHAPTER 6

A Walk In The Park

Actually, Vernon Trumboy rarely walked in the park; it was too hilly and there were too many animals on the loose. June was a busy month for Yellowstone, so he was using one of the staff-only roads that skirted the lake. Time was, visitors could actually park close to the water and get their toes wet. That was before the lake started to boil. Now it was a major attraction in its own right. Public access was restricted to the Steam Boat Billy jetties and the Super Saunas dotted around the lake perimeter.

He pulled into the cast member's parking lot behind the Planet Earth Pavilion. The ground shook. He checked his watch. It was exactly fifteen minutes since the last mini-quake. Over to his left, a groan went up from a long line of Chinese tourists snaking its way up to Earthquake House.

"Impatient assholes," he muttered, "can't you read English? It says "A Thrill a Minute" and that's what it means. You pay your money; wait forever in line, and eventually get what you pay for." That was Vernon's version of the Global-Titanic Worldwide Entertainment Corporation's motto, which, while enunciated a little differently, pretty much said the same thing, i.e. "Joy Worth Waiting For."

Ever since the National Park Service was privatized in 2023, Yellowstone had been the jewel in the crown. Under Global-Titanic management, park revenues had climbed more than eighty per cent per year—every year. Nationwide, federal parks were bringing in enough in licensing fees to underwrite the entire budget of the Department of the Interior.

Technically, Vernon was a park ranger, a federal employee. In actuality, like the park, he was licensed to Global-Titanic. Titanic paid the feds. The feds paid Vernon and provided the re-costumed uniform, the benefits, and the housing. Titanic called the shots.

The only downside for Vernon was that the floor of his house was getting warmer, and a hot spring had bubbled up in his driveway. Compared to the upside, though, these were minor discomforts. He simply drove around the spring. Ratcheting up the air conditioning and wearing Gortex slippers around the house took care of the floor problem. During the winter months, of course, it was quite pleasant. He had free under floor heating and a hot tub in his front yard.

Vernon liked Global-Titanic a lot. First, they had meetings all the time, which meant spending most of his time indoors. Second, they employed good-looking women. Best of all, he was a charter member of the park aristocracy. The feds paid well. Most of the employees, especially the younger cast members and immigrants, were on minimum wage and living in dormitories.

Today's meeting concerned plans for enhancing the lava leak. As always, there were free Dunkin Donuts and Starbucks coffee, courtesy of the makers. He helped himself to four Boston creams and a jumbo Americano.

A senior vice president of fantasy management had flown in from Global-Titanic Worldwide Universe, Beijing. He introduced himself. "Hi folks, I'm Dick Derringer, and I'll be moderating our discussion today."

Dick was spotlessly turned out in a green Park Promotions blazer, pleated gray slacks, and topsiders that artfully matched his flawless tan. He was the only male in the room other than Vernon not wearing a tie, and the only male sporting an earring. Vernon had quickly learned that not wearing a tie in Titanic management level meetings meant one of two things: the tie-less one was being sloppy, in which case he was never seen again; or he was a member of the senior creative staff, like Dick Derringer, and thus allowed small tokens of nonconformity.

"So, is everybody on top of the world this morning?" Dick demanded, with a dazzling smile. "Did we all greet a guest today?"

"Hi, Dick, sure are, Dick, sure did, Dick," chorused the gathering.

"Before we get down to business," Dick continued, more serious now, "I just want to say what a privilege it is to be here. We hear great things about the work you fine folks are doing at Yellowstone. I, for one, just want to say, Go Team, Go! Our founder would have been proud."

A modest murmur of pride rippled around the conference table.

"Over there," Dick announced, pointing to a felt covered flip chart off to his right, "is my little Yellowstone surprise, but more of that later. Now, why don't we all introduce ourselves?"

Vernon disliked this part. He was not good at public speaking, at least not in the presence of his betters; he tended to mumble and get embarrassed. Pontificating in the park was different. There, he had the authority of the costume and the golden glow of insider knowledge to prop him up.

When it was his turn, Vernon raised his hand and stared hard at the jumbo Americano. Try as he might, he could never bring himself to make eye contact with a moderator. "Ranger Vernon Jumbo, senior park liaison officer," he said in a strong, clear voice. Someone whimpered in a desperate attempt to smother a giggle. Vernon reddened. "I'm sorry, that would be Trumboy," he muttered.

"Thank you, Ranger Dumbo," Dick responded enthusiastically. "What a pleasure to meet a childhood hero. I always loved costumes when I was a small boy-still do as a matter of fact. You guys do a great job, Vernon!"

Vernon blushed again.

When the introductions were done, Dick Derringer was all business. "Today's main topic," he said, glancing down at his *MacPod* Instant Projector (*MacPIP*), "is the lava leak." He thumbed a small button on the side of the palm-sized device. A nine by twelve image instantly appeared on the wall behind him.

Vernon had seen countless versions of this diagram before. This one was by far the best. It was a typical multi-colored, 3-D Global-Titanic extravaganza.

"As you all know," Derringer began, "two years ago, government scientists at the park observatory predicted a small scale eruption here at Specimen Ridge." He moved a small red arrow to a point just east of the main ridgeline. "Boy, were we ready to reach for the brown trousers."

Everybody laughed.

"But Global-Titanic's contract seismologists weren't convinced. Their idea was that it was going to be a minor lava spill. Of course, they were right; it was nothing to be alarmed about. Even so, the Department of the Interior had the entire park evacuated. I'm sure everyone at this table remembers what happened."

Vernon raised his hand. "Total fuck-up for four days. The thing actually oozed out on day two, but we were so busy directing traffic nobody noticed. Then they sent in those volcano guys."

"Volcanologists," prompted Dick.

"Yeah, well those volcanologists. All they found was a magma trickle running down into a hole that had opened up in Pebble Creek."

"Thank you, Vernon," Dick said graciously. "By the way, and just so you know for future meetings, Global-Titanic is not comfortable with the "*F*" word." His eyes narrowed and his upper lip curled. He was through being gracious. "You should also know Vernon, as the sole federal employee at this table, that Titanic is not about to shut down the park again—ever. We lost close to two hundred million in park revenues during that fiasco, so kick *that* upstairs, will you." He didn't wait for a reply. He switched his smile back on and addressed the table. "Today, the lava leak is a so-so attraction. Tomorrow, folks, it's going to be a mega-attraction." He paused, waiting for the tension to build

"Ta-da!" He thumbed the *MacPod* expertly and an overlay slowly dissolved into view. It showed a six-lane, divided highway starting at the mouth of the leak and following the lava flow all the way down to Pebble Creek, three thousand feet below. The highway continued on to the park's northeast entrance.

"Here," said Dick, moving the arrow to the source of the leak, "is where we plan to enlarge the opening. We figure we can quadruple the flow with a single precision blast. Here, running between the new road and the leak, is a monorail with heat-shielded observation cars. You'll see we've tripled the size of Roosevelt Lodge to accommodate the extra traffic."

There was a spontaneous burst of applause.

Dick rose slowly to his feet and leaned forward, his hands pressed down hard on the table. His lips were a thin red line. His eyes glittered. "First-of-all, we're doing away with the name lava leak, which, by the way, was dreamed up by the media. The scheme you see here will be called Lava Park. This is going to be a whole new way of doing business for Titanic. When we announce Lava Park, we're also going to announce 'Global-Titanic Play as you Pay.' No more single admission price. If you don't want to see an attraction, you don't have to pay for it."

Vernon raised his hand. "What about all the extra staff you'll need to sell tickets all over the park? What about all the extra queuing up?"

Dick reached into a side pocket and held up a tiny chip. "When we scan their credit cards at the entrance, they get a forehead implant—a Global-Titanic patented design. It only takes a couple of seconds and since it's less than skin deep, it heals right away. All their personal and credit information is on the chip. All they have to do is walk up to a turnstile and in they go."

Vernon raised his hand again. "What about —"

Dick interrupted impatiently. "It's all taken care of, Vernon. The codes on these chips are unbreakable. Even White House security is using them now. Remember, this is the Global-Titanic Worldwide Entertainment Corporation. Nobody gets a free ride." He stood and flexed his arms. "Excuse me, will you? I need a break."

While Dick helped himself to coffee and donuts, excited chatter broke out at the table.

Vernon's neighbor, a heavy set blonde from Park Promotions, elbowed him hard just below his right bicep. She was the one who had almost laughed. "Vernon, why in hell did you call yourself Jumbo? Can't you remember your own fucking name?"

"Slip of the tongue. It won't happen again."

He slid the Americano her way.

"Try this if you like. I'm finished with it."

Dick took a bite from his donut and washed it down with a gulp of coconut latte, but he didn't return to the table. He walked over to the felt covered flip chart. The chatter died down. "I know you've all been wondering," he said. "Could there be more? What else could Dick Derringer possibly be hiding up his sleeve?" He lifted the felt slowly, like an exotic dancer going all the way. Then he gave a last tug to reveal his surprise. Everyone gasped. It was the final overlay. "Cast members," Dick whispered. "Say hello to Lava Lake!"

Pebble Creek was no more. The drain hole was still there but the entire creek bed had been expanded to form a shallow lake, two miles in diameter. Lakeside were clusters of heat-shielded pedestrian walkways, boutiques, and restaurants. Luxury high-rise condominiums and hotels populated a second tier. Overlooking the eastern perimeter of the lake, on a high plateau, was a sprawling sub-division of trophy homes.

Dick Derringer pointed to the subdivision. "Boys and girls, welcome to the Villas at Lava Lake. Each one has an uninterrupted view of the lake, and they all face west. When the sun goes down, what with the spectacular sunsets and the glow from Lava Lake, the residents are going to cream themselves. These babies will be the hottest properties on the planet."

At the far end of the table, Leroy Gilman raised his hand. Leroy was a Titanic construction supervisor and this was the first he had heard of Lava Park, let alone the Villas at Lava Lake. "Dick, a great concept by the way, but when is all this going to happen?"

Dick rubbed his hands. "Three phases. Phase one will be the expanded lava flow and the lake, the highway, Roosevelt Lodge, and the monorail. Phase two will be the lake infrastructure. Phase three will be the villas."

Unsatisfied, Leroy persisted. "Exactly when will it all be finished?"

"We'll finish phases one and two by Christmas. Phase three should be completed by this time next year. Actually, precision blasting will start next week for the leak and the lake so you can pretty much consider that a done deal."

Leroy gasped and turned pale.

Vernon raised his hand. "Any problems the park service can help you with, Dick?"

"I'm glad you mentioned that. It so happens the architects are a bit concerned about wild-life. The villas will be mostly a retirement community for wealthy guests, so they're anxious to avoid any intrusion by unwelcome species."

Vernon leaned back with a professional smile. "That won't be a problem," he said. "Even if it were we'd take care of it. As it happens, the bears and what was left of the wolves have all moved out. Don't know why—they just upped and left last month. Bunch of other wildlife seems to be taking off too. Mostly, what we have right now are the bison, a few of the older deer, a bunch of elks, and some prairie dogs. Of course, the jackrabbits might be a problem, but we can easily eradicate the ones in your neighborhood. Also, you don't have to worry about the elks, we put out feed for them so they pretty much stay in one place. Used to be they wandered a lot into Wyoming, but then they started infecting sheep with Mad Elk disease and Dick Cheney got upset, so these days we feed em and shoot em ourselves."

"Excellent!" Dick exclaimed, visibly pleased with Vernon's input. "Bambi in the back yard once in a while would be great. Just make sure the bison and prairie dogs stay away, will you? They'll dig up the lawns"

Vernon nodded decisively and made a note.

Leroy Gilman raised his hand again. "Dick, are we seeing much interest in the villa properties?"

"Absolutely unprecedented," Dick said. "The minimum buy in is five million. We're already eighty percent pre-sold. We're getting lots of interest from South America and China in particular. You won't believe it, but our South American guests insist on paying for everything up front. Cash and a handshake is what they call it. They don't even want any paperwork. It's amazing how trusting they are."

He grinned. "I guess they just feel it's the Titanic way. Believe me, they won't be disappointed."

Vernon's neighbor raised her hand. "Dick, are there any special promotions we should be thinking about?"

Dick almost bubbled over with glee. "You and I should be a double act, er..."

"Cindy, Cindy Greezlik."

"Cindy, yes, we should. Look here!" He flipped to the next chart. It was a spectacular rendering of a glowing lava lake framed by fireworks, with Santa's sleigh in the foreground. The title read: "A Lava Lake Christmas."

"All the celebs are going to be there," Dick enthused. "Lindsay Lohan has agreed to forego rehab that week to sing the anthem, and Bon Jovi will be released from the retirement home to do backup."

Everyone clapped, including Leroy Gilman, who was still looking dazed.

"And that," Dick cried, "is not all."

There was an expectant pause.

"Why are we here?" Dick prompted. "What do we all want? What does your corporation want? What do the shareholders want?"

It was a familiar exhortation and everyone knew the response. The room burst into a full-throated chant. "We want money...more money...more money!"

Dick raised his arms for silence. "You'll get it cast members," he said. "As of now, this park is a 24-7-365 operation. No more seasonal down time. When Lava Park warms up, winter will be as hot as summer. It's going to be August all the time!"

The cheers were deafening.

On the way out, Dick Derringer made a point of singling out Vernon. "You know Vernon," he said, with a careful smile, "I meant what I said about liking rangers and uniforms. Maybe on my next visit you can show me the park."

He squeezed the ranger's hand gently.

Vernon blushed. "Sure," he mumbled, "sure, be my pleasure." And a tiny shudder skipped lightly up his spine.

CHAPTER 7

In which Frank Dreams of his Former Self

With the exception of Margie Green, whom he would love until his dying day, Frank Chamberlain mistrusted just about everybody. That was why he was still alive. When it came to officers, he detested every single one above the rank of captain. Not that he had a problem following orders, that came with the territory. He just made it a point not to do anything suicidal.

He had been called to a mission briefing.

"This is not a suicide mission, sergeant," explained the special-forces colonel, "but you can expect some stiff opposition. We're not asking you to volunteer. We have you down as the best man for the job, so you're it. Do you have any questions?"

"Yes, do we walk or shall I call for a cab?"

The colonel raised a neatly clipped left eyebrow and sniffed. His other eye was covered by a vivid green velvet eye-patch. "I was getting to that. You will fast rope from an MH-53 Pave Low helicopter gunship supplied by Air Force Special Operations Command. Then you and your men will enter a dwelling and deal with the occupants."

Frank Chamberlain slammed the table with both hands. "You cock sucker! Those goddamn meat grinders were mothballed ten years ago. Thanks all the same, but we'll walk. They're sixty years old for God's sake."

"Hear me out, sergeant. The Chinooks and Black Hawks are grounded. Their engines are crap full of sand and we can't afford replacements. Anyway, Kellogg stepped in with a long-term lease offer we couldn't refuse. They took title to our old mothballed helicopters, fixed them up, and folded in a maintenance fee with the monthly payment. No money down and a deep-discounted buy back when the lease runs out."

Chamberlain sighed. "Okay, I give in. Just tell me where, when, and who and I'll get my squad together."

"It's an *al-Qaida* hit. Some hotshot from *al-Qaida* corporate is holding precious cargo in downtown Fallujah. We want to talk to him."

"Who's the cargo?"

"A couple of puke PIOs wandered out of the Purple Zone for lunch and got collared."

"Fine, I'm in, but somebody's going to get hurt, sir, and it's not going to be me or my boys, so I need some rules of engagement here."

The colonel sniffed again. Chamberlain had dealt with him too many times before. He was the worst kind; he kept so close behind the generals, if they stopped walking they'd be sodomized. Not surprisingly, Chamberlan and he despised one another. The colonel's name was Norman Nimegen and he was altogether too well pressed for Frank Chamberlain, including his neat sandy hair and candy-ass little moustache. Nimegen was wearing a lightweight leather flying-jacket decorated with multi-colored squadron patches. Chamberlain noticed the patches were all upside down.

"Just get the *al-Qaida* guy out. If the PIOs get wasted, don't worry about it. You're spearheading a new appeasement doctrine. We offer to put them on the payroll; they guarantee they'll leave us alone." Nimegen reached into the breast pocket of his jacket and handed over a folded slip of paper. "Just key it in, sergeant, and give me back the paper."

Chamberlain snatched his armored *MacPod* Army Model (*MacPAM*) from the table. He selected Combat Map Quest and keyed in the address. Instead of handing back the paper, he crumpled it and tossed it into the wastebasket.

Then he left.

Two hours later, he fast roped with his men down to the balcony outside a third floor apartment in Fallujah's Al-Shuhada district. They didn't knock. Before the smoke cleared, the squad was moving in. The lead man loosed three quick bursts. Chamberlain slammed him hard on the shoulder.

"Hold off, Biggs! They're just kids."

Four children in long, white nightshirts were sitting on the floor watching television. Chamberlain took a deep breath and forced himself to calm down. Sometimes, you had to let the adrenalin take over, but this was not one of those times. "Biggs," he commanded, "get the remote."

Biggs shuffled over, keeping his SCAR Heavy Combat Assault Rifle at the ready. He grabbed the remote from the smallest child and backed up carefully. The eldest child stood up then and hobbled towards Chamberlain. He was holding his severed left foot underneath his right armpit. Fresh blood was still coming out of the foot. Oddly enough, there were no bloodstains on the carpet, even where the boy had walked across it on what remained of his left ankle.

"Marge! Marge!" Chamberlain yelled, "We need a Marge here."

"I don't want a Marge, I want our remote back," the child said.

"What were you watching?" Chamberlain demanded.

"We were watching 'Little Miss Fixit' with Mandy Miller and Dirk Forrester."

"That's okay then," Chamberlain said. "Biggs, give it back."

"By the way," said the child, "if you're looking for *al-Qaida*, they're three doors down. Also, they checked out this morning."

"What happened to the hostages?"

The boy graciously accepted his remote from Biggs. "They called for a cab."

When they left the apartment, Chamberlain looked up for the helicopter. It wasn't there. Biggs tapped him on the shoulder. "Looks like they hit the deck, Frank," he said, pointing over the railing. Below, the giant machine sat groaning in the middle of the street. The ancient rotors shuddered and squealed, but they weren't moving. Chamberlain led the way down, covering the stairwells every step of the way.

The aircrew was sprawled on the back ramp of the helicopter smoking Marlboro-Lites.

Chamberlain was enraged. "What the hell are you guys doing? Don't you have an engineer on board? Get this piece of shit off the ground and let's go, for Christ's sake!"

"Whoa, whoa!" the pilot said. "We touch that equipment we void the lease agreement. Only ones allowed to fix it right now are Kellogg mission maintenance, and I already called. They're backed up with surge support in Quim. Be two weeks, minimum."

"I knew it!" Chamberlain cried. He beckoned to his squad. "We're walking." He turned back to the pilot. "Are you coming?"

"Not fucking likely, we're Air Force; we'll stick around for the search and rescue boys."

Three blocks later, the squad met a slow moving convoy of Mine Resistant Ambush Protected Joint Light Tactical Vehicles (MRAPJLTVs)—which was just another way of saying warmed over *Humvees*—and seven-ton armored trucks. Chamberlain flagged down the lead vehicle. The driver cautiously rolled down the window and pointed a pearl-handled Colt 45 semi-automatic at Chamberlain's groin.

"You guys Americans?" he inquired politely.

"Of course we're Americans. Do I look like Lawrence of fucking Arabia?"

"Who won the last World Series?"

"How the hell should I know? I watch English Rugby."

The driver snorted in disgust. "Get in. Your men can ride in the trucks."

Chamberlain squeezed into the passenger seat. Apart from the driver and the roof gunner, he was the only occupant. The rest of the warmed over Humvee was crammed to near bursting with packets of Little Debbie cakes.

"Do help yourself, by the way," the driver said. "We got Marshmallow Supremes and Fudge Brownies with walnuts."

Chamberlain squinted up at the gunner. In place of the preferred, 2000 rounds per minute .50 cal. Gatling gun, was a brand-new skeet thrower.

"What in the Lord's name are you guys doing with a skeet thrower?" he asked incredulously.

"Hey, man," the gunner said, dropping into view. "This ain't no ordinary thrower, it's an *LDLAAM*—a Little Debbie Launcher Automatic Aerial Model. It takes fifty Little Debbie's and puts em out a hundred yards, guaranteed, man."

They were approaching a bombed out vacant lot. Rubble and garbage were piled all the way to the curb and spilling into the road. A gang of boys and older youths emerged from the rubble. Some of them waved. Some started to pee. The rest of them just squatted and stared.

"Watch this," the gunner said. He climbed back to position and hit the launch button. Little Debbie cakes sprayed out ahead of the vehicle. The effect was instantaneous. Chamberlain watched in horror as one youth, racing ahead for the cakes, stepped onto a garbage bag sitting curbside. There was an ear-splitting thud and a column of dirt and asphalt erupted skyward. The youth simply disappeared.

Chamberlain threw open the door, and half stepped, half fell into the roadway. Before he could get his balance, he felt a tight, choking pain at his throat.

He knew immediately what he was in for.

Boris, his Ukrainian Spetsnaz instructor had slipped a garrote around his neck. The next move would end it. Boris would swivel and stoop swiftly, raising and twisting the garrote as he turned. Then he would bend and lift. Chamberlain would lie across the Ukrainian's back like a sack of freshly harvested Nevsky potatoes. His own weight would choke him to death. He clawed and gagged with terminal air hunger, but it was too late.

Marge grabbed him as he toppled from the bunk. "It's all right, Frank, its just another one of your night-frights, love." She helped him to his feet.

"Jeez!" he muttered, "what time is it?"

"You shouldn't be asking. You came back last night after drinking God knows what on that beach. You fell asleep the moment your feet touched the deck."

"I'm sorry, Marge."

She smiled gently. "Don't you worry. Anyway, since you ask, it's three in the afternoon, and there's a nice young man outside who wants to give us some fish. I think you'd better talk to him."

CHAPTER 8

Mistress of the Harem

When Jesús returned to his apartment after the incident with the chairs, God was back. He was sitting in the recliner watching television. Genghis Khan and Jesus One occupied the settee. As Jesús came through the door, God turned and waved. He was no longer Jimmy Carter, but the wave seemed oddly familiar. It was stiff-armed, with the hand rotating back and forth like a mechanical toy. Jesús was stymied until he saw the face-splitting grin. Then it came to him in a flash.

God was Richard Nixon.

"Please sit down, Jesus," said God. "I tuned in to everything you said at the control tower. It sounds like we have a deal, my friend." He leaned forward, still beaming, and extended his hand. The handshake wasn't like before. It didn't have the dry, reassuring firmness of Jimmy Carter. The hand was damp and desperate, as if a drowning victim had just grabbed hold of him. God gave Jesús a parting squeeze before he let go.

"Sure, sure," said Jesús, "and by the way, you pronounce my name *Heysús*. I'm from Mexico, that's how we talk down there, Jimmy Carter. By the way, didn't have a problem with that."

God threw his arms up and glared. The beaming smile was gone. In its place was uncontrollable rage. "I don't care how you talk south of the border. You're in America now, boy. I learned to speak English, and so can you. And don't talk to me about being Jimmy Carter; I don't want to hear it. You think for one lousy minute I enjoy being Richard Nixon?" All at once, the rage vanished. An expression of utter gloom came over him. He sat down, hunched his shoulders, and fiddled with the tip lever on the recliner

Jesús shrugged and found space on the sofa between the Khan and Jesus One. "What are you guys watching?"

"It's 'Little Miss Fixit' with Mandy Miller," explained the Khan. "Mandy and Dirk, her assistant, are building a twelve room mansion in Baltimore. Dirk is showing Mandy how to use the air-powered finish nailer."

Jesús sighed and leaned back.

On screen, Dirk handed Mandy the nail gun and explained the controls. Somehow, he managed to stare without blinking at the camera and smile continuously while he talked. Dirk had the look of a man who has just been French kissed by an angel. Subtle hints of sun bleaching edged his carefully spiked brown hair.

"So what's this one for again, Dirk?" Mandy asked, with a bright smile and a girlish toss of her gleaming blonde tresses.

Dirk turned to look at the gun. "Back is bump fire, Mandy. Forward is for sequential. You push the little button forward like this, then when you pull the tool-free trigger, you get one nail at a time."

"Oh, Dirk, you make it all seem so simple," Mandy exclaimed, and pulled the trigger.

Dirk turned to the camera with a vacant smile and a two-and-a-half inch, sixteen-gauge finish nail embedded in the middle of his forehead.

The show went to commercials.

Jesus One fished for the remote and hit the mute button.The Khan turned to Jesús. "We're surfing for virgins," he said. How about Mandy Miller? She's such a sweet young thing. She can't be more than nineteen and, boy, is she innocent, or what!"

Jesús shifted position so he could look the Khan squarely in the eye. "Mandy Miller is twenty-nine and twice divorced. Not to mention she's had a serious nose job, Kevlar breast implants, and gets bi-monthly curve renditions at Lipo-World in Las Vegas."

"Don't knock it," the Khan retorted. "Me and him have been getting regular organ boosts and bio-sonic skeletal re-growth for close to two thousand years. Anyway, how come you know all this?"

"I read *Star* magazine in the break room."

"Who makes this *Star* magazine?"

"Listen, I don't buy em, I just read em. How the hell would I know who makes em?"

"There's more than one?"

"Sure there's more than one; it's a weekly." Jesús paused and scratched his head. "I think."

The Khan looked puzzled. "Why would you want to read about Mandy Miller every week?"

Jesús sighed. "First of all, let's get one thing straight. I don't give a flying Frisbee about Mandy Miller. Secondly, I only read the damned things because they're lying around. Personally, I prefer really old copies of *US News and World Report*, but somebody must be sneaking that one out, because it's hardly ever there anymore."

The Khan leaned forward with an intense look."Can you sneak out some *Star* magazines? I'd like to know more about Mandy Miller."

"Hear me out," Jesús said patiently. "I've only ever seen that one piece about Little Miss Dipstick. Mostly it's all about washed up movie stars battling cellulite and screwing one another."

"I'm still interested. Maybe it'll have stuff about virgins."

Jesús grinned and gave the Khan a fatherly pat on the knee. "Listen son, the only virgins you'll read about in *Star* magazine are the ones that have just been born. But if it will make you happy, I'll see what I can do."

"The thing is," interjected Jesus One, "and not wanting to get you off *Star* magazine, but the Khan is now saying it's more than just a matter of finding the virgins; you'll need staff."

Jesús frowned. "What is this, bait and switch? I thought you said you never had a problem."

"That's just it," the Khan said defensively. "I personally never had a problem. The reason being I never had to actually manage the girls. That was someone else's job. I always had a harem mistress, and then I had a lady of the robes, a keeper of the baths, a protector of the jewels, a guardian of the imperial turbans, and so on. It's a lot more complicated than you might think."

God hunched his shoulders and glowered. He crossed his legs then leaned forward and stabbed a curiously long index finger at the Khan. "You get one goddamn harem mistress, and that's it. It's always the same with you: Give you an inch, you take a mile."

"Okay," the Khan said, "have it your way, but I'll tell you this: whoever it is, she's going to have to be the mother of all bitches."

God turned to Jesús, who grinned. "Don't even ask," he said. "Boy, do I have a candidate for you."

"Call her up," God demanded.

"You've got to be kidding. I'll need time. I can't just pick up the phone and ask."

God cracked his knuckles and flexed his eyebrows. When he spoke, his voice was deadly calm. "Don't screw with me, mister; we don't have time. You're in or you're out. You shit or you get off the pot!"

Reluctantly, Jesús picked up the phone.

"Put it on speaker," God commanded. "I want to hear this."

Muriel answered on the second ring. "Speak!" she snapped.

"Hey, Muriel, it's Jesús, Jesús Martinez."

"Do you think I don't know your voice? Do I seem stupid to you, child? What you up to, Martinez?"

"Well, right now, I'm sitting here with Richard Nixon, Genghis Khan, and Jesus Christ. We just watched Mandy Miller drive a finish nail into Dirk Forrester's forehead."

There was a pause, followed by a soft click. "Got you, you son-of-a-bitch," Muriel said in a silky voice.

"What do you mean?" Jesús asked, suddenly feeling queasy.

"You're on tape, lover boy. You are all mine. You want to keep your job, you just report to Muriel first thing in the morning and we'll talk about your mental health problem. Maybe then, you'll start to see things my way."

"That's not fair, Muriel."

"You think I care? Why were you calling me anyway?"

"I want you to be mistress of my harem."

Muriel hung up.

Jesús turned to God and shrugged. "See what I mean."

God stood and folded his arms. He was wearing a dark blue suit with heavily padded shoulders. When he crossed his arms, the shoulders of the suit lifted like giant bat wings.

"She's perfect," he said, smiling enthusiastically. "Sign her up!"

"Shush!" interrupted Jesus One. "The show's back on."

God sat down again, arms still folded. He crossed his legs and retreated into a brooding silence.

Mandy Miller was on camera. She was sitting across from a good-looking young man of Indian descent. She turned to the camera with a perky grin. "Hi," she said, "this is Mandy Miller. Welcome back to 'Little Miss Fixit' with Mandy Miller. Now, as you know, just before the break, Dirk had a little accident. Doctor Prashant Nagpal is our resident physician. He's going to tell you how Dirk is doing."

The camera went to medium close on Doctor Nagpal, who smiled shyly. "Peoples are getting nails in the head all the time," he announced. "Not to worry, you see. Only last year, I can tell you, a hundred thousand peoples were treated for foreign bodies in the head. Ninety four percent of these peoples went home in the same day. All I am having to do for Dirk, is taking these Black and Decker power-assisted chain-nose pliers from his tool bag, and pulling out the nail."

He held up the heavy, motorized pliers. "I think we should all be having pliers just like these in our very own tool bags." He laughed infectiously. So much so that Mandy joined in.

"Come on in Dirk," Nagpal said, "and let us see how you are now doing." He stood up to welcome Dirk as the camera pulled back to medium wide. Dirk wandered onto the set wearing a black tee shirt that showed off his bulging torso, tight jeans, a low-slung tool belt, and hand-tooled Moroccan suede work boots. The nail gun drooped from his right hand. His smile was happier now, and the nail was gone; in its place was a small Band-Aid.

"So how is it now going with you, Dirk?" the doctor asked, vigorously pumping Dirk's free hand. Dirk turned on cue as the camera zoomed in to a full-face headshot. He didn't say anything; he just continued to smile happily, showing two rows of perfect teeth. A tiny dribble ran from the corner of his mouth. The camera immediately panned tight to Mandy.

"Well, that's all for this week, and remember, Doctor Nagpal is a trained physician. So if you find a nail or anything else in your head, don't try to remove it at home. All you have to do is visit your nearest emergency room. They'll be so pleased to see you." She tossed her hair and smiled brightly for the camera. "This is Mandy Miller for 'Little Miss Fixit' with Mandy Miller, saying goodbye folks. See you next week."

Jesús reached behind him for the remote and turned off the TV. God stood up again and yawned.

"I'm done," he said, "time to go."

"Just a minute," Jesús protested. "You heard what Muriel said. She recorded everything. Now I'm her bitch. It was supposed to be the other way around."

God grinned malevolently. "Don't you worry, Jesus," he said, "I'll remote erase the tape."

Then he was gone.

CHAPTER 9

Bringing Home the BACON

Writing for a penny a word is ridiculous. If a man really wanted to make a million dollars, the best way would be to start his own religion.

L. Ron Hubbard, science fiction writer and founder of The Church of Scientology

Billy Ray Bixbee's Baptist Adventist Church Of Nature (*BACON*) was his best idea, ever. The cross-denomination consumer demographic was a stroke of pure marketing genius. It joined evangelical fervor with an unstoppable demand for anything and everything green. It was a vision sent by the Lord—and he made sure everyone knew it.

During his first guest appearance on 'Little Miss Fixit' with Mandy Miller, Billy Ray came up with the line that really got him started:

"The Lord is thy shepherd, and the Lord sayeth unto me, 'Billy Ray, now ye shall be mine shepherd on earth. Lo, and shall thee not then lead thy flock unto green pastures?'"

"Oh, Billy Ray," Mandy exclaimed with an adoring smile. "I just love it so when you talk religion. It's so like, like it was the written down truth from the Bible." Then she set aside her Black and Decker soft-recoil jackhammer and hugged him.

After that, Billy Ray could do no wrong.

Frequently questioned about his lack of affiliation with the established Adventist and Baptist churches, Billy Ray had a quick smile and a ready answer, "They got their testimony, and I got mine. And, believe me, I talk with the same fella they do."

Within six months of his appearance on "Little Miss Fixit", Billy Ray was discussing a rent-to-own option on the NASA Vehicle Assembly Building (VAB) at Kennedy Space Center, Florida. NASA, bought by Virgin Galactic during the privatization initiatives of 2021, had been renamed North American Space Adventures, with Virgin retaining all rights to the original NASA name and logo. Since privatization, Virgin's Near Space Adventures (*NSA*) had rocketed, but it was struggling to make money with its Mars Trekking Venture (*MTV*).

Billy Ray was a godsend.

"This is how it's going to be," he explained to the Virgin executive board. "This here VAB is going to be repainted and fixed up inside and out. I'm going to name it Pastureland, after the calling I got to lead my flock to the pastures. The whole ceiling will be done in sky blue with clouds and angels. We'll have a theme park inside I'm calling Pastureland Farms. Then we'll have a big ass auditorium with its own IMAX where I get to preach. I'm talking big, big, and I got all the backing I want."

What really caught Virgin's attention, was the Archer McDaniel deal.

"We got a line of pure food products ready to go under the Pastureland Farms label." Billy Ray continued. "Archer McDaniel supplies dang near everything from frozen soy turkey lasagna to fresh-killed, fresh-baked, free-range soy chicken-pot-pie. Them Wal-Mart fellas handle point of sale. Oh, and by gosh, did I forget to mention, Global-Titanic will design and manage the whole indoor park shebang."

Richard Branson, still looking startlingly youthful despite his advanced years, rubbed his hands and leaned forward eagerly. "Forget the rent, Billy Ray. You name Virgin as Pastureland's exclusive travel partner and the VAB is all yours."

"It's a done deal," said Billy Ray. "Just so's I get to fly in that fancy Fanjet Falcon airplane y'all's got parked outside."

"No problem," said Branson, with a boyish grin that all but swallowed the rest of his face, "I've got a spare. You can pick up the keys on your way out."

***

Eight months later, on a frighteningly hot day in June, Billy Ray surveyed his handiwork. Relative humidity was at one hundred percent and the heat index had soared to 125°. Billy Ray wasn't perspiring because he was sitting in an immaculately restored 1956 V-8 Chevrolet Belair sedan, retro-fitted with total wrap-around climate control. He carefully placed his limited edition George W. Bush active senior sunglasses on the dash and squinted up at the VAB. His companion did the same, although her sunglasses were a good deal more feminine than his. They were Paris Hilton gold signature frames, with personalized laser-touch self-tinting lenses by Versace.

"Hell, Mandy, that there is the biggest goddamn air conditioned property on Earth and it didn't cost me but a half hour's worth of bullshit. Eight acres of prime indoor real estate and I got it for a dollar less than a buck. Now what do y'all think about that?"

Mandy Miller turned to Billy Ray and offered one of her most dazzling smiles. "Why, Billy Ray, I think the good Lord must have given you the gift of gab for a very good reason. You just shouldn't be putting yourself down that way."

Billy Ray seemed puzzled. "I wasn't running myself down, honey cake. I was just mouthing off like I always do."

Mandy reached across and stroked the lapel of Billy Ray's five thousand dollar, free-range Japanese silkworm, hand-spun and hand-stitched silk Brioni suit. "Well, when you preach to the faithful, just you remind them God has a purpose for us all."

Billy Ray leaned back and laughed. "Now, Mandy, don't you be giving me that prime-time religion. They know, and I know, the only purpose God gave them is to dig down, dig deep, and hand it over to Billy Ray Bixbee."

"Oh, Billy Ray," Mandy giggled, "the things you say."

Billy Ray shifted into drive and the Chevy smoothly gathered power, heading for the looming portal of the VAB's north entrance. Painted on one side of the building was a gigantic American flag. The blue field was the size of a regulation basketball court. Each star was six feet across. The stripes were as wide as a one-lane highway. The gargantuan metal door was close to five hundred feet high and six hundred feet wide. When they were exactly a half-mile from the building, Billy Ray reached for a garage door opener clipped to the driver-side visor.

"Watch this, gal," he cried, and hit the button.

The massive wheeled door started to inch open at considerably less than a snail's pace.

"I got it timed so I drives in from right here at six miles an hour. When we gets there, I can squeeze her in with a half inch either side."

He was as good as his word.

Mandy Miller was accustomed to far-out interior set design, but the inside of the Vehicle Assembly Building blew her mind. As they entered, the concrete apron gradually narrowed to become a winding country lane. They drove serenely past flower filled meadows framed by reinforced fiberglass willow trees and populated by electromechanical farm animals. Plump cows steadfastly munched on Astroturf. Mechanical birds twittered in the trees. Smiling goats looked up as they passed. Lambs frolicked happily by a gurgling stream. Ducks swam in neat circles around a millpond, carefully avoiding Styrofoam lily pads occupied by singing frogs. "*Whatever the weather, we'll all be together. We'll all be together, forever*," sang the frogs.

They sounded like early recordings of Mario Lanza.

Billy Ray pulled up to a solitary parking space at the entrance to a two-acre shopping mall at lane's end. "Only person drives in here is Billy Ray Bixbee. Every other sucker gets to stand in line."

"Well, Billy Ray, are you saying you're a sucker too?" Mandy inquired, with a disingenuous smile.

"Get out," said Billy Ray," and don't be a smart ass. I want to show you something."

They walked to the far side of the shopping mall and past the entrance to the Ministry Of Reborn Evangelicals of the Baptist Adventist Church Of Nature (*MORE-BACON*). The Ministry was a huge building within a giant building. Through the wide-open gilt embossed doors, Mandy caught a glimpse of a towering IMAX screen that must have been close to twelve stories high. Fronting the IMAX were tier upon tier of close-packed green canvas lawn chairs. The entire floor area was covered in green indoor/outdoor carpeting.

It started to rain.

"What the hell!" Mandy cried. She reached up instinctively to protect her hair.

"Ain't nothing Titanic can't fix," grinned Billy Ray. "This building is so big it has its own weather. When it gets humid outside, it rains inside and plays hell with the sound system and the cameras. Titanic has its own climate change control system though. They put it together for

Titanic World in Orlando. Works like a charm. Goddamned park gets sunshine *24-7-365*. Welcome to Wonderland, baby."

Billy Ray led Mandy to a three-acre vacant lot behind the ministry.

"But, Billy Ray, there's nothing here," she said.

"That's just it, babe, there ain't nothing here but concrete. But you are looking at the most valuable real estate on God's green earth." He walked over to a stack of green lawn chairs and picked one out. Stenciled on the canvas back in bright pink was the legend, *AARP-PRE-TRIB-RAP SEAT 8462*.

"But, it's just a frigging lawn chair," Mandy pointed out.

"This 'just a frigging lawn chair' as you so eloquently put it, is going to rake in close to a half million bucks before some fat asshole blows the bottom out of it." He pointed to the legend. "You any idea what this means?"

"No."

"This, babe, is going to be the biggest thing ever to hit faith-based marketing. It stands for Pre-Tribulation Rapture. Y'all know that before the time of the tribulation there will be the rapture of the faithful."

"What of it?"

"So, *Pre-Trib-Rap* will be the cornerstone of *BACON*. We timeshare the lawn chairs so the faithful can have somewhere to sit down, bring the kids, and read *Star* magazine while they wait."

"What about the *AARP*?" Mandy inquired.

Bixbee grinned. "Aw, shucks, honey, that's just Billy Ray's little joke. It stands for American Adventist Rapture Program. So, let em sue me."

"But, what if all these people show up, and there's no rapture, Billy Ray? What then?"

Billy Ray beamed. "That's the beauty of it, little darlin. See, because Al Gore invented the global warming and the old NASA found all them killer asteroids, and the honeybees all vanished, and you got worldwide flu just around every goddamned corner, and Muslims is blowing the shit out of white folks, not to mention each other. Why, everybody's got their own danged theory about how and when the world's going down."

Billy Ray was a big man, and he was apt to perspire whenever he was excited or sermonizing. For this reason he always carried at least two Gucci one hundred percent silk twill handkerchiefs on his person. He took off his Knudsen hand-formed, authentic Boss of the Plains Stetson and mopped his forehead. "Now, you just answer me this, sweet honey pie. If y'all had a choice between scratching and puking yourself to death from bird flu, or sitting in a lawn chair reading *Star* magazine and waiting for the end, what would you be doing?"

He unfolded the lawn chair and sat in it. "Believe me when I tell you, this here lawn chair is where they'll come. When you and me tie the knot July Fourth, we kick off the whole shebang. After the ceremony, we open the doors with a one time special: no money down and interest only payments for three years, and all I got invested is a bunch of cheap lawn chairs. The suckers pay for the timeshare. They choose the interval. When it comes their actual rapture time and it don't happen, why then, we'll do an interval swap and collect the broker's fee. We'll sell a full range of rapture merchandize, plus care and feeding while they're here. When the rapture doesn't happen, *BACON* will offer fee-based consolation, collect for park dues and incidentals, and clean up for the next bunch of morons."

"Oh, Billy Ray, you're so brilliant," Mandy gushed. Then she frowned. "But what if it actually happens, Billy Ray? What if the world really is going to blow up or something? Won't you be overbooked?"

"No," said Billy Ray, "we'll be totally fucked like everybody else, sugarplum."

CHAPTER 10

Believe in Jesus

Muriel was waiting for him.

After getting off the elevator, Jesús made straight for the break room, hoping to lift some *Star* magazines for the Khan. He opened the door furtively and popped his head in. The room was empty. He looked behind him to make sure he wasn't being watched. That's when he spotted Muriel.

She was sitting at the far side of the lobby by the giant window, leafing through an old issue of *Puget Sound This Week*. Suddenly, she threw the magazine down, stood like a drill sergeant, and headed his way. He wasn't sure he had been seen, but he was sure of one thing: Muriel Banks was hopping mad. A dark hole opened up beneath his rib cage and something scary wriggled out. He could feel it gnawing at his stomach, trying to get back in. He did the only thing he could: he entered the break room, closed the door quietly, and prayed.

Despite his ongoing collaboration with God, Jesús' prayer went unanswered. Muriel came through the door like the front man on a special weapons team. This was the first time Jesús had ever been attacked by a woman. All she did was poke him repeatedly in the chest with an index finger, but it was enough to send him cowering behind the break room sofa. Muriel's other hand brandished a tiny *MacPod Insta-Greet* (*MacPIG*) module.

"When Muriel's home, Muriel does the greeting, but this thing is plugged into my phone 24-7, smart mouth. I do the talking, and it does the listening." She marched around the sofa and grabbed him by the arm. "I got you taped. First off, you get yourself some kind of religious phobia, now you're leaving freaked out messages on my phone." She dragged him towards the door. "I've had enough. You and I have a meeting downstairs, right now."

He knew exactly where they were headed. Descending in the elevator, Muriel didn't say a word and didn't move a muscle. She was like a viper poised to strike. Jesús thought furiously, casting about in near panic for plausible half-truths and outright lies. Nothing convincing came to mind. He was going to have to wing it.

Muriel didn't wait to be announced. She barged past a stone-faced executive assistant and marched Jesús straight into Roy Upstart's office. Upstart was the FAA Northwest Regional Administrator. He was as high as you could go in the building without actually climbing onto the roof. He was also as scared of Muriel Banks as everyone else in the tower.

Upstart looked up from his desk with a tight smile. "Good morning, Muriel. Shirley gave me your message. Why don't you two just make yourselves at home?" He gestured to a squat, dark haired woman sitting across from him. He seemed faintly surprised, as though he had only just realized she was there. "Oh, and please let me introduce Doctor Agnes McDrab. She's the head of Psychiatry and Behavioral Sciences at University of Washington Medical Center. She's an old friend, and wouldn't you know it, she just happened to be in the building. Bearing in mind your concerns about the mental state of Mister Martinez, Muriel, I've asked Agnes to sit in, if you don't mind."

The woman smiled modestly and greeted the arrivals.

"Hi, don't you mind me, and by the way you can call me Aggie. Everybody else does."

Upstart chuckled approvingly, which struck Jesús as odd since the man was definitely not known to be a chuckler. "How come you have a Scottish accent?" he asked. "McDrab doesn't sound Scottish at all. It's like it was made up or something. You don't mind my asking do you?"

She chuckled along with Upstart. "Och, mon! I dinna mind a wee bit. The McDrabs are actually an old Scottish family. We've been around since the time of William Wallace. You're right though, in a way. I'm descended from the first Lord Drab. He supervised Wallace's drawing and quartering. In gratitude, Edward the First made him an honorary Scot and bestowed all of Wallace's lands and possessions on him. We've kept the McDrab name and the castles ever since."

"You know," said Jesús, with a thin smile. "I've got a friend who would just love to to have a word with you."

Muriel sat down and glanced sideways at the doctor with the cold, calculating stare of a professional assassin. "Cut the social chit-chat," she said in a dangerously quiet voice. "We're not here for history lessons."

She slammed the *MacPIG* down on Upstart's desk and jerked her head angrily at Jesús. "We're here to listen to this and talk to him!" She thumbed a tiny button on the side of the *MacPIG*. There was a short pause filled with low-level static, then Richard Nixon's voice oozed out of the micro-speakers. "Believe in Jesus," the voice said.

"Play that again, will you please?" asked the doctor.

"Believe in Jesus," repeated Nixon slowly.

"You know," she murmured, "that voice sounds creepy, and it's oddly familiar. I could swear I've heard it somewhere before."

"Me too," agreed Upstart.

Sensing a chance to ingratiate himself, Jesús chimed in. "Yes, by golly, you're right. There is something faintly familiar about it. I'll be darned if I know who it is, though."

"You know perfectly well who it is," Muriel cried. "That's you putting on some smarmy voice you think I won't recognize. Well, as a matter-of-fact, I recognized it right away. It's a lousy imitation of Richard Nixon. Do you think I'm some kind of ignorant fool who never took history lessons?" She glared at Upstart. "What you have here is a seriously deranged individual. Last night he called me and said he was watching 'Little Miss Fixit' with Jesus Christ, Genghis Khan, and Richard Nixon. I recorded the whole thing. When I played it back this morning, all I got was this sick message. Not only that, he asked me if I wanted to be mistress of his harem."

"Excuse me," interposed Upstart, "would that be Richard Nixon, or Mister Martinez?"

Muriel looked at him in amazement. "I'm talking about this sorry sack of nonsense sitting next to me. Who else would I be talking about, child? Don't you ever listen?"

Upstart looked down and discreetly shuffled papers.

"I see, I see," the doctor observed. "And would you perhaps have a recording of the part about you being his mistress, Muriel?"

Muriel stared at the other woman with eyes full of contempt. "That would be Miss Banks to you. I'd turned the thing off by then. And you can just wash that Scottish peat from out your ears, woman. He didn't ask me to be his mistress; he asked me to be mistress of his *harem*."

Roy Upstart and Agnes McDrab turned to Jesús—eyes wide open. Torn between coming clean or denying everything, Jesús realized he had only one option. He made his move. "I said no such thing." His tone was decisive as he slipped easily into his favorite fantasy, one that was an inexhaustible well of believable lies. "I mean, I did call, but just to see if she'd mind me swapping shifts next week. A close friend just died in a snowboarding pileup, and I said I'd like a couple of days off for the funeral. To be honest, I'm just as confounded by all this as you are."

It worked; it always worked. It worked because deep down Jesús saw himself as a world-class snowboarder. This was one of many teenage dreams that never materialized. He had persuaded his Auntie Carmen to buy him the board for his thirteenth birthday. Then he had set out for the slopes with the thousand-yard stare and the easy swagger of a future world champion. In the event, a perfectly natural fear of dying young, coupled with a puzzling inability to master nose and tail rolls, sent him in other directions. But the dream lived on as a deeper part of him; a pleasing alternate reality, if you will; so he could never quite let go.

"Tell me, Muriel," the doctor asked in a soothing tone, "have you been experiencing any other dreamlike sensations or perceptual distortions recently?"

Muriel pounded the desk then and made a lunge for Jesús. He leaned back in fright.

Without seeming to move, Agnes McDrab spun Muriel's chair around and clamped thickly muscled fingers around Muriel's forearms. Her knees pressed hard against Muriel's legs, immobilizing her from the waist down. All Muriel could move were her head, her hands, and her toes. The doctor continued speaking as though nothing had happened. "Do you have difficulty sleeping, lassie? Do you seem to panic without cause? Do you have this feeling something really bad is about to happen, and you're powerless to prevent it?"

Muriel screamed.

Upstart reached for his phone. The doctor shook her head gently. "That willna be necessary, Roy, I'm just establishing precursors. If yourself and the young man will kindly leave us alone for a while, Muriel and I will be having a wee chat. I have this feeling she might be needing a little time to herself."

As he left, Jesús sneaked a guilty look over his shoulder. Muriel was glaring at him with a curious mix of childlike desperation and implacable rage. Half of her seemed lost and betrayed (with good reason); the other half was all too obviously out to get him. He wasn't sure which half disturbed him most. He was sure of one thing, though: as far as Muriel was concerned, the gloves were off; playtime was definitely over.

Sharp teeth got going again in his lower intestine as he headed for the elevator.

Foreboding descended like a dark veil.

CHAPTER 11

Chicks and a Violin

Jesus One and the Khan stopped watching television within a week of reading the *Star* magazines Jesús had pilfered. Although intrigued by "Hot Gossip" and "Star Style", the sight of cellulite so sickened the Khan he also stopped reading the magazine. For his part, Jesus One was appalled by Rosie O'Donnell's persistent feud with Larry King. Larry was ninety-three years old by this time, and it seemed to Jesus One he was just a confused old man, undeserving of Rosie's unrelenting attacks. Worst of all, both the Khan and Jesus One were astonished and disillusioned by the shocking off-screen antics of their on-screen heroes. So, instead of channel surfing, they switched to surfing the web.

Not to mention, the clock was ticking loudly on the quest for virgins.

Jesús had snatched the *Star* magazines from the break room immediately after leaving Roy Upstart's office following his session with Muriel. A week later, he returned to the scene of the crime. He had wandered in casually, hoping to snare some more magazines. He didn't see any, but was happy to stay.

Since Muriel had been encouraged to take indefinite medical leave, the place was greatly changed. Instead of her anti-trade union tirades, soft jazz played in the background. Chess playing and online poker were enjoying a renaissance. CNN Distractions ran continuously with the sound off. The coffee was always fresh, and someone always remembered to pick up three boxes of Dunkin Donuts at the start of every shift.

Dennis Floyd fixed Jesús a double cream mint latte and joined him by the fireplace. Already, he seemed ten years younger. With a sigh of contentment, he lowered himself into the open arms of a fireside Chesterfield.

"Only one thing missing, Jesús," he said, with a reminiscent smile.

"And what might that be?" Jesús asked, sipping his latte gratefully.

Dennis looked around to be sure no one was listening. He leaned forward confidentially. "Hate to say this," he whispered, "but I really miss having those *Star* magazines around."

"Oh, really," Jesús replied innocently.

"Only nice thing Muriel ever did."

"What do you mean?"

"Well, she's the one used to bring em in. I guess she must have taken them all back when she got busted. That would be typical of the bitch."

Jesús remained as calm as he could, but a fearful presence slowly sucked the air from his lungs. "Gee, Dennis, I'm sorry to hear that. Maybe we should take out a joint subscription to *Global World News* or something." He set down the latte. "Anyway, sorry I can't stay to finish this. I'm running late for a snowboarding convention."

All the way home, he was torn by guilt for betraying Muriel and his growing fear of the consequences. Dennis had unwittingly and forcefully reminded him that Muriel was very definitely going to come after him; it was just a matter of time. Fear eventually overcame guilt; it was like a bread knife slicing his liver. "My God, what have I gotten myself into now?" he repeated over and over, punctuating each outburst by slamming his head against the steering wheel.

By the time he got back to the apartment, Jesús was an emotional wreck, and God was back for the first time since Muriel had been furloughed. He happened to be closest to the door, enveloped by the recliner, his elbows just visible, so he caught the brunt of it. "I've got a bone to pick with you, mister," Jesús growled.

God put down the *Star* magazine he was reading and got to his feet. His eyes twinkled. His face was lit with a mischievous smile. "For why must we to pick this bone together my young friend, and so where must we go to pick it?" God asked jokingly.

Jesús recognized Him instantly. He was Albert Einstein.

Jesús put his head in his hands. "I just don't fucking need this right now!" he groaned.

Einstein smiled fondly. "You know, when I see you to do this, I am to reminded of my little Hans Albert." A distant look came into his eyes. "You see, one time I have promised him we shall go for hiking at Seelisberg. He was so happy. Alas, it snowed, and I have explained to him we will therefore to stay in the hotel for discussing the non-Euclidian geometry. The sturdy little chap was holding his head just as you are." Einstein chuckled at the memory. "He has also said what you have said. Of course, he has said it in the good German. This was, many years before he came to America and discovered this other word you have used."

Jesús looked up. "When you erased the tape, what possessed you to leave that frigging message?"

Einstein fumbled for his pipe and looked off into space. He continued to stare at the ceiling for close to a minute before coming back to Earth. "Have you to seeing my matches?"

"No, I just came through the door. I was asking about the message."

"Ah, yes, this message I am leaving with Muriel," Einstein said, with a childlike smile. "It was to bring the lovebirds once again together. So I have asked her to believe in you."

"What you asked Muriel to believe in was Jesus One. She thought it was some kind of freaked out religious crank call and hauled me downstairs. You pronounced my name wrong again—and don't say I didn't tell you about that."

By now, Einstein was tamping tobacco in his polished briar pipe, seemingly oblivious to the reprimand.

"Well, did you find your matches?" Jesús inquired, giving up on his obviously futile protest.

"So why should I be to looking for my matches?" Einstein said with a bemused smile. "When I need matches I can to finding them in the pockets of my overcoat."

A long, beige Burberry was draped over the back of the recliner. Sitting on top of the coat was a navy blue wool seaman's cap. Jesús walked over to retrieve the matches. Half way across the room, he almost stepped on Einstein's violin case, which was lying on the floor not far from the recliner.

"Gee, I'm sorry," he exclaimed. "I wasn't expecting a violin in the middle of my living room. I guess that's what happens when people show up uninvited. They just dump their frigging stuff all over the place and expect you to step over it."

"Please, you must not to worry about this silly old violin of mine," Einstein said with a warm smile. "If it gets broken, then so shall it be. I will just to find another one."

He leaned forward then, and peered closely at Jesús with a puzzled look. "By the way, my boy, for why do you have this furrow in your head?"

Jesús picked up the battered old violin case and placed it on top of the television. He felt his forehead and ran a finger in the groove created when he had recently taken to bumping his head against the steering wheel. "Jeez, your right. How about that? Listen, Doctor Einstein, I'm not myself right now. Just bear with me, will you please?"

"Ach, my little *bubeleh*, it is nothing," Einstein said, stoking his pipe. "And, you must to calling me, Albert. I have never liked it to be called, Herr Doktor by my friends."

"Yo, Jesús," the Khan beckoned, "come on over here. I think we just hit pay dirt."

Einstein sat down and picked up the *Star* magazine, puffing happily at his pipe. On the far side of the living room, Jesus One was sitting at Jesús' workstation. The Khan was leaning over his shoulder.

"What is it now?" asked Jesús, wandering over.

"It's a nightclub in Gainesville called Chicks in Paradise," the Khan said with an excited grin. "All this time we've been searching for virgins and not finding anything, except a whole bunch of stuff about his mother." He pointed to Jesus One. "Anyway, I got this idea to search for chicks instead, and bingo!"

Jesús stroked his chin. "Gainesville, Gainesville? Of course, that's a university town. I remember now—University of Florida. It was always number three or four on the top twenty list of best party colleges. It should be a great place to look for virgins. Although, come to think of it, when it comes to virgins, maybe we should be thinking Brigham Young. It was always voted most sober."

"Nah!" the Khan opined. "Remember, we don't have much time. And we don't just want virgins; we want willing virgins. We need to score fast. Which was number one?"

"Most of the time it was WVU, West Virginia, but believe me, you wouldn't want to go there dressed the way you are. People in West Virginia don't take kindly to strangers showing up in funny clothes."

Jesus One turned with a look of protest. "Incidentally, it wasn't entirely his idea. I already had chicks on my list. I just hadn't gotten to it yet. By the way, you have a large indentation in the middle of your forehead."

"Yes I know. It's nothing, I just bumped my head on the steering wheel. Don't worry about it."

"Where have I heard that before," Jesus One said with a compassionate smile. He stood and gently placed his hand over the groove. Jesús felt a warm, joyful glow suffuse the top of his head. Jesus One removed his hand. "How's that feel?" he asked.

Jesús carefully felt his forehead. Not only was the groove gone, but also the tiny frown lines he had been worrying about. "Man," he said, "you should take out an ad in *Star* magazine. You could make a fortune as God's answer to Botox."

"I don't think so," Jesus One replied. "It only works with certain people. I can tell when I look into their eyes. They're either more or less selfless or totally self-obsessed. I'll give you one guess as to which ones respond. Anyway," he said, sitting back down, "I'm done with *Star* magazine. Rosie just won't let up on poor old Larry and I can't bring myself to read about it anymore."

"That's all to the good," Jesús said, "because I'm taking them all back."

CHAPTER 12

Jimmy the Fish

By mid afternoon, Noahu was pleasantly warm, though a little steamy. When Chamberlain stumbled on deck the moisture breathed all over him. Fortunately, out in the lagoon the air was rarely still. Every night, a cooling breeze drifted down from the heights of the old volcano. Every afternoon the process was reversed. Today, though, it wasn't so much a breeze as a cool tap on the forehead.

Marge was pouring a glass of her cranberry vodka for a young man who was the spitting image of Barry, except that he had what might be described as a bit of a Roman nose. Also, his right arm was intact, and his head wasn't painted.

It must be said that Marge Chamberlain's cranberry vodka was legendary. Her recipe was treasured along the shores of the tropical North Atlantic, throughout the Caribbean island chain, and, more recently, among the remote archipelagos of the South Pacific.

"Grandma was all for calling me Alfred, after Granddad," the young man was explaining to Marge, sipping the vodka with evident enjoyment, "but my Mum had been having it off with this Italian from Brisbane, so she wanted Alfredo."

"That's nice, only, I was wondering. I understand about the old missionary names, but Alfredo threw me for a bit of a loop."

Chamberlain rubbed his eyes and yawned. He was having trouble seeing and sitting down. Sitting down was a problem because Hilda, their eight-year-old Irish wolfhound, was taking up ninety percent of the available space. Chamberlain was also having difficulty managing his legs. "If you don't mind my saying so," he interrupted, "you're the spitting image of the chief, and I happen to know his name is Barry."

"Right," Alfredo said, "he's my granddad."

"Then why aren't you called Barry?"

"Because his Christian name is Alfred, his real name is *Noahureake*, but everybody calls him, Barry."

Chamberlain wiped his forehead with one of the nautical napkins Marge liked to hand out with her vodka. "What kind of a name is Alfred, anyway?" he grunted. "That was Batman's butler. I like Alfredo even less. It's too frigging foreign. How about I call you Jimmy: Jimmy-the-Fish?"

"Yeah, all right, mate." Alfredo grinned. "You enjoy that kava then?"

Marge raised an eyebrow. "So that's what it was. How did you know, Alfredo?"

"It's not so hard, missus. He's walking like he has six legs. Anyway, Barry mentioned he'd had enough to keep him out cold for a week."

Marge gave Frank an accusing look. "How many times have you promised me, Frank Chamberlain?"

Chamberlain reached into the cooler for a beer. "Sorry, I was just being sociable."

Marge leaned over and snatched the nautical napkin from him. "And how many times have I told you not to use these for wiping your nose."

"I wasn't wiping my nose, Marge, I was just dabbing my head."

"Well, it amounts to the same thing. You can dab your head on one of your dirty old tee shirts."

Sensing discord, Alfredo gestured to the canoe. "Anyway, come and have a look at the fish. I did all right this morning. You can have what you want."

The tiny canoe was brimming with reef fish, most of which looked as though they had just been lifted from a very large, very expensive aquarium. Lying by the prow was a beautifully carved, teak spear gun. Alfredo climbed down and sorted through the fish until he came up with a bumphead wrasse that must have weighed close to ten pounds. He held it up proudly and offered it to Marge. "I'd usually keep this for my auntie, but she's gone off somewhere, so you can have it."

Marge carefully took the fish and handed it to Frank. "How much do we owe you, Alfredo," she asked.

Alfredo grinned. "You don't owe me anything—I've got all I need for right now. When I want money I'll ask you for it."

He surveyed his fish. "You want any more?"

"No thanks. You just come and finish your vodka, and tell me how I should cook this."

"I'll tell you what, missus," grinned Alfredo as he climbed back on board, "I'll tell you how to do my fish, if you'll tell me how to make your vodka."

Back in the cockpit, under the shade of the Bimini top, Marge carefully wrote down her recipe and handed it over. "Now it's your turn," she prompted.

"Well, first, you scrape out the insides. Then chop it up, but keep the head whole. Then we always pack it in a basket, put the top on tight, and boil it all up. If you don't have a basket, put it in a pan. A basket's best because it's self-draining. When it's done, all you have to do is take the top off and pick the meat from the bones. Of course, you can sprinkle on whatever spices you like first, and a bit of coconut butter on the fish helps a lot too."

Chamberlain was already licking his lips. "Sounds good, Marge. You want me to clean out one of your flower baskets?"

Marge turned on him as though she had a kitchen knife in her hand and was getting ready to use it. Ever alert to the slightest hint of domestic unrest, Hilda closed her eyes, put her head between her paws, and pretended to be sleeping soundly.

"You leave my flowers alone, Frank Chamberlain. I've got a perfectly good basket we bought in Panama that I can use."

"Anyway," continued Alfredo, every bit as alert as Hilda when it came to signs of friction, "the head's the best part. It's got fat all over so it stays juicy. Just make sure you cook it while it's still fresh." He leaned back and surveyed the boat. "She's a nice boat, sure enough. Good thing fiberglass came along. My lot's been building boats from wood since before the flood. I made my own canoe you know, dug it from a tree trunk. For all the time it took, I might just as well have bought a bloody plastic kayak."

Chamberlain rapped the side of the cockpit. "Believe me, Jimmy, all this stuff has going for it is that it's cheap, strong, and easy to fix. Somebody once said it's like making boats out of frozen snot. Of course, he probably wasn't on a budget. You stick with wood, though. There's already enough frigging plastic out there."

Alfredo seemed unconvinced. "All the same, it must be nice, being rich. Having a big boat like this to sail off in whenever you feel like it."

Having heard this many times before, Marge was quick to reply. "We're not rich. All we have are our Army pensions and the boat. We don't have a house and the boat is forty years old. Also, it's not that big when you have to live in it."

"Looks like new, though." said Alfredo with an admiring smile.

"Yes, well, Frank's handy, and I clean a lot."

"Were you in the Army then, both of you?"

"We were," Marge smiled fondly at her husband. "He was my action hero. He's more of an old fart now, but he's still my hero."

"What did you do then?"

"What we did was the Islamic wars for twenty years," Frank replied, looking grim. "Then we cashed in the first chance we got. Marge was the best goddamned combat nurse ever enlisted, and they treated her like shit."

"Yeah," Alfredo said, "we used to get the wars a lot on the telly." He sighed. "Not any more though. We're not watching it these days."

"Why not?" Marge asked, looking concerned. "Did it break?"

Alfredo's face opened up with a big, ear-to-ear grin. "Believe me, you don't want to know."

"Try us," Chamberlain muttered. "We lived on Army bullshit for twenty years. Another shovelful won't hurt."

Alfredo leaned forward. "Well, we've had the telly on the island ever since I can remember. It's Barry's and we'd watch it every night. Last week though, the mail boat dropped off his *Star* magazine and he had a fit."

"I thought he didn't speak English?" queried Chamberlain.

"Well, he doesn't, and he can't read it either, so I read them for him."

"I've got some old *People* magazines I can let you have," Marge said.

"Marge, please be quiet and let him finish," Frank said impatiently.

"Anyway," Alfredo continued, growing serious, "we all like watching 'Little Miss Fixit', with Mandy Miller, especially Barry. Then I read him last week's *Star* and he got so mad he said nobody on the Island can watch television anymore. Barry's the chief so we've got to do what he tells us."

"That's amazing," Chamberlain said. "I just dreamt about that old show. It's not still going, is it?"

"Very much so. In fact, Mandy Miller was the problem. She stuck a nail in Dirk Forrester's head. The worst part, and this is what really pissed off Barry, is that she might have done it deliberately. We all thought it was an accident, but *Star* revealed she was jealous of Dirk."

"We haven't watched television in a long time, Alfredo," Marge explained. "That's one of the reasons we decided to get the boat, so if we're a bit slow on the uptake, you'll just have to bear with us. Now, exactly why did Mandy Miller put a nail in this young man's head?"

"It was ratings. She's been down in the ratings ever since *Star* revealed she was no longer a nineteen-year old virgin. Show's been on for ten years too, so what was the big bloody surprise about that? Anyway, she was about to be laid off and Dirk was going to be the main man. The new show was going to be called *Doing it with Dirk*. Mandy found out, and somebody caught her saying she'd nail him first chance she got. When he heard that, Barry got so upset he said he'd never watch television ever again."

Marge winked at Chamberlain with a satisfied smile. "It sounds as though we made at least one good decision, Frank."

CHAPTER 13

Extinction Event

The general uplift of the Yellowstone caldera is scientifically interesting and will continue to be monitored closely by YVO staff.

Yellowstone Volcano Observatory (YVO)

When the Global-Titanic Worldwide Entertainment Corporation re-costumed the Yellowstone Park Rangers, they took as their inspiration a 1958 Paul Newman movie called *The Left-Handed Gun*. By 2023 there had been twenty-seven more screen epics depicting the life of William H. Bonner. Bonner, born Henry McCarty, actually preferred to be known as Billy the Kid, and apparently suffered from some kind of identity crisis. Nonetheless, Billy was an enduring western legend. Titanic chose the Newman character as their role model because his was the most neatly turned out and the only one without a trace of facial hair. A real plus was that Newman was thirty-three years old when he played the teenage outlaw. Titanic executives thought this better reflected the image of authority they wished to project with the new costume.

To begin with, Vernon Trumboy didn't like the costume; he thought he would be laughed at. In particular, he was uncomfortable with the gun on his left hip because he was right-handed. Female rangers filed a protest when they discovered they would be required to dress as

Newman's co-star, Lita Milan. As it turned out, the dresses were unanimously given two thumbs up by park-visitor focus groups.

So that was the end of that.

As it turned out, the first time Vernon wore his new costume in public he was greeted by gasps of admiration and asked for his autograph. From then on, he was more than happy with the idea.

The only downside was the themed audio that came with the clothing.

Shortly after the release of *The Left Handed Gun,* Marty Robbins recorded the hit ballad, *Big Iron*, as in "Big Iron On His Hip". The song told the tale of a lone Arizona ranger gunning down Texas Red—a dastardly outlaw modeled after Billy the Kid. For some unexplained reason, the showdown happened in the song at eleven-twenty in the morning, as opposed to high noon. Other than that, Vernon thought the rendition was great—until he had to hear it eighty times a day. Fortunately, sewn-in sensors muted the music every time he spoke and whenever he entered a building or climbed into his truck.

Just as fortunately, he wasn't expected to ride a horse, or actually draw his weapon.

***

Two weeks after the Lava Park briefing, Dick Derringer returned. He flew directly from Beijing on a Titanic corporate jet, bringing with him a Chinese VIP guest. In his capacity as the senior park-liaison officer, Vernon was responsible for hosting the visit. He left his park service truck in the cast member parking lot behind the Planet Earth Pavilion. Parked nearby was one of Titanic's VIP vehicles: a compressed air drive Toyota Homelander Special Edition Maxi-Cab truck with All Wheel Muscle-Traction. Making sure his big iron was firmly strapped to his left thigh, Vernon climbed in and headed for the airstrip.

Although Vernon was not one to be struck by nature, there were days when even he marveled. Today was such a day. It was no more than ten miles to the airstrip—a former pasture favored by the bison for sunning themselves on cool fall days—but enough of a distance to immerse yourself briefly in the wilderness. Within minutes, the single track road was the only sign of man's intrusion. Ahead of him, rugged, snow tipped mountains looked like a child's cutout pasted over a too-perfect sky; as if the child had painted the sky with her most brilliant blue; as if she had thought her usual dumpy clouds and round, yellow sun would have spoiled it this time. Between the blue-gray cutout mountains and the road, the child had brushed in bold strokes of meadow green. Trees, in long lines as they followed water, or in clumps and copses, grew out of the painted green grass.

Too perfect by far, you might say, if you didn't know it was real. Over all to soon, you would say, if you were Vernon Trumboy and for once thanking your lucky stars you're alive and in the world and enjoying a day such as this.

The Fanjet Falcon was barely at a standstill when the door swung open. Dick Derringer bounded down the steps. Following sedately behind was a slightly built Chinese man wearing rimless George W. Bush signature eye-wear and an expensive, but cleverly understated business-suit by Brioni.

Dick greeted Vernon like an old friend, clasping the ranger's right hand in both of his and flashing a hugely delighted grin. "Vernon, it's so lovely to see you."

Vernon hesitated awkwardly. He wasn't sure if he should lean in for a peck on the cheek. Instead, he settled for a shy smile.

Derringer introduced his companion. "Vernon, this is Jung Shi-Zhe, chairman of the Honest Electrical Engineering and Office Furniture Factory of Pingyang. He is a valued business partner and future guest of the Villas at Lava Park." He turned to his guest. "Shi, this is Ranger Vernon Dumboy of the United States Park Service."

Shi-Zhe bowed formally and shook hands. "It is so very nice to meet you, Ranger Dumboy. Please, in America I like to be called, Steve."

"Gosh, Steve, it's a real pleasure, and you can call me Vern," Vernon gushed.

Dick Derringer climbed into the front seat of the Homelander with Vernon, while Shi-Zhe settled in the back. "You know where we're headed, Vernon, I take it," Dick said, with one of his trademark smiles.

"Sure. Straight for the volcano observatory. Everybody's expecting you; although they're all a bit curious as to why you're here."

Dick turned to Shi-Zhe with a conspirator's grin. "Well, I guess they're about to find out. Isn't that right, Shi?"

Shi-Zhe responded politely. "Yes, Dick, very soon they find out."

Operated by the U.S. Geological Survey and the University of Utah, The Yellowstone Volcano Observatory (YVO) was the sole remaining federal facility in the park. Like the Park Rangers, the YVO scientists enjoyed government salaries and benefits. Unlike the rangers, they also enjoyed autonomy from day-to-day park operations. Their job was to monitor and report on seismic, geodetic, and hydrologic activity within the park—nothing more, nothing less—and they took the job very seriously indeed.

Just before the infamous lava leak of 2024, the YVO had moved to stunning new quarters atop one of the highest peaks overlooking Yellowstone. Since then, the observatory had been under siege. Taken to task by the media for overstating the danger of the event, YVO scientists had suffered deep budget cuts and the scorn of disenchanted park visitors.

Life on the mountain was not so good anymore.

Vernon maneuvered the Homelander skillfully up the steep, winding road leading to the northern rim of the park. As they climbed, the indescribable magnificence of Yellowstone extended below and beyond, as far as they could see. He spoke with the practiced ease of a park professional. "What you see here is the result of more than seventeen million years of volcanic activity. Last big one was somewhere around six hundred thousand years ago. There were two more before that, and they were all about six hundred thousand years apart. So the next one will be number four, and it's due. It could easily be another thousand years or more before it blows, though."

Shi-Zhe leaned forward with a polite smile. "How big have they been, Vern?"

"Well, they all start with massive outpourings of lava and volcanic ash, then you get the mother of all eruptions. They don't come any bigger. Billions of tons of ash particles and sulfuric acid droplets could spread across the entire upper atmosphere in weeks. It might go dark for years. Temperatures would drop, and then all that ash would start to come back down. Pretty much everything on the planet would die off eventually, including us. It's what we call an extinction event—right up there with them giant asteroids."

He took his left hand from the wheel and pointed out the open window. "Down there is what we call the caldera, which is just a fancy name for a giant crater. That's from the last eruption. It was so big it blew this ginormous hole in the earth's crust. The entire park is well over two-million acres." He turned to grin at Shi-Zhe. "And that, Steve, is near as big as the state of Connecticut."

"Eyes on the road, and hands on the wheel, Vernon," Derringer muttered nervously.

Vernon did as requested. "We're almost there, folks."

They turned into a wide driveway leading up to the Frank Lloyd Wright inspired observatory. The architect had used Wright's famed organic approach, in which buildings seem to be born of their surroundings. Great cubes and rectangular forms of sandstone, granite, and volcanic rock emerged from the mountainside. Framed by massive logs of treated pine, a gracefully curved observation deck topped off the edifice.

Derringer gasped. "Titanic couldn't have done it better."

"I like it very much," Shi-Zhe murmured.

Vernon smiled proudly. "Wait until you see the inside. By the way, under this baby is a nuclear hardened safe room the size of my house. They put it in so the scientists can observe major volcanic activity up to the last minute. Be the greatest show on earth if you were stupid enough to stick around."

Waiting by the hand-fashioned, eco-harvested, redwood doors was the YVO chief scientist, Doctor Edward Clump. He seemed nervous.

After the hand shaking and ceremonial exchange of business cards, Clump conducted them to the observatory conference room. The senior staff stood in gloomy silence around the conference table, an eighteen-foot by six-foot slab of polished Welsh slate. "I'm sorry we have no chairs," Clump mumbled apologetically, "but the old ones were declared unsafe by OSHA. The Department of the Interior confiscated them and we're still waiting for the new ones."

Derringer turned to Shi-Zhe. "You make chairs don't you, Steve? Anything you can do for these folks?"

There was a long pause while Shi-Zhe scrutinized his shoes. "I sincerely hope new chairs come very soon," he whispered apologetically.

Derringer shot a disappointed look at the chair manufacturer, but brightened immediately. "Anyway, gentlemen, let's look on the positive side shall we? If we all have to stand, the meeting won't last very long, will it?"

"I sure as hell hope not," someone muttered.

Derringer ignored that. He reached into a side pocket of his blazer and came up with a small hand-held device that looked remarkably like a *MacPod*, save for two tiny triangular black ears poking from the top. He nodded proudly to Shi-Zhe. "Say hello to the *MousePad*, gentlemen—a joint venture of the Pingyang Honest Electrical Engineering and Office Furniture Factory and Global-Titanic Entertainment,

Worldwide. Our lawyers say we can get away with the little mouse ears because, after all, we've called it the *MousePad*, which is a name no one can copyright, and the ears aren't round like Disney's. Ours actually look like mouse ears."

He casually thumbed one of the tiny ears and a brilliant white flash erupted on the far wall. A loud buzzing noise sounded from inside the *MousePad*. Shi-Zhe leaned over, took the device from Derringer, and slapped it hard on the table. Immediately, the buzzing stopped and the blinding white patch dissolved into a crystal-clear, nine by twelve image of another tiny device. Derringer retrieved the *MousePad* from Shi-Zhe and held it up. "This is a prototype *MousePad* Instant Laser Entertainment System, otherwise known as *MousePILES*. It has a built-in stereoscopic camera and projector with multi-phonic audio playback and it can project a nine by twelve image, in broad daylight, from as far away as two miles. It also retails for less than half the price of the *MacPIP*." He gestured to the projected image. "And over here, gentlemen, is your future. We call it the *MousePad* Earth Seismic Tremor System, or *MousePESTS*."

The scientists craned forward to examine the displayed image. Dick Derringer handed the *MousePILES* to Shi-Zhe, who continued. "You see, we scatter *MousePESTS* all over park and they send back seismic signal via satellite to Pingyang. Then we employ student from Pingyang Polytechnic to read signal and make report."

Doctor Clump raised his hand. "Excuse me, Mister Jung, but don't you mean students, plural?"

"No, we have calculate we only need one person."

"But what about all those signals and all those reports you'll need to process?"

Shi-Zhe smiled indulgently. "We also calculate one signal and one report."

Clump reddened and clenched his fists. "I believe, sir, I will talk to the secretary of the interior about this."

Dick Derringer smiled slyly and handed the scientist an envelope. "That won't be necessary, Doctor Clump, the secretary has already made her decision."

Clump slowly opened the envelope and read the enclosed letter. He looked up and addressed his colleagues with a grim expression. "It says here the observatory will cease operations, effective immediately. Henceforth, all monitoring and reporting activity will be conducted by the Honest Electrical Engineering and Office Furniture Factory of Pingyang." He let out a prolonged sigh. "I guess that's it, boys. You can't say we weren't expecting something like this."

The senior staff growled threateningly.

"Read on," Derringer urged, his voice edged with panic.

Clump continued reading. Suddenly, his face lit up with a broad smile. "Hey!" he exclaimed. "It's not all bad. It says here that senior staff is reassigned forthwith to the volcano observatory in Hawaii."

He looked up with relief written all over him. "That's a hell of a lot closer to the beach than this place." The senior staff cheered. Clump turned to Derringer and held out his hand. "I'd say you have yourself a deal, Mr. Derringer." Then he frowned. "But what about all our equipment and sensors? And there's nothing in here about the observatory employees."

"Don't worry about it. You can leave the gear, or you can take it with you; we don't care. Also, I'm sure we can find work for suitably qualified employees as junior cast members."

Clump nodded happily and made eagerly for the door with the rest of the senior staff.

"Just one thing, doctor," Derringer called out. "Don't forget to drop off the keys when you leave."

After the staff had departed, Derringer turned to Shi-Zhe. "Now that's what I call a win-win situation. The boys in the backroom are happy, the government saves a whole bunch of money, and we look like heroes."

Shi-Zhe raised a cautionary hand. "But all we have, Dick, is first prototype. Also, still no student is volunteering from Polytechnic."

Derringer patted Shi-Zhe on the shoulder. "Don't you worry. You heard what Vernon said. We're good for another thousand years at least. That will give you all the time you need to iron out any bugs and find your boy." He hitched his trousers and hoisted himself onto the conference table. "By the way, that was a golden opportunity I gave you with those chairs. How come you didn't run with it?"

"It is because we are ones who made first chairs already. They are sent back and now we must deliver new, improved chairs."

"Gee, I'm sorry, Shi, I didn't know."

Shi-Zhe beamed. "Oh, we are very happy—only not happy that new, improved chairs not yet ready. We sell six million first chairs for eighty dollar each, and only cost fifteen dollar to make. Then we forced to buy back at our cost of fifteen dollar less five dollar restocking fee. Then we do secret deal with *al-Qaida* global operations to resell like new still in plastic return chairs at forty dollar. After, we sell American government new, improved chairs for ninety-five dollar. Same type chair, different type cheap glue."

Vernon tried desperately to do the arithmetic in his head and failed miserably. "That's a whole bunch of money," he said admiringly.

"That's my boy," Derringer said with a happy grin. "How else could he afford to buy into ten villas, five million each, cash on the barrel?"

Vernon looked around the conference room, took off his Paul Newman replica hat, and scratched his head. 'Talking of property, what you plan to do with this place, Dick?"

Derringer shrugged.

"I'll be darned if I know. We just aren't that far in our thinking yet."

"I buy," Shi-Zhe said eagerly.

Derringer glared at him. "You're already committed to the villas. You know, at Titanic we take our contracts seriously. If you don't mind my saying so, it's a bit late to be backing out, Steve."

Shi-Zhe smiled inscrutably. "I keep the villas for rental property. This place I use for myself."

Derringer breathed a sigh of relief. He leaned forward and shook the other man's hand. "You've got yourself a deal, sir, and don't worry about the price. When the secretary hears we've already disposed of the property, she'll be ecstatic, whatever we sell it for. Just don't forget to pick up the keys on your way out."

Walking down the driveway ahead of Shi-Zhe, who had lingered to admire his purchase, Dick Derringer put a confiding arm around Vernon's shoulders and pulled him close. "Nice costume, ranger. You know, I haven't had the chance to tell you, but you look ever so nice in those jeans. Tell you what," he continued in a whisper. "July fourth I have a VIP invitation to the grand opening of Pastureland in Florida. I was the senior Titanic design consultant. I'm allowed a guest. I know it isn't much of a heads up, Vernon, but do you think you can come?"

Vernon blushed and nodded shyly.

CHAPTER 14

Einstein's Theory

The world's most famous scientist looked less than Godlike. He wore an old khaki army sweater with shiny leather patches at the elbows, faded corduroys, and bathroom slippers. His hair was famously wild and he was, of course, enjoying his pipe. He chuckled as though he had just thought of something unbelievably funny.

"You must to forgiving me, I am just to completing this new thought experiment," he said, when he had composed himself.

Jesús cringed. "Please, not another one. I never could figure them out, and believe me, I tried."

Einstein laughed merrily. "*Ach*, my little *bubeleh*, when I have first come to America, I have heard this same thing by everybody we have met. Do you know what I have told to them?"

"No," Jesús answered. "I must have forgotten. What did you say?"

Einstein seemed disappointed. "That is a shame, my boy, because I also have forgotten. I was to hoping you would have remembered." He puffed thoughtfully at his pipe before continuing. "It is no matter. In this, my latest thought experiment, I am using the same premise I have used for calculating the $E=mc^2$."

Jesús groaned and reached for his beer.

"Imagine, my young friend, you are trapped in an elevator somewhere in space. Now, imagine that you are bringing with you some marbles in a paper cup, like this kind you get from the *Burger King*. Only you have lost the top."

Jesús leaned forward. Despite himself, he was intrigued.

"Now, when the elevator is at rest, and you spill the cup, these marbles, they will float beside you, no?"

Jesús nodded in comprehension.

A triumphant gleam appeared in Einstein's eyes. "But if you are now to pressing the button for the penthouse, the elevator will go up quickly and all of your marbles, they will fall to the floor, yes?"

"So what's your point?"

"My point," Einstein said with a deadpan expression, "is that if you are trapped in this elevator in the middle of the space, you will soon to losing all of your marbles." He laughed uproariously.

"That's really not very funny," Jesús said. "Anyway, what I want to know is why choose me, Jesús Maria Martinez, as the savior of all life on this planet? Furthermore, what's so special about the Seattle presidential hideout, apart from it having enough food for three zillion years and comfy beds?"

It took a while for Einstein's shoulders to stop shaking. Even then, he couldn't get rid of his mischievous smile. He crossed his legs, losing one of his bathroom slippers in the process. "You know, the last time I have to help in saving the world, it was not so pleasant. I have had to find a sturdy young chap like you, but with the good skills for building the boats." He sucked hard on his pipe, then took it out of his mouth and examined the bowl closely. Then he looked up with a vacant expression.

"You don't mean, Noah, do you?" Jesús prompted.

"*Ach*, yes, Noah. So I must tell to him it will soon to flood for one hundred fifty days because of the giant tsunami and the endless rainings, so he better to build, how do you say, a big ass boat for to saving the world. He was, of course, most happy when I have explained to him about the forty virgins."

"So what was not so pleasant?"

"Next, I have to tell him about the animals."

"Oh!" Jesús said.

Einstein nodded. "So this time, there will be no need for the shovels. You see, your government has put into this bunker beneath your tower a frozen embryo and seed bank, which is containing all of the animal and plant species. So, all you will need when the time comes is to incubate the embryos and to planting your little seedlings."

"Jeez!" Jesús exclaimed.

"Also, they have in this bunker a giant *MacPod* Ultimate Knowledge Explorer, which they call the *MacPUKE*. This giant *MacPUKE* can know everything you ask it."

"Jeez," Jesús said again, "but why me?"

"Easy. We have remote brain-scanned all of the peoples with access to the tower. You are the one who is the least disturbed in the head."

"Gee, thanks. That's a real compliment."

"Believe me, my young friend, if you have seen what I have seen, it is a very big compliment." Einstein tapped his pipe on the edge of the plastic cup Jesús had provided. After emptying half the contents into the cup and the other half onto the carpet, the world's most famous scientist looked up expectantly.

"Okay, I'll buy all of that, but tell me this," Jesús asked, not knowing whether to feel flattered or insulted. "How is it you seem to be the only one who can come and go in a flash? Like right now for instance, Jesus One and the Khan suddenly get this craving for Little Debbie's Marshmallow Supremes, but they had to walk all the way to the Korner-Wal-Mart, the same as I do. You just vanish and reappear at will."

Einstein nodded his head vaguely and stared into space. Jesús wasn't sure he had heard the question, but then Einstein came back to earth. "In answer to your question, I am being reminded, you see, of my good friend, Erwin Schrödinger," he said. "He has had this clever thought experiment, in which his cat is to being shut up inside the steel chamber. This chamber is so small you cannot even swing Erwin's cat around, and she has no way out. Which, I must say, is the best part of his idea. If you know Schrödinger's cat, you must also know she will to eating your intestines after such abuse."

Jesús had learned to be patient when listening to the world's most famous scientist, so at this point he walked over to the fridge and helped himself to another beer. "Go on," he said, "I'm listening."

Einstein chuckled. "Well, also inside this chamber was to being a flask full of deadly acid. I think perhaps it was hydrochloric, but sulfuric is also good, because this will also dissolve the cat."

Jesús sat down and twisted off the top of his Michelob. "I'm not sure I like where you're going with this, Albert. Anyway, what the heck does Schrödinger's cat have to do with teleportation?"

Einstein waved his briar pipe like a baton and hummed a few bars of Mozart's *Eine Kleine Nachtmusik*. "Everything, my young friend, as you will see. For also connected to the flask is the very smallest Geiger counter in the Universe, containing just one tiny atom. As the tiny atom decays, it will to discharging inside the Geiger tube. Erwin, the cunning fellow—who I am persuaded is not so fond of his cat—has imagined a tiny hammer at the end of the tube. The hammer will to breaking the flask when the tube discharges. Then, Erwin's cat, she will to be smeared all over the insides of the chamber."

Jesús rolled his eyes. "That's gross!"

Einstein smiled enigmatically. "But, you see, this may also not to happen because there is the equal chance this tiny atom will not to decay. So, if we are to combining these two outcomes, we will to have both a cat that is alive and is also smeared." He leaned back and smiled triumphantly.

"So that's it?" Jesús said, shaking his head in disbelief, "that's how you explain teleportation? It's just as fucking incomprehensible as quantum mechanics, if you'll pardon my French."

Einstein nodded his head in agreement. "It is funny how you should to mentioning this. I myself have invented the quantum mechanics, and yet I have never quite understood how it can work. Happily, my good fiend, Niels Bohr has persisted with the calculations. After many years these calculations have made the teleportations possible."

The world's greatest scientist helped himself to Jesús' Michelob and sipped it reflectively. "You know," he said, with a faraway look, "they have to smearing a lot of cats in those early days."

"But how come you're the only one getting teleported?" Jesús persisted.

Einstein rubbed his thumb and forefinger together. "Because, *bubeleh*, it is to costing an arm and a leg for to doing it. Even these days it is for taking the two years for one person's DNA to being fully ionized. During all of that time, you must to being by yourself inside this machine for the eight hours of every day. You cannot believe what it costs just to leasing this ionizing machine. Not to mentioning, these peoples are to being paid more even than my nephew, the proctologist."

Jesús shook his head in puzzlement.

Einstein scratched at a toe. He took another sip of beer before continuing. "You remember these marbles I have told you about?"

"Sure."

"Well, you must to thinking of your DNA molecules as to like they are being these tiny marbles, and you, *bubeleh*, are to being the cup. Now, we must to spilling all of these marbles, and also to chopping them up into the tiny atoms, then we must to slicing the tiny atoms up into the tiny packets of light for to being transported."

"I get it. So you spill the cup, you stomp on the marbles then you grind all the pieces to dust with the heel of your boot. Then you throw the dust out the frigging window. It sticks to a light beam and somehow ends up in my living room as a cupful of marbles. What was I thinking? No wonder you smeared a bunch of cats along the way."

Einstein clapped his hands. "This is good, so now you have understood the principles. With this process, we are to scanning a person's DNA molecules and to placing the ionized markers inside them at the subatomic level. It is like to putting the tiny address labels on each particle. Can you not see, *bubeleh*, why this is for taking such a long time?" Einstein closed his eyes and rocked back and forth with a dreamlike smile. He continued speaking without opening his eyes. "So you see, my young friend, these tiny particles are like little postcards we send. When they are in the post office, they are mixed up with all the other postcards. But when the postman comes to your house, they all arrive together because they are to having the same address."

"Great, just tell me how much it costs and I'll order one. However, I still don't understand how come you keep changing into these other old guys from the past."

Einstein stopped rocking and his eyes opened abruptly. As was often the case, he seemed to be focused somewhere on Jupiter. But he was overcome with excitement. "I have it," he chortled, standing suddenly. He picked up his empty pipe and sucked at it vigorously. Then he immediately sat back down and stabbed excitedly at Jesús with the pipe. "This, my boy, is a question that Niels and many other of the peoples have struggled with, and also why so few have volunteering. Now, I have the theory. Oh, you cannot imagine the joy of finding the new theory. It is for like I am to rolling down the hill in springtime. Now, it is all seeming to be quite simple."

"This theory wouldn't involve a thought experiment would it?" Jesús asked, "Because I have some laundry that needs folding." He picked up the now empty Michelob and started to move away.

Einstein put out a restraining hand. He had the look of a small child who has just discovered ice cream. "Speaking of the foldings: You are, of course, knowing all about the foldings together of the space-time continuum?" He asked eagerly.

"Oh, space-time folding," Jesús said, "sure, I think about it all the time." He held up the empty Michelob. "I'm getting another. Would you like one?"

"For why must you ask if I drink this American maiden's water," Einstein sniffed. "You know I only like the good German pilsner, or even what is better, the Czechoslovakian."

"Okay, suit yourself," Jesús said, heading for the fridge.

When he returned, Einstein reached for the beer. He raised it in salute and launched into his new theory, forgetting to take a drink. "You see, when it is that we are riding the light beams we must eventually come back to the same time and the same place. Along the way, we can meet up with these other light beams coming from the other directions. Such light beams can only be coming from our past, you see, *bubeleh*. These other light beams from our future are for always ahead of us and so we cannot to catching them."

"Hold that," interposed Jesús. "I hate to interrupt, but maybe a thought experiment might not be such a bad idea after all."

Einstein nodded enthusiastically. "Yes, of course, we must to making another of the thought experiments."

The world's most famous scientist leaned back and sucked slowly on his empty pipe. Then he snapped his fingers. "I have it. Imagine myself as a clever young chap with his first real job. I am working in the patent office near to the railway station in Bern. I have just left my young wife in the house. She is so proud that after all this time I am finally to doing something for the money. Imagine I have just to getting off the train and I am in a hurry to get to the work." He paused reminiscently. "Although for why I am in a hurry to get to the work, I cannot imagine."

Then Einstein closed his eyes and was silent for such a long time Jesús thought he had fallen asleep. Finally, Einstein opened his eyes and continued as though there had been no interruption. "Coming the other way are all of these other peoples wanting to get on to the train. Imagine I bump against one of these other rushing peoples. Do you know what then happens?"

"Do tell."

Einstein shook his hair vigorously. A shower of tiny white particles descended gracefully onto the arms of the recliner. "You see, my dandruffs is to falling on to his shoulder, and his dandruffs is to falling on to mine."

"This is almost as gross as the cat," observed Jesús with a grimace.

Einstein was undeterred. "So, when I am getting to my office, I am finding some few tiny particles of the other person's dandruff mixed so with my own. It is like this with bumping into the light beam coming the other way. When all of my tiny particles are to mixing with these few tiny particles from the past, I am to carrying them with me. Then, you see, when I am arriving, like this little postcard from heaven, some of these past particles are recombining in my DNA."

Einstein could barely contain himself at this revelation. He removed his remaining slipper and scratched his foot vigorously. "It is not enough for the smearings, you understand. It is also not enough for Albert Einstein to becoming Marilyn Monroe. It is just enough past particles for Albert Einstein to becoming some other old man, like Jerry Falwell, or perhaps Mahatma Gandhi. Of course, if you are to remembering Erwin Schrödinger's cat, it may not happen that I bump into these past particles at all. In which case I am also Albert Einstein"

The world's most famous scientist sat back with twinkling eyes and an ever-so-satisfied grin. "If only my old friend, Niels Bohr were here, he could help me to calculate the past particle equations."

Jesús scratched his head in a passable imitation of the world's most famous scientist and smiled sarcastically. "Where you lost me, Albert," he said, "is when you switched from science to grammar. Now, how exactly do past participles fit into all of this?"

CHAPTER 15

Nailed

Billy Ray was furious. Mandy Miller wept. He threw down the *Star* magazine in disgust. Emblazoned across the cover was the headline: "*NAILED*". Beneath the headline, a tight-lipped Mandy was being led in handcuffs from her partly finished mansion in Baltimore. Also on the cover was a photo of a smiling Mandy in her future wedding gown. Beside that was Billy Ray's photograph. He was wearing a dove-gray Brioni wedding tuxedo, offset by a bright pink, one hundred percent hand-fed silkworm vest by Gucci. A still frame from the now infamous episode of "Little Miss Fixit" completed the montage. It showed Dirk Forrester smiling vacantly at the camera with the finish nail in the middle of his forehead.

The rest of the cover was taken up by trivia: "Fifty Best and Worst Dressed Space Tourists"; "Twenty Fifth Annual Cellulite Awards"; and a side bar proclaiming: "World Exclusive: Rosie O' Donnell's Secret Brain Implant, Larry King says, About Time!"

Mandy picked up the magazine and stared blankly at the cover. "Honest to God, Billy Ray, I didn't mean to hurt him."

"Now don't you piss down my leg and tell me it's raining, honey pie. They got a witness says different. Not only that, she caught you on her cell-phone camera while you were saying it." He snatched back the magazine and leafed to the center spread. "See here, what it says: "Phone Recording Reveals Shocking Truth in "Fixit" Scandal. 'First

Chance I Get, I'll Nail the Son-Of-A-Bitch,' says Mandy Miller in Taped Shocker."

"But I didn't know the phone was on, Billy Ray. You have to believe me. Why, I wouldn't do anything to spoil the wedding, and besides, it was just a figure of speech."

Billy Ray stared down at her in disbelief. The gleaming blonde tresses were gone. In their place was a flattened straggle the color of old piano keys. Her eyes were puffy. Without makeup, her face was pale and pinched with worry.

"Look at you," he exploded. "Y'all's eyes like to be two pee holes in the snow. Your God damned hair done shriveled up, and y'all's got Larry King's ass for a face."

Mandy sniffled. "I am truly sorry, Billy Ray, I truly am."

Billy Ray hitched up his trousers and squatted down to where he could look her in the eye. When he spoke, his voice was deadly calm. "I'm telling you straight, honey, don't nobody fuck with Billy Ray Bixbee. We got a wedding and a grand opening coming up in a week that set me back five million, not to mention a hundred grand to your bail money. I've been billing you as the New Prophetess of Pastureland, honey, but that done changed as of right now."

He gripped Mandy's chin and forced her to look at him. "From here on in, sweet child, we bill you as the Repentant Bride Of Heaven, for ye shall be forgiven in the Pastures of Heaven." He flourished the magazine. "Money can't buy this kind of promoting, little pumpkin seed. When they hears we're going ahead with this wedding, and y'all shall repent of your sins in the presence of the faithful and be purified in the flesh and the blood of the Holy Spirit, they'll come running. Why, we'll be the biggest thing since Larry decked Rosie in 'World Celebrity Face Off." Billy Ray's smile returned then; it just didn't make it to his eyes. "If y'all pull jail time, though, you can repent on your sweet lonesome, sugar pie, and we gonna get that in writing, along with them other covenants I done drawn up."

Thus it came to pass that Billy Ray Bixbee prepared to take unto himself a wife.

CHAPTER 16

Snatched

Not only was the nearest Korner Wal-Mart out of Little Debbie's Marshmallow Supremes, but no one there recalled seeing the Khan or Jesus One. Jesús had to check out six more Korner Wal-Marts in the neighborhood before he got lucky. The checkout girl definitely remembered the Khan.

"Yeah, funky looking dude in a bath robe. He had two baskets full of Little Debbie's. He done near cleaned us out, and he couldn't take his eyes off of me, neither."

"Yes, well, he doesn't get out much. When was this?"

"Be about an hour ago."

"Was he with anyone?"

"Yeah, thin kind of dude with a beard, kept smiling all the time-and them two nice black gentlemen."

Jesús' heart skipped a beat. "Really, two nice black gentlemen. How about that? Did you happen to see where they went?"

"Got in the black dudes' car and drove off."

"So what was so nice about the black gentlemen?"

'Well, for starters, they was wearing nice suits, and they was ever so polite and quiet spoken, considering how big they were."

"Oh, they were big guys, uh?"

"Oh yeah, they were real big, all muscles and shoulders. You could tell from the way their jackets was fitted."

"Well, thank you so much. You've been very kind."

Walking back to his apartment, Jesús had lots of time to think. What was going on? He could think of only one logical explanation (he didn't want to consider the alternatives): Muriel had made her move. She must have had someone watching the apartment. But did even *she* have the nerve to abduct the Khan and Jesus One? He remembered the last time he saw her; he remembered the look in her eyes. The answer, much as he hated to admit it, was obvious: of course *she* had the nerve—*she* was Muriel. And *he*, Jesús Maria Martinez, compulsive liar and betrayer of innocents, was in deep yoghourt, and rightly so. He had gotten complacent. Muriel had been out of sight, and he, moron that he was, had put her out of mind. "Oh, shit!" he muttered, "she'll want a full confession, immediate dismissal, and maybe a little jail time thrown in for good measure. I'll be out of a job for sure."

But the self pity didn't last long. The professional future of Jesús Maria Martinez was the least of his worries. In less than six months the entire world was going down the pipes. Once again, the sheer enormity of what was about to happen hit him like a hammer. "What the hell am I thinking?" he said to himself. "A few months from now, *no one* will have a job. They'll be lucky if they're still breathing. No more Marshmallow frigging Supremes; no more me; no more anybody, unless I get this show on the road."

By the time he made it back to the apartment, Jesús Maria Martinez was a man possessed—mostly, by fear and apprehension. Albert Einstein, on the other hand, was back to reading *Star* magazine and puffing happily on his pipe.

"I have a question, and I'd like a simple answer," Jesús said,

Einstein looked up in amusement. "If you are wanting the simple answers, my boy, you should not be talking to Albert Einstein. For the simple answers you must for going to the Post Office."

Jesús made for the settee. "If I lose my job, am I off the team? This could be very important."

Einstein thought for a moment. "If you are to losing your job, we can definitely have the problems."

"Can't you just re-program my chip to get me back in?"

"No."

"What the heck do you mean, no?"

"You have asked for the simple answer. This is for being a simple answer."

"Well, you're God aren't you? You have all that frigging technology up there. You can pretty much do anything you want, can't you?"

"What I have said," Einstein answered patiently, "is we are to being much more advanced than you, but these chips for the forehead and in the arms have now to being perfected by the Global-Titanic Corporation. When Titanic says no free rides, they are absolutely to meaning it. The coding is now unbreakable and has been sold to the government, who has to changing all of the locks. This code cannot be penetrated, not even by me—Albert Einstein—not even by the very best minds in all of the known galaxies. Not to mention we have also to asked for the help from Brian Flatbaum."

"Who, for Pete's sake, is Brian Flatbaum?"

"He is a twelve-year old from Murfreesboro, who last year is hacking into Al Gore's money market accounts."

Jesús put his head in his hands. "I really don't need this right now."

Einstein got to his feet with a faraway look in his eyes. "You know, when I see you to do this, *bubeleh*, I am reminded of my little Hans Albert."

"Don't start that again," Jesús warned, with a murderous look. "Look, what I've been working up to is Jesus One and the Khan are missing. I think Muriel Banks just had them kidnapped. I least I hope it was her. If not, we are well and truly screwed. Well, I mean they are, anyway. The point is, She'll want me to come clean with Roy Upstart, and you know what that's going to mean: I'll lose my job for starters."

The phone rang before Einstein could answer.

"Please sit back down, Albert," Jesús said, "I think we're about to get the bad news." He picked up the phone, nodded several times, and wrote down an address.

"So what was to being the bad news?" Einstein enquired.

"Some guy saying, if I want to know where my friends are, I should listen up. He wouldn't say anything more. He just gave me an address and said to be there in twenty minutes."

Einstein's face lit up. "So, finally, I get to ride once more in your fine automobile."

"Well, he did say to come alone, but what harm can it do? Who could possibly object to Albert Einstein showing up? Get your coat."

"Perhaps, you can teach me how to driving the automobiles on the ways," Einstein suggested as they left the apartment.

"It's just a twenty minute drive, Albert, and we're in a hurry," Jesús replied, with all the patience he could muster. "You sit in the back. You say nothing on the way. You say nothing when we get there. For once, please to keeping your opinions for yourself."

"In that case," Einstein replied, "I must to going back for my pipe."

Jesús grabbed his arm. "For Christ's sake, now *I'm* starting to talk like you. You will not go back for your pipe. You cannot smoke in my Toyota. Please, for once, just do as I ask without starting a frigging debate."

"Perhaps we can then to stopping along the ways for to buying the Little Debbie's for the journey," Einstein suggested, throwing his scarf over his shoulder.

"I'm going to scream, Albert," Jesús said through clenched teeth. "Just one more word from you, and I will scream my goddamn head off."

The address was not far from the corner of 23rd and Union, at the center of what had once been a predominantly black neighborhood. Jesús had read somewhere the neighborhood had also been home to a polyglot mix of Jews, Swedes, Chinese, Filipinos, and Italians. By the time he arrived in Seattle, though, gentrification had long since taken its toll, so he wasn't sure what to expect.

He found a church. More precisely, he found an old synagogue. The Star of David was carved in stone above the original wooden doors. Beneath the old carving, a simple neon sign advertised: *The Church of God's Global Divinity – Bishop Ron P. Wilmus III, presiding*. By the doors waited two large, well-dressed black men wearing dark suits and sunglasses. The eye-wear struck Jesús as strange, since it was close to midnight.

He drove past slowly, looking for somewhere to park. Eventually, he had to settle for a spot in a vast underground parking garage three blocks away. He handed Einstein the address. "Stay put and hang on to this, Albert. If I'm not back in an hour, think of something."

"For what am I to think?"

"I'll be darned if I know. You're the one with the brain; use it."

Five minutes later, Jesús approached the synagogue doors.

"Yes sir," murmured the larger of the two guardians. "You would be Mister Martinez?"

"Yes, I was told you have a message."

The other man reached into his pocket and brought out a slip of paper. Jesús held out his hand, but was ignored. "I'm supposed to read it, sir."

"Oh, yes, go ahead. Should I take notes?"

"I don't believe that will be necessary, sir."

The guardian removed his sunglasses and peered at the note. "It says here, Miss Muriel Banks wants you to go to Mister Roy Upstart and tell him everything. Then you will get your friends back."

"Where are they?"

"I can't say, sir."

"Where is the bishop? I'd like to talk to him."

"He already left with Miss Muriel Banks in the church bus—for the rehearsals, sir."

"Exactly what rehearsals might these be, if I may be so bold?"

The guardian of the doors grinned with pride. "Why, sir, Bishop Ron shall be officiating at the wedding of the Reverend Billy Ray Bixbee to the Repentant Bride of Heaven. Miss Muriel Banks is our choir mistress. She will be singing lead solo with the Global Divinity Choir at the ceremony in Florida on July Fourth. You can read all about it in this week's special issue of *Star* magazine, sir."

"Most interesting," Jesús said. "Jeez, that's this coming Sunday. If you don't mind, I have to leave right now. I'm defending my world snowboarding championship first thing in the morning, so I really should get some bed rest."

"The Lord's most divine blessings go with you, sir," the two guardians chanted in unison.

As Jesús turned to leave, one of the main doors opened and Albert Einstein came out of the church. Guns miraculously appeared. Jesús froze. Einstein smiled innocently.

"What the fuck you doing in the Global Divinity Church, old man?" demanded the larger guardian.

Einstein pointed to the ancient carving. "I am visiting to the old synagogue, for where I am coming as a sturdy young chap for the Bar Mitzvahs. *Oi Vey!* For what is it now you have to doing in there? I think I am for finding the temples of Solomon." He shook his head in mock amazement.

The second guardian turned to Jesús. "Is this old Jewish motherfucker with you, White Bread?"

"Never saw him before in my life," Jesús said.

CHAPTER 17

Time Off

Jesús waited for Einstein around the nearest corner. The world's most famous scientist showed up two minutes later, whistling the opening to Mozart's *Rondo Alla Turca*.

"I thought I told you to stay put," Jesús whispered angrily.

Einstein shrugged. "When you have left I am getting bored without the pipe, so I have teleported into this address you have given me to looking for the Khan and Jesus One. And for why must you be whispering so?"

"Did you find anything?"

"No, I am to finding nothing."

"Then why the hell didn't you just teleport back?"

Einstein shrugged again, looking embarrassed. "I am forgetting to where we have parked the car."

Jesús extended his left arm. Penciled on his palm were the level, row, and parking spot number for the Toyota. "You should write it down. That's what I always do. I've been caught too many times."

"*Oi Vey*! So what a clever little chap you are."

"All it takes, Albert, is a little common sense, which I've noticed some of us don't seem to have much of. You can also put a stop to this *Oi Vey* business. I personally thought that was overdoing it."

"*Oi Vey!*" Einstein repeated obstinately, revealing the small boy still trapped inside..

Jesús sighed and shook his head. "Listen, if I know Muriel, she's not letting those two out of her sight. My guess is they're on their way to Florida with the church choir, and that's more than three thousand miles from here. Why else would she be taking the bus?"

"Perhaps like me she is not liking to fly. Also, I am to thinking it is too expensive to take the airplane with all of these peoples from the choir."

"What do you mean, you don't like to fly? Not long ago you teleported half-way across the frigging Universe just to pay me a visit."

Einstein grimaced. "It isn't the same. When I am to flying in the airplane it is an agony for my stomach."

"Albert, flying is our best way to go. Look, it's almost Tuesday midnight. That's a three-day trip minimum, driving round the clock. We'd barely make it in time for the wedding."

"So if you have listened to me in the first place, by now you will have teaching me how to drive the automobiles and I can help. We also are not to caring about this wedding. We are caring for to find the two *dumbkopfs* and to bringing them back."

Jesús reluctantly had to agree, but a couple of things still bothered him. "Okay, so I'll get the time off and we'll drive, but answer me this. Why can't you just teleport back and run some kind of tracking program? That way we'd know exactly where they are. I'd hate to drive all the way to Florida and find out they've been here all along."

Einstein frowned and removed his seaman's watch cap. He nervously smoothed his hair. Given the nature of Einstein's hair, this was a futile gesture at best. He was clearly worried. Before speaking, he contemplated his shoes. When he looked up, he was pensive. "You are remembering when I am explaining my new theory, which I am now to calling the Postulate Of The Particles Impacting Einstein by the way, since I cannot yet to be calling this a proper theory until my calculating it is to proving the idea. For short you can be calling this concept the *POTPIE*."

"Albert, this is no time to be splitting scientific frigging hairs. A year from now there won't even be any science down here, let alone rules and protocols. What exactly is the problem?"

"The problem, my little *bubeleh*, is that if I am to teleporting once again in space, Albert Einstein's *POTPIE* may to finish up in the head of Jerry Fallwell."

"Oh, shit!" Jesús observed.

"Yes, and I have just to little testing this postulate by the teleporting in the local area. As you can see, by avoiding these past particles traveling on the light beams in the outer space, I am not to bumping into them. This I am calling the Intermediate Near Earth Particle Theory, which is *INEPT* for short. Also, I have to say that being Albert Einstein is not half so bad in any case."

"So what you're saying is: you stay down here as Albert Einstein, or you pop up for a quick visit to the mother ship, and when you get back I could be dealing with Jerry Falwell or Mahatma Gandhi."

"Yes, or perhaps Erwin Schrödinger, which can be a good thing, or perhaps Benito Mussolini, which is not so good a thing in any way whatever."

"Oh, darn!"

"It is what we have used to be calling the Hobson's choice."

"Call it what you like, Albert. It seems to me we have only one option."

Einstein's good humor returned. He put the wool cap back on and chuckled. "Yes, my little intellectual giant—exactly, so I am to believing you must ask for this time off and we shall to drive across America."

Jesús gave it one last try. "Don't you have some sort of instant communication device so you can just call up and keep in touch?"

Einstein shook his head gravely. "Not any more. It is something we can no longer safely do. After your government has passed the American Right To Intercept Future Alien Communications Traffic act, which you are calling the *ARTIFACT*, then your National Security Agency is being authorized for listening to every single phone call in the entire Universe, including of course, every one on Earth. Not to mentioning the emails. So all I have now to bringing with me is the emergency recall button. In case I am to wanting immediate help, I am simply to squeezing the button three times. When it is they are for wanting me back to the mother ship, the button is to chirping like these Australian budgerigars they have had at the hotel in Seelisburg."

He fished in a trouser pocket and came up with a grimy mother-of-pearl trouser button. "It is to being disguised of course, and only to being used in the dire circumstances. Not even the Khan and Jesus One are to having one of these."

Jesús accepted it like a man. It seemed they had no choice but to drive—all the way to Florida.

***

The following day, Jesús was scheduled for the seven a.m. to three p.m. shift. He arrived early. Dennis Floyd, who had been promoted to acting supervisor in Muriel's absence, was already in the break room. Dennis was a changed man. He arrived early, left late, and never stopped smiling. In recognition of his promotion, he had received a brass plaque and a four hundred dollar management award from Roy Upstart. The award commended him for outstanding excellence, dedication, professionalism, personal integrity, good personal hygiene, superlative communication and inter-personal skills, civic awareness, and selfless commitment to superior air-traffic-control-management. This was in place of an actual pay raise, which would have increased his pension.

Nevertheless, Dennis Floyd was a happy man. "Good morning, Jesús, what can I do for you, sport?"

Jesús pointed to his ears.

Dennis nodded sympathetically. "You telling me you caught a tone in the goddamn headset?"

Jesús handed Dennis a note. It read: *Dear Teeth: I can't hear a thing, I caught a tone in my headset yesterday, and now I seem to be deaf.*

Dennis read the note thoughtfully and gave Jesús a speculative look.

"It's true, Teeth. I can't hear a thing. I can see your lips move, but I'm not getting a word.

"You couldn't have picked a worse goddamn time, Jesús. We've got July fourth weekend coming, and you know what that means."

Jesús wasn't falling for it. He shook his head blankly.

Dennis shrugged, took out his pen, and initialed the note before handing it back. "What the hell. Here, take this to the doc. I'll call him and tell him you're on the level."

Jesús stared back quizzically. Dennis rotated his index finger and made a funny face. Jesús smiled, nodded, and made for the door, glad he wouldn't have to go though Upstart's office and possibly end up seeing Agnes McDrab.

The resident airport doctor had an office behind the Delta Crown Room on Concourse Eighty-One, and he was a very busy man. "Sit down, please Mister Martinez," he said, without looking up.

Jesús remained standing.

The doctor glanced up and gestured for Jesús to sit down. He glanced back at his work record. "According to this, you've only had eight days off in the past six months, and that includes weekends."

Jesús stared back intently and frowned.

The doctor leaned forward. "Let me see the note," he whispered.

Jesús frowned some more.

The doctor leaned back with a grin. "You won't believe how often that pays off. I whisper like that, and some imbecile will say 'why are you whispering, Doc, didn't they tell you I was deaf?'"

He gestured to the note clutched in Jesús' right hand. Jesús handed it over.

The doctor initialed the note, placed it in the file, made a notation in the records, and pointed to the door. "I'm giving you three weeks medical leave: two for temporary loss of hearing, and one because you've earned it. We'll forget about the tests. If you're faking it, they're useless anyway."

Jesús remained mute and didn't move. The doctor scribbled intently on his notepad and handed the note over. Jesús read it carefully, smiled, and shook hands. Just as he was leaving, the doctor called out. "See you in three weeks time, Mister Martinez."

Jesús kept going.

CHAPTER 18

Einstein's Duck

The quickest way to drive to Central Florida was to head south on Interstate 5 for a thousand miles, then east on Interstate 10 for two thousand miles, then south on Interstate 95 for the last two hundred miles or so. This route also had the advantage of being absurdly simple. Even so, Jesús was reluctant to use the Toyota's Automatic Instant Navigation and Total Entertainment Device (*TAINTED*). In the first place, staring at a screen is what he did for a living; on vacation, he preferred to look out the window. Secondly, he had an irrational fear of taking his hands off the wheel.

Einstein, on the other hand, had no such inhibitions. When Jesús explained the controls, the world's most famous scientist shook his head in wonderment. "You know, my first and only car was to being the 1937 Studebaker cruising sedan, which I am to buying for four hundred seventy five dollars from my friend Zuckerman. The Studebaker I am never to getting out of my driveway, and so I am giving it back to Zuckerman. This Toyota from you is more to like the Confederation mother ship, which is to having the Instant Intergalactic Hyper-Drive. With this I am having no problem."

"Good," said Jesús. "In that case we'll split the driving two hours on and two hours off. Just try not to fall asleep at the wheel.

Einstein frowned. "For what kind of *farkuckt* machine is this? With the Intergalactic Hyper-Drive, you can go to sleeping all you want."

"Yes, well, instead of cruising past big ass planets every six or seven light years, we'll be dodging garbage convoys and pizza dough trucks on the interstate. Anyway, if you do happen to fall asleep there's a Fully Automatic Reawakening Trembler—*FART*—built into the back of your seat. All you have to do is switch on the *TAINTED*, keep your hands off the wheel, and try not to activate the *FART*, because it also vibrates the passenger seat to alert the passenger, which would be me."

Einstein nodded enthusiastically. "I have one question."

"What would that be?"

"When you have to awakening for· how are you to stopping the *FART*?"

"You roll down your window and keep it open for at least fifteen seconds. Just let us not have to do that, okay?"

It didn't take them long to get going. Einstein's only luggage was his violin case. Jesús threw a change of clothing and a toothbrush in a tote bag and took the last two bottles of functional drinking water from the refrigerator. "When we get hungry we can grab a bite along the interstate," he explained.

Einstein smiled in anticipation. "I am remembering when I was at Princeton for all those years we have had the best of the American hamburger and shakes I can ever remember."

"Well, just don't get your hopes up. We'll only have two choices most of the time. It'll either be Petro-Pizza at a gas station, or all you can eat at a Shovel House."

One of the best features of the Toyota was how quiet it was on the highway. Once the propulsion drive reached critical compression, the engine was virtually noiseless. With regular sixty-five percent ethanol priced at thirty four dollars per gallon and hybrid plug-ins not much cheaper for long distances, compressed air drives were rapidly gaining in popularity. The only real downside was that every four hours or so you had to find a gas station with a compressed air hose that worked. For this reason, Jesús always carried four spare dive tanks in the back.

***

It took close to two hours to escape the sprawl formerly known as the fruit basket of the Pacific Northwest. Then they wound their way through the breathtaking peaks and steeply wooded slopes of Oregon and Northern California. As they descended, they saw endless green fields of soy and switchgrass stretching as far as the eye could see.

Einstein gazed in fascination at the panorama. "Only in America can you see so much food to be planted. You know, my little *bubeleh*, without all this grain you have sent, Europe and the rest of the world will have starved after the war."

"Yeah, well that was a long time ago, Albert. These days we use ninety five percent of the grain for domestic fuel and corn syrup. All of this used to be vineyards. Now everybody's growing fuel crops, soy, or potatoes. We get all of our vegetables and fruit from Mexico. If you don't like Petro-Pizza or flavor of the month soy and potatoes, you're either shit out of luck or you've got more money than the Gates Foundation."

Two hours later, they decided to eat. Jesús pulled up at an Exxon-Shell station that advertised a working air hose. "Looks like Petro-Pizza," he muttered. "There's nothing else to be had."

The gas station was painted entirely in green: a green concrete forecourt; green pumps; and a shiny green, reinforced fiberglass, dining module. Perched on top of the dining module was a giant illuminated pizza with a vivid yellow crust and bright red pepperoni toppings. Inside, were three people eating pizza, a solitary server, and a small cage housing two mallard ducks. Propped against the cage was a hand-written sign that read: *Ducks Available On Request.*

When they were seated, Einstein perused the illustrated pizza choices printed on the table. Then, he eyed the ducks hungrily. "I think I will to ordering the duck," he said.

Jesús sighed. "You don't eat them, you feed them."

Einstein shook his head in confusion. "So for why am I to be feeding the ducks when I am the one to be hungry?"

Jesús rolled his eyes. "Ever since we started mixing gas with bio-mass ethanol, the oil companies have been up in arms. Five years ago, they declared war on the food conglomerates. They came up with an edible derivative of polyester made from South Louisiana crude oil. They use it for making cheap pizza dough. The major downside is that the pizza polyesters can suppress progesterone secretions in the adrenal gland."

"So for why should Albert Einstein be concerned about what is in the pizza dough?"

"For why, Albert, is that in some individuals, diminished progesterone can lead to epileptic seizures, screaming fits and worse. Not to mention it can play havoc with a woman's reproductive system."

"So for why do you have this Food and Drug Administration if for not to protect from such things?"

"Six years ago the FDA was privatized. The pharmaceutical and food companies were deemed to have a conflict of interest, so Big Oil bought the agency. The first thing they did was to simplify drug and food testing by going back to the fifty-plus standard the country had back in 1954."

"I remember this," Einstein said. "We have to feeling very safe back then because of this rule. If more than fifty percent of the hamsters have died from the eating of a food, we have to banning it for humans."

"Exactly, and that's why we have the ducks, because based on the new, well old, standards the FDA declared petroleum pizza fit for human consumption. If you're not sure how you might react to a particular pizza, you can feed a slice to a mallard duck. For some reason, mallards react instantaneously to progesterone levels in edible polyester. Fortunately, they love pizza crust. If they eat a piece and fall over quacking like crazy, you might not want to eat it."

"I shall request a duck," said Einstein, "and I am also to ordering two slices of the Petro-Pizza Supreme."

CHAPTER 19

On The Road Again

Einstein's duck didn't fall over; it just waddled back to the cage and fell asleep. This should have raised a red flag, because the pizza had the same effect on Einstein. He slept all the way from Sacramento to beyond San Bernardino, thus missing most of southern California.

At first, Jesús was glad of the break. The Toyota quietly ate up the miles. He played softly muted selections of old jazz vocals as sunlit fields of soy and switchgrass whizzed by. He overtook a few garbage convoys headed for New Orleans. Coming the other way were return convoys loaded with Petro-Pizza dough from South Louisiana. The traffic was moderate and orderly.

Then night came and Jesús approached the infinite black void that was Los Angeles. Roadside lighting disappeared. Unlit buildings and traffic signs were swallowed by the darkness. Worse, the entire Los Angeles basin was blanketed by a temperature inversion that had moved in ten years previously and refused to budge.

His choice was simple: he could put on a smog mask, or breathe in a lethal mix of hydrocarbons, exhaust fumes, grease particles, nitric oxide, and sulfur dioxide. His only defense against the ozone would be to hold his breath for two hours or strap on one of his dive tanks and a regulator.

It was also raining.

South of Bakersfield, Jesús switched on the *TAINTED*. He grabbed two carbon-filtered masks from the driver's door pocket and donned one of them. Then he reached over and gently fitted the other mask to the sleeping Einstein. He switched back to manual steer, turned off the music, and prayed to the patron saint of windshield washer fluid.

Northeast Los Angeles didn't start out so bad, although the garbage convoys were building. By now, it was close to three a.m. Jesús was amazed at the amount of local traffic still on the road. Because the city could no longer afford to illuminate traffic signs, everybody was switched to full beam. Not to mention, no one had used a turn indicator in Los Angeles since 1958.

Before long, the combination of psychotic drivers, lumbering garbage rigs, non-stop rain, and glaring headlights started to get to him. No matter how hard he clenched the wheel, he was convinced he was about to have an out-of-body experience. Leaving Los Angeles compounded the nightmare. Transiting garbage convoys merged with hundreds of garbage rigs escaping the city. The Toyota was engulfed by a horde of articulated thirty-six wheelers. Those behind wanted to overtake. Those ahead wanted to slow down. The rigs on each side fought to change lanes.

Despite the constant gasps and whimpering of his companion, the world's most famous scientist continued to sleep like a foundling child. He woke as they breasted the San Gorgonio Mountain Pass in clear weather. Pale pink clouds dusted the sky high above Palm Springs.

Einstein carefully removed the smog mask and yawned. "For why, am I to having this thing on my face? " He turned to hand over the mask and caught sight of his companion. Jesús had the desperate, half-starved look of an escapee from Devil's Island. Einstein cried out in alarm. "What am I saying to you? Have I not said you must also to feeding the duck? Now, this pizza has turned you into a dying person. You're eyes are to sliding off your chin, and your face is to being whiter than Erwin Schrödinger's bottom."

"How the heck would you know about Erwin Schrödinger's bottom?" Jesús asked, struggling to stay awake.

Einstein smiled mischievously. "One time, I have placed Erwin's cat into the bathtub while he is in there dozing."

Jesús couldn't answer. His brain was rapidly losing the will to survive. He pulled into a viewing area, thumbed the drive control to park, and immediately fell asleep.

When he woke, Einstein was gone. Jesús panicked. He tumbled out of the Toyota, near blinded by the desert glare. He felt like a prairie dog surfacing after years underground. Still dazed, he heard someone whistling the overture to Mozart's *Magic Flute*. He calmed down.

Einstein was sitting on a concrete post contemplating four thousand unmoving windmills. Without a hat, his white hair floated gently in the constant breeze. Jesús sat on the ground and leaned his back against the post.

"I have a question," murmured Einstein, fumbling for his pipe.

"It's on the back seat. Remember, I explained about not smoking. So what's the question?"

Einstein gestured to the windmill farm. "We have observed many of these giant windmill places from the mother ship. In the other countries, they are for always working. In America this is not so. They have not to be turning at all for years."

"Ah, yes," murmured Jesús. "Welcome to the post industrial stone age." He stood up."I think you're going to need your pipe, Albert. Hang on while I go get it."

When Jesús came back with the pipe, Einstein was standing, entranced by the green vistas of switchgrass covering the entire Coachella valley and beyond. He gratefully took the pipe and tobacco, sat against the post to shelter from the breeze, and prepared his smoke. Jesús sat down beside him. "Once upon a time..." he began.

"*Ach*, this is good," said Einstein, lighting the pipe, "for now you are to tell me a fairy tale."

"It's for sure a fairy tale. Anyway, back in 2006, or thereabouts, the FAA and the Pentagon claimed the windmills interfered with aviation and long-range air defense radars, thus being a threat to national security. Of course, they had absolutely no evidence to support these claims, but Congress stalled a whole bunch of permits anyway. Well, there was a big protest and as usual the Pentagon tried to mumblefuck its way out of the situation. Then the FAA was forced to admit aviation radars had no problem whatever separating a windmill on the ground from a jetliner at thirty thousand feet. So the blades started turning again."

He looked up at the sky. The early morning clouds were gone. It was a typical day in Palm Springs: warm, dry, and unbelievably sunny. Later in the day, the wind would strengthen and funnel down through the pass.

He continued. "So, eight years ago, the Pentagon, which never forgives and never forgets, came up with a new one. They said they had rock-solid information from a water-boarded Pakistani sewing-machine-salesman. He had confessed that *al-Qaida* was about to invade. The plan was to attack from the Pacific with waves of refurbished Goodyear blimps fitted with Army surplus Gatling guns. They would arrive at night and slip in under the air defense radar, using the windmill farms as cover. Congress immediately declared Goodyear an enemy of the state, shut down all the windmill farms, and deployed the National Guard. If you look closely enough, you can see the guard shacks and the perimeter wire." He pointed to the disused windmill farm.

Einstein didn't bother to search for the guard shacks. He joined with Jesús, who was back to gazing at the heavens. They sat in comfortable silence and it was a while before the scientist said anything. "I am noticing you to watching the sky a lot, *bubeleh*. Is it that you are missing your airplanes?"

Jesús lowered his gaze to survey the green expanse of valley and desert plain. "No, Albert. What I'm thinking is it's a good thing we're making the trip after all. This is the last chance I'll get to see the country. Somehow, sky-gazing makes me appreciate it even more. By the way, I did a little reading. You ever hear of Marie's disease?"

Einstein shook his head.

"It's what you get from breathing in volcanic ash. The ash is like ground glass. When you breathe it in it eventually shreds your lungs. You know, the holy rollers are going to say that sort of thing is divine retribution. We both know that's not true, but sometimes you have to wonder, don't you? We're certainly guilty of screwing up planet Earth every way we could." He turned to Einstein. "Are they all like this? I mean, these other planets you've visited. Have they all been taken over and shit-canned by certifiable frigging lunatics?"

Einstein sucked thoughtfully on his pipe. "*Bubeleh*, this is the way with your planet. It must now and then to cleaning itself, like the fox with too many fleas. For the fox, he is simply to walking in the stream backwards and so the fleas are all to jumping off his nose and drowning. For the planet, it must explode or to spreading the deadly disease like these plagues you have had. You should also know this Earth of yours is a very small and not so important planet when you look at all of the galaxies. Most of the larger planets are to being very virtuous and very happy." Then he grinned. "But they are not to being half so much fun."

Jesús glared. "Well, that's great to know. I'll pass it on when the lights go out. What I'm trying to say is it's so ridiculous. Talk about throwing out the baby with the bathwater. When it's over there's going to be nothing left but me, forty virgins, and a ten-year supply of Meals-Ready-to-Eat. Not to mention hundreds of certifiable lunatics in private and government bunkers just itching to do it all over again."

His expression softened. "You know, when we first met, when you were Jimmy Carter and you gave me the bad news, I said I almost felt like crying. Well, I'm telling you, I feel that way right now."

"I think it is time I drive the Toyota," Einstein said.

CHAPTER 20

Your Basic Breakfast

Before they left, Jesús maneuvered the Toyota so that it faced the exit. After settling in the passenger seat and buckling Einstein's belt, he pointed to the floor. "Forget about your left foot. That's the accelerator pedal to the right, brake pedal on the left. This little lever in the middle is the drive control. To move forward you keep your foot on the brake and thumb it into drive, which is the "D" position. When you are stopped, you keep your foot on the brake and thumb it into park, which is indicated by the "P". Never, ever use the "R", because if you do the car will go backwards. Nod your head if you understand."

"I have just to doing this yesterday," complained Einstein. "For why must I be told again like I am to having no brain? Are you not forgetting this is Albert Einstein to which you are talking?"

"That's just my point. There's a very good reason you never could get Zuckerman's Studebaker out of your driveway. You make me nervous. Behind us is a seven hundred foot cliff, in front of us a six-lane highway. I'm too young to die."

Einstein grunted, stared intently ahead and selected Drive. Seconds later, he took his foot off the brake and stepped hard on the accelerator pedal. The Toyota surged forward like a drag racer. Jesús opened his eyes as they merged. Einstein casually steered between two passing convoys and settled into the center lane.

Jesús sighed with relief. "Nice, just watch the speed, okay? You're doing a hundred miles an hour. This is not the intergalactic frigging highway. You're in America now, Albert. See those signs with 70 MPH written in big letters? That's the speed limit."

Einstein grinned happily. "I have thought this was for the big trucks. These are the only ones to driving at such a speed."

"Playtime is over, my friend." Jesús thumbed the drive control to *T*, for *TAINTED*. "Now, let go the wheel and sit back. I hope you like staring at switchgrass, because that's all you're going to be seeing for the next two thousand miles."

Einstein pointed to his stomach. "Sometime in these next two thousand miles I wish to eating. Down here it is saying breakfast."

Jesús nodded. "I'm up for that, but no more Petro-Pizza for you, pal. Tell you what, we'll drive until we cross the Colorado River into the Mojave Desert, then we'll stop at a Shovel House."

The first sign after the river indicated Quartzsite to the north and Yuma to the south. Jesús checked the *TAINTED* display. "Quartzsite is at the junction of Interstate 10 and U.S. 95. Yuma is close to eighty miles south. We definitely don't want to go there. Put your hands back on the wheel, Albert." He reached over and deactivated the *TAINTED*. "Now, please slow it down, and take the next exit."

Before they reached the exit, Jesús counted forty-five trailer parks north of the highway. To the south was an unending vista of tall, green switchgrass. A single sign advertised food and lodging. The left arrow indicated Shovel House. To the right was the Love Motel. "Whatever you do, Albert," he said, "don't go right at the intersection,"

The restaurant was marked by a giant Johnny Appleseed statue made of green plastic, with a green shovel on his shoulder. Luckily, there were only six cars in the parking lot, since Einstein's final approach was considerably less than perfect.

"Now, I don't know what you're used to up there on the mother ship," Jesús cautioned, "but down here, it helps to be real hungry when you eat out."

They entered through double swing doors made from imitation-teak fiberglass. Each door was decorated with a four-foot high plastic palm tree. Jesús held one of the doors open. "After you, Albert," he said graciously.

Welcome to the Shovel House, chanted a recording. *Remember to push and twist, push and twist, push and twist. Have a nice day. Have a nice day.*

Jesús grabbed two large trays from a stack. He handed one to Einstein. "Here, just slide this along after me, and do as I do."

Einstein looked about in amazement. The interior was decorated jungle style, even down to a tiny jungle pool in the middle of the restaurant. Two plastic crocodiles faced off in the water.

"It's time to pick a shovel, Albert. You can check the place out later." Jesús stopped in front of three vertical racks containing green plastic shovel blades. "These are all regular square-mouth tree digging shovels and they come in three sizes. You've got your number fourteen large, your number twelve medium, and the active senior, which I think is an eight."

"For why is there all of this plastic jungle in here?" Einstein whispered.

Jesús pointed to the far wall. Reaching from floor to ceiling was a faded photograph showing a short, stocky white man flanked by two natives. Each of the natives carried a rusty shovel blade. The native to the right had only one arm and his head was painted red and blue.

"That's the founder of Shovel House," Jesús explained. "He's an Italian from Brisbane, Australia. Apparently, he spent a lot of time in the islands near New Guinea. That's where he got the idea."

"For what kind of *farkuckt* idea is this, where you must come to eating with a shovel?" Einstein whispered in bewilderment.

"It seems these natives worship a crate full of shovel blades dropped accidentally on their island by an Australian supply plane during World War II. Since the crate had no shovel handles in it, the natives figured the blades were white man's dinner plates. They've been eating off shovels ever since."

Einstein looked at the photograph again and scratched his head. "You know, while I am not to believing a word of your story, this man with the red and blue face I think I am having to seen before. But, how can this be?"

Jesús ignored him. He selected two fiberglass shovel handles from a bin and handed the smaller one to Einstein "Forget about the shovel king. Just take this then push and twist, it'll click right in."

Einstein did as he was told and followed Jesús to a row of heated vats filled to the brim with food.

"I'm going for a medium shovel full of the basic breakfast," Jesús explained. "That's a mix of soy sausage patties, soy scrambled eggs, soy cheese, soy bacon, soy hot cakes, and soy whole-wheat toast. You get jumbo ketchup and corn syrup dispensers at the table. This next vat is home fries. If you want breakfast plus fries, you grab an extra shovel blade. Once you've paid, you can come back as many times as you want. At twenty-nine dollars ninety-nine cents for a number fourteen shovel, that's not half bad"

Einstein watched in fascination as Jesús helped himself. He then clipped the loaded blade to a bracket built into the base of the tray and removed the handle, which he dropped into a used shovel handle bin. "These handles are beautiful," Einstein said. "They are to looking as wood but are so light, and such carvings they have."

"Hand carved fiberglass done by the natives. You can buy them as souvenirs. Believe me, the Italian has made a fortune. He started out in Australia. Now, he has Shovel Houses all over the world. He came to the States five years ago. Since then, he's bought out Wendy's, McDonalds, Burger King, Dairy Queen and just about all the rest, except Subway—they're oil company owned now and big into Petro-Subs. He's got to be the world's first shovel billionaire."

Einstein shoveled his own breakfast and inquired, "For what can we drink?"

Jesús pointed to a row of drink dispensers by the cash register. Stacked on the floor next to the dispensers were three towers of green plastic buckets. "You have large jumbo buckets, extra large jumbo buckets, and the mega-jumbo. Same as the food: once you buy a bucket, you get unlimited refills. They have Mountain Dew regular or Instant Energy Boost, or you can have the South Louisiana Lite Sweet Crude Classic Cola."

"I think I take water," Einstein muttered.

"They don't serve water, and you're not allowed to bring your own."

Einstein shook his head and followed Jesús to the checkout. As Jesús was reaching for his wallet, Einstein tapped him on the shoulder. "Where am I to finding the knives and the forks?"

Jesús pointed to the tables. "They don't have knives and forks. You'll find garden trowels at the table."

On the way out Einstein lingered at the giant Johnny Appleseed statue.

"What is it now?" Jesús asked.

"I am to wondering for why they have this giant plastic man here."

That's Johnny Appleseed. He's an American folk hero. Way back when, he wandered about the country planting apple trees." Jesús pointed to the giant green shovel. "Legend has it, he used the very same number fourteen large they have inside."

"I am not to believing this," Einstein scoffed.

"Nor do I, but just about everybody else does. They think it gives the place a patriotic flavor. It's like when you're in there, you're eating for America."

CHAPTER 21

Rolled Up

The thing to know about switchgrass is that it grows year round and it doesn't need much water. Throw in a liking for warm weather and you have a fuel crop that will thrive just about anywhere south of Wichita. In his 2006 State of the Union address, George W. Bush revealed that switchgrass was right up there with the second coming of Christ in terms of liberating America from foreign oil. After that, it was only a matter of time. The great American switchgrass crusade of 2017 was a triumph of national resolve matched only by the Apollo space program of the nineteen sixties. By 2019, more than two hundred million acres were planted and five thousand biomass refineries constructed across the nation. Coincidentally, this was also the year worldwide oil production fell into permanent decline.

Once again, America was the envy of the planet.

The major downside was that cheap labor from Mexico was the only way to bring in the switchgrass crop—so the fence had to come down. Stretching all the way from San Diego to Brownsville, Texas, the fifteen-hundred-mile blast proof fence had just been completed at a cost of twelve billion dollars. Yet, all was not lost. Canada, overwhelmed by thousands of elderly baby boomers fleeing the American healthcare system, came to the rescue. The fence was dismantled and shipped to plug a hole in the northern border at absolutely no cost to the American taxpayer.

Another drawback, of course, was that pretty much wherever you went south of Wichita, all you saw was switchgrass. For Einstein, that lost its appeal somewhere between Tucson and Willcox, Arizona, after which he stared straight ahead and commenced to hum his way through Mozart's entire life work. Jesús, on the other hand, was spellbound. He gazed contentedly at the tall springy bushes for mile after mile. "I'll tell you, Albert," he said lazily, "it's green, it grows, and you can smell it. All I've seen for the past three years is blips on one screen, and bullshit on the other. The way I feel right now, I'd be just as happy if they were growing stinkweed out there."

Einstein stopped humming, checked the mirror, and looked down at the *TAINTED* display. "For you, I am so happy, my boy, but you know, I am now observing two things I am not to having seen before."

"What might those be?"

"On the screen I am to seeing this red flashing light for where it says El Paso, and behind in the mirror I am to seeing two motor cycles, also to showing this flashing red light."

Jesús sat bolt upright. He searched furiously in his pockets then rummaged through the glove compartment in a panic.

"These gentlemens on the motorcycles are now on each side and to waving," Einstein said, and waved back.

"Shit!" Jesús exclaimed. "I meant to ask for cash back at the Shovel House, but you made me forget with all your silly questions."

Einstein looked offended.

"I'm sorry, Albert, I didn't mean that, but we could be in big trouble here. Just pull over. It's an *NAACP* patrol."

Einstein de-activated the *TAINTED* and carefully pulled over. One of the riders stopped a few yards ahead and unsheathed a combat shotgun. The other dismounted behind the Toyota and approached slowly. Both men sported Zapata style moustaches and fringed black bike leathers. The bikes were identical Harley Davidson Fat Bob custom specials.

"For what kind of trouble, is this?" Einstein whispered urgently.

"Between watching switchgrass and listening to your frigging Mozart, it clean went out of my mind. That red light on the *TAINTED* is a reminder to have cash ready. El Paso is *NAACP* controlled. We'll have to pay a toll. Just roll down the window and leave this to me."

Einstein rolled down the window and blinked at the unwavering barrel of a Sig-Sauer P226 nine-millimeter semi-automatic pistol.

The biker smiled politely and showed a badge with his free hand. "Welcome to El Paso Sunland precinct, Mexican Mafia Brigade, man."

Einstein nodded silently and pointed to Jesús.

"Good morning," Jesús said, with a bright smile. "Did we do something wrong, officer?"

"Not yet. I wanna see your wallet, man."

"You don't want registration and proof of insurance?"

The biker grinned. "Hey, Holmes, we don't mess with no shit like that."

Jesús made to hand over the wallet. The biker shook his head. "Don't work that way. You open the wallet, take out the cash, and hand it over. Also, you got a brake light, she not working too good, man."

"Er, I'm sorry, but all I seem to have is forty dollars."

The biker's lips tightened into a thin smile. He pocketed the badge, holstered his pistol, and brought out a citation pad. "I want you names, where you coming from and where you going, man."

"That would be Martinez and Einstein. We're driving from Seattle to Cocoa Beach, Florida."

The biker wrote down the details, tore off the top copy, and handed it to Jesús, who stared in dismay. "Eight hundred and fifty dollars! You've got to be kidding."

The biker shrugged. "Five hundred dollar fine for having not enough cash and three fifty for the brake light. You just got yourself rolled up. You coming with us. You don't got the dead presidents in twenty four hours, we confiscate your ride, man."

"Please to excusing us for a moment," Einstein said. Then he closed the window and turned to Jesús. "So, just to putting down the window and leave it to me," he mimicked sarcastically.

Jesús stared back forlornly. "There was nothing I could do. Now, we're well and truly screwed. I can't just stop at the nearest ATM and withdraw the money because the banks no longer operate in El Paso. It's strictly a cash economy—so, no cash, no Toyota, and no way out. You'll have to teleport back to the mother ship. I'll either have to walk the rest of the way or sell my body for bus fare."

"Why is it that these *NAACP* gentlemens they can do this so?" Einstein asked, looking perplexed.

Jesús let out a slow sigh. "About five years ago some cities were in such a mess that local governments just gave up. Then the gangs took over. One of the first things they did was change their name from gang bangers to *ACs*: Accredited Criminals. To be accredited you have to be a registered gang member with at least two years in the slammer and/ or three felony indictments. They formed the National Association of Accredited Criminal Precincts and they've been running things ever since. El Paso is one of those cities. They also rule in Detroit, Cleveland, most of LA, and Trenton, New Jersey."

"Just to passing me my violin case, if you please."

"This is no time to be rehearsing Mozart sonatas for Christ's sake."

"Just to be passing the case," Einstein repeated patiently.

Jesús reached back to the rear seat and handed over the battered leather case. Einstein put the case on his knee, opened it, and brought out a tightly wrapped bundle of new one hundred dollar bills. "Here is ten thousand dollars. Now you can pay the gentlemens."

Jesús peered into the case and gasped. "Jeez, Albert, there must be close to a half million dollars in here."

"Exactly—the half million dollars, less the ten thousand I am just giving you."

"Well, I'll be a son-of-a-gun, and here I was thinking you all you had in there was a violin."

Einstein responded with a sly smile. "Do I look like some crazy old man for to be coming to America with just a violin and the clothes upon my back?"

"But, how in hell did you come by all this cash?"

Einstein chuckled. "When I am to winning the Nobel Prize for Physics in 1921 I am giving it all to my first wife, Mileva Marić."

"Why would you do that? Wasn't that a bunch of money?"

"Yes, but I have promised her so we can get the divorce, and also it was for the children. But then she has spent it all, and I have to say most unselfishly."

"Then where did all this come from?"

Einstein wagged an admonishing finger. "Just to listen to me, *bubeleh*. When the Nobel Committee has heard of my generosity, they are very impressed. Also, they have been feeling guilty. You know, these good German Swiss have had the problems admitting a little Jewish patent examiner of no importance is to becoming the world's most famous scientist. Because of this, they have denied me the Nobel Prize for many years. When they are finally to making the award, it is for something I have thought about while sitting on my toilet—the law of the Photoelectric Effect—instead of my greatest work, which is the General Theory of Relativity."

He paused and looked reflectively at the passing traffic. "So, for feeling guilty they have secretly paid me a second prize amount to a numbered bank account in Zurich. It has been there now for one hundred and five years. I have stopped there on my way to see you, and taken out a little cash."

Jesús cocked a disbelieving eyebrow. "You expect me to believe you just walked into this Swiss bank more than half a century after you died and took out a little cash, and nobody said anything?"

Einstein shrugged. "This is to being the Swiss bankers we are talking of. If you have the pass codes and the signature, you can to having your money, no matter for how long you are dead. They are used to it and are for never asking the awkward questions."

"Good Lord!" Jesus cried. He was still skeptical, but it was awfully difficult to argue with half a million dollars. "So, how much do you have now, if you don't mind my asking?"

Einstein pretended to count off the amount on his fingers. "Well, in 1921 I am being paid thirty two thousand and two hundred and fifty dollars for the prize. Then it has to being accumulated with the clever German Swiss investments since that time at about thirteen percent every year. I now have twelve billion, seventy one million, six hundred and forty thousand, two hundred and fifty eight dollars, and the five cents."

Jesús shook his head in disbelief. "Just answer me one thing. Did you really work all that out in your head?"

Einstein snorted with amusement. "*Nein*, I have had to ask the bank teller and he is to writing it down for me on the back of my withdrawal slip."

For some reason this struck Jesús as excruciatingly funny. He laughed until tears rolled down his cheeks, and Einstein joined in. When they were done, Jesús reached over and sounded the horn. Then he cheerfully peeled of a thousand dollars and handed the rest of the money back to Einstein. "Put this back, stow the case, then roll down the window and leave the rest to me."

Einstein replaced the money and put his feet on the case. Then he snatched the thousand dollars from Jesús, stuffed half in the driver's door pocket, and rolled down the window, still giggling. "This time, I think I am to do the talking."

He waved.

The biker had already put his bike back on the stand and was walking over. He was clearly irritated at the long wait. "What you want, old man?"

Einstein meekly handed over the five hundred dollars. "I am just to remembering, officer. I have this money saved by my little blind granddaughter for the vacations in Florida."

The biker thumbed through the banknotes. "I wanna see you ticket, man," he demanded, looking decidedly mean.

Jesús passed the citation to Einstein, who handed it to the biker, who tore it up and threw it away, looking meaner than ever. Then he laughed and handed two hundred dollars back to Einstein. "You some piece of work all right, Holmes. We forget about the brake light. This time I just charge you for the toll, man."

"Please to having a nice day, man," Einstein answered politely.

CHAPTER 22

The Human Bomb

Three miles west of Fort Stockton, just before dusk, Jesús dozed off in the fast lane while cruising at a steady ninety miles per hour. He slumped forward, activated the *FART*, and woke in total shock at the wild, jarring motion. His eyes jerked wide open. His body shook uncontrollably. Muriel Banks was screaming, "Martinez, you crash one more airplane, I'll glue your fat ass to your chair."

Einstein thumped his right shoulder. "For please to open the window," he yelled. "This seat is to shaking off the ears from my head." Jesús punched the window open and the air blast immediately pinned him to the vibrating seat back. Fifteen seconds later he rolled the window up and wiped the tears from his cheeks.

"Let's pull off at the next exit" he said calmly. "I think I'm ready for a cup of coffee."

At the Fort Stockton exit, the road took them under the interstate and headed east into town. Jesús tapped the wheel rhythmically, glancing from side to side for a place to eat. Apart from a brand new Shovel House and three gas stations advertising Petro-Pizza, nothing leaped out.

"I am not to visiting either the pizza or this Shovel House," declared Einstein emphatically.

"Me neither," agreed Jesús. "I'm still digesting the basic breakfast. But don't get your hopes up. I stayed overnight here once on my way to Seattle. It has the nicest public library I ever saw, the worst Mexican food I ever ate, and the scariest motel I ever stayed in. Other than that, I don't remember much."

They were into town and almost over the railroad tracks when Einstein pointed to an illuminated sign for the Happy Daze Diner. It advertized: *Mexican – Burgers – Sandwiches – Delivery*.

"Hey, sure, we'll try that," Jesús nodded. "It's probably the last Mom and Pop in America."

The diner was bright, clean, and almost empty. A young migrant couple was quietly tucking into fajitas at a corner table. Sitting at the counter was a slightly built older man with uncommonly large ears and no hair. Jesús scanned the menu behind the counter. "I'm just having coffee. You want any food Albert?"

"Yes," said Einstein, "I take the burger."

"It's probably made from soy."

"I don't care, just so it is not like this food we have had at the Shovels House."

"Excuse me, sir," interrupted the server from behind the counter, "we raise our own beef hereabouts. That's the finest burger ya'll will find in Pecos County."

"Make that two," said Jesús, having an abrupt change of mind, "and two coffees with."

The server was right; the burger was one of the best Jesús had ever tasted. Einstein didn't say a word during the entire meal, he didn't have to; his eyes spoke volumes. When they were finished, Jesús ordered two coffees to go and settled the bill at the register.

"Excuse me, folks," intervened the hairless man at the counter.

Jesús paused, about to pocket his change. His instinct was to pretend he hadn't heard. Einstein settled the matter by answering for him. "Good evening, I am Albert, this is my friend Jesús. How can we to being of help?"

The other man extended his hand. "Howdy, Albert, pleased to make your acquaintance. The name's Chittenden, Johnny Chittenden. If y'all are from South Texas and into thrill driving, y'all might remember me. I used to be the Human Bomb."

Getting no reaction, he shrugged. "Anyhow, y'all can call me, Johnny." He glanced down at a small tote bag by his feet. "I was wondering. If you folks is heading out on the interstate, I'd be mighty grateful for a ride."

"Which way would you be going?" Jesús asked.

"Whichever ways you is," replied the Human Bomb. "All I'm figuring right now is on leaving town first chance I git."

"So, you are liking to drive?" Einstein enquired with a calculating look.

"Yes, sir, I've been professional thrill driving since I was turned sixteen."

"I hope you don't mind my asking," Jesús said, "but why were you known as the Human Bomb?"

Chittenden smiled modestly and reached for his tote bag. "Used to hose the car down real good with gasoline then drive her through the steel wall of death. Sparks lit her up like she was a fireball from hell." He pointed to his head. "That's how come I got no hair."

When they reached the Toyota, Einstein insisted on sitting in the back. "From now, I do what I am doing best. I am to sitting here and thinking only to solve some of these many problems we have."

Jesús topped up at the one gas station with a working air hose and mentally prepared himself for a long night's drive through the rest of Texas and into Louisiana. Johnny Chittenden settled quietly in the passenger seat and didn't speak unless spoken to. Three hours later, Einstein was fast asleep and Jesús was fighting to keep his eyes open. Not wanting a recurrence of the *FART* experience, he turned to his passenger. "Done much night driving, Mister Chittenden?"

Johnny turned to him with a wry smile. "Why, yes, sir, I done a little. Time was I drove with Sammy Blackwood's Hell Riders then with Joe Jericho and his Drivers of Death. Did that for nigh on thirty-five years. Back driving with Joe is where I first seen a human bomb act. After that, I took up with my own show, which I called Johnny Chittenden: The Human Bomb, and his Hellions of Doom. I'm here to tell you, sir, we done real good till them monster trucks showed up. Too late to change, I guess."

He looked ahead and stared reflectively into the darkness for a while before continuing. "We'd go from one town to the next most nights. Then we'd do setup all day and thrill driving to midnight. Never took more than a couple hours sleep at a stretch for close on forty-five years. Still don't, to tell the truth."

He paused again, and Jesús had the distinct impression he had more to say. Instead, the Human Bomb contemplated the road ahead in silence. He wasn't smiling anymore. Jesús had the feeling there was something deep down in Johnny Chittenden that he couldn't, or wouldn't, put into words.

Jesús broke the moment. He de-activated the *TAINTED* and pulled over to the hard shoulder. "Be my guest," he said. "Are you familiar with these auto-navigation drives, Mister Chittenden?"

Chittenden scrutinized the drive control and the *TAINTED* display. "No, sir, I cain't say as I am. Last car I owned was a 1969 Oldsmobile Hurst I done rebuilt. I just sold that to the fella used to run the Comanche Tortilla Factory back in town. You got no cause to worry though—ain't a car made Johnny Chittenden cain't drive."

***

They passed Houston six hours later, and the garbage convoys started to merge again. Unbroken columns stretched for miles at a time. The roar of the big rigs and the constant buffeting from the downdraft woke Einstein.

Johnny Chittenden was still driving. He had quickly figured out the auto-steer, but like Jesús, he was happier with his hands on the wheel. Staring at oncoming headlights and a sea of red taillights for hour after hour didn't seem to bother him. Jesús' only complaint was his choice of music. "Mister Chittenden," he observed, "please don't take this the wrong way, but if I hear one more redneck whine about losing his truck, his job, and his Peggy Sue, I'm going to roll down my window and throw up."

The Human Bomb grinned happily. "Dang good listening, though, ain't it?"

Jesús closed his eyes and tried to sleep. The world's most famous scientist leaned forward and tapped the Human Bomb on the shoulder. "Excuse me, Johnny," he whispered, "for where are all these trucks going to? Jesús has said they are filled with the garbage."

"Right on, Albert. They all loaded up with garbage and headed into New Orleans." He glanced back at Einstein. "How come you don't know that? Next to all that dang switchgrass, that hole in the ground is the biggest thing ever happened in the South since Sherman done burned Atlanta."

"It must have been when I am to going back for the re-ionizing," Einstein murmured. "Also, I should prefer talking to the back of your head than to the front."

"Gotcha," Chittenden concurred with a grin, turning to face forward. "Y'all remember the monster hurricane flattening New Orleans, though, right?"

"Which one? They have had so many after this *Katrina* has destroyed everything for the first time."

"I'm talking number fourteen: *Katrina's* bad-ass sister, *Karen*."

"Yes, I am to remembering this *Karen*. She has to totally destroying what is left of the New Orleans."

"Yep, was like fourteen spoonfuls of prune juice going through a pig: first thirteen cleaned her out real good. After number fourteen, weren't nothing left but a burp and a fart."

Einstein shook his head. "So what is it with these peoples, Johnny? Even if you are to being a visitor from space, you can see it was crazy what they have done, to keep building again the same way. What is worse, they are not listening to the clever Dutch peoples who know about such things."

"Yep, well, be that as it may, they sure done took one hell of a whuppin. Anyways, after *Karen*, the Feds said y'ain't getting no more free stuff this time around, you done spent all your gittin. So, first off, as usual, they starts to digging a big hole and filling it with all them smelly refrigerators and dead animals. Then somebody in the government figured out if they dug this hole thirty six mile square by a mile deep, they could fill it with the country's entire garbage for the next three hundred years."

Einstein sucked on his empty pipe. "This was to being brilliant. Even I cannot imagine such an idea as this."

"Yep, it also happened that was the exact size of New Orleans. Seems this Chinese fella as sells chairs paid the mayor a bunch of money to lease the city. Then the mayor done took off for Panama and then they dug them a hole bigger'n hell."

He nodded at the garbage rigs. "That's where they's all going to, Albert. Best damn thing ever happened to the state of Louisiana. On top of them sales taxes, now it gets to collect all them garbage taxes. The trucks'll turn off soon, and once we're out of Louisiana, won't be but a day's drive to where y'all is going."

The Human Bomb glanced back again. "Only problem is, when we get closer to New Orleans, we'll need a shit load of washer fluid to wipe off the flies. Also, y'all might want to be holding y'all's nose for a spell."

CHAPTER 23

Lunch

Frank held his mask and rolled backwards over the side of the dinghy. Before descending, he had re-rinsed his mask, purged his regulator, and given Alfredo two thumbs up. As soon as he hit the water, he released air from his buoyancy compensator and headed straight down, head first.

Ten seconds later he was completely disoriented.

He had almost forgotten this part: that first plunge into an alien world so staggeringly complex and beautiful the senses have trouble keeping up. He instincively stopped breathing, but then relaxed and touched bottom ever so gently, giving in to the rhythmic sway of the wave surge. He smoothly pushed himself up and over so that he was standing. He stayed put, resisting the temptation to move into and join with the spectacle that was all around him.

It would be easy to forget why he was down here, to lift off and glide forth with no destination and no purpose. First, though, he let his sense of time reassert itself. Then he looked up to reclaim his sense of place. The dinghy was way over to his left, yet it seemed close enough to touch. Even forty feet down the water was full of light and life, energizing and bringing color to everything it reached.

Frank stood in a glade of sugar sand near the base of a looming coral head. Above him, and just beneath the waves, stretched a massive canopy of honey colored giant fan coral. The supporting trunk was a gnarled accumulation of coral and delicate plant life. Beneath the canopy were hordes of small, multicolored fish. In places, the coral colonies had intertwined to form a honeycomb labyrinth of caves and tunnels, some of which were big enough to swim into.

Still, he wasn't here to observe, he was here to find edible fish. To do that he had to behave like one. He had to join with the jumbled fantasy of dead and living coral and become a part of it, to rediscover the instinct for separating the animate from the inanimate. He also had to be careful not to shoot himself in the foot.

Alfredo, who did this sort of thing every day and had no need for life support, darted down with a mask on his face and a spear gun in his hand.

***

"I'm a bit worried about the crocodiles," Marge had said just before Chamberlain and Alfredo left for the reef.

"No problem, missus,"Alfredo reassured her. "The crocs stay on the island side of the reef; we'll be on the other side, where the sharks hang out."

Her mouth turned down at the edges, but she managed a smile. Chamberlain knew the expression well. It said, *All right Frank Chamberlain, go do what you have to do. I'll be fine, but just make sure you come back in one piece, and if you can't do that, then for God's sake, please get back any way you can.*

"I'll take a shark over a crocodile any day of the week," he said, and immediately realized he should have kept his mouth shut.

"I hope it doesn't come to that," Marge said carefully.

"Nah," intervened Alfredo, "there's enough fish down there for everybody. He'll just want to keep the catch away from his body on the way up."

"I know that," Chamberlain said. "It's not as if I haven't done this before."

"All right, mate," urged Alfredo, with a grin that said it was time to go. "Let's bugger off then."

***

Chamberlain had bought a used Darryl Wong spear gun in Hawaii. It was the short, three-banded model, and it was beautifully made. He could tell Alfredo was envious and made a mental note to offer it as a parting gift when they left the island.

For now, though, he is clumsily attempting to band the spear and stay upright. Alfredo dropped his own gun onto the sand and deftly loaded Chamberlain's weapon for him. Then he picked up his gun and vanished into a nearby cave. Seconds later, he came out of a different entrance, brandishing a large parrotfish at the end of his spear. He waved briefly then shot to the surface with the joyful exuberance of a young porpoise.

Chamberlain felt old, slow, and out of practice, but he wasn't worried. He knew the feeling would soon pass. He headed for the reef wall, making his way towards a point opposite the dinghy. Despite Alfredo's total lack of concern about such things, he wanted to find the anchor and make sure it wasn't stuck, or likely to drag, finding it set next to a brown boulder of brain coral that reached almost to his waist. Framing the coral was an array of purple hued sea ferns, swaying lazily with the tide surge. He moved farther along the reef wall, noting other landmarks as he went, glancing back from time to time to locate the anchor line.

Mesmerized by the teeming reef life around him, Chamberlain failed to distinguish between the reef wall and the protruding stump of a partly fallen coral head. His shoulder bumped against the obstruction and he felt it move. He froze immediately, but it was too late. He heard a muted roar above him, like an approaching freight train. Falling coral rocks tumbled past in slow motion and a mushrooming cloud of silt enveloped him. One of the rocks bumped violently against his dive tank. The tank protected him, but the force of the blow tipped him over. He immediately lost all sense of what was up and what was down.

That changed when his back hit bottom.

Without thinking, he had clutched his regulator and held it firmly to his mouth. It was as well that he had, because the silt was so dense he couldn't even see his bubbles. If he had let go, the regulator would now be suspended somewhere above and behind, floating at the end of its hose, impossible to see and almost as impossible to reach. He kicked with his legs and nothing happened.

He wasn't in pain; he just couldn't move.

He calculated he had at least another thirty or forty minutes of air, unless his regulator feed sprang a leak. He wasn't too worried, because soon the silt would clear and he would be able to see what was pinning him down. Until then, he would lie still. Struggling would only bring up more silt and make matters worse. He had to do something though, so he tentatively explored the seabed around him with his free hand. What he found was mostly silt and small pieces of dead coral, but he did come across a good-sized rock. In a strange way, the rock was comforting; it was like a newfound friend, so he held on to it. It was all he had.

Something moved towards him in the murk. His first thought was that Alfredo had found him. He soon revised his thinking.

He couldn't make out the shark until it was nearly close enough to touch. It had to be less than five yards away, emerging from the gloom like some nameless horror from the deep—which, of course, is exactly what it was. The huge mouth opened slowly, revealing a dark cavern filled with rows of big, saw-like teeth. Although the eyes were wide open, the nictitating membranes were closed—the shark had the sightless stare of a ghastly living corpse. Then the membranes flickered open and two shiny black, utterly expressionless eyes gazed straight at him. He felt his heart pump as the shark moved in, nudging him, exploring this new thing it had found that was Frank Chamberlain.

Survival instincts kicked in then and Frank denied the adrenalin rush of fear. He stayed calm. He slowed his heart rate. He imagined he was a clam. The shark slid past and faded slowly into the silt fog.

Great white sharks are solitary creatures, but they can be sociable unless, of course, they happen to be hungry or provoked—in which case it definitely pays to be a clam.

Alfredo found him within minutes. He tugged gently at Chamberlain's fins. Frank wiggled them in response to show there was no loss of movement. Two heavy pieces of fractured coral lay across his knees. Alfredo struggled, but eventually managed to move the fallen coral away from Chamberlain's legs. He pointed upward with his thumbs.

They came up close to the edge of the reef, about fifty yards from the dinghy. Alfredo removed his facemask and grinned. He wasn't even breathing hard. "Hey, Frank, next time you want to feed the fish pick something a bit smaller. That was a great white, mate. You're lucky he didn't have you for lunch."

Frank realized he was still holding the regulator to his mouth. He removed it and gasped a response. "Thanks, Jimmy, I owe you one, you sarcastic son-of-a-bitch."

He was also still clutching the rock, which suddenly seemed a lot heavier—this being hardly surprising, since his spear gun was looped around the same wrist. Just as he was about to pitch the rock back into the water, Alfredo waved frantically. "Hey, Frank, don't throw that away, you silly sod."

He swam over and took the rock from Frank with both hands. It was actually a huge oyster. Alfredo kissed it lovingly. "It's a black-lipped oyster and a big bleeder too. There must be a colony down there you broke up. These things are rare as shit these days. They farm them in the Cook Islands, but I've never seen one wild like this."

Frank peered at the encrusted mass. "So it's a frigging oyster, so what?"

"So frigging what, mate, is there could be a black pearl in there. That's why I kissed it. You do that, it's supposed to make a pearl."

Alfredo handed back the oyster. "Here, you give it a kiss."

"What the hell," said Frank, and kissed the oyster full on the lips, "just so long as I don't turn into a frog."

Back in the dinghy, Frank inspected his legs. There was one long scratch just above his right knee. Other than that, there was no discernible damage. "I'll get Marge to put some peroxide on that when we get back," he muttered.

Alfredo ignored him; he was too busy opening the oyster with his dive knife. Frank watched skeptically. Thirty seconds later, Alfredo whooped with delight. He held up a black pearl the size of a Swedish meatball. "Fucking Norah, will you look at the size of that? You're looking at two thousand quid easy, you lucky bastard."

"What do you mean?" Chamberlain said. "It's your reef, you keep it."

Alfredo shook his head. "No, mate. Finders keepers. This one's for your missus. You give this to her, you'll be made for life."

"Jeez, thanks Jimmy, not a word to Marge though, I'll keep it as a surprise." He put the pearl in the side pocket of his buoyancy vest and zipped it tight. Alfredo retrieved his spear gun and made to leave the dinghy.

"Just a minute, wait for me," Frank protested.

"Nah, you've had enough for one day. You stay here. I need to catch a few more for tomorrow's big do."

"Not likely," Chamberlain said, leaning over the side to rinse his mask. "I can out fish you any day, Jimmy. But don't you dare say anything to Marge about the big one that got away, *capiche*?"

Alfredo grinned. "Not one word, Frank." He drew two fingers across his throat. "I'm not daft, mate. If I said anything, about that shark, she'd kill me and not think twice about it."

CHAPTER 24

Party Time

Frank Chamberlain owned three kinds of shirts, three kinds of shorts, and three kinds of hats. To help him dress appropriately, Marge sewed labels on each garment. The labels were numbered from 1 to 111. As Frank's garments aged or were otherwise degraded, Marge added a 1 with her indelible pencil. Frank was discouraged from mixing labels. Unfortunately for Marge, this hierarchy of nautical fashion was difficult for Frank to figure out, even with the labels to help him. Driven by some perverse instinct, he was unable to grasp that number 1 or 11 shirts were not be worn while cleaning the bilge or topping up batteries. Equally confusing to him was the edict that number 111 garments were not allowed ashore.

"All you have to do," Marge had explained patiently, "is look at the label before you put anything on. Most people know to dress nicely on social occasions and not wear their good clothes for grinding fiberglass."

'I'll do my best," he continued to respond earnestly, and did mean it, and did try. Often, though, despite the labels, he still got it wrong. On those occasions, Marge was obliged to bite her lip and resist the temptation to throw him overboard.

Today was July Fourth and they had a shore invitation to boot, so Marge was optimistic. Of course she was disappointed when Frank presented himself, yet not greatly so.

"Nice, Frank," she observed. "I like that shirt ever so much on you, and the shorts will do, but that's not a shore hat, it's not even a boat hat. As you very well know, it's a work hat. It has rust all over it. It looks like you just used it to wipe off the anchor chain."

"Oh, shit!" said Frank. "Talking about the anchor chain just reminded me. I picked up a little something for you while I was checking the dinghy anchor yesterday."

He disappeared up the companionway steps and came back two minutes later carrying his buoyancy vest. "Close your eyes and hold out your hand," he said.

Marge did as requested and Frank removed the black pearl from the pocket of the vest. He gently took her hand, placed the pearl in her palm, and closed her fingers. "You can open your eyes now, and take a guess."

Marge opened her eyes wide and fluttered her eyelashes. "Why, Frank, darling, you finally bought me that glass eye I've always wanted."

Frank grinned. "Open your hand and see what Uncle Frank got you this time.

Marge unclenched her fingers, took a deep breath, and looked up at Frank with wide eyes. "Is this really a pearl, a black one? It's the biggest I've ever seen."

"Straight from the biggest oyster I ever saw, and with Margie Green's name written all over it."

Marge hugged Frank as though he had just returned from the wars. He felt like a poker player betting a full house against two straights and a flush. Jimmy was right: he was made for life, or at least for the rest of the week.

Marge reached up and removed his hat. "I'll love you forever, Frank Chamberlain," she said, her eyes all misted over, "but don't think for one moment I'm about to let you ashore wearing this hat."

While Frank selected a category 1 hat, Marge found a small freezer bag for the pearl and placed the bag in the refrigerator between a half pound slab of New Zealand cheddar and an aging pot of barely used nutmeg jelly from Grenada.

"So, are we taking Hilda?" queried Frank, after receiving the necessary nod of hat approval.

"No, we are not. If you will remember, Hilda's job is to guard the boat when we're not here."

"But she doesn't have a frigging clue. As soon as we leave, she goes to sleep. Every time we leave her, we have to wake her up when we get back."

"She's a dog, Frank. When the time comes, she'll know what to do. Just you wait. One of these days you'll be surprised."

They had had this discussion many times. Frank was firmly convinced the dog was not right in the head. Hilda, however, was an Irish Wolfhound and Marge remained steadfast in her belief that deep down the dog had the ferocious instincts of her Irish forebears. Centuries ago, wolfhounds were bred as war dogs by the Irish high kings. It was the custom back then to offer the dogs as a token of friendship, especially to visiting Viking chieftains. This served to placate the Vikings and remind them that he who has the biggest dogs usually wins.

Hilda knew none of this and was about as ferocious as a piece of plywood.

Two years before they set sail Marge had rescued the dog from a trailer park in South Florida. Marge's then hairdresser, a woman with a nose for such things and a fierce love of animals, had discovered Hilda chained to a tree outside a doublewide. Both women agreed this was intolerable, so they borrowed Frank's bolt cutters one afternoon and made off with the dog. Hilda had been more than happy to go along.

Hilda's greatest advantage as a guard dog was that she was big and she looked mean. Other than that, she was more or less useless, not to mention she took up too much living space. By the time her owners were in the dinghy, she was fast asleep. The noise of the outboard starting up had no affect on her whatsoever.

Frank and Marge loved Hilda to death.

***

Nothing much happened on Noahu. On most Sunday mornings, nothing happened at all. The Presbyterian Church was long gone. There was no bar. There was no restaurant, no highway, and therefore no traffic. There was no airstrip, and therefore no aircraft. There was no boat dock, and therefore no boats tied up. There were no shops, and therefore no shopkeepers. Most importantly, at least for Frank Chamberlain, there were no offices of any kind, and therefore no one employed to mind other people's business.

Incongruously, perched atop the old volcano was a solar powered cell-phone tower—incongruous because no one on Noahu had ever asked for phone service, let alone had the wherewithal to pay for it. The other incongruity was a fifty-yard long chain-link fence. The fence, with a locked gate in the middle, was situated at one end of the beach, a good half-mile from the village.

Frank had asked about these oddities. It seemed that for the main island (Vanahu) to qualify for American military assistance—e.g., free helicopters, trucks and so on—all the islands had to consent to two things: the first was a perimeter fence to guard against border incursions, whereby terrorists might take out strategic targets, such as cell-phone towers. The second thing was a cell-phone tower, so that in the event of such an assault, the Pentagon could be notified at once.

The islanders on Noahu had agreed in principle, but countered by pointing out that putting a fence around the entire island, albeit with a gate in the middle, would seriously jeopardize beach access. Not to mention the ocean view. The crocodiles were none too pleased either. The islanders also protested that the old volcano was sacred. Why not, they suggested, erect a partial fence somewhere out of the way, and put a box on the gate with a satellite phone in it; then they could easily change out the batteries once a month. The State Department refused to budge on the tower, but eventually compromised on the fence.

There was, nevertheless, a meetinghouse and a chief on the island, both of which were significant on this particular Sunday morning, because the chief had called a meeting. The meeting was being called because commerce was finally coming to the shores of Noahu. A factory was to be built. Therefore a dock, a road, a small airstrip, and a store would also be constructed. In addition, there would be at least one office for minding other people's business.

On the way to the beach, Chamberlain voiced his concerns—yet again. "No good can come of it, Marge," he said. "It's going to be downhill all the way from now on, just you mark my words."

"Stop being negative," Marge said with a stern look. "Anyway, if we don't like it, we can always pull up the anchor and move. And you never know, you might just get involved."

He laughed. "What, get involved in making fiberglass shovel handles? You must be joking."

Marge couldn't help but smile. "Well, I have to admit, it would seem a bit odd—from decorated war hero to running a shovel handle factory. Still, you have to admit, if anyone knows anything at all about working with fiberglass—especially hereabouts—it's got to be you."

Chamberlain chuckled. "Not a chance. The only two things I run these days are a seventy-seven horsepower marine diesel and this little baby here." He patted the cover of the outboard motor. "Other than that, you're in charge."

"And don't you forget it, Frank Chamberlain," Marge replied, somehow managing to look strict and forgiving at the same time.

Alfredo and George were occupying the beach chairs when Marge and Frank pulled in. They set down their *Tusker* beers and willingly helped beach the dinghy. When Frank offered two cases of Fosters for the party, they accepted gleefully, shouldering the cases with accustomed ease.

"Looking extra special smart there, Frank," said George as he helped Marge from the dinghy. "It's not formal you know missus. We're just having a party."

"Yes, I know, George, but Frank happens to be with me, so he's going to look nice, and you're not to be sneaking him any of that disgusting kava, either."

"What's the drill, Jimmy?" Chamberlain asked as they walked to the beach table.

"Barry's going to say a few words, then we'll have a party. A bit later the Italian is going to show up on his yacht and say a few more words then we'll carry on with the party."

"Is this the same guy you told me about? The one that was screwing your mom?"

"Yeah, well that was a long time back. He didn't have two halfpennies to rub together in those days. Now he's a billionaire."

"What, from shovel handles?"

"Nah, Frank, he's got restaurants all over. You must have seen them in the States. They're called Shovel Houses."

Chamberlain shook his head. "Must have been after we left. But what does that have to do with Noahu."

Alfredo laughed. "He spread this story he got the idea for his restaurants here in the islands. He even had his photo taken with Barry and George holding a couple of old shovels they'd found."

Alfredo paused to pull up chairs for the visitors. Undaunted by Marge's edict, he offered Chamberlain an early cup of kava.

"Not likely," said Chamberlain. "You heard what Marge said. Do I look stupid?"

"No comment, Frank." Marge sat down, accepting a beer from George. "You can offer him a beer though, Alfredo. He can drink those all day."

"Thanks, Jimmy," said Chamberlain gratefully. "What I don't understand though, is if this guy wants to make shovel handles, why doesn't he go to the Chinese like everybody else?"

George spread his arms wide and leaned back in the chair. "It's this tropical paradise, mate. It's all about his image. Desert islands are what people like to think of when they eat his food. So he passes off his bloody shovel handles as hand-carved native art. Alfredo's auntie carved the first one from teak, just like she does the spear guns. He had moulds made from that. He already has one factory on Maehu. Between you and me, it might just as well be in Lithuania for all the bloody native carving that gets done."

Alfredo leaned forward. "Also, he gets to hide his money. The central government on Vanahu says since he brings work, he doesn't have to pay a penny in taxes."

"Anyway," intervened George, "he did go to the Chinese. They're the one's putting in the factory and everything else."

Frank and Marge exchanged glances. "If I were you," Frank said, "I'd be asking what comes next."

Alfredo shrugged off the comment. "Who'd want to come here, Frank? We've got bugger-all to offer."

"We came, " Marge said.

"Yeah, well you two are different. Anyway, if it were up to me, I'd tell the Italian to stick every single one of his shovel handles up his bum. But it's not up to me; it's up to Barry and the prime minister. They're the ones in charge."

Alfredo finished his beer and nodded in the direction of the reef. He grinned and beckoned to George. "They're here, mate. We're in luck. It looks like they decided to give it a go." Both men put down their beers, politely asked to be excused then jumped up and ran whooping and waving to the water's edge. Marge and Frank settled back to watch.

More than a dozen large outrigger canoes crowded through the reef passage. The canoes bumped, weaved, and tipped as they fought for position. The oarsmen hurled insults. The passengers hurled anything they could lay their hands on. Chamberlain recognized fresh fish, mangoes, tomatoes, toilet paper, and bits of clothing. It seemed they were also throwing shredded chicken livers smeared with ketchup. He was later to identify these latter items as fresh-killed fruit bat innards marinated in balsamic vinegar. This marinade was the brainchild of the *Melanesian Gourmet,* an islander who had departed as a three-year-old to Pittsburgh, and who was now a Food Channel regular. Before the *Melanesian Gourmet* showed up on island TV, fruit bat innards were traditionally fed to the pigs or buried sensibly out back.

There was no winner of the race. All the canoes coasted into the beach at the same time. The oarsmen shipped paddles, stepped out smartly, and hauled the canoes onto the sand. George and Alfredo slapped a few backs and yelled a few greetings, but were clearly not focused on the oarsmen. They were too busy taking care of the passengers: most of whom were excited nut-brown maidens, all with brightly decorated faces, all giggling, and all more than happy to be assisted.

"Frank," Marge observed with a smile, "you'd better go fetch another case of beer and two more bottles of my cranberry vodka. I think the party just got started, and I think it just got bigger."

CHAPTER 25

Hormones

Not only was Barry's short speech incomprehensible to Frank and Marge, he could barely be heard because he was standing between the generator and the icemaker. Everyone listened intently, though, and the gist of it wasn't hard to figure out.

The Chamberlains were recognized, along with the three cases of Fosters and four bottles of cranberry vodka: applause. The four men and six boys who had been up since five a.m. spit roasting six pigs were acknowledged: enthusiastic applause. The location of the bush toilets was pointed out: laughter and cheers. The women who had spent two days preparing *lap-lap* and other side dishes were thanked: applause and whistles. Directions were given for the shed set aside as a *nakamal* for the quiet contemplation of kava: silence, since all the men, including Frank Chamberlain, knew exactly where the *nakamal* was, and were not about to seem overeager. The pigs were honored: a soaring harmonized chant with rhythmic handclapping, during which Barry pointed at the pigs with a decorated stick and gazed up at the wooded heights of the old volcano. The oarsmen were greeted: lusty cheers. Finally, a welcome was extended to the visiting maidens, now busily mingling with their homegrown counterparts: screams, cheers, giggles, whistles, wild applause, whooping, waving, and much leaping about.

Barry then headed for the *nakamal* with a half dozen or so cohorts while Marge gently but firmly restrained Frank.

Barry, incidentally, was truly magnificent. In addition to his workaday blue and red, he had vivid yellow circles around his eyes, and diagonal white stripes under his cheekbones. He wore a polished silver nose ring with matching earrings, intricately carved upper arm rings made from wild boar tusks, a masticated pigskin penis sheath, and solid gold ankle bracelets. All of this was topped off by a headgear that defied description.

Marge asked Alfredo if she could take a photograph. Alfredo said sorry, but no. In addition to being chief, it seemed Barry was also a *klever*: a man possessed by magic—a witchdoctor. Some days he was amenable to being photographed. On this day, he was not. On this day, Alfredo explained, Barry felt a camera might make off with his magic.

The maidens on the other hand clamored to have their pictures taken—all forty of them. Like Barry they too were possessed by magic: the beauty magic painted on their faces, and this other, more urgent magic they carried within. The maiden's magic, unlike Barry's, however, was clamoring to be revealed. Marge was invited to share the magic: to have her face painted, to join with the maidens, and later to dance. Like Frank, she was afraid of nothing, although usually a good deal more cautious. On this occasion, it being a feast day, she was prepared to throw caution to the winds and have fun. Alfredo gently held her back.

"No," he said earnestly, "that would not be a good idea, missus. When the dancing starts you'd be better off sticking with Frank and shutting your eyes."

"Alfredo, I was an Army nurse for twenty years. Believe me, there isn't much I haven't already seen."

"Or done," interjected Frank, immediately realizing he had spoken in haste.

"That wasn't very nice," Marge said, looking hurt.

Frank studied the wooded heights of the old volcano and secretly vowed never again to utter another word in the presence of his wife. However many times he made this vow, though, it never seemed to stick, so instead of keeping quiet, he dug himself in a little deeper.

"What I meant was..."

"Don't even go there, Frank."

Frank made a small course correction. "Going to get a bit raunchy is it, Jimmy?"

"It'll get raunchy all right, but don't get me wrong, mate. This isn't something we do every weekend. If we did, we'd be out of virgins in less than a month."

Marge contemplated the maidens. "I hope you don't mind me saying so, but as nice as these girls are, some of them aren't exactly without experience."

Alfredo grinned. "That's the least of our problems. When the lads get going, they'd have it off with a friendly pig if it got close enough." He winked at Frank. "I'd even keep an eye on young Frank if I were you. Some of our girls aren't that choosy, either."

Marge gave Alfredo one of her looks.

"Welcome to the club, Jimmy," Frank chortled.

It was Alfredo's turn to make a course correction. "What I was saying was, we don't do this all the time. It's supposed to be just once a year, but if enough girls feel like it, we do the ceremony more often."

Marge handed Alfredo a cup of cranberry vodka. Frank, being temporarily in the doghouse, was left to fend for himself.

"It sounds like quite the occasion," Marge said. "And what, exactly might we be celebrating, apart from an over abundance of hormones and a new factory?"

Alfredo squinted up at the heights of the old volcano. "Up there is where Noah landed when the flooding stopped." He pointed to the crocodile beach. "Over there is where he built his boat."

Frank put down his beer ever so slowly. "Sure, and I've got this bridge in Brooklyn I'm trying to get rid of."

"No, Frank, I'm dead serious. The missionaries didn't believe it either. That's why the first two got baked."

"I thought you put them in cauldrons?"

"Nah, that's just a story. The way you cook people is, you dig a pit on the beach, then you get a nice wood fire going in it. After the flames die out, you wrap the body in fresh palm fronds or banana leaves, put it in the pit, sprinkle some sand over it, and let it smoke for a while."

"Next thing, you'll tell us is it tastes just like chicken," grinned Frank.

"Actually, it's more like pork," Alfredo replied, ostentatiously licking his lips. "Mind you, and I'm not just saying this to scare you, there's some on the islands would revert back to the old days at the drop of a hat if they had half a chance."

Frank took a long, thoughtful pull at his beer, suddenly feeling the need to change the subject. "Okay, so what you're saying is, this whole Biblical story about Noah and Mount Ararat is a bunch of baloney."

"That's right, Frank," Alfredo confirmed. "Noah's actual name was Noahu, our island god, mate. Barry is his direct descendant and so am I. This ceremony commemorates Noahu summoning the virgins. They came from all the neighboring islands so he and his crew could choose the ones they liked best. Legend has it he only had room for forty, so that's the ideal number, although these days we'll take however many we can get. And we're not too fussy about them being virgins either."

Frank and Marge took a few moments to digest this frontal assault on one of the Bible's all time favorites. Frank, not having opened a Bible since third grade, had no problem accepting an alternative version, particularly since he was getting it first hand, so to speak. Marge politely avoided the issue. She sat down and examined the nearest food dish, which happened to be a plate of flame-broiled fruit bat, minus the innards.

"I have one question," Frank said. "How come Noah made it into the Bible if he was a South Sea Islander?"

Alfredo shrugged. "No idea, mate, and here's another one for you, while we're at it." He nodded in the direction of Barry's hut. "The Italian never knew how close he was when he came up with his story about the shovels. He said we ate off them because they were dropped from a plane during the war and they had no handles, so we thought they were white man's dinner plates. Well, he was making all that up, naturally, but there's something else."

Alfredo looked about to make sure no one was listening then lowered his voice. "You're the first white man to ever hear this, Frank, so please don't repeat what I'm about to tell you."

Frank nodded and leaned close.

"Noahu actually invented the world's first shovel," Alfredo continued in a whisper. "Over there in Barry's hut is Noahu's sacred shovel. It's been handed down from chief to chief ever since Noahu got back from the flood. Legend has it that when his boat landed on top of the old volcano Noahu marched out swearing blue murder and waving this shovel. Then he hurled it down the mountain. He never touched another shovel for the rest of his life."

"So, why did he invent it?" whispered Frank.

"On account of all the animals on the boat, especially the pigs. Can you imagine scooping up pig shit with your hands for a hundred and fifty days?"

"You've got to be kidding."

"No, I'm not." Alfredo was deadly serious. "In fact, when Barry dies and I get to be chief, we perform the secret shovel hurling ceremony. All the chiefs from the other islands come over and I get to hurl the sacred shovel from the top of the old volcano. Whoever gets to it first is named guardian of the shovel. His family gets first pick of the virgins every year until the next hurling."

"So who gets first pick these days, Jimmy?"

"I do," Alfredo said with a broad grin. "Barry's no fool. When he hurled the shovel he had his brother hiding behind the nearest tree."

"You know," Marge said, looking up, "this fruit bat isn't half bad. Doesn't taste a bit like chicken, though, more like venison. You'll have to jot down the recipe, Alfredo."

Giovanni Garibaldi, the Italian, showed up just then and put an end to the conversation. More accurately, his eighty-eight foot motor yacht showed up. Five blasts of the ship's horn sounded her arrival. Frank Chamberlain, being a licensed captain, was aware that five blasts signified an emergency. Everyone else assumed it was a summons to dash to the water's edge and gasp with admiration. Of course, everyone else was right.

The yacht approached the crocodile beach like some fantastic alien craft commanded by unimaginable beings. She gleamed and glinted, moving carefully, silently, and with deadly intent. Frank understood how the islanders must have felt when the first white explorers arrived in their amazing vessels, i.e., totally and utterly screwed. He watched with interest as a tender emerged from the stern and raced ahead of the bow. Two hundred yards from the beach the tender stopped and settled in the water. The helmsman looked casually over the side then waved to the yacht. Frank heard the great chain rattle briefly before the anchor splashed down.

Now, the longboat was in the water, the amazing vessel was secure, and soon the captain would come to the island bearing cheap gifts and the usual false promises.

Nothing much had changed, really.

CHAPTER 26

Shovel World

Apparently, Garibaldi, who couldn't care less, was no longer in Barry's good books. This stemmed from the photograph. Back when it was taken, Garibaldi had obtained a signed release from George, together with Barry's notarized mark in exchange for a new TV set for Barry and fifty dollars for George. At the time, it seemed like a good deal. At the time, neither George nor Barry knew about Garibaldi's Shovel House idea. Ever since Barry had found out, he could fairly be described as a disgruntled former employee. George on the other hand, was happy to forgive and forget. Consequently, Garibaldi wasn't about to visit the *nakamal,* and Barry wasn't about to come out until he was good-and-ready, so Garibaldi was obliged to address the partygoers on his own.

First, he displayed his contribution to the party: four large coolers crammed with beer and wine, two dozen or so roast chickens, and a crate full of number eight active senior shovel blades to serve as plates (no trowels). Then he introduced his guest—a slightly built Chinese man wearing rimless George W. Bush active senior eye-wear and an expensive, but cleverly understated seersucker tropical suit by Brioni.

By this time, George had set up the sound system and was trying out dance tunes. He generously passed the mike to Garibaldi and muted the music.

"First, I would like-a you to meeta my friend, Mister Jung Shi-Zhe, chairman of the Honest Electrical Engineering and Office Furniture Factory of a Pingyang. He willa be building you-a factory."

Polite applause. Shi-Zhe smiled politely in return.

"I also wanna say you gonna be getting a gooda deal here. You getta work; you getta paid; you getta benefits; and you also getta two weeks offa with-a pay."

Alfredo raised his hand. "Two weeks off doesn't sound like much to me."

Garibaldi smiled condescendingly. "You also getta thissa extra day for every year you-a work. You worka for twenty years, you getta sixa weeks off."

"Right now I get fifty two weeks off."

"Yes, but you donta getta paid."

Alfredo turned to Frank. "What do you think?"

"I think it stinks."

"What about you, missus, what do you think?"

"I think it stinks too, Alfredo, unless you really need the money."

Alfredo raised his hand again. "Thanks all the same, mate, but I'll pass."

When all was said and done, all the men said no, and all the women said yes (which was more or less what all the men and all the women had anticipated all along). Therefore, everyone was happy; everyone had reason to celebrate. The men would celebrate manliness and not having a regular job; the women would celebrate having financial independence for the first time in their lives; and Giovanni Garibaldi would return to his yacht to celebrate the advent of yet another profitable venture.

***

When it became clear that maidens were about to be hoisted aloft and fondled, Marge decided it was time to leave. Not that she and Frank were prudes—quite the opposite. Nor was Marge afraid her own feet might shortly be leaving the ground, despite having received her share of amorous glances. No, Marge was afraid of what Frank might do if someone decided she was fair game for hoisting. Frank was not prone to violence, but his protective instincts and close combat skills were finely tuned when it came to his wife.

Not to mention, Frank was receiving more than a few amorous glances of his own.

Therefore, Marge gladly accepted the Italian's invitation to sit out the rest of the event on his yacht. The Chamberlain's stayed just long enough to retrieve a bottle of cranberry vodka and wave farewell to Alfredo and George. The two islanders were vigorously hoisting and fondling their first willing virgin and thus in no position to wave back—but they did nod a joyful acknowledgement.

Garibaldi's yacht was called *Foxy Lady III*. She was a raised pilothouse Ferretti 881, which was another way of saying, "get out of my way". Neither Frank nor Marge had ever set foot on a vessel that luxurious, nor ever wanted to for that matter, which is not to say they were not impressed and amazed. Nonetheless, Garibaldi apologized, assuring them that had the lagoon been deeper and the reef passage a good deal wider, he would have brought his flagship, *Foxy Lady I*. Not wishing to be utterly overwhelmed by envy and amazement, Frank and Marge didn't enquire as to the size and make of the flagship. Frank did observe, however, that during their passage from Florida to the South Pacific, they had observed a multitude of *Foxy Ladies*, ranging in size from nine feet to well over two hundred. "They wouldn't all belong to you, now would they?" he inquired disingenuously.

The Italian threw back his head and laughed. "You havva the joke with me. I like-a that."

Frank and Marge were sitting on a white leather settee in the cockpit, which was situated behind the main salon and above the hydraulically operated drop-down swim platform. Shi-Zhe had excused himself, murmuring that he wished to change into something more casual. Garibaldi's steward had served beers, and was now tending bar, trying not to notice Marge's unlabeled bottle of cranberry vodka. The bar, needless to say, was stocked with a kaleidoscopic display of high-priced tipple. Frank had already calculated that the cockpit alone was twice the width of the *Mary Rose* and half as long, i.e. almost the size of a regulation squash court.

"You wouldn't be in the market for a well behaved Irish Wolfhound would you?" he said, edging away from Marge.

She discreetly kicked his right shin, which hadn't quite made it to safety. "What Frank is trying to say, Mister Garibaldi, is that we have a large dog on a small boat, which can sometimes be a bit trying."

The Italian leaned forward and nodded sympathetically. He jerked a thumb over his shoulder, indicating the vast, over-polished interior behind him. "Believe-a me, this I understand—except, I havva the opposite problem; I havva the big boat witha the smalla dog. My foxy lady, who has-a this headache and is-a lying down for now, she has-a this Lhasa Apso." A vein started to pulse in his forehead. "You cannot a train-a these-a dogs. They sheeta anna they pissa everywhere, and when they are not-a sheeting, they are a doing a yappa yappa all-a time in you-a face."

"Jeez," murmured Frank, "life's tough all over."

"Well, at least we don't have that problem with Hilda," Marge observed. "We have a piece of green indoor-outdoor carpet on the aft deck and she's very good about using it."

Like most borderline personalities, Garibaldi had stopped listening the instant he stopped talking. He ignored Marge and snapped his fingers. The steward stepped forward smartly. "Getta me a plate of these-a Buffalo wings anna glass offa the Chianti, anna after that I wanna some Tiramisu."

He turned to Frank and Marge. "You wanna food?"

"No thanks," said Marge stiffly. "We've already eaten."

Shi-Zhe showed up then wearing the pale blue seersucker trousers from his Brioni suit together with a worsted wool and cashmere-serge navy blazer by Hickey Freeman, hand stitched Brazilian steer-hide topsiders, and a dark olive casual cotton sateen shirt by Gucci. Artfully draped around his throat was a silvered-silk cravat accented with a filigreed Croatian braiding motif.

Frank was mystified. He couldn't fathom why anyone would want to wear such a getup, especially on the water. Yet, he was ever alert to the possibility he might be expected to learn from such fashion encounters, so he glanced furtively at Marge. She caught his glance with one of her own that said, *Don't worry, Frank, you're in the clear on this one.*

Garibaldii signaled the steward to wait. "You wanna food, Steve?"

Shi nodded politely. "Please, I will have same as you."

"Excuse me," Marge said, "I hope you don't mind my asking, but how come you're called Steve. That's not a Chinese name is it?"

Shi settled himself carefully next to Garibaldi, trying unsuccessfully to avoid wrinkling his trousers. He nodded briefly as the steward asked him if he would care for his usual. "When I was little boy in Shanghai we have watched all the time this movie *The Great Escape,* with Steve McQueen, and also *The Magnificent Seven*, also with Steve McQueen." He paused while the steward set down a glass containing two ice cubes. Next to the glass, the steward placed an unopened bottle of twenty-five year-old Balvenie single malt scotch whiskey. Shi slowly swirled the ice cubes to cool the glass then leaned back as the steward removed one cube with elegantly fashioned antique silver tongs. Shi sat in reverent anticipation as the steward opened the bottle and carefully poured. At exactly two fingers, he raised his hand. "That is enough, thank you."

After savoring the whiskey, Shi set the glass down and turned his attention back to Marge. "So, I have always like to be called Steve, especially when I am in America."

He nodded to Garibaldi. "This is where we have met: in America."

"Yess-a," said the Italian enthusiastically, "we havva been special invited by the Global-a-Titanic Corporation to look atta these hotta properties in Yellowstone Park."

"Oh, I see," Marge said with a dangerous smile, "so now our national heritage is for sale, as well as most of our politicians. Did they offer a package deal: buy one property, get two congressmen and one senator at half the normal price?"

Garibaldi didn't answer. Instead, he pointed to the crocodile beach. "When you havva the money, you can buy whatta you want. Thissa beach, and thissa island for example, issa all mine."

The statement caught Frank's attention because he had naively assumed the island belonged to the islanders—forever, in perpetuity, ad infinitum, and so on.

Not so.

Marge and Frank exchanged glances.

"I hope you don't mind my asking, Mister Garibaldi," Marge said, "but, exactly how does one buy an island like Noahu?"

Garibaldi beamed. "You go to-a the prime minister of-a the islands and aska how much. Inna the case of Noahu, I cannot buy, but I gotta ninety-nine year lease for-a commercial purpose only." He winked. "Anna the prime minister, he gotta nice place onna Lake Como."

"Yes," said Marge, "I see. Well, we didn't think for one moment the factory would be the end of it. So, now that you own the island, Mister Garibaldi, what will you do, next?"

Garibaldi seemed unaware Marge had spoken. He finished his beer and impatiently summoned the steward—who, in all fairness, was already on the move. The Italian pointed angrily at the table. "Whatta you see?"

"Nothing, sir."

"Then you go getta something. You go getta my food, which been-a sitting in-a kitchen for a half an hour. But first you getta me wine."

Garibaldi didn't raise his voice and he didn't look directly at the steward until he was finished, at which point he picked up his empty beer glass and tossed it overboard. Then he looked at the steward and yelled. "Anna iffa you don't-a move a you-a lazy ass you also-a going inna the water."

Garibaldi punctuated his remarks by slamming a meaty fist on the table. Evidently accustomed to such outbursts, Shi-Zhe had placed the Balvenie and his glass on a side table the instant the Italian had put down his beer. Marge and Frank were not so enlightened. Frank, however, was blessed with lightning reflexes when it came to rescuing endangered beverages. He grabbed both glasses before they even had a chance to wobble.

Garibaldi leaned back as though nothing had happened. He beamed at Marge. "What willa happen next is-a Shovel World. First we getta rid of this-a crocodiles. Then we builda this-a theme park designed by a Global-Titanic, anna hotels, anna cruise a ship terminal, anna alla that."

He turned to Shi-Zhe. "Is-a same thing Steve is-a doing in-a New Orleans for thissa Garbage World he is-a building."

The steward returned with Garibaldi's wine and hastened to the kitchen, leaving the bottle on the table. The Italian reached over and raised his glass in a toast. "So, I wanna we alla drink to Shovel World."

Frank set down his beer. "I think it's time we left," he said.

Garibaldii persisted. "First, I wanna you drinka with me."

"No thanks," Frank said firmly. "To be honest with you, pal, I think this Shovel World of yours is a totally fucked up idea."

Once again, Giovanni Garibaldi was transformed. Rage billowed upwards and outwards like a mushroom cloud. His wine glass went overboard. The vein in his forehead pulsed. His eyes bulged. He stood, marched over to the bar, grabbed Marge's bottle of cranberry vodka, and launched that too. "Okay, so you don wanna drink with me. Then also I don wanna drink with you."

"Suits me," Frank said, rising slowly to his feet. "By the way, that was my wife's cranberry vodka you just ditched."

Garibaldi folded his arms and puffed his chest. "You wanna the vodka, you canna looka for it when you-a leave."

"I've got a better idea," said Frank. "Why don't you go look? But be sure and mind the crocodiles; they've been known to bite."

Giovanni Garibaldi was a heavy-set man with a low center of gravity, i.e. his build wasn't conducive to being tossed overboard from the cockpit of a Ferretti 881 luxury motor yacht. Frank Chamberlain however, managed the feat with ease, having been well tutored in such matters.

The steward returned just then with a plate full of Buffalo wings, which he placed carefully on the table between the two settees. He accepted Marge's empty glass with an appreciative smile. "Would that be all, Ma'am?"

"Yes," said Marge, "that will very definitely be all, thank you." She turned to Shi-Zhe. "It was nice to meet you, Steve. I do so hope you enjoy Yellowstone. Oh, and perhaps you could mention to Mister Garibaldi when he gets back that Frank was acting on impulse. He wasn't angry or anything. Believe me, you really wouldn't want to be that close to Frank when he's angry."

CHAPTER 27

Mandy Meets Muriel

At the very moment Frank Chamberlain tossed Giovanni Garibaldi overboard, Johnny Chittenden launched Billy Ray Bixbee's 56 Chevy at the inside of the north door of the Vehicle Assembly Building. This event occurred at three a.m., Eastern Daylight Time, July Fourth. In the car with the Human Bomb were Albert Einstein, Genghis Khan, Jesus One, Jesús Maria Martinez, and Mandy Miller.

Here's how it happened.

First, though, it's important to be aware that the 56 Chevy was one of the all-time favorites of professional thrill drivers. Few other cars ever came close, unless you count the 57 Chevy. Alas, the 57 soon became a prized collector's item, which made it way too expensive for nightly ramp jumps and multiple rollovers. Furthermore, Chevrolet added anodized aluminum side panels to the 57, thus making it risky for human bombs and other stunts involving extremely high temperatures.

For thrill drivers, what mattered most was a rock-solid combination of steel, weight, power, unbreakable suspension, and damn good brakes. The 56 Chevy delivered in spades. Her all-steel frame, chassis, and massive outrigger springs weighed close to two tons. A two hundred twenty-five horsepower super turbo V-8, with twin four-barrel carburetors took the car from zero to sixty in less than ten seconds. Moreover, Joie Chitwood, the most famous thrill driver ever, was heard to say, "You can stop this car on a dime, and she'll give you a nickel in change."

Was that a great thrill driving car, or what?

***

When Billy Ray Bixbee first set eyes on Muriel Banks Mandy Miller knew she was in trouble. Like most thunderbolts, Muriel showed up when least expected. Well, that's not strictly true, since Mandy *was* expecting Muriel, but not as a thunderbolt.

It was the Friday evening before the wedding rehearsal, which was scheduled for the following morning, and Mandy was anticipating the arrival of Bishop Ron P. Wilmus, accompanied by the Global Divinity Church Choir under the direction of lead soloist Miss Muriel Banks.

That was certainly no cause for alarm.

Bishop Ron was officiating based on his growing popularity with black congregations in the Pacific Northwest. Sensing an opportunity to broaden *BACON's* appeal and not wishing to share the stage with anyone remotely resembling competition, Billy Ray had put it this way: "Lookit here, Bishop Ron, y'all do me and the Repentant Bride of Heaven the favor of officiating, and y'all will go national faster than green grass through a goose—guaranteed!"

Who could refuse?

Thus, it came about that Muriel Banks unknowingly embarked on a new chapter in her life when she emerged from the Church bus in the VAB parking lot. For there was Billy Ray with his bride-to-be, waiting to greet Bishop Ron. Not to mention the VAB itself, sans flag and newly adorned with floodlit scenes from the idyllic pastures of heaven. Trumpeting angels floated in an impossibly blue sky. Endless green fields vanished into a royal purple haze. People of all sizes and shapes, and the occasional plump child, wandered the meadows among a host of happy lambs.

Muriel was bowled over by it all. She paused artfully in the doorway of the bus, her face uplifted in awe, her bosom uplifted for a different reason. Billy Ray also looked upwards—spellbound by a sight vastly more appealing than the pastures of heaven.

That was when Mandy knew she was in trouble.

The following day at the dress rehearsal, it became clear to most of those present, that Mandy Miller was yesterday's news. Billy Ray had discovered his New Prophetess of Pastureland. Muriel was a shoo-in.

She wore a figure-hugging crimson gown that flowed like a gathering pool of sacrificial blood. Her eyes shone with a fanatical combination of fury, conviction, and seductive promise. She sang as though Jesus Christ himself were perched atop the IMAX.

She also showed lots of cleavage.

While Muriel was performing her life-changing solo and transfixing Billy Ray, Mandy prepared for her processional into the Ministry of Reborn Evangelicals with Dirk Forrester. Mandy's father had passed away some six years previously, so Dirk seemed the logical choice. He had, after all, been her closest male companion until Billy Ray showed up and she got her hands on the nail gun. Despite Mandy's legal problem with Dirk, their respective advisors were unanimous in believing this arrangement was best for both of them. Having Dirk give Mandy away to Billy Ray was not only richly symbolic, but also a brilliant play on the twin wedding themes of repentance and forgiveness: she repented; the two men forgave; and a book deal, possibly a movie, waited breathlessly in the wings.

Dirk had happily agreed to the arrangement because he no longer had the mental capacity to disagree with anything. His only request was that he be allowed to bring his nail gun to the ceremony. Since the accident, the gun had been his best and only friend, so Mandy had tearfully consented. "After all," she said. "It's only right. It's the least we can do considering what I put him through."

When they heard this, the advisors almost fell off their respective chairs with glee. In their wildest dreams, they could never have conceived of such a PR masterstroke. Even before the mishap, Dirk Forrester had been dumber than a box of rocks, but they had to admit his nail gun idea smacked of pure genius. *Star* magazine would eat it up. Maybe, they speculated, the finish nail had somehow transformed Dirk into some kind of idiot savant.

Not a chance.

Mandy had no family in attendance. Her only surviving relative was her father's younger brother whom she hadn't seen or heard from in twenty years, even though she had written him after her father died. All she had to remember him by was a scrapbook of newspaper clippings that had been sent to her father for safekeeping at a time when Uncle Johnny was said to have lost it.

"Johnny's done gone and lost it," her father had said, upon receiving the scrapbook. "Dang, if he weren't right up there with the likes of Joie Chitwood. Then them monster truck pulls showed up and human bombs wasn't what folks wanted no more, so Johnny took to the bottle. Could have been the best thrill driver ever was, your Uncle Johnny. Instead, he got drunk and set hisself on fire."

But, back to Mandy, waiting to make her entrance. She could hear the Ministry's organ—the very same one that had played at the 1847 marriage of Dorothy Carew to Tom Daniel at Saint Peter's Church, Tiverton in Devon, England. This was significant, because Tom and Dorothy were the first bride and groom *ever* to choose Mendelssohn's *Wedding March* for their ceremony. (Billy Ray would stop at nothing to feed the gaping maw that was *Star* magazine). For the recessional, he had chosen that other wedding favorite, the *Bridal Chorus* from Richard Wagner's *Lohengrin*, thus reversing tradition, since the *Bridal Chorus* is usually played when the bride arrives.

Entering the Ministry arm in arm with Dirk, who lovingly clutched the nail gun in his other hand, Mandy noticed all eyes were on Muriel Banks. Billy Ray, in particular, was transfixed. At that very moment, Mandy felt that just about everything was instantly miniaturized, Mandy Miller included. The only normal, and therefore giant, objects left in the entire Ministry were Billy Ray Bixbee and Muriel Banks. Mandy's two hundred foot white satin train was suddenly the size of one of Billy Ray's silk twill handkerchiefs. Her shimmering nine-carat diamond ring (on loan from Tiffany) could have been a glass bead from a Barbie Bowtie. Her twelve-tier wedding cake was smaller than a six-pack of Little Debbie's cakes. Even the IMAX was no bigger than her living room TV.

Giant Billy Ray looked down at her in profound disbelief that anyone could be so tiny. The Giantess that was Muriel Banks had sung so loud the roof was gone.

Exit Mandy Miller.

Of course, she was obliged to continue with the rehearsal. She was through crying though. As she left the altar, two thoughts were uppermost in her mind: stay out of jail, and get the hell away from Billy Ray before the axe fell, which was only a matter of time, the Repentant Bride Of Heaven notwithstanding.

Therefore, Mandy was on full alert when she noticed Jesus One and Genghis Khan. She saw them as Billy Ray escorted her down the ramp leading from the great stage to the center aisle. They were sandwiched between two of Bishop Ron's giant helpers. Even had Mandy not been miniaturized the two escorts would still have been giants. They were too bulked up to be basketball players, and way too tall for the NFL—but spot on for ushering and guard duty.

Mandy and Billy Ray descended to the gathering tempest of Wagner's chorus. The holier than heaven siren calls of the Global Divinity Choir cut like chariot blades through the triumphant climax. Then Muriel Banks trumped Wagner and the choir. She sang for the Lord; she sang for three thousand invited guests; and she sang for a TV audience expected to be in the tens of millions.

Most of all, though, Muriel sang for Billy Ray Bixbee.

Jesus One and the Khan were clearly enjoying the spectacle, and just as clearly didn't belong. The Khan was the first to catch Mandy's attention. To begin with, he was staring at her in total adoration—and right then that counted for a lot. The other eye-catching thing about the Khan was that he looked like an ancient Mongol chieftain, even down to the wine stains all over the front of his robe. The Mongol's companion was cleanly and conventionally dressed, yet there was something different about him too. Mandy couldn't fathom what it was right away. Then it came to her: he radiated peace and goodwill—something else that counted a lot for her right then.

Mandy asked about the misfits over post-rehearsal cocktails in the shopping mall forecourt. Billy Ray had just finished polishing a small blemish on the hood of his beloved Chevy. He carefully re-folded his twill handkerchief and tucked it back into his breast pocket.

"Do tell, Billy Ray. Who were those two gentlemen I saw being escorted by the bishop's young men?"

"That there's nothing to worry y'all's pretty little head about, honey pie. All I've been told is they's some kind of folk musicians the bishop done hired to play after the wedding. Evidently, they showed up late and got no place to stay." Billy Ray removed his Boss of the Plains Stetson as a cover for glancing furtively behind him, hoping—no doubt—to catch a glance of Muriel Banks. At least, that's what Mandy assumed, not being the least bit fooled by the maneuver. "So I offered the bishop they could stay here with the VIPs, just like you and me. We get the Epiphany Suite in the Lord God's Evangelical Retreat; Miss Banks, Bishop Ron, and their party will be staying in the Heaven's Rest Duplex. And them two weirdo fellas, they'll be sleeping in the same room with the IMAX projector."

Just then, Muriel came into view, walking past the singing frogs with

Bishop Ron and looking like she owned the place; or so it seemed to Mandy Miller. Billy Ray, all too blissfully aware of his impending fate at the hands of Muriel Banks, put his hat back on, not even pretending anymore. "Now, you got to excuse me, sugar pudding," he whispered urgently. "I got wedding business to talk over with Miss Muriel and Bishop Ron. And remember y'all need to be changing into y'all's shroud for the Repentant Bride of Heaven autograph signing." With that, Billy Ray scurried away, without so much as a backwards glance.

Mandy watched him leave with trepidation. In less than twenty-four hours, she had gone from home free to seriously screwed. She dabbed at a solitary tear and fretted about the mess she was in. Ahead lay a highly uncertain, likely impecunious, and possibly incarcerated future. She was broke from sinking all her money into the Baltimore mansion; she was without a job; and there was no way she could afford a decent lawyer.

Mandy saw no way out.

She needn't have worried, at least, not for the foregoing reasons. Because Mandy Miller's future, along with everyone else's on the planet, was about to take care of itself.

Doesn't it always—sooner, or later?

CHAPTER 28

Frog Hair Split Four Ways

True to its journalistic roots, *Star* magazine's "Wedding of the Century" special edition was relentless in its research and meticulous in its presentation of the facts. Of chief interest to Jesús was the revelation that Mandy Miller's real name was Doris Chittenden. Also that she had been born with ears the size of storm shutters—just like Johnny's—at least if the childhood photograph was anything to go by. Clearly, in Mandy's case, there had been some corrective surgery along the way. Jesús didn't have the temerity to point out the likeness, but he did share his new knowledge. He handed the magazine to Johnny, who was sitting across from him.

They were enjoying breakfast at a Waffle House just off Interstate 10, not far from Baldwin, Florida. The Waffle House chain was one of the few enterprises to have survived the Shovel House onslaught. In Waffle House strongholds breakfast loyalties ran deep. This was country where recently slaughtered pig in the form of genuine pork sausage and real bacon meant almost as much to a person as family and the Baptist church.

The décor was strictly functional: dark brown veneer everywhere, except for the tables and countertops, which were covered with spotless white Formica. No pretense here—if you wanted false promises, fake food, and fancy looking servers, you belonged someplace else.

Not wishing to seem over inquisitive, yet dying to know why Johnny wasn't at the wedding, Jesús went for the oblique approach. "Here,

Mister Chittenden. Look at this. Mandy Miller has the same name as you. Now that's a coincidence isn't it? Are you related in some way?"

Johnny took the magazine and stared impassively at the center spread for several moments. Then he started to cry silently. Tears welled and trickled down his cheeks. Jesús looked away, at a loss for words.

Einstein, who was sitting next to Johnny and seemingly unaware of the tears, put down his raisin toast and leaned over to get a better look at the magazine. He chortled. "*Gevalt!* You must only to see these ears on the little girl to know it. They must to being the size of the storm shutters."

Albert Einstein was known for speaking his mind, usually when it might serve him best to bite his tongue. He was also a noted prankster. Thus, in common with most pranksters and small boys, he was drawn like a moth to a flame by extreme bodily functions and oversized anatomical features. Not that he ever meant to offend. On such occasions, the world's most famous scientist just didn't stop to think.

Johnny reached for a paper napkin and dried his eyes.

Realizing his *faux pas*, Einstein was mortified. "Why am I always to saying these things? Please, Johnny, you must to forgive. I am only meaning this to be the little joke."

Johnny turned to him and smiled tolerantly. "Dang, Albert, if I done got mad every time my ears got talked on, I'd be crazier than pork in a pumpkin pie. Y'all don't pay it no mind now."

"I had no idea," Jesús lied, happy the ears were now off the table, so to speak, but still seeking an answer to his unspoken question, and suddenly feeling much bolder. "To tell the truth, I thought it was pure coincidence. But if you *are* related, I hope you don't mind my asking, how come you're not going to the wedding?"

Johnny's smile vanished. For a moment, Jesús thought he had gone too far. Then Johnny shrugged, as though accepting the inevitable. "Well, sir, last time I seen little Doris must have been twenty years gone—just before they upped and moved to Baltimore. When my brother Danny passed away, she wrote me. I never did write back. Guess I figured she had troubles enough without hearing about mine. I kept the letter though." He reached into his shirt pocket and took out a neatly folded, well-worn sheet of pink notepaper. He looked at it briefly, then shrugged again. "I reckon Uncle Johnny don't count for much no more in certain quarters."

Einstein and Jesús exchanged glances.

Jesús was the first to speak. He carefully made space to rest his elbows then leaned forward confidentially. "Mister Chittenden, there's a couple of things you need to know."

Johnny pocketed Mandy's letter with evident relief. Suddenly, he was all ears (so to speak) and all business.

"Shoot."

"Well, first, we want to get into the wedding, but we don't have an invitation."

"Why, you fans of Mister Bixbee, or something?"

Einstein rolled his eyes. "I ask you. Are we to looking like fans of this *Kolboynik*?"

"What's a *Kolboynik*? Johnny enquired with a look of genuine interest.

Einstein scratched his head. "I am not having the proper English, but this *Kolyboynik* is a man who is to taking the dog droppings and selling it as gold from the end of the rainbow."

"Oh, sure," Johnny grinned knowingly. "I met me a whole bunch of those fellas along the way. Usually, they was selling me shit on wheels and calling it Shinola."

"Anyway," Jesús continued, "the point is, we think a couple of friends of ours are being held against their will, and they might be somewhere in Pastureland."

It was Johnny's turn to lean forward. "What, you mean they been abducted, like they been forced to join one of them religion cults?"

Jesús saw no reason to disagree. The alternative was to tell the truth, and Johnny Chittenden clearly wasn't ready for that; nor was he for that matter. Apart from which, they still hadn't come up with a viable plan of action, despite Einstein's thinking spell in the back seat. Now, thanks to Johnny, it was all fitting together beautifully. He dropped his voice to a whisper. "You don't know the half of it. Bixbee's people have brainwashed them so bad one thinks he's Genghis Khan and the other is convinced he's Jesus Christ. We have to get them out of there. That's where we're headed."

Johnny let out a low whistle of amazement. "Man, you must be kiddin me!"

"I wish," Jesús said, with a look of acute concern.

"Well, now how you intending on springing these fellas?"

"That's just it," Jesús said. "Before we can get them out we need to get in. We were sort of planning to buy tickets and mingle with the crowd for the Pastureland grand opening after the wedding."

Einstein intervened. "This, of course, is to being a problem because we are not to knowing exactly where they might be."

"Also," Jesús added, "one of Bixbee's associates knows what I look like, so that could be an even bigger problem."

Johnny saw the light. "So y'all is telling me you need somebody on the inside."

"Er, yes, in a manner of speaking," Jesús said, thankful he hadn't had to spell it out.

Johnny pondered his plate. He had ordered a sausage and cheese omelet with bacon, accompanied by raisin toast, fried potatoes, freshly baked country biscuit with sausage gravy, sausage patties, baked beans, and grits. Having eaten heartily, there wasn't much left to ponder, so it wasn't long before he looked up. He seemed troubled. "Y'all should know I'm mighty grateful for the ride and all, but I really don't see as I can help."

"Well, we could drop you off at Pastureland," Jesús prompted. "I'm sure Mandy—sorry Doris—would love to see you. Then maybe you could sort of make a couple of discreet enquiries and report back."

Johnny's expression hardened and he shook his head. "I'm sorry, sir. I'd sure like to help y'all, but I just cain't bring myself to it. It ain't proper, seeing-as-how I never done right by Doris."

As usual, whenever defeat or dismay was staring him in the face, Jesús put his head in hands.

Einstein smiled fondly. "You know, when I see Jesús to do this, I am reminded of my little Hans Albert." A distant look came into his eyes.

Jesús covered his face and groaned.

Einstein turned to his companion. "Hans Albert was not the only child, but he was my favorite. These little ones, you know, they are to being our most precious things in the world."

Johnny nodded solemnly. Jesús peeked through his fingers.

Einstein continued. "So, Johnny, I must say that now you are not so far from Doris you should be thinking in this way: Even if you have not to writing, I am sure she would want it that you see her." He reached for his pipe and tobacco and went through the motions of tamping and sucking on the stem, pretending to smoke, giving Johnny time to reflect.

Johnny, however, seemed lost in space. He had the glazed eyes and blank face of man in acute denial.

Einstein glanced at Jesús, who returned the look with an imperceptible shrug. Einstein nodded decisively. He carefully placed his pipe on the table and turned to his contemplative neighbor. "Johnny, if these were to being your last days on the Earth, then what should you do?"

Johnny came out of his reverie with a slow smile. "Hell, that's easy, Albert. I'd be off to that wedding so fast the devil hisself couldn't catch me."

Einstein picked up his pipe and leaned back with a mischievous grin. "Well, I have to tell you, I happen to know the world is to exploding very soon. So for why are you waiting?"

Johnny slapped his knee and grinned. "Dang, Albert, if you cain't split frog hair four ways come Sunday. Y'all got a point though. Could be I ain't got but this one chance. All right, then, I'm with y'all. You just tell me what y'all want done and we'll git right to it."

"By the way," Jesús concluded, "I've been meaning to say this. If you promise to stop calling me, sir, I'll promise to stop calling you, Mister Chittenden."

Johnny reached across and shook his hand. "Done deal, but y'all will have to settle for Jesus, Jesus. I just cain't pronounce it t'other way."

CHAPTER 29

Nervous

When Jesús and his two companions arrived at Pastureland, they were obliged to join a long line of vehicles waiting to get in. Everything seemed larger than life: the immensity of the VAB, the heavenly décor splashed all over it, most of all the sheer scale of the parking lot. It was a viciously hot July day and Einstein wasn't inclined to walk, so he didn't think he had much choice when it came to the forehead implant: the argument was simple, yet compelling.

"Well sir," explained the parking associate to Jesús, all cool, calm, and collected in his air-conditioned booth, "of course, you can walk if you like, but it *is* highly recommended you get parking implants, at the very least. With parking this full, you'll be a good half-mile from the entrance. For our senior and well-proportioned guests, we advise against walking, on account of it being ninety-nine in the shade and a hundred percent humidity."

"Excuse me," interrupted Jesús, "but don't you have a parking shuttle?"

The associate nodded condescendingly. "Yes sir, that's what I was trying to explain. In order to have vehicle to vehicle transfer, you will need the forehead implants."

"So, how does that work?" Jesús enquired warily.

"You get the implant. When you park your vehicle, the nearest *DRIVEL* will register your location and come right over for the pickup."

"What, if I may be so bold, is a *DRIVEL*?"

"That would be a Driverless Robotic Interactive Vehicle sir."

"So, you're going to stick GPS transmitters in our heads?"

"I wouldn't know about that, sir, I just do the implants. Don't you worry, our Global-Titanic chips are state-of-the-art: never been known to fail. Even the Reverend Billy Ray has one in his head for opening and closing Pastureland. Without him, nobody gets in and nobody leaves.

"Well that's a bit dumb isn't it? What happens when he's not here?"

"That's classified, sir."

Einstein tapped Jesús on the shoulder. "For why must you argue so? I am liking to hike in the snow, but I am for sure not to walking in this heat."

"Albert, with that thing in your forehead, Titanic will be able to track you 24/7."

"What, you mean also when I am to being in the mother ship?"

"Well, maybe not up there, but certainly down here. Who the hell knows anymore?"

Johnny Chittenden turned slowly, looking puzzled. "Excuse me, Albert, what did y'all just say?"

Jesús clenched the wheel. "All I want to do," he muttered, "is park the frigging car!"

"Excuse me sir," said the Titanic associate, sounding friendly, yet looking firm. "There are people behind you waiting to get in."

Jesús nodded in defeat. "Okay, you've made your point. Make that three parking implants. We also want to purchase three tickets for the preview and one autograph signing. How much will that be?"

The associate was all smiles again.

"Would you like to super-size the implants, sir? If you go for the all-in-one implant it comes with free parking at all participating Titanic facilities, free HBO for a month, ten percent off your admissions, and entry in our Yellowstone Park Lava Lake Christmas weekend for two super sweepstakes."

Einstein nudged Jesús eagerly. "This is sounding like the good deal, especially for getting the free Christmas weekends for two at the park."

Jesús turned with a frown. "Aren't you forgetting something, Albert?"

Einstein put his head in his hands. "*Oi vey!* What was I thinking of? You are right. So, we must to have only for the parkings."

"Also, for anything more than the parking he's probably going to want your social security number and a photo ID," Jesús pointed out.

"The social security I don't have since I was dying. All I am having now is the Bio-Secure Molecular Augmentation, which is good, because I have no more to remembering this crazy number."

Johnny Chittenden's expression went from puzzled to downright perplexed.

"Somehow," Jesús observed, with a wry smile, "I don't think your molecular augmentation explanation would go over too well."

He turned back to the Titanic associate. "We'll have three implants—parking only."

"Would that be the twenty-four hour basic option, sir? I can also offer lifetime parking, which comes at a one-time cost of eleven hundred sixty-nine dollars and ninety-nine cents, also payable in nine equal installments of a hundred twenty-nine dollars ninety-nine cents. Plus, you get the Lava Lake Christmas promotion." He now had the smile of a sadist contemplating his next victim.

Jesús pointed to his forehead. "Twenty four hours, right here, right now. Just tell me how much I owe for the parking, plus the tickets to get in and the autograph."

"That will be two thousand, eight hundred and seventy nine dollars and ninety nine cents, sir," replied the man with a smirk. "I'll want five hundred each for the admissions, twelve hundred for the autograph token and complimentary photograph, and seventy nine ninety-nine for the parking." He was about to say more, but Jesús ignored him and turned to Einstein.

"Albert, did you get that?"

"Yes, so you are wanting the violin case?"

"No, just fish out twenty-nine hundred and hand it over."

Einstein opened the case and obliged. Johnny Chittenden stared straight ahead as though he were willing himself to dematerialize. Jesús paused before handing over the fistful of bills. He glanced up at the associate, smiling dangerously. "By the way, if you now tell me you don't take cash, or if you make one more frigging sales pitch, I will rip out this steering wheel and implant it personally, and it will not be in your forehead."

The associate glanced briefly from side to side, then leaned forward. His eyes had the cold, dead stare of fish on a slab; the dark underbelly of Global-Titanic was showing itself. "Listen, buddy, I deal with jerk-offs like you every fucking day of the week. And I don't need your aggravation. All I need to do is pick up the phone and say I've been threatened by a guest and you're dead meat, *capiche*?"

"Good," Jesús said. "Now we're talking. You win. So give me my stuff and we'll be on our way."

The associate wordlessly handed over three tickets, an envelope containing an eight by ten photo of Mandy Miller and the autograph token, twenty dollars, a receipt, and three implant packages. Jesús looked up expectantly. "They're just like Band-Aids. Remove the wrapper. Stick the tape to the middle of your forehead. Slap your forehead once as hard as you can. Then count to three and peel off the tape. To remove it, you press a piece of duct tape on your head then rip it off, or you can just leave the fucking implant where it is. You can forget about the penny. Now, get lost."

Sure enough, two minutes after parking the Toyota, a *DRIVEL* showed up with a family of six on board. Four small children were stuck to the inside of the bubble glass like tree frogs. Johnny Chittenden got out of the Toyota, looking thoughtful. He still didn't say anything though. In fact, no one had spoken since leaving the parking kiosk.

Jesús leaned across. "Thanks once again, Johnny. Anything you can find out would be great, and good luck with Mandy, I mean Doris. Just take your time. We'll be waiting right here."

Johnny looked Jesús squarely in the eye. "I don't rightly know how to say this, Jesus, but I'm getting to be a mite nervous."

Jesús smiled reassuringly. "That's all it is, just nerves. To be honest, if I were you, I'd be quaking in my shoes. I mean, meeting Doris after all this time."

"That ain't what I'm nervous at."

"Oh, really," Jesús nodded, indicating the *DRIVEL,* which was suddenly flashing a blue roof lamp and beeping impatiently, "well, we're all feeling nervous right now, Johnny. Maybe we can talk about it later."

When the *DRIVEL* was gone, Jesús leaned back with relief. "Jeez, Albert, that was close. I think he's getting cold feet." Then he frowned. "Now, *I'm* the one feeling nervous.You know what, he might just make up with Mandy and wave us goodbye, and I can't say I'd blame him."

"I can tell you," Einstein said confidently, "Johnny is to being a man of his word. He will come back. I know it."

Jesús yawned. "I hope you're right. Anyway, now that he's gone we really need to talk. I'll join you in back."

When he was settled, Jesús relented about the smoking. "Listen, Albert, I know how much you miss your pipe, and you've been very good about it, so why don't you go ahead? Just don't overdo it, okay?"

Einstein grinned with delight. "*Ach*, this is so wonderful, *bubeleh*. You know, without the pipe I am only to having half the brain." He fumbled happily for his pipe and tobacco pouch.

"Believe me, you having half your brain is the least of my worries. My main concern is how much time we have left before word gets out about Yellowstone."

Einstein nodded vaguely while he searched for his matches. When he was done lighting up, he puffed happily and stared into space.

"Albert," Jesús persisted. "How much time do we have?" He sniffed at the gathering tobacco fumes. "By the way, maybe I'm just getting used to it, but that stuff is starting to smell pretty good. Actually, I think I have a little buzz going. What the hell are you smoking, Albert?"

"It is a special Schermerhorn mix I am having made with the Black Perique and the Zimbabwean Orange tobaccos. It is also being soaked for eight weeks in the Balvenie single malt whiskey. Then it is to matured in these oak barrels they have used for making the sherry."

"Good Lord! No wonder it puts a smile on your face."

Einstein nodded appreciatively. He enjoyed the pipe for a few moments before speaking. "As for how much time we are to having, well, now is the beginning of July. If this observatory in Yellowstone is to having the best of the equipments, they will to seeing the first indications at the beginnings of September."

"So you're saying two months."

"Yes, it is to being perhaps two months, by which time you must be ready. If you wait for them to announcing, you will have no more than seventy-two hours before the breaking down of the society."

Jesús folded his arms, leaned back, and joined Einstein in contemplating Jupiter. "So, all we have to do in that time is spring Jesus One and the Khan from the clutches of the scariest woman on the planet. Then we must somehow score forty willing virgins—just like that. We then keep said virgins entertained and out of harm's way until the time comes. Next,we take over the control tower of one of the biggest and busiest airports in the nation. We crack the most impregnable code in the entire frigging Galaxy. Then we break out the champagne and celebrate the end of all life as we know it."

He turned with a look of polite enquiry. "Am I forgetting anything?"

"Yes," Einstein replied with a chuckle. "You are to forgetting the mistress of the harem."

"Oh, shit, Muriel!"

"Yes, your Muriel, who I am to thinking is no longer the candidate for this job."

"Damn right. Jeez, Albert, this whole thing goes from bad-to-worse."

Einstein was unconcerned. "*Ach, bubeleh,* you should not to worry so. I am sitting here in the back to thinking and I am only to finding two problems."

'Do tell?"

"It is how we can rescue the Khan and Jesus One and to find this new mistress for the virgins." He turned to Jesús with a philosophical smile. "But, you see, this is the way of it. These problems of today are for always to being harder than the problems of tomorrow. For example, on the day I am postulating my Special Theory of Relativity, I am unable even to finding my own socks."

Jesús nodded thoughtfully and gazed out at the vast parking lot. Vehicles crammed with the faithful wandered about like lost souls in search of redemption. *DRIVELs* dodged the meandering traffic with uncanny precision. Nobody walked.

He turned back to Einstein, feeling a little more hopeful, but far from convinced. "Well, at least we've got Johnny working Jesus One and the Khan. But how in hell, if you don't mind my asking, do we manage to round up all those virgins and get into that bunker if we can't crack the code?"

Einstein puffed joyfully at his pipe before answering. "The day I am leaving the mother ship I am running the special programs. You see, we are to having this program called the Civilization's Response to the Apocalypse Predictor, which is to being called the *CRAP* for short. For this, I have only to identifying the planet, the different countries, and for what kind of the apocalypse. For example, whether it is the alien invasion, or the spreadings of the deadly virus, or the nuclear annihilations. Then the *CRAP* is telling what will to happen in each country and is also to giving us the timelines and the major milestones."

"So that's how come you know we'll have no more than seventy two hours after the word gets out?"

Einstein nodded sagely. "Exactly, yes, and after this time will come the rising up of the armies, which is how we are getting into this bunker under your tower."

"What do you mean—armies? What would be the point of that if the whole frigging world is going down the pipes?"

Einstein shrugged. "I am only to explaining what the *CRAP* has said will happen for your planet. For the control purposes, I am also running this same scenario for the planet Zorgon. These Zorgons have accepted calmly and are organizing the block parties." He paused reflectively. "This, of course, is why planet Earth has yet to being invited for joining the Confederation."

"What about the Zorgons?"

"They are already having the provisional membership."

"Gee, thanks a lot," Jesús said disconsolately. "But what does all this have to do with getting into the bunker?"

Einstein waved his pipe like a baton and hummed the opening bars of Mozart's *Die Zauberflöte*. "Well, after the *CRAP* I am running the Heuristic Organizational Latency Indicator, which is to being called the *HOLI* for short. With this program, we are to seeing exactly which organizations are having the most potential for starting the troubles. The *HOLI* says in America you will have three armies to rising up. You will have the organized criminals, like this *NAACP* we have seen, then what is left of your military peoples, and you will also have the big religious army from the Christian televangelists."

"Holy Crap!" exclaimed Jesús.

"Exactly, it is the *HOLI CRAP* which is telling us. You see, from this we have learned that one of these armies is predicted to attacking the White House. Then they are taking over the shelter under the back lawn. So, your president must for fleeing to Seattle."

"And he'll have the access code, so that way we get into the bunker. Jeez, Albert, that's brilliant!"

Einstein smiled broadly in acknowledgement. Then he revealed his plan for the virgins. "I think everybody wants to being in these reality shows," he said enthusiastically. "So, we tell some girls, which you perhaps can find, we are to producing a new show we are for calling *Virgin Beach*. In this new show, you see, forty virgins are to being stranded on the beach of a desert island. They must to compete for winning impunity and the quality time with the sturdy young men."

Jesús stared at the world's must famous scientist in pop-eyed amazement. "How the heck did you come up with that?"

"Well, it was not to being easy. I have considered this problem for many hours. First, I have asked to myself if these virgins are something you will for sure be needing, since you will also be having the embryos."

"Well, hatching embryos won't be much fun, will it?" Jesús muttered.

Einstein eyes gleamed. "So, we are no longer objecting to these girls, eh, little *bubeleh*?"

Jesús reddened. "I'm just agreeing with what I was told. I mean, the Khan seems to know what he's talking about."

"Exactly, the Khan is to having more experience in this matter. We must also consider that even with the embryos, you will need some girls for making and raising the babies."

"But *Virgin Beach* for Pete's sake?"

Einstein nodded eagerly. "Yes, the virgins on the beach. I have come up with this idea from watching the televisions and reading the *Star* magazine."

"Do you think they'll go for it?"

"Of course they are to going for it."

"You know," Jesús said thoughtfully. "I'm still not totally convinced, but the more I think about it, the better it sounds."

Einstein shook his head in wonderment. "What do you mean, you are not yet to being convinced? Are you to having the better ideas than Einstein?"

"Well, no."

"Good, then this is what we shall do. The Khan, he can be the producer. You and Jesus One will be for the cameras, but for you it will be only until going back to work. Albert Einstein will be for what *Star* magazine is calling the on-camera-talent."

"Boy, you really thought this through, didn't you?"

Einstein grinned. "Sometimes, I am surprising even myself with such ideas that I have."

Someone rapped on the side window.

CHAPTER 30

The Second Coming of Christ

According to *Star* magazine, Mandy Miller would be signing autographs in the forecourt of the Gifts from Heaven Shoppes shortly after post-rehearsal cocktails. Invited guests were entitled to one free signature. Everyone else was obliged to wait for the doors to open and pay for the privilege: five hundred dollars for the Grand Opening Preview, plus another twelve hundred for an autograph token. Jesús dipped into Einstein's Nobel Prize fund to purchase admission tickets and an autograph token (plus one complimentary photograph) for Johnny.

They waited for him in the Toyota.

***

Mandy looked a lot more angelic than she felt. All she lacked was wings and a harp. Billy Ray himself had said so when she first tried on the signing shroud. Knowing Billy Ray, Mandy promptly put her foot down. "Billy Ray, I happen to know for a fact there is no such thing as a girl angel. I also happen to know that angels have six wings and if you think I'm going to sit there and sign autographs smothered by a bunch of feathers, you can find yourself another prophetess."

This, of course, was said before Mandy was busted and Muriel Banks showed up.

Not that Mandy was a biblical scholar, but some things do stick. Her insight into the equipage and gender of angels stemmed from sixth grade. Back then, one of the forbidden, and therefore hot topics after Sunday Bible class, was the subject of angel genitalia. Norma Flatley, whose father was an Episcopalian minister, knew where to look for this kind of stuff and came up with the goods. Norma should definitely have been a biblical scholar.

It seems that in *Isaiah 6:2* (King James Version) the Bible says that angels have six wings and refers to the seraphim as *he*—so they have to be guys, right? But wait, it gets better, because one pair of wings is for covering the feet, one for covering the eyes, and one for flying. But, according to Norma, the ancient Hebrew word for feet (רגל) was the same word you would use for private parts. "So if you were an angel and you had to fly around with no clothes on, not seeing where you were going and you didn't cover *it* up, you'd for sure get into big trouble. You certainly wouldn't be hiding your feet." Norma observed.

Then she clinched the whole thing by showing them *Ezekiel 16:25:*

> *Thou hast built thy lofty place at every head of the way, and hast made thy beauty an abomination, and hast opened thy feet to every one that passed by, and multiplied thy harlotries...*

...which was juicy, if only for "harlotries", since they all knew what *that* meant. "Why" asked Norma, "is opening your feet such a big deal? I bet Ezekiel was really talking about showing off your *thingy.*"

Ever since Norma's revelation, Mandy had often wondered about all that foot washing in the Bible, which is probably why she never forgot about the angels.

***

Before Johnny got to Mandy, he was stopped dead in his tracks by the 56 Chevy—the Holy Grail of thrill driving. He couldn't touch the vehicle because she was roped off with gold tasseled silk braid, which he thought only fitting. Johnny was mesmerized. He knew this car the way Leonardo must have known the *Mona Lisa*. She wasn't merely an object of beauty; she was a creature of motion and momentum. More than that: she was steady as a rock. As Joie Chitwood once said, "Driving a car on two wheels is like balancing an egg on a toothpick, and nothing does it like a Chevy." The Human Bomb could testify to that. He had performed the two-wheel tightrope a thousand times and the car hadn't wavered once.

Mandy glanced up from her signing and recognized Uncle Johnny immediately. She didn't have a photo of him with no hair, but she knew all about his going up in flames, and she *had* seen photos of the Hellions of Doom, so it wasn't hard to imagine why he was so obviously taken with Billy Ray's pride and joy.

The ears, of course, were a dead giveaway.

Mandy realized Uncle Johnny moved about a lot, and she knew he wasn't one for writing. In all honesty, she never did expect a reply to her letter. Eventually, she forgot about it and consigned Uncle Johnny to a back shelf. She wasn't bitter or resentful; she just didn't think about him much. Occasionally she searched for thrill drivers online, but Johnny Chittenden existed only in the deep cyber-past, along with the likes of Joe Jericho and Joie Chitwood. In other words, he was forgotten. Johnny, as we know, was unaware of Mandy's unconcern. In his mind, she was a wounded soul and he was the culprit. Well, Mandy Miller *was* a wounded soul, but certainly not on Johnny Chittenden's account.

The upshot was that Mandy was overjoyed to see her uncle, but the longer Uncle Johnny admired the Chevy the more his courage withered. Fortunately, she got to him before he could beat a retreat.

She tapped him on the shoulder. "Uncle Johnny, it's me, Doris."

Behind her, what had been an orderly line of expectant autograph seekers was rapidly shape-shifting into a formless mob. When Mandy downed tools, so to speak, and walked off the job *sans explication*, she failed to consider the consequences. Thus, when Johnny Chittenden composed himself and turned, looking suitably contrite, his moment was irretrievably lost. Doris was there all right, but large parts of her were being consumed. Finally, all that was left was her head, bobbing wordlessly back to the signing table in a sea of indignation. They owned her, you see. She was bought and paid for.

Johnny got the idea. He clutched his token and his complimentary photograph and stood in line like everybody else.

Mandy was genuinely frightened. She put her head down and signed as though her life depended on it—which apparently it did. She smiled, she murmured vacantly, and she was careful not to show favor by lingering over dedications.

Finally, Johnny made it. He handed her the photograph, which showed the bridal couple in full wedding regalia posed in front of the cavernous portal to Pasture Land. "If y'all could write: *For Uncle Johnny from Mandy Miller,* I'd be much obliged," Johnny ventured hesitantly. Mandy switched on her "Little Miss Fixit" smile, wrote the dedication, and smartly handed back the photograph. The dedication read: *For my Dearest Uncle Johnny from your ever-loving niece, Doris Chittenden.*

For the second time that day, and the second time in his life, Johnny Chittenden struggled unsuccessfully to hold back tears.

That was enough for Mandy Miller. She put down her pen, marched around the desk, and hugged her uncle. To the next in line she announced: "Y'all and the rest of the people that paid can go get your money back, or y'all can consider yourselves invited to my wedding. Either way, I'm done signing. This is my Uncle Johnny. He's here for the ceremony and we've got some catching up to do." Then she smiled warmly and tossed her tresses. "Would y'all be so kind as to pass that along, please?"

Now, that would have wrapped things up nicely if Jesus One hadn't lost it right then, smack in the middle of the Gifts from Heaven Shoppes. Mandy realized something was seriously amiss when a side window exploded and a three-foot gilded bronze crucifix sailed out. She grabbed Johnny's hand and they joined the exodus swarming into the Shoppes. Before the statuette hit the sidewalk, the forecourt was already half empty.

Inside, as many people were fleeing as were eagerly rushing in to get a better look.

The cause of it all had already downed one of his guardians. He was using a nicely antiqued Cross-of-the-Calvary floor lamp to fend off the other. Mandy Miller had never seen anyone so enraged. Behind him, the Mongol was gleefully hurling things. Peace and goodwill had apparently sailed out the window along with the crucifix.

"Good God Almighty!" Mandy cried. "They've gone mad!"

Johnny gulped.

"Don't you people ever learn?" yelled the lamp wielder. "What's worse is you're selling all this crap in my name."

With that, he jabbed the guardian in the midriff, dropped the lamp, and upended a display cabinet of handcrafted mahogany Singing Jesus Dolls. That was as far he got. Billy Ray rushed in at that moment with reinforcements. Muriel Banks and the bishop were hot on his heels.

What surprised Mandy was the ferocity of the Mongol and the abrupt change in mood of his enraged companion. All at once he was back to smiling gently and radiating peace and goodwill. The Mongol, on the other hand, continued to fight with superhuman strength. Three of Billy Ray's security men tried to grab him. He threw the first one to the floor. He head butted the second. Then he dispatched the third with a vicious punch to the throat.

"Thank God he doesn't have a weapon," Mandy whispered to Johnny, who seemed thunderstruck.

Billy Ray finished it. He hit the Mongol just above the right ear with a solid bronze Head of John the Baptist bookend. The Mongol didn't go down, but all the fire went out of him. He shook his head slowly, looking puzzled.

Billy Ray had the two miscreants handcuffed. But before they were taken away, the formerly enraged one had the last word. He looked up at Billy Ray and spoke calmly. "I said this once a long time ago and now I'll say it again. If you're going to put God's name on the shingle, everybody is welcome and nobody pays, and I do mean everybody. You, sir, are a bigot, an idolater, and a thief."

That being said, He turned to leave, glancing at Mandy as he passed by.

All the breath seemed to go out of her. His gaze was a loving embrace. Peace and goodwill poured from Him like a great river in flood. A sense of utter joy permeated her entire being. She wanted to sing. She wanted to fly with the angels— despite the confusion about the wings.

"It's *Him*," she cried out. "It really is *Him*. He's back!"

Hearing this, Billy Ray marched over in a fury. "You, little lady, can haul your sweet ass back to Baltimore, or you can shut your mouth right now and pick up your goddamn pen."

At first, Mandy ignored Billy Ray; she was still entranced. Then she came out of it with a deep sigh."Well, y'all can tie me to a pig and roll me in the mud, Billy Ray. I had no idea you was so upset. Now, this is my Uncle Johnny. If you will excuse us, we have lots to talk about."

Johnny looked bewildered, but somehow managed a nod and a polite smile. Billy Ray paid him no attention. He glared at Mandy. "Y'all can talk all you want, sugar pie, but you just remember I got plans for you, and they don't include no Jesus freaks. I'm locking up that son-of-a-bitch. When this wedding's over, he's going to jail. And if y'all don't watch out, y'all will be in the cell next door."

"Why, Billy Ray," Mandy replied, smiling even more sweetly, "whatever do you mean?"

Billy Ray leaned in close and lowered his voice to a whisper. "What I mean, honey pot, is you got as much chance of fucking with me as a no legged dog. I got you hogtied. You don't be getting any ideas. You hear?"

Mandy stopped smiling.

Muriel Banks wasn't smiling either. She stared angrily after the captives as they were marched out. When they were gone, she turned her eyes on the bystanders. A flamethrower couldn't have done it better. The Shoppes cleared in seconds.

"Billy Ray!" she called out. "I'd like a word."

Billy Ray nodded dismissively at Mandy and her companion. "Now, I do believe Miss Banks wants to explain about them two crazy fellas. So y'all will have to excuse *us*."

Johnny wasn't bewildered anymore. In fact, he was downright angry. He started to say something, but Mandy forestalled him gently. It was time to leave. "Now, Uncle Johnny, don't you pay no mind to Billy Ray. This is all just a fuss over nothing."

When they were outside, Johnny spoke out. The anger was gone, but there was a hard edge to his voice. "I don't know about this all being a fuss over nothing, Doris. I don't take right kindly to what that Billy Ray fella was saying in there."

He frowned. "Or oughtn't I to be calling you, Mandy?"

Mandy smiled back serenely. "Uncle Johnny, I was Doris. Then I was Mandy. To tell the truth, since *He* looked at me, I feel like I'm this third person I just met."

Johnny shrugged. "I guess then, I'll call you Doris, until y'all three can decide."

Mandy nodded in agreement. She was decisive now. Her jaw was set; her eyes sharply focused. "Doris will do just fine. That doesn't matter anymore. What really matters is we need to help those poor men get away from here."

Uncle Johnny let out a long-suffering sigh. "Y'all tell me about it," he said.

CHAPTER 31

Busted

It was Johnny Chittenden, looking worried. Behind him, waiting patiently, was an empty *DRIVEL*. When Jesús stepped from the Toyota, he was assaulted by heat and light. The heat stole his breath; the light bleached his eyeballs. Other than that, he felt pleasantly woozy—so much so, that he staggered slightly. Johnny frowned suspiciously and backed away.

"Jesus, have y'all been drinking in there?"

Jesús shook his head, as much to clear it as in denial. "No, no, it must be Albert's pipe. I'm just a little off balance from sitting in the car."

Johnny didn't seem the least bit persuaded, so Jesús opened the door as wide as he could. "Here, stick your head in. See for yourself." He wanted to giggle, but suppressed the urge.

Einstein leaned across, waving his pipe in greeting as Johnny bent down. Johnny breathed deeply, then retreated with watering eyes. "Albert, y'all best not be going any place with that pipe lit. Dang tobacco grabs your ass worse than week-old Texas moonshine."

Einstein didn't argue. After exiting, he stooped and emptied his pipe on the concrete. The tobacco flared briefly before giving off one last savory spiral of smoke. He looked up at Jesús with raised eyebrows as the tiny, symbolic mound flickered and burned out. Then he straightened, squinting in the harsh sunlight. "I am for sure not to walking," he gasped. "In this heat, I can hardly to breathe."

Jesús helped Einstein into the *DRIVEL*, with Johnny bringing up the rear. Once they were inside, the sliding door closed silently and a gentle flow of deliciously cool air flooded the interior. The Mormon Tabernacle Choir soothed them with a surround-sound rendition of *Hymns for God's Peculiar People*. Delicate scents of jasmine and honeysuckle wafted forth. Einstein settled contentedly into a softly cushioned white leather seat as the *DRIVEL* effortlessly moved out. "It is like for finally dying in a nice way and going to heaven," he whispered.

"I think that's the general idea," Jesús whispered back—normal speech seeming somehow disrespectful.

Johnny Chittenden broke the spell. "Well, y'all for sure ain't going to heaven, Albert, and that's a fact. I seen Doris and I seen your friends and I'm here to tell you, y'all's got yourself one helluva situation here."

He didn't have time to elaborate because the *DRIVEL* slowed to a stop at that moment and the door slid open to admit two more passengers. For the first time ever, the Tabernacle Choir found itself competing with Marty Robbins. Then *Big Iron* mercifully faded, and the choir was redeemed.

Forever curious, Einstein spoke first. "I hope you don't mind me to asking, but for why does the music play so when you are outside?"

The heavier of the two blushed. He was wearing western garb with a Colt. 36 Caliber, Sheriff Model strapped to his left thigh. On his head, tilted rakishly to one side, was a flat-topped, narrow-brimmed black Stetson. His companion wore a green blazer, pleated gray pants, and an accessorized smile that reminded Jesús of Dirk Forrester with the nail in his head. The smiling one answered and stuck out his hand. "Vernon is a Yellowstone Park Ranger. The music is part of his costume. Hi, I'm Dick Derringer with Global-Titanic Worldwide Entertainment, and on behalf of Titanic, I'd like to extend a heartfelt welcome to Pastureland."

"You know," said Jesús, "before today, I had no idea Titanic was into faith-based fun. Between redesigning nature and perfecting heaven, you must be a busy guy."

"Oh, you don't know the half of it," Derringer replied with a modest smile. "As of tomorrow, Pastureland will officially be a done deal. Yellowstone, of course, will always be a work in progress. On top of that, we're busy fantasizing a huge project called Shovel World in the South Pacific, and then I'll be starting work for a Chinese client on Garbage World in New Orleans."

"How appropriate," Jesús observed, which seemed to be a suitably neutral response, since he wasn't sure whether to laugh or to cry.

"I'm sorry," Derringer murmured suspiciously. "I don't know what you mean."

"Oh," Jesús said, trying to muster an engaging smile, but only managing a self-conscious smirk. "I mean, like shovels being right up there with garbage?"

Derringer didn't get it. He nodded vaguely and switched his Dirk Forrester smile back on. "Well, you know, each of our guests is our most treasured resource. We strive at all times to maximize Guest Value per Visit. We call that GV^2." His smile grew wider in a passable imitation of Richard Branson. "Now, if there's anything at all I can do to enhance your own guest experience, all you have to do is ask."

"How about you provide cocktail waitresses and on-line poker in the *DRIVELs*?" Jesús responded, coming up with a full smile.

Branson vanished. Derringer stared at Jesús like a body snatcher confronting a coffin full of maggots. "Yes, sir, a wonderful idea, but hardly appropriate for the Pastureland demographic, don't you think?"

Before Jesús could reply, Einstein intervened. "Mister Vernon, so for how are things being in the Yellowstone Park these days?"

Vernon touched the brim of his hat respectfully. "Well, sir, I have to say things are just fine. We've got ourselves another record summer season, and thanks to Mister Derringer here, come Christmas, we'll be all set to blow the lid off of the greatest show on earth."

Derringer down shifted his smile to neutral. "What Vernon is referring to is Titanic's Lava Lake Christmas show."

"Oh," Jesús murmured, "we heard about that. How jolly. You wouldn't by any chance be planning fireworks afterwards, would you?"

"Absolutely—a fabulous fireworks finale, and God Bless America to kick it all off. Not to mention the lava glow."

"Good golly," Jesús said admiringly, "'God Bless America,' glowing lava, and fireworks. How can you go wrong?"

"You bet," Derringer agreed enthusiastically. "When it comes to engineering the enhanced nature-based entertainment event, Global-Titanic is unbeatable."

"Speaking of the enhanced nature-based entertainments," Einstein enquired, "for how are you these days to forecasting the eruptions?"

"Funny you should mention that," Derringer said. "We just upgraded to a new portable sensing system from China that shows absolutely no disturbance whatever. Apparently, all those readings in the past must have been overstated, or more likely fudged. Also, our friends at the park service assure us we're in the clear for a long time to come."

Vernon nodded confidently. "The park is good for another thousand years, minimum, guaranteed."

"So, we have not to worry for visiting the park?"

"No, sir, you should have no worries whatever."

"Well that's a relief," Jesús said. "Only, I'd hate to pay for a ticket and find myself burnt to a crisp before the fireworks got started."

Derringer gave him the body snatcher look again. Einstein added a warning frown.

"Just kidding," Jesús said. "Anyway, it seems we've arrived. Good luck with the Christmas show, Mister Derringer. Unfortunately, I doubt I'll be able to make it. That's the week I'll be defending my world's snowboarding championship in Zermatt."

The *DRIVEL* dropped them off at a side entrance where they handed over their admission tickets. Derringer and the park ranger waved VIP passes and bypassed the turnstiles. By the time Einstein had fumbled for his ticket and Johnny's re-entry voucher had been scrutinized twice, the Titanic executive and his companion were gone.

Einstein watched them go with amusement. "I don't know for what kind of the sensing system they have from these Chinese peoples, but I am now thinking they will know nothing until much later than I have thought."

"So we have some relief then?" Jesús asked.

"Oh, yes, perhaps until the middle or the endings of September, when even the small child can see something bad is to happening."

"Great," said Jesús, relieved, "so let's go find Mandy Miller."

Ten paces in, he froze at the sound of a familiar voice. "Jesús Martinez! You stop right there. You and I got some talking to do, mister."

Jesús put his head in his hands. "Shit, I completely forgot about the implants," he cried. Then he looked at Einstein and raised a cautionary finger. "And not one word from you about little Hans Albert, if you don't mind."

Einstein scrutinized the distant ceiling. Johnny started to edge away but didn't get very far. Two giant security guards blocked his retreat. Muriel Banks emerged from behind a reinforced fiberglass live oak tree with two more guards in tow. She tapped her forehead. "You can run, child, but you sure can't hide." She held up a palm-sized device with a blinking display. "I got facial recognition when you paid for your tickets, and this little *MacPod Micro-Sleuth* tracks that chip stuck in your head. You're mine, Martinez. You and your friends are coming with me."

She led them past the entrance to the ministry building. Through the open doors, Jesús glimpsed the IMAX screen, towering above the stage like a silver coated replica of the Four Gorges Dam. Standing alone onstage, miniaturized by the IMAX, was a forlorn looking figure wearing a white, gossamer shroud. It was Mandy Miller. She managed a surprised wave as they passed. Johnny nodded glumly in acknowledgment. Jesús couldn't take his eyes off her.

"Look, Albert," he whispered. "It's Mandy Miller. You know, in person, she doesn't look half bad. Give her a couple of wings and a harp and she could pass for an angel."

Einstein wasn't impressed. "For an angel, by the way, she is to needing six wings, and also there is to being no such a thing as the girl angels. Since I am God, this I know for a fact."

"Okay, so no harp and no wings, but right now we could use a little help from heaven, and she's the closest thing we have."

Jesús managed one last lingering backward glance, before Muriel took them to a flight of stairs leading to a small door. "Up the stairs, Martinez, and don't try anything. You and your crazy ass friends are staying here tonight. After we get through with the wedding tomorrow, you'll be leaving a message for Roy Upstart and then I'm calling the cops. Billy Ray Bixbee is filing charges for assault and willful destruction of property. You're in big trouble, Fly-Boy. I hate to do this, but you've only got yourself to blame. What you did to me was as low as a man can go. You should know, Muriel never forgives and she never forgets."

"Yes, well, that comes as no big surprise. You're just about as full of loving kindness as the frigging Pentagon. Okay, so I apologize, and I guess I'll have to call Upstart, but how the heck did you come up with assault and destroying property?"

Johnny spoke up. "That's what I was about to tell y'all. The one as thinks he's Jesus Christ broke a whole bunch of stuff, and the other laid into them security guards like he was a pissed-off pig in a Waffle House."

"Oh!" Jesús said, which was about all he could say, given the circumstances.

Jesús mounted the stairs thinking furiously. Muriel followed quietly behind. She didn't need to speak; he could feel her eyes feeding off the back of his head. Of course, if the back of your head is being eaten away it *is* difficult to think clearly. Although Samuel Johnson did observe that jail (or was it the prospect of hanging?) concentrates a man's mind wonderfully. It must be said that Samuel Johnson prevailed, because by the time the door at the top of the stairs opened, Jesús Maria Martinez was as clear headed and alert as a stalking panther.

Not that he had the slightest notion of what to do next.

CHAPTER 32

Hellions of Doom

Jesus gaped at the IMAX projector in awe. Sitting on a massive turntable next to it were two film platters that could have been wheels from a combine harvester. "Good God!" he exclaimed, "that thing is twice the size of my Toyota."

"Just don't get in front of the lens when it's running," said Jesus One. "The gentleman that was in here earlier to do the maintenance said he's always very careful. You could be incinerated—just like that."

"Let's hope he doesn't buy a ticket for the Lava Lake Christmas show then," said Jesús. "Boy, would he be upset."

The projection room was barely big enough to house the projector, a maintenance station, a film storage rack, a small closet, and a manual forklift used to stack the film platters. There were no chairs. The front wall was all glass, though, so at least they had a view of the auditorium. Jesús had prompted Jesus One's observation by pressing up against the glass, hoping for a glimpse of Mandy Miller, but she was gone; the stage was deserted.

Jesus One, the Khan, and Johnny Chittenden were perched on the maintenance table. Einstein prowled around the giant projector, poking and peering at it as though he had just stumbled across a tranquilized elephant.

"Anyway," said Jesús. "Johnny says Mandy wants to get us out of here, so we're not totally without hope."

"Sure," the Khan replied. "All she has to do is take out the goon they left by the door, lift his keys, then smuggle us out. In case you hadn't realized, we don't exactly blend in too well with the rest of the flock out there."

"Well, maybe she'll wait until they close up and everybody's off the floor."

"Jesús," said Jesus One, "we've been stuck in here for hours. Don't think we haven't racked our brains, and don't think I don't know about Mandy Miller being converted when I walked by. I've seen people react like that before; twelve times to be precise. The best we can hope for is that she will intercede with Mister Bixbee. After all, they are about to get married."

"Somehow," said Johnny, still looking glum, "I don't think that's likely. That Billy Ray fella gave her a right good talking to. She's lucky she ain't in here with the rest of us."

"I have a plan," Einstein announced cheerfully, looking up from his examination.

"Do tell," said Jesús.

Einstein had a plan. Life was good again.

"Well, you are remembering for when we have searched for the Khan and Jesus One and you have left me in the parkings?"

"Sure, who could forget?"

Einstein ignored the sarcasm. "Afterwards, you are to lecturing me on how clever you are for always writing down the parking numbers."

Jesús rolled his eyes. "So?"

"So, little *bubeleh*, if you can to give to me these numbers, I can teleport to the car for the violin case. Then I can use this money to pay the damages for Mister Bixbee, and maybe, a little more, no?"

"Albert," Jesús muttered, "you're not going to believe this. When I put that chip in my head, I figured there was no need to remember, so I didn't write anything down."

Einstein didn't get mad right away. First, he took out his empty pipe and sucked at it furiously. *Then* he got mad. "So, I am to having not two, but the three *dumbkopfs!* Must Einstein to think for the entire world, now?"

Jesús couldn't resist. "Well, you *are* the world's most famous scientist, Albert. Isn't that what you're supposed to do? Besides, do you seriously think Muriel's going to let us buy our way out of here? Not to mention Bixbee."

***

Four hours later, Billy Ray and Muriel showed up—apparently to gloat; certainly to confirm hell would have to freeze over before money changed hands.

"I'm here in person," Billy Ray began, "because I want y'all to know Billy Ray Bixbee don't tolerate being fucked with. And I'm here to tell y'all, the only way y'all will be leaving here is in a goddamn paddy wagon. Miss Muriel told me all about you, Mister Martinez. Y'all ought to be ashamed for taking advantage of such a fine God-fearing young woman."

Jesús decided a little groveling might be in order. "Well, I did apologize, and I will most certainly call Roy Upstart and explain everything. Please let me assure you, we will be more than happy to pay for any damage, plus whatever you think is reasonable for your trouble."

Billy Ray leaned in close. "I also got you taped, boy, threatening one of my employees and using offensive language in a place of worship. I don't need your money, sugarplum. I don't give a shit about restitution. What I'm looking for, and what Miss Muriel wants, is *retribution*."

Then Billy Ray stretched to his full height, carefully removed his hat, and opened his arms beseechingly to the heavens. He cried out with the rabble-rousing indignation of a born preacher. "I humbly beg of the righteous Lord above to visit his wrath upon these sinners. For so sayeth Nahum, that the Lord is avenging and wrathful, and the Lord takes vengeance on his adversaries."

"Just a minute," interjected Jesus One. "This isn't exactly Nineveh is it? All we did was break a few baubles and crack a couple of heads. It's not as if we were raping and pillaging, or killing and eating small children. Moreover, if you're so up on the scriptures, why not quote from the Beatitudes and let us go? Wouldn't that be the Christian thing to do?"

Billy Ray responded with a long, hard stare. "This here is my church, you freak, and I'll quote whoever and whatever I damn well please. You want to preach the Beatitudes, then find yourself a hill somewhere and start your own outfit."

Jesus One shrugged sadly. "Yes, well, as a matter of fact, I already tried that, but I'm not so sure it's worked out quite the way I thought it would."

Recognizing his groveling ploy was a non-starter, Jesús gave divide-and-conquer a try. "Muriel," he implored, "I know you're a deeply devout person. Can't you find it in your heart to forgive? After all, Johnny and Doctor Einstein really haven't done anything wrong. The other two were just overwrought from being abducted. I mean, when you picked them up, they hadn't done anything either."

Muriel folded her arms and commanded her eyes to eat the middle of his forehead. She was still wearing her rehearsal gown, so the arm folding was, to say the least, a significant distraction. "You've had your chances, fool. I told you one of these days you were going down the pipes, and I'd be there when you did, and I'd nail you. Well, today is the day, Martinez. Consider yourself nailed. And don't you dare tell me you don't deserve it. I worked damned hard to get where I was."

Realizing his divide-and-conquer ploy was going nowhere, Jesús took a deep breath and went for broke. "What if I told you it's all true? This gentleman here really is Jesus Christ, his friend really is Genghis Khan, and Doctor Einstein, although he seems to be Albert Einstein, the world's most famous scientist, is actually the being you would normally refer to as God."

Einstein nodded. "This I can vouch for. We are coming down to help Jesús for to saving the humankind. So, for doing this we should prefer not to be in the jails."

Johnny Chittenden sighed and put his head in his hands.

"Prove it to them, Albert," Jesús urged. "Teleport somewhere and then come right back."

Einstein looked at him severely. "For the teleporting demonstrations I must these days to have the prior written authorizations. Even when I have done this for you, it has taken four months before they are agreeing. This is because the God before me has been using the demonstrations for hitting on the young virgins and to giving them free rides in the mother ship."

"But, Jeez, Albert, this is an emergency."

Einstein shook his head. "No way. After the William Wallace thing with the Khan, I am to getting the final warning. One more problem and I will be reassigned as full-time Messiah for the planet Gronad, where they are still to eating their firstborns."

Jesús threw up his hands in disgust. "That's it, I'm not saying another word, but I'll tell you this: Roy Upstart and you, Muriel Banks, can kiss my ass. Call your frigging paddy wagon and we'll plead guilty and pay the fines. Now, go read up on your Beatitudes and leave us alone."

Billy Ray chuckled. "Listen, son, I got the fix in here. Billy Ray is the big man on campus in these parts. If I say you're going to the slammer, believe me, that's where y'all will go, and that's where y'all will stay. And I'll see to it you get a couple extra special boyfriends to make nice while you're in there."

Johnny Chittenden raised his hand high like a man on the verge of drowning. "If y'all don't mind, Mister Bixbee, I'd just as soon leave right now and keep going. I promise I'll be gone faster than a duck on a June Bug, and I ain't never coming back. You got my word on it."

Billy Ray removed his Stetson, wiped his brow with a twill handkerchief, and smiled warmly. "Why, sir, I do believe you're related to my bride-to-be, Miss Mandy Miller."

"Yes, sir, I would be her Uncle Johnny."

Bixbee put his hat back on with a flourish and pocketed the handkerchief. He wasn't smiling anymore. "Well, Uncle Johnny, I'm here to tell y'all, y'ain't going no place. I don't want Miss Mandy getting any bright ideas. So, until this wedding is done and over, y'all is staying right here."

Johnny gulped.

The Khan stepped forward then, raising his hands in surrender. His lips were drawn tight. His eyes glittered with menace, yet when he spoke he sounded uncommonly affable. "Very well, Mister Bixbee. The pleading is over; let the bargaining begin. Just tell me what it will take to get us out of here."

"Listen, Chinaman, I'll say it one more time: you ain't going no place. I got you wrapped tighter than a flea's ass over a rain barrel, so whatever you're offering, the answer is no."

"Okay, that's fair enough, but let me tell you a little story," said the Khan. "I tried being Mister Nice Guy once before, just after I'd gotten together my first barbarian horde. I wanted to open a trade route past a certain city, and they said no. Anyway, to show good faith, I sent over two ambassadors with camel caravans as gifts. They kept the camel caravans and beheaded the ambassadors. Then I sent an envoy with an even better deal. They cut off his beard, which was as bad as chopping his head off, and sent him back. Now, I'll tell you what I told them."

The Khan folded his arms and he was no longer affable. "You, sir, have chosen war. And by the way, I'm not Chinese, I'm from Mongolia."

Billy Ray laughed. "You know what, Chinaman? I'm scared. What's going to happen? You going to put me over your knee and spank me?"

The Khan smiled evenly. "What will happen, you fat asshole, will happen. I will tell you this, though. When I was done with those other guys, someone wrote I had left not a single eye open to weep for the dead."

"Well, let me tell *you* something, Chinaman," Bixbee snarled. "Where you're going you'll need both eyes open all day and all fucking night, and you won't be watching for no camel caravans neither."

Billy Ray and Muriel sauntered out then with nary another word, nor a backwards glance.

(Of course, dismissing Genghis Khan in such a cavalier fashion was not very smart—as Billy Ray would ultimately discover. But we'll get to that later.)

***

The Repentant Bride of Heaven made her move at two-thirty in the morning. By then, the clean up crews were long gone, Pastureland was locked down, and the Epiphany Suite and Heaven's Rest Duplex resonated with the important dreams of sleeping VIPs. Mandy's only problem was how to deal with the six-foot-four, three-hundred-pound watchdog guarding the IMAX projection booth—which wasn't that difficult really. She climbed the stairs, smiling innocently until she was up close. Then she zapped him with her leopard skin trimmed Teaser-Taser. The guard collapsed as much from surprise as loss of muscle control—it certainly didn't hurt much—but he was down long enough for her to remove his law enforcement special from its holster, zap him for real, and take his keys.

Mandy knocked and paused for the sake of decency before letting herself in. She needn't have bothered. Not only were the inhabitants fully clothed, they were wide awake and wide eyed with fright—all, that is, except the Khan, who had gabbed the maintenance toolbox and was all set to hurl it.

Jesús snatched the toolbox, set it on the table, and took out a fistful of cable ties and a roll of duct tape. "Move it!" he yelled. "We need to truss this guy and get him inside." The Khan rolled the guard face down and sat on him while Jesús wrapped ties around his hands and ankles and pulled them tight. "Roll him back over," Jesús said. He tore off a length of duct tape and covered the guard's mouth. Then they dragged his considerable bulk over the threshold and maneuvered him under the table.

"Uncle Johnny, are you all right?" cried Mandy.

"I'm fine, Doris, and I'm mighty beholden, honey, but unless y'all can get us out of this building real fast, y'all can stick us with a fork, cause we'll be well and truly done. Them keys you got ain't worth a damn when it comes to opening the big doors."

"Oh!" Mandy cried, with a squeak. "I assumed one of these keys would get us out."

"Shit!" said Jesús. "He's right. Remember what the parking guy said about Billy Ray's implant." He turned to Mandy. "Excuse me Miss Miller, but is there any way you can sort of get to Billy Ray and persuade him to let us out?"

Mandy Miller didn't say a word; instead, she gave him the Dick Derringer body snatcher look.

"I have a plan," Einstein announced cheerfully.

All heads turned. Einstein was looking at Johnny Chittenden with a calculating smile. Johnny stared back suspiciously. "Johnny," said Einstein, "when we are to being taken here, I have seen a nice motor car near the shoppings."

Johnny brightened. "Sure, Albert, that's a 56 Chevy—best danged thrill driving car ever built."

"Then can you not to driving such a car through the big door, like you have done with this steel wall of death?"

"You've got to be kidding!" Jesús cried incredulously.

Einstein shook his head in wonderment. "So, is it *now* you are to having the better idea than Einstein?"

Johnny wagged a cautionary finger. "Just hold on there, I'm thinking." He walked over to the glass wall, closed his eyes, and leaned his head against it for several moments. Then he opened his eyes and spoke to the darkened auditorium. "Last time I done that, I swore I'd never do it again lest somebody else was to get hurt." He ran both hands slowly across the top of his hairless head, paused for a moment longer, and turned to face Einstein. "Considering the circumstances, though, I reckon I'm willing to try it one more time—but we got ourselves some problems, Albert. First off, that steel wall of death weren't steel, it was aluminum; we'd a been crazy to try it with real steel, though I'm willing to bet that big ole door ain't steel neither. My guess is it's steel-framed with aluminum panels. I'll need a screwdriver and a hammer to find out. Second problem is, we ain't got no keys for the car, and it's for sure locked and fixed up with some fancy alarm. Third problem is, when you drive through the wall of death y'all has to jump off a ramp. That way y'all can keep momentum with the engine switched off, and y'all can hit it at the right angle. If you come at it on the ground, the dang wheels will sure as shit get stuck on the door frame."

"Good God!" cried Jesús in a near panic. "You're not seriously considering this, are you?"

Johnny smiled. "I think I got it licked. If them door panels is big enough we're outa here. All I need to get the Chevy started is that there film stacker, a coat hanger, and some needle-nose pliers."

"But where, for Christ's sake, are we going to find a frigging ramp?" Jesús demanded.

Johnny grinned and pointed to the auditorium. "I seen a ramp coming off that stage when Mandy done waved at us. My guess is its got lock-down wheels. If it ain't, then it'll be about as much use as a wet dream in a whorehouse, and we won't be going nowhere—that's for sure."

"Oh, Uncle Johnny," cried Mandy, "it does have wheels. I remember them bringing it in and locking it down for the ceremony, and also so Billy Ray can use it when he does his laying on of the hands thing."

"Piece of cake!" said Johnny Chittenden.

"This can't be happening," Jesús muttered desperately. "I'm about to jump in a vintage Chevy through the biggest doorway in the world with Albert Einstein, Jesus Christ, Genghis Khan, and Little Miss Fixit. Not to mention, the Human Bomb is at the wheel and the frigging door is closed."

He was ignored. The Khan was busy introducing himself to Mandy, who couldn't take her eyes off Jesus One. Einstein puffed happily on his empty pipe. Meanwhile, Johnny Chittenden rifled through the toolbox for needle-nose pliers, a screwdriver, and a tape rule. With these in hand, he went to the closet, where he discovered not one, but a half-dozen intertwined metal clothes hangers. "Albert," he directed, "y'all grab that duct tape, and you'll find a flashlight in the toolbox, then y'all is coming with me."

He turned to Mandy. "Doris, honey, can y'all tell me iff'n the Chevy's got itself one of them add-on car alarms."

Mandy nodded. "Why, yes, I do believe it has. I've seen Billy Ray switch on something under the dash then a little red light starts blinking."

Johnny grinned with satisfaction. He gestured to Jesús. "Jesus, y'all three is going to have to lift that stacker and take it downstairs to the

Chevy. After y'all has done that, go git the ramp and wheel it fast as y'all can to the big door. Mandy can show you the way."

***

Johnny and Einstein were still measuring when the ramp arrived. Johnny glanced over his shoulder with a happy smile. "Wheel it right up to the door, dead center. We're in luck, fellas. This door is like I thought: it's got two feet of steel running along the bottom, then it's aluminum skinned all the way up. We measured each panel at ten feet wide. I'm danged if I know how high, though."

With the ramp against the door, Johnny walked up it with his measure and hammer.

"Ten feet wide?" Jesús whispered. "I saw that car. We'll be lucky if we've got an inch clearance on either side."

Einstein silenced him with a frown. Johnny tapped lightly to locate the frame then extended the tape rule as high as he could. When he came back down, he was nodding happily. "Well, that just dills my pickle. Them panels go up at least thirty feet. My guess is they're ten by forty. And I'll be danged if I know why, but this here center panel can't be but an eighth of an inch thick."

"I think I know why this is so," observed Einstein. "When we have been measuring, I have noticed some of these other panels also to being thin like this. I think it must be so that when they have hurricanes they will blow out for to equalizing the pressure on the building."

Jesús carefully pushed against the panel and smiled with relief. "I think you might just be right, Albert. If I hit this hard enough, I'll bet I could put my fist through it."

Einstein's shook his head and rolled his eyes. "Perhaps if you are to putting your head through it instead, you will for once to believing what Einstein is telling you the first time."

Johnny handed Jesús the tape rule and duct tape. "Here, since y'all's the tallest, I want you to get dead center on that ramp, reach up and tape the biggest cross you can in the middle of the panel. Make sure it's dead center because that's where I'll be aiming the Chevy. When y'alls done, we'll wheel this ramp back just over a car length and lock her down. I want to hit that danged door with the nose up so's the windshield don't hit." Johnny took two paces back and proudly surveyed the ramp and the door. "I'm telling you folks, I ain't had this much fun since I had me a head full of hair."

Heisting the Chevy took less than two minutes. Johnny instructed Mandy to keep an eye on the alarm while Jesús and the Khan lifted the front end with the stacker. At exactly eighteen inches off the floor, the lamp went out and Mandy squealed with delight. "Why," she said, eyes sparkling, "how ever did you know to do that, Uncle Johnny?"

"I drove a tow truck once. These alarms is usually set so they dies when the front end gets lifted. Iff'n they wasn't, they'd sound off like a stuck coyote every time y'all tried a tow."

That being said, Johnny straightened the coat hanger, leaving a hook at one end, fished open the driver's door, and reached in to turn off the alarm. He held out a hand to Einstein. "Now, Albert, if you would kindly give me the flashlight and them pliers. In the meanwhile, y'all can let her back down."

Johnny stood quietly while Jesús and the Khan lowered the front end of the Chevy. Then he beckoned them all to gather round, looking deadly serious. "I'm only going to say this once, so listen up good. Before I hotwire this baby, I want y'all inside and belted up. Mister Genghis, you can sit beside me. I want you others sitting in the back, with Albert and Doris in the middle."

He tapped his forehead and grinned. "I ain't planning to set light to this topknot no more, so y'all can relax. This time, when I hits the wall of death, I'll remember to have the engine switched off. Now, git yourselves inside and hang on. Johnny Chittenden and his Hellions of Doom is back in business!"

Jesús held up the duct tape. "Hold it. Speaking of topknots reminded me. We need to get rid of these frigging implants. He tore off three strips and handed one each to Johnny and Einstein. Jesus One and the Khan looked on in amazement as they slapped the tape to their foreheads then ripped it off.

"Don't even ask," Jesús said.

Two minutes later, they reached the top of the ramp traveling at eighty miles an hour and accelerating. As the front wheels cleared, Johnny wrenched apart the two red ignition wires he had twisted together. The engine died, and for the smallest fraction of a second, they defied gravity. They were suspended magically in some silent realm of time and space. Einstein puffed furiously at his empty pipe with his eyes shut tight. Jesus One put his arm around Mandy Miller, who closed her eyes and smiled as if in the depths of some delicious dream. Taking no chances, Jesús Maria Martinez prayed fervently to a God he no longer had reason to believe existed. Johnny Chittenden and Genghis Khan whooped like Rodeo cowboys.

Then Billy Ray's pride-and-joy rocketed clean through the VAB door; well, more or less. That is to say, she kept going, but the thunderclap of the impact, and the agonized screams of metal torturing metal were probably heard in Ecuador. She also briefly caught fire as five-thousand-dollar's worth of paintwork was ignited by sparks and melting aluminum. A moment later she hit the concrete like a flaming meteorite, and they were no longer suspended in time and space, and it sure as hell wasn't silent anymore.

CHAPTER 33

Holy Vows

Mandy Miller never would have agreed to go along with the *Virgin Beach* idea if she hadn't believed in Jesus. Mind you, it didn't take much Lordly persuasion. It made sense. She was, after all, a bona-fide TV personality and she *did* need the work.

After the escape from Pastureland, they holed up in a Cocoa-Beach motel. Anxious about Billy Ray's reaction, Jesús stayed awake and checked all the early news broadcasts. There was nothing about the breakout. In fact, the lead story locally and on *Star TV* was still the wedding of the century.

At eight a.m. that first morning, Billy Ray broke the news of Mandy Miller's miraculous departure. He made the announcement live on *Star TV's* Sunday with the Stars breakfast hour. Flanked by a radiant Muriel Banks and a devout looking Bishop Ron, Billy Ray was solemn, humble, and forthright. You could tell though, that beneath his composure, Billy Ray Bixbee was a deeply troubled man—anguished if you will—close to tears as a matter of fact.

This was true. Billy Ray *was* anguished, and he *was* having trouble hiding it. His anguish, though, stemmed less from Mandy's departure than the blistered wreck that had formerly been his pride and joy. His reaction to Mandy's absence had actually been to breathe a sigh of relief. When he beheld the still smoking Chevy, however, he broke down and wept. Bishop Ron, himself a vintage car man, consoled Billy Ray by pointing out the damage was largely cosmetic. "You gets yourself a new paint job, a front bumper, and four new tires, she'll be right-as-rain, man," Bishop Ron opined.

"You don't understand, Ron," Billy Ray sobbed. "I feel like I been violated. Y'all hear this: I'll hunt down them sons-of-bitches and they'll pay for this, if it's the last thing I do."

Billy Ray pulled himself together then and prepared to face the cameras. By the time he had worked things out with Muriel and Bishop Ron, he was almost his old self again. If it hadn't been for the Chevy, he would have been smiling like the cat that got at the cream.

Billy Ray's story was that, right after the embarrassing fracas with the Jesus freak, Mandy had been visited by six angels. Evidently, the angels had told her to forget about the wedding and check into a remote mountaintop convent somewhere in southern Latvia. Once there, they insisted she submit to sacred vows of poverty, chastity, and obedience. Not to mention they sternly demanded she top it all off with a vow of silence.

"I am also announcing," Billy Ray continued, moving along at a good clip now, "directly them angels ascended back to heaven, the good Lord appeared before me in all his glory, and the Lord sayeth unto me: 'Billy Ray Bixbee, thou art a righteous man. Yea verily, so shall righteous men receive the wisdom and the word of God,' and His word was: 'Billy Ray, thou shalt right away join in divine and holy union with thy New Prophetess of Pastureland, which would be Doctor Muriel Banks. So shall it come-to-pass.' Our Lord works in mysterious ways. The show must go on."

"So, since when did Muriel get to be a frigging doctor?" Jesús asked incredulously.

Bishop Ron looked him squarely in the eye from the TV screen and answered, "Doctor Muriel, our blessed child, is a summa cum laude graduate of the Global Divinity College of God, with a PhD in choir management. Yet on this glorious occasion she aspires to a higher calling. Today our deeply beloved Muriel will be sanctified as a holy Prophetess of the Lord God on high, yea, Jesus, Hallelujah, and Amen."

Et cetera.

***

They didn't bother to watch the wedding.

Instead, they checked out of the motel and headed for Gainesville. Along the way, Jesus One was obliged to assure Mandy the Virgin Beach scheme was very definitely above board. As to the matter of Billy Ray almost certainly revoking bail, Einstein showed her the contents of his violin case. After that, she calmed down.

Of course, there was still the unresolved issue of finding a suitable beach.

"Ideally," Mandy pointed out, "we should have a tropical, desert island sort of place. Viewers pretty much insist on exotic locations. I mean, you wouldn't want to put forty virgins in doublewides on Boynton Beach, now would you?"

"Why not," Jesús said, "I *was* sort of thinking we might invest in an oceanfront trailer park. After all, we're already in Florida."

Mandy, who was crammed in the back seat of the Toyota with the Khan, Jesus One and Uncle Johnny, silently bored holes in the back of Jesús's head.

Einstein suddenly slapped his forehead. "*Gevalt!* Am I not also to being the *dumbkopf*. For why am I not to thinking of this before?"

Jesús glanced sideways and sighed. "Don't tell me, Albert. Whatever it is, I'm not sure I want to hear it."

"*Nein, nein,* this is to being the perfect idea for finding the beach. I am remembering now to where I have seeing this gentleman with the red and the blue head." He turned excitedly to Jesús. "When we have been in this Shovel House, was I not to saying I am to knowing this man from somewhere?"

Jesús fixed his eyes firmly on the road and nodded reluctantly.

"And are you not also to remembering when I have told you about Noah and the building of the big ass boat?"

Jesús gripped the steering wheel as tightly as he could. "Yes, Albert."

"Well, Noah is to looking just like this Shovel House man. Even for having the red and the blue head and to holding the shovel. So I am to thinking this is a direct descendant of Noah." Einstein paused to gather his thoughts. "You know," he reflected, "there are few people knowing it, perhaps only Einstein, but Noah is the first man to inventing the shovel. I am thinking for why should he not be as famous for this wonderful idea as Einstein for inventing the Relativity?"

Jesús spoke through clenched teeth, "I'll be darned if I know. Now, pray-tell, apart from being right up there with the guy who figured out knitting, what, for Pete's sake, does Noah have to do with Virgin frigging Beach?"

Einstein's flexed his eyebrows in a passable imitation of Groucho Marx and waved an imaginary cigar. "Well, you see my little *bubeleh*, Noah is coming from this beautiful desert island which is for having such a beach like you cannot imagine."

"Oh, Christ," Jesús muttered, without thinking. He glanced furtively over his shoulder.

"You're forgiven," Jesus One said, with an indulgent smile. "Anyway, it sounds like a great idea. All we have to do is find the virgins. Then we can fly a charter to the island."

Mandy Miller looked puzzled.

Uncle Johnny reached over and patted her hand reassuringly. "Don't y'all get to worrying, Doris," he whispered. "Sometimes, Albert's just a mite strange, is all."

CHAPTER 34

Chicks in Paradise

"This is going to be tough," Mandy yelled. "The good news is that most of these girls are less than twenty years old. They're using fake IDs and nobody cares. The bad news is there are close to two hundred of them in here and so far I've only spotted six virgins."

Jesús squinted. Music pounded. Panicked images from dozens of giant plasma screens darted across his retinas. Taste buds had mysteriously sprouted in his esophagus and stomach. These were newborn growths. They had little experience of life; all they knew was gastric stew was about to be served and they sensed it didn't bode well.

This gastric stew recipe called for mixing a liter of cheap cola with two jumbo English Toffee diet lattes, adding a half-pound of masticated green chili hot dog with mustard, stirring in three handfuls of salted bar peanuts, then flavoring with two glasses of no-name rum and the remains of a half digested lunchtime Petro-Pizza. Simmer gently in stomach acids for an hour or so—then taste.

"Excuse me, Mandy," Jesús said. "I have to close my eyes for a moment. I don't feel so good."

Mandy didn't seem to hear. She leaned in close and lowered her voice. "It's a pity you're not looking for boy virgins, Jesús. Ninety percent of the guys in here never made it past first base."

Mandy being near helped a lot. Suddenly, at their first taste of life, his infant taste buds shriveled and died. Suddenly he felt much better.

He opened his eyes. "Well, who's screwing all the girls, then?" he asked, trying to sound as if he didn't know.

"The other ten percent," she confided.

He sighed. "Well, isn't that the big surprise. Some things never change! Anyway, since we're here, we may as well get it over with. Point me at a virgin and I'll go fish."

Her name was Destiny and she wanted to know the real reason Billy Ray Bixbee had married the New Prophetess of Pastureland and not Mandy Miller. First, though, Jesús offered to buy her a drink. She asked for a White Zinfandel. Now, it so happened, Jesús had made a study of sorts concerning the drinking preferences of approachable young women in bars. His take on White Zinfandel was this: he would tell her his great grandfather on his mother's side was Ezekiel Inglenook, the man who invented Merlot. Clearly, he would say, you are a woman who appreciates the finer things in life. Personally, he would say, I prefer the Merlot, but I have heard good things about the Zinfandel—so I'll have one too. If he couldn't stomach the Zinfandel, he would go for something he could keep down, but stick with wine at all costs, and not worry about tripping himself up—she'd never notice.

"Well, how about that?" Jesús said, as he set down two Zinfandels. "Like, I can tell you appreciate the finer things in life, Destiny. By the way, my great grandfather was Ezekiel Inglenook, like, you know, the man who invented Merlot?"

This random use of *like* together with the misplaced questions was a deliberate nuance; it was a cunning use of Valspeak and uptalk (otherwise known as the moronic interrogative). By freely sprinkling *like* and delivering every statement as a question, he was cleverly adopting the favored speech pattern of his audience.

"Like, pass me a napkin—my hands are sweating?" Destiny replied. "Also, like, how come Billy Ray Barf Bag went for this New Prophetess of Pastureland? Like, it was so totally, like, GAG *me*? I'm, like, so totally grossed to the max when I heard it?"

Mandy did her best to explain. It had been a heart wrenching decision, she said, especially on the eve of her wedding, but in the end, her career had to come first, despite Billy Ray's announcement she had fled to a convent and taken holy vows. Not even *Star* magazine knew the truth. "No, Destiny," she said, "I'm not in seclusion. What I have, you see, is a new show I'm working on. That's why I'm here. We're scouting for talent. Jesús is my executive producer. Now, Destiny, I want you to promise me you won't say a word about this to anyone. If you sign up, the whole thing will be confidential. You won't tell a soul, will you?"

Destiny carefully wrapped her napkin around the plastic cup of Zinfandel. She clutched the cup under her chin and leaned forward. Her eyes wide as wagon wheels. "As, if," she whispered solemnly.

"You see," continued Mandy, "I'm looking for really attractive young ladies for a new reality show. It's going to be called *Virgin Beach*. You *are* a virgin aren't you?"

Destiny put the cup down and glanced nervously at Jesús. At first, she blushed, then raw ambition kicked in. She smiled coyly, "Fer sure!"

Ashley was next. She demanded a blue bayou, which is made by blending ice, vodka, blue Curacao, pineapple and grapefruit juice, and tossing in a couple of chunks of pineapple and a beach umbrella. The Jesús take: a ball breaker. Run, don't walk for the nearest exit, and whatever you do, don't look back. Of course, in the line of duty, he delivered the blue bayou, and patiently nursed his untouched white Zinfandel until the deal was done.

Jesús avoided all eye contact with Ashley.

All Madison wanted was a beer. She didn't even care about the brand. Jesús downed the Zinfandel and treated them both to a Michelob. He scanned the club, instinctively searching for a dartboard or a pool table. Madison was all right. He could hang out with Madison.

Mandy Miller, aka Doris Chittendenon, on the other hand, was nursing a Perrier. Jesús hadn't quite figured out the Perrier, but he had a nagging suspicion it was a sign of difficult times ahead.

Ava got to him before he could get to her. Jesús was actually en route to Trinity. Ava took him by the arm and walked him to the bar.

"So, what are you drinking?" he enquired politely.

"Well," she said, "you can call me Ava, and I'm drinking Gina's Pussy."

He looked blank. "It's raspberry liqueur and orange soda, with lots of ice. Now what's going on? I've seen you pick up three girls, and that looks like Mandy Miller at your table. Whatever it is, I want in."

Jesús take: say no more; hang on tight; do what she tells you; enjoy the ride; just don't drink the Gina's Pussy—stick with beer at all costs.

He had to drag Trinity away from what seemed to be some kind of fertility rite in which she was cast as principal chalice holder. By now, Jesús was well into the swing of things. It was strictly get-up-and-go as far as he was concerned. He didn't even ask what Trinity was drinking. He ordered tequila shots for two and marched her over to meet Mandy. Mentally, he was getting naked at Trinity's place.

"Are you sure?" he asked as he sat down. "I mean, are you really sure?"

Mandy nodded grimly. "Positive," she said. "I'd stake my life on this one. By the way, I've been watching you, Martinez," she continued with a mocking smile. "You think you're something, don't you? Quite the lady's man."

Jesús didn't say anything. He didn't even put his head in his hands. Instead, he sipped his tequila with narrowed eyes while Mandy tried to break through to Trinity. Despite his continuing field study of approachable young women in bars, he wasn't happy being tagged as a lady's man, let alone, a would-be lady's man—for some perverse reason that was an even lower blow.

Brianna, his next assignment, considered herself a wine connoisseur. He knew this because she was drinking from a real glass and the wine was red. She was the last one. Suddenly, he felt weary. He just couldn't force himself to fabricate lies about rare Croatian knee-pressed ice wines—which would have been the classic connoisseur ploy. Apart from which, Mandy's putdown still bothered him. She was starting to sound like Muriel Banks, which was discouraging to say the least.

"Hi," he said to Brianna, "I'm Jesús. I'm actually a world famous designer of motorized snowboards, but tonight I'm auditioning attractive, intelligent women for a new reality show. Interested?"

That was it for the night. All they scored were the six virgins. Mandy had each of them sign a participant contract, which they all did eagerly, thus committing themselves to six months of indentured servitude, a ban on all outside contacts during production, and a legally binding promise to henceforth only have sex that was directed by the show host, and on camera.

Jesus promised the girls he would be in touch within a matter of days. It was clear, though, that whereas scoring the virgins was a lot easier than he had thought, finding forty of them was something else entirely. "Listen, Mandy," he pointed out as she was finishing her Perrier, "I don't want to put a damper on things, but at this rate we'll have to check out close to fifteen hundred girls just to score forty. I'm not sure I'm up to it. Also, I have a day job."

Mandy was unmoved. She took a last sip of Perrier and sniffed. "Welcome to show business! You seem to be forgetting this was your genius idea in the first place."

"It was actually Albert's, and he really is a genius, by the way."

"Listen," she said, "don't get me wrong. It's a great concept and you can count me in one hundred percent. Now, why don't you stop sniveling and get us out of here? I'm hungry. I could really go for a couple of cokes and a hot dog."

CHAPTER 35

Crocodile Magic

Barry recognized Mandy Miller right away. Although he seemed strangely shy at first, considering he was chief of the island and not so very long ago she had seriously gotten his goat. Jesús couldn't care one way or the other. Ever since getting on the plane with the virgins he had been greatly overwhelmed by events. Not to mention he was jet-lagged from flying close to nine thousand miles in less than twenty-four hours. Despite standing perfectly still, he felt he was drifting backward. He looked down. Sand had blown across his sneakers. His feet seemed far away, as if he had grown an extra yard or two, but at least they were firmly planted on the beach and still attached to his ankles.

"Who am I?" he wanted to ask.

Looking at the sand all around him, he was reminded of the legendary Ferkarewe tribe: a mythical band of Arabian nomads, so named because whenever they arrived somewhere, the chief would halt the tribe, dismount from his camel, gaze majestically at the far horizon, and invoke the sacred chant: "Where the Ferkarewe? Where the Ferkarewe?"

Whereas Jesús was not actually a Ferkarewe, it seemed to him he could rightfully claim membership of the Ferkameye tribe, who were close relatives of the Ferkarewe, but of a more solitary nature.

Yet, on the mail boat from Vanahu, he had felt quite normal. Life was relatively good. They had twenty-three virgins happily sequestered in

Mama Lu's Golden Sunset Club under the watchful eye of Jesus One. With help from the Nobel Prize fund, Einstein and Mandy had swiftly negotiated a six-month lease of Noahu's premier beach spot. The only fly-in-the-ointment, according to the prime minister, was the attitude of the indigenous saltwater crocodiles. That was why they were meeting with Barry. (As it turned out, there was a second fly-in-the-ointment, something the prime minister had failed to mention when he collected the lease payment: this would be the attitude of Giovanni Garibaldi. But we'll get to that soon enough.)

Jesús started to unravel the instant the launch hit the beach.

Sitting in lawn chairs at a much-abused plastic table under a faded beach umbrella, were the two men from the Shovel House photograph. Eagerly helping Mandy disembark was a younger, smiling version of the man with the red and blue head, except that he had both arms and his head wasn't painted. Villagers clustered around the launch, chattering nonstop and making off with everything they could lay their hands on.

All at once, Jesús had felt invisible. The villagers didn't seem to know he was there in the launch. Even Einstein seemed no longer aware of his presence. The world's most famous scientist had been first off the boat. Now, he is standing in the surf, his trousers rolled up, marveling at the view of the old volcano. The Khan was also oblivious, or flat out didn't care. He had spied drinking accoutrements on the table and was hastening in that direction.

Jesús floated unseen from the launch, trailing behind Mandy and the Khan like an anonymous blob of ectoplasm. When Mandy reached the beach table, the chief was standing in dignified silence. Word of Mandy's arrival had apparently preceded her. Barry was in full regalia, including the headgear that defied description. There was an awkward pause before he spoke. "*Hulo,* Mandy Miller," he said shyly.

"I'm so pleased to meet you, sir," responded Mandy, with her trademark toss of the tresses and dazzling smile.

Barry shook his head (ever so carefully, on account of the headgear). He seemed puzzled. "*Wasmara yupela no long haus mater long Latvia?*"

Alfredo translated. "He wants to know why you're not in a convent in Latvia. We read in last week's *Star* magazine you'd been banished there by six angels."

"Billy Ray lied," explained Mandy. "That's the reason I'm here. I left him because he lied all the time. Now I'm producing a new reality show and we need a beautiful, deserted beach. The prime minister leased us the one over there, but he said we might have a problem with the crocodiles."

Alfredo grinned. "Isn't that the truth, missus."

Barry interrupted, looking agitated. *"Wasmara yupela putum finish nail long het bilongim Dirk?"*

"He wants to know why you stuck a finish nail in Dirk Forrester's head."

"It really was an accident," Mandy explained, looking suitably forlorn, "for which I am truly sorry. But what about the crocodiles? The prime minister said Barry would take care of them."

"No wari!" announced Barry, clearly much relieved by Mandy's declaration of innocence. He pointed proudly to his stump with his good hand. *"Wataim dispela, ya puk-puk kaikaim han bilong mi, ol gat dinau Barry plainti."*

"He says, not to worry. For eating his arm the crocodiles owe him plenty," explained Alfredo.

Barry shook his stick at the crocodile beach. *"Long Mandy Miller, Barry wokim bloody gut majik poisen long puk-puk"*

"He says, for Mandy Miller, he'll work some bloody good magic against the crocodiles.

"Ol stap gut, fer sure, oltaim yupela hia!" Barry exclaimed, swirling the stick three times.

"He says, they'll stop misbehaving for sure as long as you're here."

"Well, I'm glad that's settled," said Jesús, no longer feeling invisible and not drifting backward anymore. "I'd hate for us to be embroiled in a turf war from day one."

He was ignored.

George did eventually find him a spare lawn chair, though. By this time, Tusker beers were flowing freely and Mandy had presented Barry with one of her signed photographs (not the one standing in front of the VAB with Billy Ray). Alfredo handed Jesús a beer and pointed to Einstein, now paddling happily with a band of giggling toddlers. "Excuse me for asking, mate, but that old bloke's the spitting image of Albert Einstein. Who is he, then?"

Jesús took a grateful swig of the Tusker. "He *is* Albert Einstein, as a matter of fact. Anyway, how come you know about Albert Einstein?"

Alfredo laughed. "What, like with me being an ignorant native from Timbuktu?"

Jesús shook his head. "No, I didn't mean it that way. It's just odd. We've traipsed half way across the United States and you're the first person that's bothered to ask."

Alfredo gazed reflectively at the surf line marking the reef. "Truth is, I did physics at Brisbane University for a couple of years. Then I got bored and came back here."

His face lit up. "This is great though. I can ask him about his thought experiments. I agree with most of it, but I think his quantum mechanics was a bit shaky."

"Are you kidding me?"

Alfredo shook his head emphatically. "No way."

"Tell me something else then," Jesús persisted. "Why don't you think I'm making it up about Einstein?"

Alfredo nodded at Barry, who was deep in conversation with George, the Khan, and Mandy. "This old bloke is my granddad. He's a time traveler like your mate, Albert. He doesn't know how it works; he just does it sometimes. He does mind-melding and magic too, when he feels like it. You just watch him with the crocodiles."

Jesús started to drift backward again.

Mandy stopped him with a sharp stare. "Are you feeling okay, Jesús? Ever since we landed you've been looking even dopier than usual."

"I've got jet lag."

"Well, get over it. We're talking about where we can stay on the island and what kind of shelter we can provide for the girls."

"Not my problem. If you need money, talk to Einstein. Otherwise, you're in charge. Remember, I'm leaving. I'm the one with the day job."

Mandy leaned closer. "I don't get it. Albert has all this money; you're his number two, and you won't give up your cruddy airport job. It doesn't make sense."

Jesús stood and beckoned her to follow him. He walked until he was out of earshot of the table then waited for her to catch up. He pointed to Einstein, still frolicking in the surf. "Does *any* of this make sense? Here you are in the absolute back of fucking beyond, if you'll pardon my French, being bankrolled by the world's most famous scientist. You're sitting on a beach knocking back beers with Genghis Khan and a time-traveling, mind-melding witchdoctor with a red and blue head. On another island you've got Jesus Christ babysitting every single surviving virgin from the University of Florida." He flopped down on the sand. Mandy joined him. "Listen," he continued, "if you want explanations, you're talking to the wrong guy. Just go on believing in Jesus and everything will be fine. That's all I'm at liberty to say right now. By the way, what's the deal with the seventeen virgins we still need?"

Mandy smiled knowingly. "I had a word with George. Albert was right: rounding up virgins isn't exactly new around here. If we sweeten the pot, George can put out the word. Apparently, they have some sort of ceremony where they summon virgins all the time. George isn't sure he can guarantee all seventeen because they had a gathering not too long ago, but he says we'll be close."

"There you go then. George is your man. What about finding somewhere to stay?"

"George says the islanders will cut down some trees to make beach shelters for the girls. When we do our establishing shots, we'll make it look like the girls did it. There's a spare hut Barry uses for drinking kava where Jesus and the Khan can sleep and store the video gear."

"What about you and Albert?"

Mandy pointed to the sailboat anchored in the lagoon. "George says there's a nice American couple living on the boat out there. He says they have a couple of spare cabins they might be willing to rent to us. At least we'd have showers."

She glanced around and dropped her voice to a whisper. "Guess what, though."

"I'm all ears," Jesús said, mentally preparing for the worst.

"Albert will have to bail out the captain and his wife—also their dog apparently. It seems they've been jailed for a month on Vanahu for throwing Giovanni Garibaldi off his luxury yacht."

"Who, if I may be so bold, is Giovanni Garibaldi?"

Mandy gasped. "What, you've never heard of Giovanni Garibaldi? He's only one of the richest men in the world. He owns all the Shovel Houses."

"Oh, him. Sure, I know him. I've seen his picture; I just didn't know his name. Short, fat Italian, friend of Barry's."

Mandy shook her head. "Not any more. That's why the captain tossed him overboard. It seems Garibaldi is all set to get rid of the crocodiles and develop the entire island as a cruise ship destination. He could start any day according to George. The islanders are thoroughly pissed off because they weren't consulted, especially Barry."

Jesús closed his eyes and put his head in his hands. "I just don't need this right now!" he muttered despairingly. "You must be talking about

Shovel World. We met this guy from Global-Titanic at Pastureland who said he was building it." He looked up. "You must know him. He said his name was Dick Dingbat or something. Tell me, why, of all the islands in all the oceans in all the world, did I have to wash up on this one?"

"Oh, grow up!" Mandy said, with an expression of utter disdain. "As I said, welcome to show business. Anyway, I've dealt with a whole lot worse then Giovanni Garibaldi and Dick Derringer. You can leave them to me." She jabbed him in the ribs, not forcefully, but enough to make him wince. "You know, Jesús, it might be best for everybody if you *do* get on that plane. You're just so negative all the time."

Jesús let out a long-suffering sigh. "Tell me about it," he said.

CHAPTER 36

Incarcerated - Well, Not Really

When the police sergeant arrived from Vanahu to arrest Frank Chamberlain the first thing he did was apologize. In his opinion, the whole thing was backwards: Giovanni Garibaldi should have been the one going to jail instead of pressing charges. The sergeant had heard about Shovel World from the prime minister's wife and he was appalled. Moreover, before calling on Frank and Marge he had visited Barry to pass on the news. Barry, he said, just about went through the roof. Frank was less than comforted, and to make matters worse Marge put her foot down, refusing point-blank to let him leave without her and the dog.

The stalemate was resolved when the sergeant explained that as the jail was full they would be obliged to do time under house arrest at Mama Lu's Golden Sunset Club. That didn't seem so bad, especially since there was a pool, and pets were allowed. Not to mention complimentary cocktails were served every evening between five and seven. Apart from which, no one seriously expected Frank to pay the fine.

Thus, when Einstein showed up and offered to bail them out, Frank and Marge didn't exactly fall all over themselves with gratitude. "It's like this," Frank explained. "We've only been here two weeks, and, to be honest, it's a welcome change from the boat. By the way, has anyone ever told you you're the spitting image of Albert Einstein?"

"Believe me," said Einstein, "you don't know how close you are coming to the truth."

By this time, Frank and Marge were well acquainted with the virgins. Indeed, the entire population of Vanahu was agog. What with word of Shovel World and Virgin Beach breaking the same week, *and* Frank and Marge being arrested, the doings on Noahu were an overnight sensation. For the first time ever, the Vanahu *Global Reporter* had more than one headline to contemplate. Not since the prime minister's wife had diverted foreign aid to subsidize her online poker habit, had there been news this riveting.

"What I don't understand," Marge said, "is how those poor girls are going to cope with the crocodiles."

"Barry is taking care of this," Einstein explained. "He is to waving his magic stick and these crocodiles are for behaving like the perfect gentlemens."

Frank was unconvinced. "If I were a virgin, I'd take a long, hard look at what's left of Barry's right arm. When it comes to salt water crocodiles, he's batting a big fat zero, if you want my opinion."

"Oh, you're always so negative, Frank," remonstrated Marge. "Mark my words, there's a lot more to Barry than meets the eye. Besides, the crocodiles probably feel they owe him."

"Oh, so that's how it works," Frank scoffed. "Only, I've often wondered about his magic stick and that oil drum he puts on his head."

Marge silenced him with a glare.

They were sitting poolside. The pool had been fashioned to resemble a jungle hideaway. At one end a waterfall cascaded over giant rocks. Lush tropical foliage reached to the water's edge. Bright-eyed sparrows darted everywhere, chirping with delight when they were offered table scraps. Hilda was the only competition. Not that she had much of a chance. She was nowhere near as alert as the birds, and a heck of a lot less adorable. Mind you, Hilda wasn't doing so badly. Like Frank and Marge, she was getting three-square a day, and the food definitely didn't come from a can.

Not far away, Jesús was downing beers with Madison. He needed a day to fly back to Seattle, which left one more day to hang out at Mama Lu's and relax. The star attraction for Jesús, of course, was the close proximity of twenty-three virgins. The downside was the hawk-like presence of Mandy Miller. She had traveled back with him from Noahu and made it clear she would tolerate no hanky panky. Madison, moreover, was acutely conscious of her obligations. While not averse to his company, she quickly reminded Jesús she was under contract.

"Remember," she said, "all those papers *you* had me sign? Just because *you* didn't sign them, doesn't mean *you* can do as you please."

"I'm cool with that," Jesús lied. "There's nothing wrong with just hanging out though, now is there? Where could be the harm in that?"

Still hopeful, however, he did ply her with a bunch of beers. Madison matched him drink for drink. Unfortunately, she was in the same league as Mount Rushmore when it came to a simple nod of the head.

"What I can't understand," Madison pointed out just before complimentary cocktails, "is how come you don't spend more time with Mandy Miller? I mean, she's not a virgin is she? So she's not off limits. Also, she's more your age."

"Good God!" Jesús cried. "So that's it. You think I'm old and smelly. It's not about the contract, is it? It's all about being obsessed by youth. If I were a pimply adolescent with no chest hair, you'd be all over me."

"Oh, chill out and get a life," Madison countered, suddenly bored. "I was just trying to be helpful. Anyway, I've seen her look at you. You know, like she thinks you're cute or something."

"Oh!" Jesús said.

He sneaked a look at Mandy. She was over by the Tiki bar explaining the rudiments of videography to the Khan and Jesus One. She had assigned Jesus One the butterfly-cams. The Khan was saddled with sound, lighting, hauling stuff, and whatever else cropped up that involved heavy lifting. Whereas the Khan was clearly challenged by tripods, Jesus One was in his element. He manipulated the controls of the tiny airborne cameras with ease. The cameras swooped and hovered. They tracked sideways in auto-dolly mode. Then they followed behind two darting sparrows with laser-like precision.

Jesús watched Mandy covertly for a while before responding to Madison. He was confused. On the one hand, he was definitely attracted. On the other hand, he was terrified of falling prey to another Muriel Banks. "Are you sure? Because, to be honest, she talks to me like I'm some kind of imbecile."

"You just don't get it, do you?"

"No," Jesús admitted with a rueful shake of his head. "I most definitely don't get it."

Madison sighed impatiently. "It's us, dork brain! It's the girls! She's jealous!"

Jesús absorbed Madison's revelation slowly. "How could I not have seen this?" he asked himself. "What clues did I miss?"

He settled on the Perrier. "So I overlooked the Perrier," he said, as much to himself as to Madison, who was also looking at him as though he were some kind of imbecile.

"What Perrier?" she asked. "Didn't you hear a word I just said?"

Still lost in thought, Jesús ignored the question. "I knew there was something going on," he muttered, "and there it was, staring me in the face. But I missed it. Obviously, I need to work on my technique."

"Oh, really," Madison offered, with a wry smile. "And just exactly what technique might that be, Romeo? I can't say I'd noticed."

Madison had to go change for cocktails then, so Jesús was left to contemplate her intriguing disclosure: this new idea that was Mandy Miller. The problem was he had only the one day left before boarding the plane for Seattle—the airplane, incidentally, that he now owned.

The matter of the plane had come about while he and Einstein were exploring contingencies on the flight from Florida to Vanahu. Einstein pointed out that if he were recalled in the event of another intergalactic emergency, someone would have to keep the ball in play on Earth. That someone, of course, would have to be Jesús. Jesús agreed, so Einstein promptly placed an in-flight call to Zurich. Thus, it came-to-pass that not long after his thirty-third birthday, Jesús Maria Martinez found himself in possession of a twelve billion dollar fortune. Unfortunately for him, the world was about to end. Not to mention, when the word got out, money would most likely lose its appeal overnight.

"So we must not hesitate to spending it," Einstein insisted. "For example, this aeroplane we have chartered we will also need to fetching the virgins back from the beach."

"Makes sense to me," Jesús agreed. "I'll take care of it when we get to Vanahu. I'll also arrange for hangar space at Sea-Tac. The charter company we're using has an aviation management branch in Seattle. They can provide everything we need: pilots, waitresses, in-flight movies, free drinks, online poker—"

Einstein interrupted eagerly. "Yes, yes, all of this, and also please to ask them for these little chocolates with the green in the middles, like we are getting from the Olive Garden."

Et cetera.

***

Given his new status as suitor, Jesús took a leaf from Madison's book and changed for cocktails. Suddenly, he was charged with boundless optimism. "No more Mister Negative," he declared to the bathroom mirror, showing his teeth in a broad smile, and managing to talk at the same time without blinking—just like Dirk Forrester. "See here, Martinez," his new, confident self beamed back at him. "What's your problem, my friend? You have this movie star drooling all over you. You have twelve billion dollars in a Swiss bank. You rescued the two *dumbkopfs* in the face of impossible odds. You came through with the virgins. You're hanging out in a tropical paradise. You have Jesus Christ, and Genghis Khan backing you up. Not to mention God and Albert Einstein all rolled into one. What could possibly go wrong?"

Jesús decided not to dwell on that last question. He had, after all, been through a lot. What he didn't need right then was another crisis. An adoring Mandy Miller was just what the doctor ordered. He hummed happily as he finished dressing, surprising himself with his unconscious choice of music, namely, Mendelssohn's *Wedding March*.

"That's it," he grinned. "We'll get married. She can be empress of my new world order *and* harem mistress. It'll be a two for one deal, just like God and Einstein."

Who, you might ask, would have thought the world was about to end?

When he spotted Mandy, she was sitting at the bar with Ashley. They were both drinking blue bayous. He joined them and ordered the same.

"I had you figured as a Michelob kind of guy," Ashley observed suspiciously.

Jesús promptly turned his back on Ashley and focused his attention on Mandy. He was remembering another key finding from his study of approachable young women in bars. To wit: *go ugly, early.* The good news was Mandy was by no means ugly. The other good news was it was still early. "So, Mandy," he began confidently. "I've been meaning to thank you for stepping in like this, helping us escape, and the virgins and all. You've been a real trooper."

"So what prevented you?"

"I'm a shy person," he lied. "Also, what with you being so famous and me being just an air-traffic-controller, I didn't want to give you the impression I was sucking-up."

Mandy stirred her blue bayou thoughtfully. "First of all," she said, with narrowed eyes, "you are probably the least shy person I ever met in my entire life. Secondly, I had a word with Albert like you suggested. He said if I need money, I should dip into the violin case, and if that isn't enough I should talk to you. He said expense is no object."

She poked him gently in the chest. "He also informed me you own the 767 we flew over in."

"Oh!" Jesús said

Mandy stared deep into his eyes. "Just exactly what *is* going on Jesús? This air- traffic-controller thing is just another one of your stories, isn't it? It's gotten so the only person I believe any more is Jesus, but all he does is keep telling me to have faith."

Jesús shrugged. "I'd love to tell you more, Mandy. I really would."

She poked him again, a little less gently this time. "Then go right ahead. I'm listening."

Jesús struggled, casting about for a convincing lie, but the compulsion to confess thwarted him at every turn. It was a dark force within, demanding he blurt out the horrifying truth and get it over with and be done with it once and for all. "Er!" he said finally. "You probably wouldn't believe me even if I told you. By the way, you're almost finished with your drink. Let me get you a refill."

He called the bartender and ordered another blue bayou and a Michelob. The switch of drink was a sure sign of his growing panic. This conversation was not going as planned. He was less than two minutes in and already up to his eyeballs.

"Quit stalling, Jesús." Mandy urged, leaning close. Subtle scents of jasmine and honeysuckle wafted gently over him.

"You know," he said, grateful for the opportunity to stall some more, "that perfume of yours is oddly familiar. It reminds me of some place I've been recently, but I'll be darned if I know where."

"Oh, you must have been in a *DRIVEL*. It's an old folk recipe from Grandma Chittenden. Every now and then, I'll make up a batch and wear it for a while. Billy Ray liked it so much he put it in the *DRIVELs*. He even uses it for special aftershaves and air-fresheners he calls Sweet Jesus. The aftershave is the top selling stocking stuffer in his *Christmas for Christians* catalog."

Mandy leaned in even closer. "I'm so glad *you* like it."

Jesús was on the brink. A seductive parting of the lips or the flutter of an eyelash and he was done for.

Luckily, Mandy broke the spell. "You know," she whispered, "I really like you, but sometimes you can be such an asshole."

"I am," he began, taking it one word at a time, groping for a way out, "actually, I am, er, if you can believe me, er, one of the richest men on the planet."

"Oh really," Mandy whispered, still up close, still shrouding him in the deliciously exciting promise of honeysuckle and jasmine. "And just exactly how rich might that be, if you don't mind my asking?"

He couldn't resist. Just saying it was right up there with the perfume. The words slid from his tongue like silk. "Last time I checked I had twelve billion dollars in the bank, give or take a hundred thousand or so."

"Oh!" exclaimed Mandy, as if that explained everything.

Seeing his opportunity, Jesús quickly tried to get back on track. "So, Mandy, how on earth did you get to be Little Miss Fixit?"

She went for it. Inwardly, he breathed a sigh of relief.

"You can thank my Pop for that. It was all in the *Star* magazine special. Didn't you read it?"

"No," he lied. "*Star* magazine isn't exactly my cup of tea."

"There isn't much to it, really," Mandy continued, carefully removing the beach umbrella from her blue bayou. "I never had a brother, and Pop remodeled houses, so when I was a kid I got to go along and help out. He used to call me his Little Miss Fixit."

She hesitated. "Are you *sure* you didn't read this?"

"Cross my heart and hope to die."

"You're just trying to change the subject again aren't you?"

"No, no," he protested. "I'm interested. I really am. Please go on."

"All right," she said, still eyeing him suspiciously. "Well, to make a long story short, like most eighteen-year-olds I wanted to be a movie star. Only I didn't have the money to pay for my portfolio. So, I found this job at a modeling agency building the little sets and props they used for photo shoots. For each set I made, they did one free photo. Then one day, in walks this TV big shot called Bill Finkelstein looking to audition girls for some umpteenth Millionaire Bachelor show. He saw me in my jeans and tool belt, varnishing a Louis XIV loveseat I'd just made. He asked who I was and without thinking, I said, I'm just the Little Miss Fixit around here. You know, his eyes just lit right up and he got excited and said, No, what's your real name? And I said, Doris Chittenden, and he said, Not anymore, sweetheart. From now on *you* are Mandy Miller, and, boy, do I have a deal for you."

Mandy looked skywards. She reminded Jesús of Einstein contemplating Jupiter. "And the rest," she murmured, "is history. Bill thought I'd be a sure-fire hit with the unwed teenage mother demographic. Apparently, they sit around a lot watching TV, fantasizing about fixing up whatever piece of crap they're renting. Dirk was a hedge bet in case they were having fantasies of a different kind." She smiled ruefully. "I guess I outgrew my part. Dirk sure as hell didn't outgrow his though."

Jesús shook his head sympathetically. "Golly, I'm sorry, Mandy. It must have been tough on both of you when Dirk took a nail in the head."

"Well, it was, especially for him. And in case you're wondering, no, I didn't do it on purpose."

"Good Golly!" he protested, "the very idea! The thought never even crossed my mind."

She placed a hand on his arm and looked deep into his eyes for a second time. "Jesús, you are *so* full of shit. Anyway, that's enough about me. Tell me, just how did you get to be so rich, so young?"

Jesús had heard somewhere that the more spontaneous the lie, the more convincing it will sound. That goes hand-in-hand with the theory that the bigger the lie, the better. In other words, people will gag at a gnat and swallow a camel. He believed these theories wholeheartedly, so he went for the camel.

"Motorized snowboards: I invented motorized snowboards, and they took off like a rocket. Ha-ha, just my little joke."

"Listen," Mandy said patiently. "Why don't we start over? Like where you grew up for instance. Then, while we're talking you can maybe come up with something a little less pathetic than motorized snowboards"

He was a worm wriggling on a stick. In desperation, he seized on the truth. "Well, as you might have guessed, I'm not exactly a red-blooded American. I'm actually Mexican."

She stared back, unmoved. "That comes as no surprise, although I have to say the green eyes don't exactly add up."

"We think those came from my great, great grandfather. He was an immigrant Irishman, and God knows how, but he somehow strayed across the border and accidentally got mixed up in the Mexican revolution."

Mandy leaned ever so slightly closer.

Detecting a spark of interest, Jesús pressed on, avoiding the temptation to embellish. "His name was Colin Cleary. No one knows how or why, but for some reason, probably free tequila, he wound up riding with the Consitutionalists. I have an old photo somewhere that shows him sitting on a horse next to a rebel general looking dazed. Apparently, he had just helped the general capture the Federal garrison at Matamoros. That's where he met my great, great grandma. She was a *soldadera* fighting with Zapata. Eeventually, they married and moved to Cuernavaca. There are still Clearys in Cuernavaca to this day, believe it or not."

She leaned back a little. Was this disbelief? If it was, he felt cheated. He decided to ditch the Clearys of Cuernavaca and move on.

"Mind you, I myself was born in the States, so that makes me a citizen."

Mandy nodded encouragingly. "Good," she said, "so you were born in the States, so what? So was I. So were three hundred million other people."

"Sure," he shot back, "but you're parents got to live in the same frigging house you did. Mine were stuck south of the border. They were illegal. They were deported when I was four."

"Oh dear," Mandy declared, and touched his arm again.

Jesús detected the note of sympathy, but decided not to overplay his hand. He was, after all, telling the truth, and it seemed to be working. She hadn't exactly said, "you poor thing," but he sensed he was getting close. "Yes, well, I mean, apart from hardly ever seeing Mom and Dad, it wasn't that bad. My Auntie Carmen brought me up, you see. I went through high school where I was a dork brain. Then I went to college where I was a dork brained History major."

Mandy squeezed his forearm. "Oh," she said softly, "you poor thing."

Bingo!

"And your poor mother and father. No wonder so many people hate us."

Jesús was genuinely surprised. "They didn't hate anybody. They were just grateful Dad could find decent work for a while. It's ironic when you think about it. If they hadn't started on the fence, Mom would have stayed home and Dad would have hopped back over the border twice a year as usual. All that extra security didn't keep us out; it kept us in. If it weren't for the fence, I'd be wearing a sombrero right now, pulling up tomatoes in Culiacan. Go figure."

"Is that where they live, in Culiacan?"

"It was where they lived. Ten years ago, they were on a bus going into town. The brakes failed and it went over a cliff. No one survived."

She gently repeated the forearm squeeze and said it again. "Oh, you poor thing!"

Double Bingo!!

Jesús shrugged modestly. "I miss them, but you sort of get over it. At least, you've still got your Uncle Johnny,"

Her eyes misted over. "And I have you and Albert to thank for that. It's funny how things work out. If you hadn't given him a ride when you did, none of this would have happened."

Jesús reached over and gently squeezed the back of her hand. She squeezed his forearm in response.

Triple Bingo!!!

"You will keep in touch with him when you get back, though, won't you, Jesús? I hate to think of him looking after the mansion all by himself, never talking to anyone."

He was ahead. He had it made. All he had to do now was keep steering the conversation his way. A graceful transition—that was the thing. A light-hearted quip, a clever yet subtle change of subject, another gentle squeeze, then dinner, harmless chitchat, and who knows what else under the moonlight. The trouble was, Jesús was so attached to the snowboard idea his mind wouldn't let go of it. Each time he reached for something else, visions of himself as a dashing, bronzed snowboard tycoon kept getting in the way.

"So, Mandy, what's so hard to believe about me being a snowboard tycoon?"

The question came out, just like that, with absolutely no prompting at all. He watched in horror as the words tumbled incredulously and irrevocably from his mouth.

Mandy withdrew her hand.

Jesús mentally threw himself from a tall building. "Jeez!" he muttered. "How frigging dumb can you get?"

"You said it," she retorted, pushing away the blue bayou. "Anyway, when you decide to grow up and stop telling your stupid lies, just let me know. Then, maybe you can buy me another drink."

Jesús buried his head in his hands.

CHAPTER 37

Wired

When first class passenger, Gordon Grimshaw, came out of the forward toilet without his trousers, Norma Flatley suspected something was wrong. The wires dangling from his kneecaps clinched it. Before Grimshaw could cross his legs and thus activate the explosive knee implants, Norma heroically threw herself between his thighs. Grimshaw was promptly set-upon by angry passengers, who beat him to within an inch of his life. Caught up, as she was, between Grimshaw's thighs, Norma didn't fare too well either.

Norma—yes, the very same Norma Flatley who was Mandy Miller's childhood friend—was a flight attendant with Taliban World Airlines *(TWA)* at the time. Her religious conversion came about after years of uncovering Biblical ambiguities. Finally, she found herself unable to believe a word of it and crossed over.

Since its debut in 2020, *TWA* had been plagued by terrorist incidents. Grimshaw's was the latest in a string of suicide attacks by Christian fanatics bent on destroying Islam. At his trial, Grimshaw confessed to being a member of the Sacred Christian Underground Militia, otherwise known as *SCUM,* a shadowy organization rumored to operate out of Baltimore. He was found guilty and beheaded the same day.

What bothered Jesús about this episode was not so much the beheading, but the classic reaction of airport authorities. From that time on, all passengers, regardless of age, race, gender, sexual preference, or religious persuasion had to pass through security sans trousers, robes, or skirts. Not to mention shoes.

People, you see, have such ugly knees—never mind the choice of undergarments.

Thanks to the prime minister's wife, the airport authority at Vanahu no longer had sufficient funds for security—nor very much else for that matter—so Jesús was spared. Mind you, given how warm it was, most of the men wore shorts and all the women wore skirts above the knee, so he wasn't spared much.

To his surprise, Mandy insisted on seeing him off.

"I thought things over very carefully last night," she said, "and I decided Jesus was right. I really do need to have faith. I'm going to assume that when you think it's time, you'll tell me what's really going on. Just don't come up with any more of your ridiculous snowboard stories, okay?"

Jesús was elated.

"Apart from which," Mandy continued, "I'd like to say goodbye to Norma."

Yes—the very same Norma Flatley who was Mandy's childhood friend.

What happened was this: Traumatized by her ordeal between Gordon Grimshaw's thighs, Norma eventually quit *TWA*. She headed back to the States and found a job as a flight attendant with the charter airline hired to ferry the virgins. Imagine Norma's surprise when she checked the passenger manifest and spotted Mandy Miller's name. Both girls were overjoyed to see each other again. So much had happened. There was so much to talk about.

"I still can't believe it," Norma said, as Mandy boarded with Jesús. "I mean, meeting you like this, after all this time, and you being so famous. The story in *Star* magazine was fabulous."

"I know, I know," Mandy said, wide-eyed, "and you being famous for tackling that horrible terrorist. Whoever would have thought?"

Jesús stuffed his bag in an overhead bin while the girls exchanged farewells. Given that he owned the plane and he was the only passenger, he guessed he could sit anywhere. He chose first class. Somehow, the little curtain separating him from the non-existent peons in coach appealed to him. Besides, the seats up front had a heck of a lot more legroom.

Mandy didn't exactly embrace him when she left, but she did peck him lightly on the cheek. Considering how things had ended the previous night, this was very definitely a good sign. "Now, don't forget to say hi to Uncle Johnny," she said, "and you have my cell-phone number, which for some odd reason apparently works on Noahu, so you can call me if you need to. Also, remember to meet with Bill Finkelstein. Now that he doesn't have *Little Miss Fixit* paying for his ex-wives, I know he's on the lookout for a new show. Tell him I'll have a *Virgin Beach* pilot in a couple of months and he has first option."

It was like being family. He almost said, "Yes dear," but settled for, "Sure, no problem. Just keep an eye out for crocodiles."

Then Mandy was gone.

***

After takeoff, Norma fetched Jesús a perfectly chilled Michelob then fussed around in the forward galley. Now that they were alone, she seemed nervous, although it wasn't easy to tell for sure because of her veil. He supposed it had something to do with his owning the plane. More likely, Mandy had told her he was a dork brain and a compulsive liar. He was ruminating thus when the bell tone sounded.

Norma popped her head out. "That wasn't you was it?"

"No. Can't you tell? I mean, don't you have some kind of indicator panel back there?"

"No," she said. "What we do is just check for the little light flashing over your head."

He glanced above his head. "Well, there's nothing flashing here."

The bell tone persisted. They both stared at the curtain.

"There's not supposed to be anyone back there," Norma said. "Would you mind checking?"

"Not likely," Jesús countered. "That's your job."

Norma sniffed and walked past him without another word. She gingerly opened the curtain. "Ooh!" she exclaimed.

Jesús craned backwards to see what, or whom, she had discovered.

Sitting in 5E, which was the right hand aisle seat of the mid-section, second row back from the movie screen, was a good-looking young man of Indian descent. He was wearing a nicely tailored black blazer, gray slacks, white running shoes, and an open-necked striped silk shirt. On his head was a white turban with two wires poking from it.

"For the love of Allah," Norma shrieked. "Not again!"

"Oh, Fuck!" Jesús added.

Norma fell to her knees, sobbing hysterically.

Jesús didn't hesitate. He calmly returned his tray table to the upright position and reached for the call button.

Two bell tones dinged. Norma looked up in confusion, but stayed put. Jesús sighed and got up from his seat. The good-looking young man of Indian descent smiled uncertainly. Jesús helped Norma to her feet and sent her forward to summon the co-pilot. He lowered himself carefully into 5F, which was across the aisle and slightly forward of 5E, but just as cramped.

Something was bothering him. "Don't I know you?" he asked.

The good-looking young man of Indian descent shook his head. "No, I do not believe so."

Jesús frowned, and then it came to him. "Yes I do, you're the resident physician from Little Miss Fixit with Mandy Miller. Doctor Nagray isn't it?"

"Yes, yes, I was such a person, but I no longer have this job, don't you see. When Mandy put a nail into the head of Dirk Forrester, the show ended. My name, by the way, is not Nagray, it is Nagpal, Prashant Nagpal." He put out his hand. "How do you do, I am so pleased to meet you."

"Jesús Martinez, I'm pleased to meet you too. Now, if you don't mind my asking, how come you have an exploding turban on your head?"

Just then, the co-pilot poked his head through the curtain. "Anything I can do, chaps?" he asked cheerfully.

Jesús motioned him to stay where he was. "Not really," he said. "We're negotiating. Tell Norma I'd like another Michelob though, if it's not too much bother." He turned to Nagpal. "You want anything, Prashant?"

Nagpal nodded. "Please, if you have it, I am most partial to the White Zinfandel."

"You're sitting in coach," explained Jesús. "You do know that will cost you twelve dollars, don't you?"

Nagpal's shoulders drooped. "This is most unfortunate, because I have spent the last of my money to eat *lap-lap* in the Crocodile Lounge of the airport."

"Tell you what," Jesús offered magnanimously. "How about this: since I own the airplane, you can have a complimentary upgrade to first. That way it won't cost you a dime. By the way, why were you calling the flight attendant?"

"I must talk with Mandy Miller, you see, so she can be with me when I explode this turban I am wearing."

"I hate to be the one to tell you this, pal, but Mandy isn't on the plane, she stayed behind in Vanahu."

An expression of utter dejection came over the turban bomber. Jesús almost felt sorry for him. He signaled the co-pilot to fetch Norma. Then he put his head back and briefly closed his eyes, feeling the tension drain away. When he looked up, Nagpal was on his feet, heading forward. "Here, just a minute," he yelled, struggling to free his legs.

He was too late. Nagpal was already through the curtain. He heard Norma scream. Rushing into first class, he found Nagpal scrambling about on his knees. Norma was curled up in a fetal position across 2A and 2B. Luckily for her, the armrest was up. The co-pilot was nowhere to be seen. Nagpal stared up at him in desperation.

"You must be very careful where you are stepping. She spilled my Zinfandel all over the floor," he cried.

"Oh, for God's sake," Jesús exclaimed. "Look, just hand me up that can of Michelob and the cup and I'll pour you another one."

He ignored Norma, who was back to sobbing uncontrollably, and made his way to the galley. *Then* he put his head in his hands. He had the good sense, however, not to open the Michelob.

When he returned with the drinks Nagpal was sitting in 3A, the rear left-hand window seat. Norma was still lying in a fetal position. She stared vacantly at the seatbacks, sucking her thumb, but at least she was quiet. Jesús settled himself in 3B and handed over the wine. "Look, Prashant," he said, sounding as conciliatory as he could, given the circumstances, "maybe we can work this out. Why not just tell me what's going on. Then we can take it from there."

"It is too late, I am telling you. When I finish my Zinfandel, I must go to heaven. The martyrdom video is made, you see. This they have sent to my family in Rajnanipur with the twenty thousand dollars I am getting from Mister Bixbee."

Jesús lowered his tray table and calmly set down the Michelob. Something started to chew through his stomach lining. He took a deep breath. "How the fuck," he said through gritted teeth, "if you will pardon my French, did Billy Ray Ratbag get mixed up in all this?"

Nagpal explained that Billy Ray was both the brains and the money behind the Sacred Christian Underground Militia (which had, by the way, produced the video and manufactured the exploding turban). This came as no surprise to Jesús. What he didn't understand was how a good-looking young man of Indian descent—a doctor no less—could be taken in by Billy Ray Bixbee and a villainous organization like *SCUM*.

It was, he soon learned, a classic tale of redemption and revenge.

Nagpal, was not, in fact, a doctor. His only medical background was two years as an ambulance driver for the municipality of Rajnanipur. After being right-sized during a push to phase out ambulances in favor of stay-at-home surgery, he moved back in with his parents to study the want ads. Imagine his surprise when he came across the following announcement in the *Rajnanipur Weekly Job Finder*:

> Wanted: A good-looking young man of Indian descent with medical credentials for popular DIY television show in USA. Applicants must speak good English. No Green Card? No problem!

It seems Bill Finkelstein had found out that, in addition to identifying with handy nineteen-year old virgins (and fantasizing about muscular young carpenters), unwed teenage mothers also lusted after handsome young doctors of Indian descent. Finkelstein, moreover, was more than flexible when it came to the medical credentials. After all, Nagpal was willing to work for next to nothing.

Not surprisingly, when the show ended, Nagpal had trouble finding another job. He was also broke. The situation went from bad to worse when Dirk Forrester's lawyers went after him for performing brain surgery without a permit. At this point, Prashant Nagpal could fairly be described as a disgruntled former employee. Not to mention he faced arrest, possible deportation, and found himself in dire circumstances to boot.

Enter Billy Ray.

When Nagpal showed up at Pastureland bent on getting satisfaction, he was not only a dollar short, he was a day late. "So I did not find Mandy Miller, you see, and I went to Mister Bixbee to find out where she had gone to. Oh yes, and when I told him of my problems, he kindly offered to help. He said if I exploded Mandy Miller, he would send the sum of twenty thousand dollars to my family. Also, he will arrange for me to go to heaven right after the explosion."

"And you believed him?"

"Surely, you must be kidding!" Nagpal said with raised eyebrows, taking another sip of his Zinfandel. "For twenty thousand dollars I would even believe Mandy is a nineteen-year old virgin"

"Excuse me," Jesús interrupted. "I'm ready for another drink, how about you Prashant?"

Nagpal stared disconsolately at what was left of his wine. "No thank you. My next drink will be in heaven. I must do this thing right now, you see, while I have the chance. Billy Ray also has said to me, if I cannot get to Mandy then I should take out the dork brain, which I believe must be you."

"Oh," said Jesús. "Well, in that case, maybe I'll stay put."

Norma's head rose into view from the back of 2B. Her eyes were puffy, but otherwise she seemed composed. "Would that be another beer, sir?" she asked politely.

"Er, yes, a Michelob please, and would you kindly turn off those bells, Norma? I'm suddenly getting a headache."

He turned to the turban bomber. "Are you absolutely sure you won't have another Zinfandel? It's no trouble you know, and you are in first now, so they are free, and you can have as many as you like."

Nagpal shook his head firmly. "This I absolutely do not need. You see, in a few moments I will be swimming in a lake of it with forty virgins."

Norma's eyes widened with panic.

"I'll have that drink right now, Norma, if you don't mind," Jesús urged, this being hardly the time for another nervous episode. He turned to Nagpal. He couldn't take his eyes off the almost empty cup of Zinfandel. Inwardly, he was shaking with terror. "So, Prashant," he prompted as calmly as he could, "How on earth did you track us down?"

"I have read in *Star* magazine a story from the *Vanahu Global Reporter,* you see, that Mandy Miller is on the island, and so I have taken the next flight. When I arrived today, I saw you with her. So, I asked the customs gentleman which plane it is you were taking."

He leaned back with a contented little grin and raised his cup for the final sip. "This is why I was sitting behind the curtain in 5E."

"Jeez," said Jesús, apropos of nothing, eyes still riveted to the cup, "maybe next time I'll fly coach." Then it came to him. "Just a minute," he said carefully. "What was that you just said about going to heaven?"

Nagpal closed his eyes and smiled serenely. "There will be rivers and springs and lakes filled with delicious white Zinfandel, I am telling you. There will be warm *chapattis* hanging from every tree, you see. There will also be these great mountains of curried lamb's tail. Then there will be for each man in heaven, forty luscious virgins filled with desire."

"Mmm, curried lamb's tail—does that sound good or what? Maybe when you have a minute, you could jot down the recipe for me. By the way, if heaven is running a bit short when you get there, and you could have only one thing from that list, which one might it be, perchance? Assuming, of course, you didn't go for the lamb's tail."

Nagpal opened his eyes. He stared wistfully at the storage bin above 2B, rather like Einstein contemplating Jupiter, except he was a lot more joyful. "Oh, that will be no problem," he sighed. "I would most definitely choose the forty luscious virgins filled with desire."

"Boy," said Jesús, "do I have a deal for you."

CHAPTER 38

Bickering Birds

By this time, in addition to the wolves and the bears, birds and other species were leaving Yellowstone in record numbers: all three hundred eighteen species of birds, for example, had already taken flight. Signs of impending doom were everywhere. Yet the signs were either overlooked or flat-out misinterpreted.

Take the white-tailed jackrabbits for example.

Vernon's explanation for the jackrabbit exodus was that they just didn't fit in—never had, never would. He based his conclusion on the fact that the rabbits had taken off once before.

In 2007, someone mentioned they hadn't noticed a jackrabbit in the park since heaven knows when. It turned out the rabbits had been absent for sixteen years (sometimes it takes a while for these things to sink in). Still, rabbits hadn't been seen in nearby Grand Teton Park for twenty-eight years either, so the Yellowstone exodus was certainly no cause for alarm. The thing is, nobody had the slightest idea why the rabbits had left, or where they were headed—other than Vernon Trumboy. Vernon's theory was they had migrated to Minnesota to seek safety in numbers. What with wolves moving in and coyotes on the rebound, Yellowstone was definitely no place for a rabbit to be, circa 1991.

Sure enough, a report was issued by the Bronx Zoo in 2008 confirming there were no more rabbits in the park, and hadn't been for seventeen years, and no one had bothered to find out why, because no one had noticed they were gone (jackrabbits, you see, had never made it to the Adorable Species List). Moreover, as everyone knows, jackrabbits breed like crazy, especially in Minnesota. So, what was the big deal, anyway?

In 2023 a dozen mating pairs of these very same Minnesota rabbits were relocated to Yellowstone in an attempt to restore the balance (sometimes it takes a while for things to move through the system). By this time, the Supreme Court had struck down every last vestige of gun control, so heavily armed citizens were on the loose in the national park system, eager to slaughter anything that moved, including each other. What was left of the wolves and coyotes were too busy dodging bullets to pay much attention to jackrabbits. Consequently, the rabbits thrived and multiplied.

Until Sunday August 9, 2026, that is.

Unlike the birds, which were leaving in orderly fashion, the jackrabbits left the same day: all twelve million of them.

"See, what did I say," Vernon declared triumphantly. "I told them it could never work. They're going back to Minnesota to seek safety in numbers."

As far as the eye could see little white tails bobbed and bounded. An ocean of fur was on the move. Jubilant visitors were letting fly with everything from Teaser-Tazers to .50 cal Gatling guns. Some were even throwing rocks. Yet nothing could stem the tide.

"Good riddance," Vernon added. "At least, now we don't have to worry about the lawns."

As senior park liaison officer, he was escorting a party of scientists tasked to investigate the bird migrations. Among them was Doctor Edward Clump—yes, the very same Doctor Clump who had once headed the Yellowstone Volcano Observatory.

Now, wasn't that a coincidence!

The scientists were focused on the birds because the whereabouts of the bears and the wolves was no longer a mystery, and therefore of no great concern. Most of the animals had been tagged, so they were easy to find.

The bears, they discovered, had made it to the old Inuit settlement of Igdloolik, which is way past Hudson's Bay and not so very far from the North Pole. Formerly a frozen void, Igdloolik had become a popular summer resort for Scandinavian sun worshippers. Scientists theorized that when the last of the polar bears perished, somehow the Yellowstone bears got wind of it, and headed north to fill the vacuum. Igdloolik offered year round moose meat (not widely available in Yellowstone), a bountiful salmon season, and an abundance of cool river water to splash about in (Bears love to splash about a lot, especially when it's warm out). For some time, the Yellowstone River, along with the Firestone, the Gallatin, the Madison, and the Snake, had offered little more than a hot soak—another good reason, the scientists theorized, for the bears to move on. Not to mention, the Scandinavians were a lot more generous with leftovers, and they didn't carry guns.

As for the wolves, they fetched up in Anchorage and moved to the suburbs. Being few in number they had little impact, if any, on the indigenous wildlife. Most of them, in fact, were eventually taken in as household pets. A popular theory was they had actually set off for the Yukon, a former habitat, but had mistakenly kept going instead of turning right at Skagway. Anyway, the theory was moot. Nobody much cared about the wolves anymore. Ever since they had taken to howling at park visitors they had been taken off the Adorable Species List.

"Good riddance," Vernon was heard to say. Right now, though, he was standing on the west bank of the Yellowstone River, discussing birds.

A waning sun dappled myriad droplets of light on the water. Over on the east bank, a solitary bison chewed grass. Three mallard ducks drifted aimlessly, enjoying the slow movement of the river and the early evening calm. Photographers call this the golden hour. Sunlight glows at this time of day, lengthening shadows and bathing its subjects with a soft and magical touch.

All of this, of course, was lost on Vernon. As usual, he was seeking illumination of a more mundane kind. "By the way Doctor Clump," he enquired, "I hope you don't mind my asking, but how come you're here with these bird guys? I thought you were a volcanologist."

"Oh, not at all," said Clump. "As a matter of fact, while we were here with the volcano obervatory my wife and I were avid birders. When I heard about this field trip, I was the first to volunteer."

Vernon scanned the group. "So, what happened to the missus?"

"Well, ever since we moved to Hawaii, Mildred has been a keen surfer. This week there's an active senior rip curl pro surfing event on Waikiki beach. She's defending her seventy-five and over world championship. I'd just be mooching round the house anyway"

"Do you have any idea why the birds are moving out?"

Clump's idea was breathtakingly simple. "If you ask me, I think they're just tired of being shot at. Mind you, that's just a hypothesis for now; we'll need to investigate thoroughly, of course."

Vernon was unconvinced. "Are you sure? I mean, they're protected aren't they? At any rate, I happen to know for a fact that a whole lot of them are definitely on the Adorable Species List."

Clump sniggered. "Sure they're adorable. Listen, next time you see some wild-eyed bastard toting a twelve gauge Winchester Defender, go ask him if he gives a crap."

"Mmm, yes, I see what you mean. Are there any other ideas?"

"Oh, sure, Doctor Cartwright here thinks he might be on to something with the fish having to survive in hot water. You see, a bunch of these birds are waterfowl. So he tried serving freshly poached cutthroat trout to *anas Americana*. That would be the American Wigeon, to you. They wouldn't go for it. It seems they prefer dinner to be *au naturel*."

The upshot was that after a week of diligence and the occasional fly-fishing break, the scientists agreed on three areas that warranted further study. Clump and Cartwright made it with the fish poaching and shotgun ideas. The other idea, though, was considered the real winner. It was the brainchild of the only woman in the group, namely, Doctor Amanda Crass of the Bronx Zoo-based Wildlife Conservation Society, the authors of the 2008 report on Jackrabbit exfiltration.

The *Crass Concept*, as it came to be known, was as brilliantly audacious as the shotgun and poached fish ideas were breathtakingly simple. Also, in all fairness, Clump did not cast aside Vernon's idea willy-nilly. Despite the jackrabbits not being on the Adorable Species List, and being off his immediate radar, so to speak, he did give full credit in his final report, referring to the *Lepus townsendii* migration in a brief footnote, as an unrelated and apparent manifestation of the *Trumboy Syndrome*.

Vernon was thrilled.

Amanda Crass, as it happened, was married to Kaashajim—Jim for short—an activist Bushman from Botswana. This was how they met: she demonstrating for Bush People's rights, he obtaining them by more direct means. Jim and his fellow activists did this by blowing up safari supply trains; it was the least they could do in his opinion.

After being thrown off their ancestral land to make way for the Central Kalahari Game Reserve and other important stuff like digging for diamonds, the Bush people had tried for decades to get it back. Thanks to activists like Jim and Amanda, they finally succeeded in 2022. The biggest challenge they then faced (unlike the rest of the world) was underpopulation.

Whereas there had been close to a million Bush people when the Europeans arrived, by the year 2022, they numbered less than a hundred thousand. There wasn't a whole lot of big game left either. This didn't bother the Bush People because they rarely hunted anything bigger than their heads. Moreover, the first thing they did when they got the Kalahari back was to ban all weapons other than spears, slings, bows and arrows, and throwing sticks.

Still, there *were* gazillions of birds: five hundred six species to be precise. The principal reason for this being that the birds had never made it to the government's Plains Game List, apart from the ostriches, of course ("You can run, big-bird, but you sure as hell can't fly."). Thus, other than the ostriches, birds were not bundled with the Elephant Hunt Package or the leopard specials. Purists will point out that there was in fact a Bird Hunt List for those too cheap to spring for the bigger stuff. Fortunately for the birds on the list—the kind that couldn't move fast enough or were too dim-witted to get out of the way, like grouse and wood pigeons—the great white hunters rarely stooped that low.

In those good old days, when the Botswana Government was running things, bagging elephants and other fast diminishing species brought in much needed foreign currency. For example, one might do a lion or an elephant for around $25,000 US per shooter in 2008 dollars (including complimentary germ-dipping and crating). *And* the elephant shooter got to keep the tusks.

Unfortunately, they never did specials on lions the way they did with leopards. Not only that, if you signed up for the Lion Hunt Package, they would stick you with a mandatory US$200 contribution to the Lion Preservation Fund (bummer!). Shipping recently slaughtered trophy heads would understandably cost extra, depending on the destination.

At the post-study press conference in the front lobby of the Planet Earth Pavilion, flanked by her husband, her colleagues, and Vernon Trumboy (in his capacity as senior park liaison officer), Amanda Crass put it this way: "As you all know, the Wildlife Conservation Society sponsors an amazing variety of field studies. My area of expertise is ornithology. In other words, I study birds. My particular specialty is bird bickering. You may not know this, but there have been spontaneous and unexplained outbreaks of bird bickering for some years now. So much so, that two years ago, in concert with the Audubon Society we founded the Bird Bickering Consortium, otherwise known as the *BBC*, to properly address the phenomenon."

A woman reporter in the front row raised her hand. "Excuse me, Wendy Winsome from *Star* magazine. I have a question."

Amanda peered over her spectacles and nodded graciously, if a little apprehensively, this being her first appearance before the media. "Please, go ahead Miss Winsome, that's why we're here."

"Do famous people have birds that bicker? If so, who are they? Also, do you think they would go along with being hounded by the media about that, the famous people I mean, not the birds?"

Amanda smiled vacantly. Vernon was reminded of Dick Derringer greeting guests. While Amanda floundered, Jim stepped forward, looking somewhat out of place in his traditional *San* garb of sheepskin cloak and antelope hide sandals. He also carried a small spear and a stick with a jackal's tail hanging from it. Although Jim was a noted activist, a freedom fighter if you will, he was first and foremost a Bushman, so he had a hard time concealing his innate good manners and childlike candor. "Miss Winsome," he said, with an engaging smile, "we have only just got started. There will be a Q&A session afterwards. So until then would you be ever so kind and shut the fuck up?" He fanned himself briefly with the tail and stepped away from the mike, still smiling politely.

Wendy Winsome said no more.

Amanda Crass reclaimed the microphone, but not before glancing fondly at her husband. "Where was I," she murmured nervously, looking down at her flash cards. "Oh, yes, the *BBC*. Were it not for the *BBC*, we wouldn't be here. Jim would be wandering the Kalahari and I would be inspecting birdcage floors at the Bronx Zoo. Therefore, I would first of all, like to thank the *BBC* for coming up with the airfares."

"Get on with it," yelled a reporter from the *National Parks Gazette*.

Vernon stepped forward, encouraged by Jim's success in quelling Wendy Winsome. His left hand casually brushed the polished walnut grip of his Sheriff Special. He tilted the little black Stetson against the overhead lighting, casting a shadow over his face, just like Paul Newman drawing down on Pat Garrett. His eyes narrowed. He pitched his voice as low and as slow as he could. He knew how to do this from watching John Wayne tuck his chin into his chest whenever he talked mean. "Hold on there, mister," he drawled. "You heard what the man said. First off, you let the little lady have her say. Then you get to speak your piece."

Someone applauded, and then the entire audience was on its feet clapping and cheering.

Vernon blushed.

Amanda bowed her head modestly and addressed the reporters with renewed confidence. "What I want to say, is the reason I asked for Jim is that since the *San* people got the Kalahari back they haven't had a single case of bird bickering. I thought he might have some insight into what's going on here in Yellowstone. As it turned out, he didn't have a clue."

She paused for effect. Jim smiled proudly. No less proud, Amanda continued. "But this is where it gets exciting. When I explained that we'd start with the Adorable Species List, then move on to the Not So Adorable Species List, and finally, God forbid, take a look at the Flat Out Frightful List—you know, the way we always do—he was dumbfounded. He said to me, "'Amanda," he said, "'what the fuck is an Adorable Species List?' And I must apologize for the language, but he really doesn't know any better."

Jim brandished his spear. Amanda removed her spectacles and abandoned the flash cards. She grinned triumphantly. "That's when it came to me. I had previously noted the birds that bickered most were not on the Adorable Species List, but I had thought nothing of it at the time. Wow! Can you imagine what it's like when a brand new idea slaps you upside the head? Why, it's like, it's like rolling down a hill in springtime!"

The audience leaned forward expectantly. Amanda took her time now, enunciating each word for dramatic effect. "Don't you see? Jim had never heard of the Adorable Species List, because the *San* people don't keep lists. All the animals are equal. A dung beetle is just as cherished as an elephant in their world. So, unlisted birds have no reason to bicker. *Ipso Facto,"* and here she grinned like a woman possessed, "that's why all the frigging birds in Yellowstone want to move to Botswana, especially the Flat Out Frightfuls and the Not So Adorables."

There was a stunned silence. Then the reporter from the *National Parks Gazette* rose to his feet and slow handclapped. Everyone else joined in.

Amanda Crass raised her hands for silence. "Please, please everybody," she beseeched them, "we're not quite finished. First, Jim and I, and the rest of the team will need to fly to Botswana to make sure the birds are actually ending up there. I also feel it only right we should acknowledge Doctors Cartwright and Clump for their brilliant hypotheses concerning fish poaching and shotgun depletion. These are very definitely contributing factors."

The applause was deafening.

Now isn't that just typical? Not one person got the big picture. The departures of the bears, and the wolves, and the jackrabbits, and the birds were all considered in isolation. Not to mention the badgers. Convenient little theories explained everything.

Meanwhile …

CHAPTER 39

...Back On Noahu

The games had begun. At first, Einstein was put out, to say the least, when Mandy ousted him as on-camera talent. Then she explained about the nutty contests. Inventing nutty contests, she said, was *the* most pivotal job in beach-based reality entertainment. Without them, participants had no way to vie for impunity and mouth-watering treats involving pizza.

"Not so many people," she said, "have the brains and the imagination to figure out that kind of stuff. But you do, Albert. I mean, the whole idea of Virgin Beach was yours to begin with."

So at least he was mollified.

Einstein's first nutty contest called for a convincing replica of the Empire Sate Building. The islanders, in particular, were thrilled when they heard this since set construction for beach-based reality entertainment paid really well. In addition to which, the whole business of the shovel handle factory was now in jeopardy because of Barry's mounting intransigence. He had already threatened to torch the first load of fiberglass matting. What's worse: he had persuaded one of his crocodiles to move into the site foreman's tent. The islanders' dream of long-term prosperity was fading fast

Of course, for a project as big as the Empire State Building, they had to send to Vanahu for bulldozers and concrete. Then Barry put his foot down yet again. Getting the crocodiles to be nice to virgins was one thing, he protested, but no way would they go for a skyscraper on their beach. The upshot was they had to use a location on the other side of the island. As it turned out, this wasn't so bad. Barry led the production team to a nice spot above an aquifer—just a little well digging and, bingo, unlimited fresh water for all. Not only that, for an extra four million dollars, the building contractors worked overtime to install geothermal heating and air conditioning, plus a couple of penthouse suites for the crew.

Jesus One and the Khan were ever so pleased.

Naturally, the usual complaints were voiced about tearing up pristine wilderness areas and scaring off indigenous species for the sake of some stupid-ass TV show. Mandy took care of that with her customary charm, plus a two million dollar contribution to the Vanahu Fish and Wildlife Conservation Society. The prime minister's wife, who was Society chairman, along with her many other civic duties, was near speechless with gratitude. Oh yes, and there were those naysayers who scoffed at the very idea of building the Empire State Building in less than three weeks. Mandy shut them up by pointing out the structure would be only eighty feet high.

"Believe me," she said, "our demographic won't even notice, let alone care."

Einstein quickly divined that nutty contests had to combine the gathering of different colored flags with leaping off something and thrashing about in shallow water; these were the basics. Throw in rickety platforms and an assortment of Styrofoam blocks painted to look like wood and you had it made. It also helped if someone was likely to get seriously hurt while drowning in mud. Not forgetting, of course, you needed a spiffy location for pizza.

Since this was the pilot episode, Mandy wanted something spectacular. "First of all," she said to Einstein, "I want a mind-boggling centerpiece. You know, like when the viewers first see it, they'll go, "'Wow!'" Then I want you to roll up all the normal challenges into one omnibus contest. Remember," she said, "this is the very first event. I want Finkelstein to be utterly blown away."

In no time at all Einstein came up with the Empire State Building idea, and soon thereafter he delivered the rest of the goods. He had to confess, though, he was stumped when it came to a spiffy location for eating pizza, Noahu not being known for spiffiness.

"Welcome to show business, Albert," Mandy reassured him with a confident smile. "Just don't worry yourself. We'll fall off that bridge when we get to it. That's why we have post-production. We can always go back and add stuff later. Believe me, no one will ever know."

***

Here's how Einstein's first nutty contest worked.

There were four tribes of ten girls each. Five girls from each tribe ran to the top of the Empire State Building, grabbed a colored flag, and jumped off. While descending, they were challenged to come up with a cheerfully optimistic word or phrase to utter as they plunged past the second floor. The only requirement was they had to smile when they said it. Opposing tribe members judged the optimistic word or phrase. Each winner received a special one-time only bonus impunity. She would put this into play if her team came last in the Impunity Challenge and she had to go to Tribal Conclave to vote somebody off the island.

Below, holding a beach towel, were four other members of the tribe. As each virgin landed on the towel, she handed her flag to one of the other girls then took her place, the last girl down handing her flag to the first leaper. The former towel holders then braved a mud pit swarming with saltwater crocodiles. After which, they swam through the surf with their flags to a forty-five feet high platform measuring just eight inches across.

Of course, the crocodiles were actually still on other side of the island. Even Barry wasn't up to persuading them to move. What Jesus One did was tape the mud pit segment later on Crocodile Beach. Then he patched it in afterwards. You couldn't tell the difference. In fact, the way it was done you could have sworn the Empire State Building was sitting right there next to the crocodiles.

Rounding up crocodiles for the mud pit was Barry's job.

To continue:

Before jumping off the Empire State Building—and this is why there were only four girls holding the towels—one member from each tribe was chosen by an opposing tribe to go to Outcast Island (since there wasn't an island anywhere close by, Jesus One and the Khan faked this segment by taping it on a nearby beach). Once there, each virgin was paired with a sturdy young islander wearing next to nothing. The idea was they had to search for forty-six hidden Impunity Idols, only one of which was genuine. The Khan had artfully concealed cameras near each hidden idol to capture the magic moment. An added incentive was that the couples got to fondle on camera whenever they found an idol. Actual sex, while not exactly frowned upon, might result in instant banishment for the offending virgin by a specially convened panel of her peers.

Boy, was that a cliffhanger, or what!

You should also know that when the girls returned from Outcast Island they also qualified for the one time bonus impunity. Not to mention, if a virgin actually found the genuine Impunity Idol, she could use it to defend herself in upcoming Tribal Conclaves and qualify for a get-out-of-jail-free card for any and all episodes of spontaneous sex.

Meanwhile, back at the contest:

When all five girls made it to the top of the platform, without falling off, they waved their flags. This was the signal for the virgins left holding the beach towels. The towels, you see, when spread out, were cleverly patterned as a template for interlocking chunks of Styrofoam painted red and blue. If assembled correctly, the pieces made a face that was the spitting image of Barry.

So, where does the pizza come in? Well, that's the easy part. The first team to assemble Barry's face would be ferried somewhere spiffy for pizza. The last team to finish was stuck with Tribal Conclave and voting.

Einstein wanted Tribal Conclave to be in a cavern at the summit of the old volcano so there would be a nice view. Since the old volcano had no cavern, the contractors obligingly blasted one out. The cavern was fitted with candleholders, a torch snuffer, a bunch of flat boulders to sit on, and a very large earthenware pot for counting votes. A major snag was that to get there involved a full day climb through steaming jungle, followed by three hours of clambering up rocky slopes. The girls were horrified, especially Ashley, who had already broken one fingernail getting to the top of her platform.

The Vanahu Volunteer Defense Force (*VVDF*) saved the day. For a four million dollar contribution to the mess fund, they offered up their fleet of donated US Army helicopters, plus the entire battalion as helpers. All Jesus One and the Khan had to do was tape the girls departing gloomily for Tribal Conclave and arriving triumphantly at the summit. In between, everybody enjoyed the helicopter rides and the nice view.

By the way, the cavern also had an antechamber stocked with enough booze, water, and supplies to feed the entire *VVDF* for two months (not to mention a dartboard). This was in case the weather turned bad and the troops were stuck up there for days on end with various virgins and nothing to do.

Einstein had thought of everything.

Well, almost everything, since there was still the problem of a spiffy place to enjoy pizza. Oh, yes, and there was that first challenge of coming up with something cheerfully optimistic to say while plunging past a second story window. We won't go into all of the utterances since they mostly involved ballroom dancing or riding naked on the beach. Destiny was the one who really nailed it—most likely because she had written down her phrase and was thus able to read and rehearse it on the way down.

"So far so good, so far so good ..." she repeated seven times, remembering to smile cheerfully as she plunged past each window.

Mandy was over the moon, despite the fact that Destiny missed the blanket and only had the use of her left leg for the remainder of the contest.

***

Appropriately enough, it was Giovanni Garibaldi who unwittingly solved the pizza problem.

As they were hosing down the crocodiles after the mud pit segment, Garibaldi showed up in his Ferretti. On the way in, *Foxy Lady III* inadvertently veered off course and sideswiped the *Mary Rose,* taking out her rudder and half the stern. Garibaldi, who was gleefully observing from the bridge, was crestfallen when he realized no one was aboard.

"Uh, oh!" Alfredo muttered when he saw the yacht. He hastily turned off the hose and shooed away the last of the crocodiles. "Now we're in trouble."

Mandy, on the other hand, was jubilant. "That's it!" she exclaimed, turning excitedly to Einstein. "Didn't I tell you it would work out? The yacht will be a perfect location. George and Alfredo can welcome the girls aboard wearing next to nothing then serve them pizza and pitchers of Michelob. Not only that, we can get the contractors to over polish everything and put in a bunch of white leather settees."

Meanwhile, Garibaldi was observing the activity on Crocodile Beach through binoculars. His first reaction had been to blow his top. He was feeling vengeful to begin with, and it hadn't helped a bit when Frank and Marge failed to emerge when he sideswiped the *Mary Rose*. Seeing his beach occupied by interlopers put the cap on it. Then he spotted the girls. There they were: forty luscious virgins, some smeared promisingly with mud, and all of them presumably filled with desire. Best of all, to a man—so to speak—they were wearing next to nothing.

The Italian's anger evaporated instantly.

He turned to his captain. "Getta me my launch, anna you can also tella my foxy lady issa all right now to have thissa headache."

As motivated as he was, Garibaldi didn't move fast enough. By the time he had changed from his commodore whites into something a little more virgin-appropriate, Mandy and Einstein were already half way to the yacht, with Alfredo at the helm. To tell the truth, Mandy wasn't all that happy. She had been bunking in the aft cabin of the *Mary Rose* during Frank and Marge's absence, so she wasn't too pleased, to say the least, when a goodly part of her living quarters went down with the rudder.

Garibaldi was soon to be dog meat.

Of course, he was not immediately aware. In fact, his delight at spotting the virgins was almost surpassed by his awe at meeting Mandy Miller in person. When Alfredo brought the Virgin Beach tender skillfully to rest at the hydraulic swim platform, the Italian was there to greet them. To say he was effusive would be the understatement of the century.

"I have seena you coming, and I must say I amma so very, how you say, so honored that this mosta famous Mandy Miller issa visiting Giovanni Garibaldi. I will make-a you so very welcome to thissa humble little boat of-a mine." Then he frowned. "But when I wassa last reading thissa *Star* magazine, whicha you understand actually-a belongs-a to my foxy lady, I havva read you was inna Latvia?"

Mandy gave him Dick Derringer's bodysnatcher look. "Mister Garibaldi," she said, "it's a long story, and I will be happy to explain later. Right now, I have a bone to pick with you. I do believe you have just ruined four of my best frocks. That back cabin you redesigned happens to be where I was staying." She tossed her gleaming blonde tresses and flashed her impossibly white teeth in a dazzling smile. "However, you have such a fine reputation for kindness and generosity, I'm sure we can work something out."

Giovanni was done for.

Mandy introduced her companions. "I'd like you to meet my senior executive producer, Doctor Albert Einstein, and this is my personal assistant, Alfredo, whose mother, I believe, is an old acquaintance of yours."

Einstein bowed graciously, while Alfredo stuck out his hand.

A momentary look of panic flickered over the Italian's face, and then it was gone—as though it had never been. He shook Alfredo's hand vigorously. "I amma so sorry I did not talk to you atta the party. I havva not seen you since you havva been a *bambino*. *Mamma Mia*, how you havva grown! And how issa you mamma, and also my old-a friend Barry?"

Alfredo grinned mischievously. "Well, after you left, my mum had to go back to waiting tables in Brisbane, and Barry is pissed off at you over Shovel World. Other than that, they're doing just fine."

Meanwhile, Einstein, as usual, was scrutinizing anatomical features. He turned to Mandy, looking puzzled. "*Gevalt!* For how can this be so? If you are to seeing closely, you can be sure these two noses are for looking exactly the same."

Being Einstein, of course, he failed to communicate this delicate observation discreetly, i.e. he didn't whisper. All at once, Garibaldi bounded up the steps to the cockpit. Alfredo, on the other hand, thoughtfully fingered the tip of his nose.

Giovanni, it seemed, was double done for.

When Mandy reached the cockpit and saw the yacht's interior, she squealed with delight. She turned gleefully to Einstein. "It's perfect, Albert. It's like it was meant to be. I mean, the yacht showing up at just the right time, and we don't even have to worry about the settees and the over polishing."

Einstein nodded enthusiastically and reached for his pipe. "Yes, yes, *maideleh,* and I also can see this Balvenie he is for having at the bar."

Garibaldi was already bearing down on them with his steward in tow. There was an air of what can only be described as eager anxiety about him. He beckoned to Mandy. "Please, you must-a sitta down onna this white leather settee I havva special made by the Gucci. Anna my steward, he will getta whatever you wanna to drink." He pointedly ignored Alfredo, who by this time was lounging happily in a white leather armchair and ostentatiously helping himself to a super robusto cigar.

The steward smiled gratefully when Einstein asked him to just fetch the bottle of Balvenie and a glass—no ice. "For why cannot I to helping myself?" the world's most famous scientist asked, with the trademark twinkle in his eyes. "Is it that Einstein is now too feeble to pour a good whiskey? And for such a shame it is to always spoil the taste by the putting in of the ice."

It was a slam-dunk.

Not only did the Italian willingly volunteer his yacht as the spiffy location, he also organized the catering. Mind you, after that, he did seem uncommonly anxious to leave, not to mention avoiding Alfredo like the plague.

"Issa most unfortunate," he explained, "but I musta go now for the grand openings of-a the new Shovel Houses I havva just built inna Yellowstone Park."

This was just as well, because when Frank and Marge got back from Vanahu, Frank was understandably fit to be tied. He spotted the damage as they came in on the mail boat. "Don't get mad, Frank," Marge cautioned. "Remember what you always say: 'if man built it, man can break it, and man can fix it.'"

"Yeah, sure," Frank muttered angrily, "but this man didn't break it, did he? We both know who did this, Marge. As soon as you and Hilda get settled, I swear, I'll track the bastard down and take him out once and for all."

"Now, now," Marge said soothingly, with one of her fonder smiles, "just calm down, and be positive. Right now, what you need to do is find some way of patching up the aft cabin and rebuilding your rudder. You can worry about Mister Garibaldi later."

Thank heaven Barry hadn't followed through on his threat to conflagrate that first load of fiberglass matting.

CHAPTER 40

Fatal Attraction

When Roy Upstart got involved with Agnes McDrab, he was headed for more trouble than he could possibly imagine. As these things usually do, it all started out innocently enough. There was that first meeting at a Chamber of Commerce luncheon where Agnes was the featured speaker. Then there were those chance encounters in the elevator lobby. Right then and there Roy should have thought to enquire how come she visited the Sea-Tac Tower so often—*his* tower, no less—but he never did, poor fool.

Until he met Agnes, Roy had been utterly faithful to his wife of twenty-seven years, the former Janice Grapnel; he had never even contemplated another woman, let alone dabbled. He had not imbibed even the smallest tipple, and he had never sucked on anything more potent than a Dairy Queen Buster Bar.

Agnes McDrab, on the other hand, was a she-devil driven by a compulsion to seduce powerful men. Of course, given her credentials, she had long ago self-diagnosed her problem—except that she didn't see it as a problem, she saw it as a crusade. The thing was, from childhood, Agnes had hated the first Lord Drab. Was it rooted in long festering guilt over what he had done to William Wallace? Was it because he was a man and thus could not only get away with being an absolute bastard, and be rewarded to boot? Was it because she was more than a little envious of the first Lady Drab? Agnes didn't much care.

Whenever she wrecked a marriage, she saw it as just revenge on her detested ancestor, not to mention all the other absolute bastards in line—including Dad.

Good golly, did she have issues!

Poor Roy didn't stand a chance.

It didn't take long before Agnes was suggesting lunch. Then there was the accidental brushing of hands and the occasional leg touch, and before he knew it, Roy Upstart couldn't get Agnes McDrab out of his mind and he was more or less done for, which is about where he was when she took care of Muriel Banks.

Of course, Jesús knew nothing of this. In any case, when he arrived in Seattle, he had other things on his mind—not the least of which was the intriguing question of exactly how he might seize control of the seventeenth busiest air traffic control tower in the nation (Einstein had conveniently left out that part). His intention had been to figure this out on the flight back, but what with Nagpal threatening to blow himself up and Norma freaking out, he was pretty much in a drunken stupor by the time the plane landed.

It should also be pointed out that Norma and Nagpal had fallen for each other. To speed her recovery, Norma decided a couple of White Zinfandels might be in order. After the fourth one she began to see Nagpal in a new light. Soon thereafter, the lovebirds were cooing like contented little wood pigeons in 2A and 2B. Nagpal took off his turban and seemed to lose all further interest in virgins—apart from Norma, that is. She even invited herself and Nagpal to stay over at Chez Martinez until they found something more permanent. She wanted them to be together while she turned Nagpal's life around.

Jesús just didn't get it—not to mention he ended up sleeping on the futon.

***

After everything he had been through, seeing Dennis Floyd was a welcome relief. Despite the all too familiar signs of jet lag, Jesús got to the tower a good half hour early. Sure enough, Teeth had beaten him to it. He was sitting in his favorite fireside Chesterfield with a mug of double cream mint latte and a back issue of *Global World News*. As Jesús came through the door, Dennis voiced an enthusiastic welcome. The only teeth not sticking out of his mouth were his molars.

"Hey, Fly Boy, you're back, you miserable son-of-a-bitch. Where in hell have you been, man? I must have called a half-dozen times and all I got was the recording."

Jesús pointed to his ears and frowned.

"Piss off," Dennis said, setting down his mug and getting to his feet. "Anyway, what are you drinking?"

"I'll have what you're having," Jesús said gratefully, taking possession of the opposing Chesterfield.

When they were settled, Jesús wasn't sure how to proceed. One thing, though, was abundantly clear: to seize control of the tower he needed a co-conspirator, and Teeth happened to be the obvious, if not the only choice. Unfortunately, all he knew about Dennis Floyd was he had amazing teeth and he cursed a lot—which was nowhere near enough. Not to mention, as far as he could tell, Dennis was no longer a disgruntled employee, so he could hardly be described as ripe for subversion.

So, where to begin?

Dennis made it easy for him. "Just as well for you I don't have a home life, you dead leg. I've been covering your ass for fifteen days straight, buddy. So, get ready to pick up the slack. I'm pulling three days off. First thing tomorrow, I'm headed for Vegas and the three Bs: booze, broads, and blackjack. Now, you didn't answer my question. Where the fuck, have you been?"

"I signed up for a twelve-day snowboarding package in Chile," Jesús lied with practiced ease. "I figured it was the best thing for me, seeing-as-how you get to wear earmuffs a lot. The doc said to keep my ears covered until the ringing stopped."

Dennis leaned forward, looking genuinely curious.

"How come they got snow down there this time of year? It's August, for Christ's sake."

"Chile's half way to the South Pole, Teeth. Also, it has a bunch of big-ass mountain ranges. Of course, you get snow. Anyway, what's this about throwing all your frigging money away in Vegas? Don't you have family to feed?"

"Nah, I tried that once. I married this German bitch when I was in the service. Turned out all she wanted was Frau Floyd on her fucking passport. Then it was *auf Wiedersehen,* Dennis."

Jesús mentally ticked off: 'no immediate family,' 'previous military experience,' 'soon to be short of cash,' 'enjoys card games' and 'likes virgins' on his designated accomplice checklist. Things were definitely looking up.

"Gee, Dennis," he said with all the sympathy he could muster, "I had no idea. Anyway, what the heck were you doing in Germany?"

"Military fucking Police, stationed just outside Wiesbaden. When I signed up, I thought I was going to be this super-fucking-cop with stripes. All I got was traffic duty for four goddamn years." Dennis sipped angrily at his latte. "Bastards!" he muttered.

Jesús promptly checked 'resents authority' and 'can give and take direction.' Just to be sure, though, he decided to take another stab at 'resents authority'; this being the thing you would like to see most in a designated accomplice. He nodded sympathetically. "Yeah, I can well imagine. So how's Upstart been treating you? I guess when Muriel left he lost his snitch."

Dennis frowned suspiciously. "Don't look at me, man. All I got from that bastard was four hundred dollars, a brass plaque, and kiss-my-ass. I took the money and ditched the fucking plaque."

Jesús underlined 'resents authority' with an inward sigh of relief. It was time to make his move. "Dennis," he said, "we need to talk."

Of course, he didn't explain everything. In fact, he hardly explained anything at all. To put it another way: he lied. What he said was, "You're not going to believe this, but I have it on good authority the world's about to end. Bill Gates is the one who told me. He's got inside information even the Government isn't privy to. He recruited me because underneath this tower is a secret government shelter designed for the president. Bill wants in before the shit hits the fan. I want you to help me seize control of the tower when the time comes."

Dennis calmly took another sip of his latte and smiled admiringly. "Man, *you* are good. You are very, very good." He set down the latte with exaggerated care. "Okay, so you got me with the tone in your ears, and I don't know how, but you sure as hell fixed Muriel's wagon. Just don't push your luck, Martinez. You try that Section 8 bullshit with me, and I'll have your ass in a sling faster than the speed of fucking light."

Jesus checked his watch. "Look," he said, "we still have twenty minutes before we clock in. I can prove it to you. Bill gave me unlimited funds and my own 767 so I could jet around to sort things out. The plane is parked in one of the private hangars. I'm not screwing with you, Dennis. Just give me fifteen minutes of your time. That's all I ask."

On the way out, he pointed out the double doors. The 767 clinched it. Dennis, to put it mildly, was gobsmacked. "Dennis," said Jesús, "this is Chuck Anderson, flight operations manager for Way-Out-West-Aviation. He looks after my aviation needs. Chuck, this is Dennis Floyd, one of my closest associates."

"Nice to meet you, Mister Floyd," said Chuck with a warm smile. "So, Mister Martinez, what can I do for you today?"

"Well, Dennis has some business coming up in Vegas. I'd like you to file a flight plan and take care of him. We don't want anything special, just the standard chief executive package. Oh, yes, and I'd like him to see the plane if it's not too much trouble."

"That's what we're here for, sir," said Chuck, reaching for his jacket. "She's already been cleaned and refueled, and I'll make sure Mister Floyd gets menu choices before his departure."

In addition to being gobsmacked, and for the first time in his life, Dennis Floyd was speechless.

After that, it was a cakewalk.

Jesus had barely time enough to walk Dennis back to the break room, fix fresh lattes, and set him straight. "Look," he whispered, leaning close, since the room was now filling up with the rest of the shift, "why don't you think it over for a couple of hours? I honestly can't give you any more time than that, because we need to move out on this right away. Bill says Yellowstone National Park is going to erupt sometime before Christmas and, when it does, it will be the end of all life as we know it. What we'll have to do is fix it so you and I have third shift just before they officially announce the eruption, which will probably be mid to late September. Then we stock the tower with supplies, let Bill in, and keep everybody out when they show up for work."

Dennis shook his head in amazement, struggling to get his voice back. "So that's it? That's you're plan?" he whispered urgently. "Listen up, bird brain, you'll have half of Fort Bragg blowing the doors off before you've even had time to break fucking wind."

Jesus shrugged. "Yes, well, actually, I haven't figured all the details yet, so I'm really in the market for ideas."

Dennis sighed mightily and reached for a napkin. He snatched a pen from his breast pocket and scribbled furiously. When he was done, he glanced around, then handed the folded napkin to Jesús. "Just so you know what you've got yourself into," he whispered, "this is the least of what you'll need. Now I'm no merchant of fucking death, so how you get your hands on all this crap is your problem; you're the one with the college degree and the money."

Jesús covertly unfolded the napkin and gasped. Dennis had come up with a surprisingly good sketch of the tower and the base building. Sitting on top of the control cab were two pods with gun barrels poking out, labeled *Air Defense System*. Between the pods, was a stick figure with what looked like a bazooka on his shoulder and the legend *Manpads*. On the roof of the base building, Dennis had put in what looked like two batteries of surface-to-air missiles. Around the roof perimeter were searchlights alternating with Gatling type machine guns. A matrix of black dots surrounding the tower was labeled: *Minefield—but what kind—anti-personnel or anti-tank, or both?*

"Oh," said Jesús, sarcastically, "is *that* all? By the way, what does *Manpads* stand for?"

Dennis checked his watch. "You got two minutes, then the FAA owns your ass. *Manpads* stands for Man Portable Air Defense System—a shoulder fired Stinger missile to you. When I was in uniform, you could buy one on every fucking street corner in Wiesbaden."

"But where am I supposed to get all this other stuff?" Jesús complained. "Anyway, what's Upstart going to say when I show up with a truckload of Gatling guns? Not to mention two batteries of missiles on his roof and a frigging minefield in his parking lot."

"How the hell should I know?" grunted Dennis, getting to his feet. "As I said, that's your problem. For starters, you might try calling one of those so-called security contractors the government uses all the time. You show up with twenty million bucks in a suitcase, they'll overthrow a small fucking country, no questions asked."

"Mmm," Jesús said. "Maybe you're onto something."

He finished his latte and joined Dennis heading for the door. "Er, Dennis, would you mind ever so much if I borrow your phone book so I can make some calls when things get slow?"

"Piss off," Dennis said.

CHAPTER 41

Some Nice Ideas

At least Dennis didn't assign him the busy seat. The newly delivered replacement chair was wide enough for three of him, but he didn't mind a bit. He gazed at the display as if he were greeting a long-lost love. The simple act of sitting at a computer screen was all it took to erase the past and abolish the future. Nothing was left but tiny bite-sized morsels of the present.

He liked that.

But he couldn't avoid sneaking glances out the window. Late July was prime time in Seattle. The sun had quickly burned off a light sea fog. Now, everything was etched in sharp detail. He could see beyond Puget Sound and Vancouver Island. He could almost make out every tree on the lower slopes of Mount Rainier. The snow-covered *massif* shimmered in bright, white light.

Enjoying the scenery was one thing. He just didn't want to imagine what three or four feet of volcanic ash would do to it. The trouble was once he looked out the window his mind wouldn't let go. When he closed his eyes, he saw scattered burial mounds where vehicles used to be, billowing black avalanches on the mountain, viscous gray scum covering Puget Sound, collapsed buildings, a constant black drizzle, no sun, no sound, no life.

Jesús shivered and looked around the control room. Everything looked and sounded the same, so he should have felt reassured, but he didn't. Familiar people doing familiar things, he now realized, were no longer real and no longer reachable. He might just as well have been watching ancient reruns of "Everybody Loves Raymond," except Raymond had been a heck of a lot funnier.

After two hours of scaring himself silly, Jesús was more than ready for his fifteen-minute break. He pulled a task chair up to the break room's one and only computer, logged out of Doyle's Room, and found an online yellow pages site. Dennis followed him two minutes later and made a beeline for the coffee pot.

It didn't take long to generate a short list of contractors with branch offices in Seattle. The only name he recognized was Crony Corporation—well known for sucking the defense budget drier than a witch's tit—so he decided to start there. He holed in one. The administrative professional answering the phone hooked him up right away. "Yes, sir," she said, "absolutely we can help. For secretly defending large buildings, you need to talk with Ron Childrish. Mister Childrish is director of business development for confidential critical structure consulting and contracting. I'll connect you.

The man picked up the phone on the second ring.

"Crony Corporation, Childrish here," he said in a brisk, no nonsense, voice.

"Er, Mister Childrish, my name is Martinez, Jesús Martinez. I, er, I'm with the FAA here in Seattle. We have just received cash-on-the-barrelhead funding from a wealthy benefactor who wishes to remain anonymous. He's very public spirited, so I can assure you our project is very much in the national interest. The project is endorsed by the government and is very hush-hush since it involves setting up a perimeter defense for a control tower. So we want to buy the right kind military hardware. Naturally, this will be a top secret program."

"Crony can handle that, sir. Are you talking *COTS* or purpose-built?"

"I'm sorry, what does *COTS* mean? I'm sort of new to this."

"That would be Commercial Off-The-Shelf. It's what we recommend. It's cheaper; it's available; and we can put it all together for you. We can even provide people to pull the trigger—you know, shooters, if that's what you need."

"Oh, I see," said Jesús, growing more confident by the minute. "That sounds about right, only we don't have much time, you see."

"What exactly do you have in mind, sir?"

"Um, well, I mean, that's why I'm talking to you, isn't it?"

"Yes, sir, I perfectly understand, but I'll need some idea, just so I can be sure we'll be a good fit. If you can send me the *RFP* I can have one of our *SMEs* take a look at it."

"I'm sorry, but what exactly are an *RFP* and a *SME*?"

"A Request For Proposal and a Subject Matter Expert."

"Oh, er, well, I actually don't have anything in writing, but it's pretty simple really. Our benefactor is concerned about possible terrorist attacks. Not that we aren't, but we haven't had much money lately. We were thinking of a few surface-to-air missiles, a minefield, and a couple of air defense guns on the roof. Naturally, if this project works out, we'll want to go nationwide."

There was a short pause. Jesús had the distinct impression Ron Childrish was frantically doing sums and drooling. When he came back on the line, Childrish was his very latest, very nicest, and very bestest friend. "Mister Martinez, or may I call you Jesús?"

"Jesús would be just fine, Ron. So, what do you think?"

"First off, Jesús, I can't tell you how excited I am to hear about your idea, and how proud I am you thought of Crony. It's high time we did more to safeguard the nation's civil aviation assets. You do understand, though, we will need to draft an *MOU*, and seeing as how this *is* the FAA, we would definitely want some serious earnest money—just so we know you really mean it this time."

"Sure," said Jesús, amazed this was turning out to be so easy. "I can understand you not wanting to spin your wheels, Ron. If it would make you happy, I could arrange for a hefty deposit then we could settle-up later. What's an *MOU*, by the way?"

"Oh, that would be a Memorandum Of Understanding, outlining the project and making it clear everything would be sole-sourced to Crony. Also we'd want you to sign an *NDA*—that's a Non Disclosure Agreement." Childrish chuckled. "We wouldn't want you opening your raincoat and showing all we've got to the competition, now would we?"

"No problem. I sign *NDAs* all the time."

"That's it then," said Childrish cheerfully. "I'm already getting some nice ideas for you. Right now, I can put my hands on some surplus *NASAMS* you might like. The White House is looking for a little extra protection, so they're swapping out what Dick Cheney put in twenty years ago—only one careful owner and never been used. Ha ha, just my little joke."

"What's a *NASAMS?*" Jesús asked, starting to feel a tad overwhelmed.

"Norwegian Advanced Surface to Air Missile System—still the best there is if you ask me. These babies have *AIM-120 AMRAAMs* with *TPQ-36A* radars and a Norwegian built *BMC41* fire distribution center for *ARCS*. You can say what you like about Cheney, but he sure as hell knew a top notch weapons system when he saw one."

"Sounds great," said Jesús as decisively as he could. "*BMC41* fire distribution, eh? That would definitely be the way to go, especially for the *ARCS*. Anyway, if you can give me some idea of what we're looking at price wise, I'll be happy to have you over so we can get started."

"You do realize all I can do for you right now is a *ROM*."

"Sure, I understand, but if I'm going to bring cash to the table I'd like some idea of how much to put in the suitcase. By the way, what's a *ROM*?"

At the mention of the suitcase, Childrish was suddenly cheerful again. "Oh, that stands for Rough Order of Magnitude. From what you've told me, I would think thirty or forty million should get us started." There was a meaningful pause then he innocently changed tack. "Of course, it would really help if I knew exactly which facility you were talking about."

Jesús realized it was time to counter-attack before Ron was all over him. "I'll tell you what: we'll waive the *RFP*. Just tell your *SME* what I told you. That way he can get started. Then email me the *MOU* along with the *NDA* and the *ROM*. You can reach me at *fly.boy@faa.gov*."

"Excuse me," interrupted Childrish, "but that's a bit of an odd email address for the FAA isn't it? I thought you government guys had to use real names."

"Nah!" said Jesus, "As long as you put the little dot in the middle, the system lets just about anything through. I used *get.laid@faa.gov* for almost two years before anybody caught on. All I got was a reprimand."

"Oh," said Childrish, sounding perplexed.

"Anyway, Ron, as soon as I receive your package, I'll put my people right on it. Then, when we're all signed off, I'll be more than happy to open my raincoat and tell you everything—*NDAs* cut both ways, don't you know. Of course, I'll need everything by *COB*."

"Er, I'm sorry," said Childrish, sounding distinctly less cheerful, "but what's a *COB*?"

"Close Of Business. I'm very surprised you didn't know that, Ron. By the way, be sure you stand by 24/7 on this. I'll want to kick things off on the double."

"Yes, sir!" said Childrish, chomping at the bit.

Jesús had a vision of Ron mentally donning his old uniform (whatever that was) and saluting. He moved in for the kill. "And, Ron—no ifs, ands, or buts—when I give you the green light, I'll tell you where and when and I'll want your whole team to show up."

Jesús put the phone down, feeling immensely pleased with himself. He gleefully waved Dennis over. "You won't believe this," he gloated. "I just got off the phone with this guy from Crony Corp. He was okay with not getting an *RFP* and he's sending me an *MOU*, an *NDA,* and a *ROM*, as we speak. Also, he's already got an *SME* working out the details."

"What kind of fucking pie-eyed gobbledygook are you talking now?" Dennis growled. "Listen, dork brain, before you drown yourself in alphabet fucking soup, you need to get real. There's no way you can pull this off without Upstart. The first thing these Crony bastards are going to want is a face-to-face with the big cheese around here, and that sure as hell isn't you, pal. Also, Roy Upstart isn't the sharpest tool in the fucking shed, but you start planting claymores under his Lexus, I guarantee he'll be on you like white on fucking rice."

Jesús drooped his head and groaned. "Don't think I don't know that. I was only trying to get things moving," he muttered. "You just burst my frigging bubble, Dennis. Thanks a lot!"

When he looked up Teeth was living up to his nickname. "What the hell are *you* grinning at?"

"Hey, I was just pushing your buttons, you moron. You can leave Upstart to your Uncle Dennis. Boy, have I been waiting for this day to come!"

"What … what?" Jesús repeated. Not only did he sound like a moron, he was beginning to feel like one.

Dennis glanced around and lowered his voice, even though they were the only two on break. "You remember that Scottish shrink—the one that shit-canned Muriel as a lunatic—built like a seven-ton truck, face like a madman's ass?"

"Sure I remember: Agnes McDrab was her name. I was there when it happened, but in all fairness to Muriel, McDrab didn't certify her as a lunatic; they just had a wee chat."

"Yeah, well I have it on good authority, that Agnes has been having a little bit more than a wee chat with our friend, Roy."

"No! Get out! Not Roy Upstart! I've never seen a more devoted couple than he and his wife. I was paired with Janice at last September's Sea-Tac Salmon Sushi Supper and Logroll Fest. They were so busy ogling each other, she fell between the logs in the rusty ankle event, and we got disqualified."

"Be that as it may, laddie; that was then, and this—as they say— is fucking now."

"Who told you?"

"Shirley. She sits outside his office like a fucking temple dog. If Roy so much as thinks of taking a crap, Shirley knows ten minutes before his bowels wake up."

"So, tell me, what's with you and Shirley?"

"Mind your own business. We're talking about Roy. Just keep your eye on the goddamn ball for once, will you?"

"Okay, so what's next? Don't tell me you're planning to blackmail the poor bastard."

"You got a better idea?"

"No."

"Right, so hear this. After you get the paperwork from Crony, we'll take it downstairs and persuade Roy to sign off. Then we invite him to chair the kick-off meeting and tell him to keep his mouth shut. If anybody asks awkward questions, you just look em in the eye and lie through your fucking teeth." Dennis grinned like a fiend. "That's what you do best, isn't it, college boy—lie through your teeth?"

Jesús shrugged modestly. "Well, I wouldn't go that far, Dennis. Still, I have been known to come up with a decent fib once in a while."

Dennis was already picking up the phone.

"What are you doing?" Jesús asked nervously.

"What do you think? I'm phoning Shirley to check Upstart's calendar, you numb nut."

"Can't we wait until I get the paperwork from Crony?"

"As we speak is what you said. To my way of thinking, that means right now. The computer is over there, genius. Go check it."

Jesús fumbled hastily for the mouse. Somewhere deep in his lower intestine sharp teeth nibbled ravenously. All at once, recruiting Dennis didn't seem like such a good idea. In less than three hours, Dennis Floyd had risen from mere accomplice to maniac in charge. Jesús had a sudden urge to curl up and suck his thumb like Norma. "Dennis," he ventured, "shouldn't we sort of cool off a little before we take this any further? I mean, once we talk to Upstart, there'll be no turning back."

Dennis motioned him to be quiet and jabbed a finger impatiently at the computer. "Hey, Shirley, it's me, Dennis. How are you, sugar pie?" There was a brief pause. "Great! Way to go. Anyway, Mister Martinez, and I would like a little quality time with your boss sometime today. Twenty minutes should do it." He stopped to listen, and chuckled to himself. "You want a subject? Oh, let's say building improvements. We have a couple of things we need to discuss right away." He nodded. "Sure, three fifteen this afternoon would be great. We'll be coming off shift at three. See you soon, Shirley, girly."

Jesús gulped.

Dennis grinned like a fiend.

CHAPTER 42

Plausible Denial

The thing with blackmail is you can't beat around the bush: the subject should know exactly what you want, when you want it, and what he or she can expect in return; otherwise it gets murky. Mind you, that doesn't rule out toying with them first. Jesús had to admit Dennis Floyd didn't exactly play Roy Upstart like a Stradivarius, but he was definitely no slouch when it came to intimidation.

"Yes, gentlemen," said Upstart, with a carefully mannered smile, "now, what I can do for you today?" He glanced at his watch. "By the way, I have senior staff at quarter of four, so I don't have much time to beat around the bush. Whatever it is just lay it on the line and we'll move out."

"Great," said Jesús, placing the *MOU,* the *NDA,* and the *ROM* on Upstart's desk. "We have a couple of papers here we'd like you to sign then we'll be on our way."

Upstart made no move for the documents; he didn't even look at them. Instead, he tilted his chair back and tented his hands. The smile disappeared. "I never sign anything I didn't initiate myself, unless it's been on my desk for at least a month and it's been through legal. Shirley should have explained that."

"Jeez, Mister Upstart," Dennis replied with a carefully mannered smile of his own, "I'm sorry as hell. I guess we didn't know. Problem is, this can't wait, see, and we didn't have time to give Shirley a heads up neither."

Upstart shrugged and bored a hole in Teeth's forehead. "I'm sorry too. Just leave them with Shirley and I promise I'll get back to you."

"Er, excuse me, sir," mumbled Jesús, "but Dennis is right. We need to move out on this right away. It is sort of urgent."

Upstart leaned forward, put his elbows squarely on the desk, and bored another hole. Jesús felt it right between the eyes. "Is there something about what I just said you failed to grasp, Mister Martinez?" Upstart's lips seemed to have disappeared.

"Er, no."

"Good, then please leave. Take your documents with you and don't forget to close the door on your way out."

Dennis scooted his chair closer to the desk and leaned forward confidentially. "Tell you what, Roy. You don't mind me calling you Roy, do you?"

Upstart leaned back a little, but he didn't shift his elbows. Everything went quiet while he bored several more holes in Teeth's forehead.

"The fact of the matter is," Dennis continued, apparently unfazed by the holes in his head, "you really need to take care of this now, before somebody sticks another bug up your ass."

The northwest regional administrator cradled his chin in his hands and stared at Dennis impassively. His face could have been a death mask without the makeup. For the first time, Jesús noticed Upstart's eyes were devoid of life. They were flat, hard, and dull, like roofing slate. They reflected nothing.

"Out," Upstart murmured, "right now."

Jesús almost obeyed.

"Fuck you," said Dennis, revealing the full set in all of its magnificence.

Upstart reached for his phone.

Jesus had a sudden urge to say, "That willna be necessary, Roy," but Dennis beat him to it.

"Bad move, Roy," Dennis cautioned. "Janice and Agnes might not thank you for it."

You don't get to be an FAA regional administrator without being relatively quick on the uptake. Upstart went back to tenting his hands. "What do you want?"

Dennis didn't answer right away. He got to his feet and walked over to the window. After scanning the parking lot, he turned with his arms folded. "We already told you. We want you to sign the fucking papers.

Oh, yeah, and I'm flying to Vegas for a couple of days. When I get back we'll be having a kick-off meeting; your kick-off in your office."

Upstart reached for the three documents. He looked up with a frown after reading the *MOU*. "You know, we talked about doing something like this a few years back when I was in D.C. We even got as far as putting out an *RFP*, but it wasn't this ambitious and we never really had any money. Why hasn't the director said anything to me about it? Anyway, if you don't mind my asking, how come you two are involved?"

Dennis raised his hand. "Whoa there, Trigger. Read on."

Upstart whistled when he saw the *ROM*. "Eighty-eight million and fifty million just to get started? That's highway robbery." He glanced at Jesús with a smirk. "You do realize they'll at least triple that by the time they're through with you."

"We don't care. It's not our money. Our benefactor said cost is no object."

"What benefactor?"

"Tell him, Jesús," prompted Dennis.

Jesús gave Upstart the same basic story he had given Ron Childrish. Naturally, he couldn't resist a little embellishment. "Also," he went on, "the benefactor doesn't want this leaked upstairs. He's afraid if the brass gets wind of it, they'll talk it to death. He wants the whole thing in place by the end of August. Then he'll reveal all and indemnify you of all responsibility. That's one reason we're coercing you, so if this backfires—so to speak—you can say you were forced to do it, sort of plausible denial, if you will."

Jesús paused to admire his handiwork. Upstart was definitely paying close attention now. Jesús went for the *coup de grace*. "Mind you, he's prepared to fund a whole bunch more projects like this if the first one works out, so there's every chance the FAA will be on the lookout for a new director before long, if you see what I mean."

Upstart reached for his pen. Apart from a slight tick at the corner of his left eye, he seemed surprisingly composed. Then he hesitated, pen poised. "Speaking of the director, what if he shows up while all of this is going on?"

"Old Chinese proverb, Roy," Dennis said conversationally, "'The emperor is far away and the fucking mountains are high between us.' Think about it: when was the last time that asshole showed up here? Anyway, stall him if you have to. Isn't that what you bastards do all the time—stall everything you can get your fucking hands on?"

"Also," Jesús added, "you can have senior staff sign *NDAs* so they don't go blabbing to headquarters. You know, make them feel important, like they're actually involved in something for a change."

Upstart shook his head and sighed. "Where do I sign?"

"Right there, over where I've typed FAA Northwest Regional Administrator."

Upstart signed and calmly handed back the papers. "Don't forget to close the door on you're way out," he said. Other than the tick, his eyes continued to show no signs of life.

Jesús made a mental note never to play poker with Roy Upstart unless Dennis Floyd was at the table. He started to get to his feet, but Dennis gestured for him to sit back down.

"We're not done yet, Martinez."

Dennis walked over to the desk and leaned over until he was face-to-face with Upstart. "This is for real, Roy," he snarled. "I got photos. You blow the whistle on this, you can forget all about the former Janice fucking Grapnel and you can kiss your FAA ass goodbye, because I got people I can call and we got the money to pay em. And don't think for one minute photos are all I have in my fucking freezer."

Roy didn't seem quite so composed anymore, and Jesús was getting the idea there was a whole lot more to traffic duty in Wiesbaden than waving down seven-ton trucks.

"So, do you really have the photos?" Jesús asked when they were safely in the elevator.

Dennis gave him a look of raw contempt. "Of course not, asshole."

"So there are no people you can call; nothing else in your freezer?"

"The only thing in my freezer, is an icemaker that don't work and four turkey dinners. What do you take me for, some kind of fucking sleaze-ball spook, snooping around?"

"No, Dennis," Jesús said. "There's absolutely no way I'd take you for a sleaze-ball."

CHAPTER 43

Munchkins

Childrish and his team arrived Monday morning promptly at nine. Shirley led them into Upstart's office, looking peeved to say the least. She made quite the show of leaving as the Crony team lined up to shake hands with Roy.

"Hang on, Shirley," Dennis said. "Doesn't Mister Upstart normally have you take minutes?"

Shirley shot a glance at Upstart that should have vaporized him on the spot. "Mister Upstart has just informed me my presence will not be necessary on this occasion. I brought coffee and muffins, by the way. They're in the outer office, if you gentlemen would care to help yourselves."

"Count me in," Dennis said, opening wide the ivory portals. He joined Shirley by the door and placed a consoling arm around her shoulders. "Listen, sweetheart, why don't you fetch that little notepad of yours, anyway. Mister Upstart's had a change of mind. I convinced him we really need to keep track of who says what to whom on this one."

Jesús raised a warning hand. "Excuse me, Dennis. I hope you realize Shirley will have to sign an *NDA* before she can sit in." Even as he spoke, he realized he was beginning to sound like a junior version of Roy Upstart.

Dennis glowered. "Tell you what: you can help her type one up while I find out what everybody wants.

Outside, Dennis poked Jesús painfully in the ribs. "What is it with you, Martinez? You're talking like the rest of those *WIMWACs* in there. Whose side are you on, anyway?"

"What's a *WIMWAC?*" Jesús gasped, rubbing his chest.

Dennis grabbed a poppy seed muffin and busily engaged his teeth before grunting a reply. "Woe Is Me We Are Fucking Concerned, is what it means, numb nuts. Every meeting has one. Our *WIMWAC* in-chief is Uncle Roy."

Now, whereas Dennis Floyd's teeth were unmistakably all there and a joy to behold, they didn't mesh too well. Consequently, it didn't pay to get close to him while he was eating. Jesús, of course, knew this and instinctively kept his distance. Muffin crumbs and poppy seeds came out of Dennis like weed and feed from a hand spreader. Jesús carefully brushed the debris from the remaining muffins and placed a selection on one of Shirley's paper plates.

Meanwhile Dennis was fumbling in his pockets. He produced an ornate ring set with a large blue topaz. "Here," he said, offering the ring to Jesús, "I almost forgot. Put this on. It'll come in useful when those pukes pull their dicks out of Roy ass and get around to shaking hands with us peons."

"What the hell is this?" Jesús whined. "What would I want with a ring? I don't even like jewelry."

"It's a West Point class ring I won in a poker game from some dimwit Artillery lieutenant. I got his fucking watch too. It's just as I figured it would be: they're all ring knockers in there, you ignoramus, same as Upstart. They see this ring, they'll treat you like the prodigal fucking son, no questions asked."

Dennis grabbed the ring back as Jesús struggled to work it on to his ring finger. "Here, you moron, you've got it back to front. *You're* the one that's supposed to be able to read the fucking class year."

Jesús shrugged and let Dennis fit the ring. He felt like it was his first day at school and Dennis was his Auntie Carmen.

Speaking of getting ready for school, it should be noted Dennis and Jesús were the only two not dressed appropriately, i.e. not wearing suits, because neither of them owned one. Shirley, of course, being well versed in executive office protocol, was ever so nicely turned out. She wore a cute Harris Tweed pants combination with a form-fitting pink blouse that barely left room enough for Shirley, let alone the imagination.

***

When he shook hands with Ron Childrish, Jesús was instantly aware the ring was working its magic. Childrish, a stocky sort with three chins and a shaved head, smiled like an old college chum, gave the tiniest hint of a nod, and squeezed a little harder and a little longer than was called for. Jesús quickly greeted the adjacent Crony before Childrish could get a close look at his ring finger. According to the ring, he would have to have been a twelve-year old when he graduated, which was definitely pushing the envelope—even for the United States Military Academy. Next in line were Gregg Nicely and Rick Roach. They could have easily been mistaken for twins: the same buzz cut hair, gratuitous grins, manly handshakes (with mandatory class ring), and anonymous gray suits. The fourth member of the team introduced himself as Preston Pleasant. Preston was not wearing a class ring, and Jesús had the distinct impression he was also manifestly not wearing his own suit. He looked like he might have been snatched at random from the back room of a neighborhood Radio Shack.

As everyone sat down at Upstart's small conference table, Ron Childrish explained who did what. "Gregg and Rick will keep the ball in play. I'll run interference upstairs, and Preston is our subject matter expert on secretly protecting tall buildings, so you can think of him as your running back."

Jesús had opted for soccer going through high school, and then only because it was the lesser of two evils. Contact sports just didn't appeal. Thus, while he got the idea of keeping the ball in play and could grasp the notion of running interference, he floundered when it came to the running back. He sneaked a glance at Preston, hoping for a clue, but Preston didn't seem to get it either. The *SME* looked vacantly around the room and tapped a four beat on the table. He sure as hell doesn't look like a running back (whatever that is), thought Jesús.

Childrish turned to Jesús with an unspoken question on his lips. Jesús casually indicated a suitcase sitting by the door. "Bit of a push, Ron, but I made a few calls Friday. It's all there. You can count it if you want."

Ron smiled like the cat that not only ate the cream, but had got at the cow as well. "Oh, I think we can trust you," he said. "Just don't forget to remind me about the receipt when we leave. All right then," he continued, with a little clap of the hands. "We worked all weekend on your program, especially Preston, so he'll punt you downfield. Okay, Preston," Ron signaled, "you've got the ball."

Eager to get going, Preston nodded gratefully and launched Power Point Ultra. It so happened, his pride and joy was his first topic, namely, the self-healing minefield. "Mmm, let's begin at ground level, shall we," he said, moving smoothly from modest to masterful, "then we can sort of work our way up to the roof."

Dennis and Jesús were all ears, although Jesús was careful to cover up the class ring, having noticed Ron and Roy casting surreptitious glances his way. Gregg and Rick were also casting surreptitious glances, except they were more focused on the rise and fall of Shirley's breasts.

"Excuse me," Jesús said, when he saw Preston's first slide. "When I invited Ron over last Friday all I did was tell him which building we were talking about. How come you have detailed drawings so soon?"

Preston looked puzzled. "It's my job. Crony has blueprints of every building in North America, just in case they need to be secretly protected."

"Oh," said Jesús, "I see. Well, golly, silly old me for asking. Er, well carry on then."

Preston directed the electronic pointer to the parking lot. "Now, you shold know that our government is a signatory to the Ottawa Convention banning anti-personnel mines. They signed us up around 2006 or 2007. So you might think your people-poppers are off the table." He smiled knowingly. "Not so, thanks to some very industrious and ingenious little chappies in Japan." He fast-dissolved to an individual landmine. It looked like a magician's hat—the kind you pull rabbits out of—except it was made from polished steel. "Looks a bit like a magician's hat, doesn't it? It's about the same size too. The only difference is, our hat's the one that does the hopping; not the bunny."

"What does this have to do with the Japanese," Jesus inquired. "Did they invent the mine?"

"Good heavens, no!" Preston exclaimed, looking down his nose. "They're nowhere near as clever as we are. No, like us, the first thing they did after signing Ottawa was look for loopholes. What they came up with were mines you could detonate remotely. That way, you get to decide exactly who to maim and when. They called them projectile scattering devices, so technically they weren't anti-personnel mines, which Ottawa says have to be stepped on to set them off. That's what gave us our first idea. We added heat sensors and profiling microprocessors so you don't actually have to step on them anymore, and nobody has to hang around waiting to press the button. We call them *IMDs*: Intelligent Maiming Devices. They've gotten to be very big in South East Asia, Africa, and the Middle East. Crony, by the way, owns the patent."

"Excuse me," interrupted Roy Upstart, "I'm getting a little concerned. Won't these things mess up my parking lot?"

"Hell, no, Roy," Childrish said, reaching for a muffin. "Believe me, when we're past the five-yard line with this nobody will know we were even here. Unless you get unwelcome guests. Then, sir, you'll be more than glad we *were here*."

Gregg and Rick nodded eagerly in unison. Upstart made a small notation and sneaked a glance at Shirley, who was diligently taking it all in and writing it all down.

Preston tapped the table rhythmically and went to the next slide. It showed land mines leaping about like jackrabbits. He rubbed his hands with excitement. "This is the best part. What the Pentagon did, you see, was add little pancake rocket thrusters to anti-tank mines. Somebody over there stumbled across that idea playing *what-if* one afternoon. It's what we call the Self-Healing Adaptable Minefield Environment, or *SHAME*. What happens is, when a mine goes off, the other mines know about it and the nearest one fires its little thrusters and hops on over to close the wound. It just so happens we have a whole bunch of these babies left over from the early trials. They're sitting on the shelf—just waiting to hop on over and start work."

Dennis leaned across the table and gave Preston the eye. "Listen, pal," he snapped, "we're not looking for hand-me-downs. It's my ass on the line crossing that parking lot. I don't want to get to the car and have a dozen landmines jump on my fucking head." He cringed then and glanced at Shirley—not that he even came close to blushing. Dennis didn't now how to blush. "Shoot, I'm sorry for the language, Shirley. Sometimes I get carried away."

For all the expression she showed, Shirley might well have been a granite countertop. "Dennis" she said calmly, "I am very well aware of that, but if these gentlemen can put up with your language, I most certainly can. Just don't expect me to write it down."

Dennis clapped his teeth together as if he had just been let off school for the day.

Preston coughed impatiently. "You don't have to worry; we took care of everything in the trials. At first, the mines did get a bit confused. They kept flying into one another and a few didn't make it. Anyway, Crony did a software mod so now they sort of talk things over first and decide who's going where. We called that breakthrough the Robust Optimum Maneuvering Protocol—so they can *ROMP* around, so to speak, without hurting themselves."

"Jeez!" Jesus intervened. "You make them sound like frigging tiny tots. What do you do, suit them up in little exploding diapers when you take them for walkies?"

Preston smiled fondly. "Well, yes, as a matter of fact I *have* come to think of them as children: I'm sort of like their mom in a way. And you're not far off the mark with the diapers. Before the little munchkins go out to play, we fit them with what we call *ROMPERS*. That's short for Robust Optimum Maneuvering Protocol Explosive Recognition System. That's how we really got around Ottawa, because we combined the power of the anti-tank mine with the precision of the *IMD*."

"I don't dare fucking ask how," Dennis murmured.

"Yes, well," continued Preston, transitioning back from masterful to modest, "that was one of *my* ideas, actually. You see, using thermal signatures, even in mid-hop, our little munchkins know the difference between armor plate and human tissue, so it's never too late. If it's a soft tissue target, only the top gets armed, so what you have then is what we call an autonomous *IMD*, and all you get is intelligent maiming; there's no HE wastage, just compromised human tissue. The bottom part stays intact and waits for a tank to show up. We retrofitted all those early munchkins with *ROMPERS*, so you're good to go." He glanced around the table, looking pointedly at Jesús. "I take it we all know what HE stands for," he said, with more than a hint of sarcasm.

"Yeah we do," said Dennis. "It stands for High fucking Explosive, and, yeah, we also know what it can do to a lousy tank tread, not to mention a seven-ton truck with compromised human fucking tissue at the wheel."

"Excuse me," Jesús interrupted, "I have to use the restroom."

"The key is on a hook outside," explained Shirley. "It's just to the right of Mister Upstart's door on your way out."

"Typical," Jesús thought, as he made for the door, "I finally get the key to the executive frigging wash room, and all I want to do is throw up."

Roy's restroom was scary. He could tell Shirley was in charge. Little brown wicker baskets were everywhere. They held nicely arranged bars of lavender-scented soap, fan-folded washcloths, hand lotions, facial lotions, sanitizing gels, pink and blue tissue, little bottles of men's cologne, assorted aftershaves, even a sewing kit and first-aid essentials.

Every item was unused. There was no soap in the soap dish—and probably never had been; it was that clean. Four impossibly neat and impossibly folded hand towels warned him off. The toilet seat was a white, shining plateau of unapproachable purity. If you were a germ, the floor must have seemed like Death Valley—a harsh, endless landscape of gleaming beige tile, utterly devoid of fellow bacteria. He imagined personal microbes and clothing mites leaping off him and scampering for the door in a blind panic.

Astonishingly, two wicker air-fresheners gave off the all too familiar fragrance of honeysuckle and jasmine. Sure enough, when he lifted one of the brown wicker covers, he found a Sweet Jesus dispenser. Further investigation uncovered two mini bottles of Sweet Jesus concealed among the aftershave collection.

Billy Ray, it seemed, was everywhere.

Suddenly, Jesús didn't want to throw up any more—not because he didn't feel like it—he just didn't dare contemplate the idea. Instead, he sat on the floor and counted wicker baskets, just to get his mind off intelligent maiming and compromised human tissue. He counted fifteen, but the image of landmines hopping about like jackrabbits wouldn't go away. It was time, he realized, to put his foot down.

When Jesús got back to Upstart's office the Gatling guns and surface-to-air missiles were in place, and Preston Pleasant was dropping two *PHALANX* air-defense pods on top of the tower. "We'll use a Chinook," he was saying. "There's really nothing to it. The roof is already reinforced, so we can just bolt them in place and run cable. Shouldn't take more than a day."

He looked up expectantly as Jesús came through the door. "Do you want me to explain about my *PHALANX* systems, Mister Martinez?"

"No, thank you," said Jesús. "I couldn't give a crap about your *PHALANX* systems, just so long as they work."

He sat down and locked eyes with Childrish. "I've seen enough, Ron. All I want is for this stuff to be in place and working before the end of August. If you have to, then work nights. Just make sure Gregg and Rick keep the ball in play."

Preston pouted. "I haven't finished yet. I was going to show how we concrete-skim the parking lot and disguise everything else to look like roof air conditioners and elevator machinery. Not to mention the doors."

"What fucking doors?" Dennis queried. "We already have doors. They're those big metal things you came through on your way in."

"Ah!" Preston cried triumphantly. "That's just it. I studied the specs for those doors and the rollups out back where you have the loading bay. The front ones are supposed to be blast-proof, but believe me, a couple of armor-piercing HE rounds and they'll look like Swiss cheese. The loading bay doors are a joke."

"Oh!" said Jesús, suddenly regaining interest. "Do tell."

Preston advanced to the last slide, and there, indeed, were the doors, and quite the doors they were. "They're a foot thick and made from a very special, very expensive Titanium-Kevlar sandwich material. Nothing can pierce it, nothing can drive through it, and nothing can blow it off its hinges. When not in use, they'll be elevated above the normal doors. If there's an attack, they'll drop down and lock into place in less than two seconds."

"Of course," interjected Ron Childrish, "you do understand that wasn't factored into the *ROM*. As it happens, you're very lucky. Preston found a couple of cancellation orders in the warehouse that will fit nicely, so we can actually let you have them right away. Naturally, we'll deduct the re-stocking fee since that's already been paid."

"So how much might my new doors add up to?" Jesús asked.

Childrish took a deep breath. "Oh, I'd say another twenty million or so."

"Do it."

Roy Upstart smirked.

Jesús pointed to Dennis. "Mister Floyd is my director of operations. He gets the user manuals and he gets the training. Just tell me when you need more money. No one else here is to be involved, including Mister Upstart. The end date is not negotiable." He casually rubbed the class ring and gave Childrish the look that said, "If I tell you why, I'll have to kill you."

Childrish understood perfectly. He picked up his folder and beckoned the team.

Shirley glanced inscrutably from Jesús, to Roy Upstart, then back to Jesús. "Well," she said slyly, "if that will be all, Mister Martinez, I'll type up these minutes and get them to you by *COB*. Also, I will see to it Mister Childrish leaves you a receipt on his way out."

CHAPTER 44

Not to be Alarmist

It takes a while for sufficient magma to accumulate: sometimes millions of years. Mostly, though, several thousand will do it. Mind you, for relatively minor events like Pompeii, a few decades will suffice. When it comes to Yellowstone, you have to think back three million years or so to get the big picture. Way back then, long before you had to pay to get in, the continent shifted and tore a hole in the earth's crust. The tear went from somewhere east of Salt Lake City all the way past Bozeman, Montana. Think of it as a cistern, except that it didn't fill with water. For more than half a million years, magma seeped in.

Now that is a lot of magma.

When the cistern was full, the magma was forced to go elsewhere or blow the lid off. The magma boiling beneath Yellowstone had nowhere to go but up, and it so happened Yellowstone was where the crust was at its thinnest. Experts describe the subsequent event as mega-colossal. Bear in mind, mega-colossal is at least ten times more powerful than super-colossal, which is ten times bigger than colossal, which is ten times bigger than mere paroxysmal (e.g., Mount Saint Helens), which is ten times bigger than cataclysmic, which brings us back to Pompeii.

The experts can only estimate the magnitude of a mega-colossal eruption because they have no way of knowing the full extent of the blast. It goes without saying that anybody unlucky enough to survive one would hardly have wandered about clutching a measuring stick and notebook—quite the bummer for precise science. In any case, once you reach mega-colossal it doesn't much matter how big the thing is, does it? The term ultra-mega-colossal would be academic, to say the least.

Apparently it took around six hundred thousand years before the lid first blew off Yellowstone. We say apparently, because we know it took six hundred thousand years to fill up the hole again. After the second event, another six hundred thousand years passed before the third incident. Number three happened six hundred and forty thousand years ago.

Not to be alarmist, but you might feel number four is overdue.

Furthermore, compared to six hundred and forty thousand years, four weeks doesn't even come close to a bat's blink, so let's skip most of August and move on.

***

Roy Upstart was right. By the time Ron Childrish got through with him, Jesús was out two hundred million dollars. Still, Crony did finish on time, and true to his promise Preston Pleasant left no trace. "Like a fish through water," he said when Jesús signed the completion certificate. "No one will ever know we were here."

In the meantime, Jesús found a nice apartment for Norma and Prashant, Uncle Johnny reported all was well in Baltimore, Mandy's producer, Bill Finkelstein said he could hardly wait to see the pilot, and Mandy called to say Einstein had vanished.

"I still can't believe it," she said. "We were watching final takes on the top floor of the Empire State Building when he took out this grubby little chirping trouser button and said 'I'm sorry, but I have to leave now'—just like that."

Jesús felt the rat wake up in his lower intestine. "Good golly, was that all he said?"

"Oh no, he had a quick word with Jesus One and Genghis Khan then he told me not to worry. He said, he had every confidence you would keep the ball in play here on Earth. What did he mean by that, Jesús—here on Earth? Anyway, then he just vanished. One second he was there, and the next second he was gone."

There was a long pause while the rat got busy.

"Jesús, are you still there?"

"Er, yes."

"Well, I asked you a question. What did Albert mean when he said 'here on Earth?' It sounded like he was going to heaven or something."

Jesús had known this moment might come. However, expecting something and dealing with it, are not one and the same thing—not by a long shot. He instinctively latched on to snowboarding, but quickly realized there wasn't even the glimmer of a half-truth there he could work with, not to mention Mandy would probably have him killed if he went there. He needn't have worried; when he opted for the truth, she wanted him dead anyway.

Her precise words were, "Why don't you drop dead, Martinez, and save me the bother of killing you myself? I told you, no more stupid stories. Who do you think I am, Goldilocks?"

'See,' he told himself, 'so much for being truthful. All they want is well-crafted lies, you moron. You should have been better prepared.'

"Talk to Jesus," he said, finally, "he'll back me up, especially about the virgins and Albert being God. You'll just have to take my word for it when it comes to Yellowstone, even Albert couldn't be sure exactly."

"What, you mean it might not even erupt?"

"No, not that, it's going up all right. He just wasn't sure of the exact date. Our best guess is there'll be signs and an official warning put out sometime in mid to late September at the earliest. Mind you, there's no need to worry. I'll get a flight crew and we'll pick you all up well before then."

"Then what will happen?"

"Well, you see, I was coming around to that part. I've arranged to hijack the control tower at Sea-Tac. When we land, I'll put the plane in a hangar and we'll make our way over to the tower. Next week I'll be signing off on a self-healing minefield, some surface-to-air missiles, and a few Gatling Guns for the roof, so once we're safely inside we'll be pretty much good to go."

Mandy promptly ended the conversation. An hour later, she called him back, weeping, after having had a talk with Jesus One. Jesús didn't know what to say to her, other than not to panic the virgins and the islanders. "We don't want this to get out of hand," he said. "You should carry on as normal, until I show up with the 767. Then we can say everybody is being flown back for the season finale, live on *Star TV.* So, that being the case, do you think you could you try to be down to at least the final four virgins by then?"

"You bastard," Mandy cried, tears all gone, "you absolute manipulating, lying bastard; you're just making all this up as you go along, aren't you?"

"Well, yes, but not about seizing the tower and the missiles and stuff, only about the season finale. I mean, what else can we do? If we spill the beans, we'll start a worldwide stampede for the exits, except there won't be any exits."

"And what do you think these poor girls are going to say when you get around to explaining they've been abducted?"

"Er, I sort of thought that could be your job, Mandy. You see, Albert and I discussed you being mistress of my harem, and I also had the idea you might want to be empress of my new post-eruption world order"—which, of course, ended the conversation for the second time that evening.

They did get back on track, though. After a day of mulling it over and talking some more with Jesus One, Mandy called Jesús back and apologized. She was, she said, fully aware now of the strain he must be under. Being a harem mistress and an empress were still sticking points, but she did concede that the forty virgins was probably a good idea, especially when it came to re-populating the planet. Her only concern was she thought he had failed to adequately address the girls' needs. Despite the Khan's assurances, Mandy wasn't convinced Jesús and he would be up to to the job, not to mention Dennis Floyd.

"What you want," she said, "is at least one bona-fide stud muffin." Accordingly, she proposed he recruit Dirk Forrester. Jesus was so pleased she was on board, he agreed instantly. Dirk, of course, was no longer inclined to argue about anything, so when Jesús called and suggested a short vacation in Seattle, he was more than happy to go along. The only downside was Dirk moved in and Jesús ended up on the futon for the second time in less than four weeks.

***

When all was said and done, August had been quite the month. The evening after the Crony completion sign-off, Dennis assigned Jesús and himself third shift and they checked into the break room early to celebrate. As usual, Dennis busied himself preparing the lattes. Jesús settled in a Chesterfield and had to confess he felt justifiably proud. Certainly, the world was about to end, but no one could accuse him of being a shirker. He had somehow kept it all together. Thanks to Jesús Maria Martinez, and a little help from his friends, humankind was far from doomed. He was, you might say, feeling pretty darned good about the way things were going.

"Great," he said, with a contented smile when Dennis was seated, "we're all set then. Don't you just love it when a plan comes together? I'll call Bill Gates and let him know we're ready. I fully expect he'll want us to seize the tower next week. First, though, I'll have to take the 767 overseas to pick up a couple of his friends. On the way back, I'll let you know when we're due so you can set things in motion."

"Not a problem," Teeth said, reaching for his latte. "You know, Jesús, I sure was wrong about you. I had you figured for some kind of no-load fucking college geek. You know, all brains and no goddamn balls, but you sure as hell came through on this one." He made to lean back in the Chesterfield.

"Just a minute," Jesús said.

Out of the corner of his eye, he had noticed something on CNN. Since the sound was off he wasn't getting all of it, but what he saw was enough to grab his attention. On-camera, a visibly worried Wolf Blister was pointing at a large-screen graphic. At bottom left in bright yellow with a vibrant red drop shadow, was the caption *Crisis in the Park.* In the middle of the display was a glowing red blob.

"Oh, shit!" Jesús murmured. "Er, Dennis, would you be ever so kind and pass the remote please?"

CHAPTER 45

Core Reaction

At seventy-eight, his features seemed chiseled from granite. Eight years of the presidency had not reduced him physically the way it had most of its incumbents. If anything, the office had nourished him, renewed the vigor and convictions of his earlier years. Everyone paid attention to him these days. He wasn't boring anymore. What he had to say meant more to the world than ever before, especially since becoming the 24th Google trillionaire. Yet, Al Core remained a modest man. He was forever thankful he had happened to be in the right place, at the right time, with the right message.

Right now, though, he was fervently thankful he had vetoed a bill to re-dedicate Yellowstone as Core Memorial Park. That would have been a real bummer, in addition to being a trifle premature. Instead, he had consented to renaming the Grand Canyon. Core Canyon seemed to him more fitting; more evocative of America's visionary past; more in keeping with his own passion for the wild, unspoiled places of the earth. Core Canyon conjured up the image of some intrepid pioneer, stumbling by great good fortune upon one of God's magnificent creations.

"Humbled," he had said. "I am humbled that my name shall forever be affiliated with this, the most memorable and enduring of God's wondrous gifts to our great nation."

Standing there on the canyon rim three years ago, a windswept symbol of America's rebirth, he had absolutely no idea what was coming down the pike.

Now, the oval office seemed like just another room with a TV set in the corner. Suddenly, climate change wasn't such a big deal any more. Well, it was, but not for the reasons he had been espousing for the last quarter century. He gripped the arms of his chair as if a dreadful presence were lurking in the room.

"Tell me this isn't true," he urged with slack jawed disbelief. "For God's sake, tell me I'm not hearing this. Please tell me I'm not hearing this."

As usual, CNN was putting out the news before the White House could work a spin. Actually, on this occasion, before the White House had even had the chance to fully grasp what was going on. Somehow, the news network had gotten its hands on a classified high school science project forecasting a massive eruption in Yellowstone National Park. The visibly fearful science teacher, clutching a now redundant *MacPod Earth Tremor System* (*MacPETS*), stood as far away from Core as she could. She didn't bother to answer the president.

No one did.

An elderly Wolf Blister intoned in front of a giant plasma screen with a glowing red blob at its center. At bottom left, colored in bright yellow, with a vibrant red drop shadow, was the caption, *Crisis in the Park*. Blister was stooped and more than a little shaky, but his eyes still had the bright shine of polished steel. "This red core represents a magma plume beneath Yellowstone National Park," he said. "CNN has learned. I repeat, CNN has learned, it may soon erupt. High school students on a recent field trip to the park measured significant near surface tremor activity. They have calculated the explosion will be an eight on the Volcano Explosivity Index. The Mount Saint Helens eruption back in 1980 was a five. Each point on the index represents a tenfold increase in power. In other words, the Yellowstone event will be a thousand times bigger than Mount Saint Helens—if not more."

Blister scrutinized the blob thoughtfully for a long moment before turning back to the camera. He gently smoothed his silvery gray hair, which was as thick and perfectly groomed as ever. "I don't know about the rest of you," he said solemnly, "but I believe this bad boy is about to blow us all to kingdom come. I'll be frank. I don't see any point standing here and repeating myself ad-infinitum until the shit hits the fan. I'm going to spend what time I have left with my family." With that, Blister calmly removed his earpiece, unbuttoned his jacket, and walked off the set.

Al Core surveyed his cabinet. He was composed now, his gaze clear and unflinching. "Ladies," he said, "I think we should evacuate the park."

Chelsea Clifton raised her hand. "I'm sorry, Mister President, but Global-Titanic absolutely refuses to let anyone do that."

"What do you mean, refuses? I'll invoke presidential discretion. Don't they realize this is a national emergency?"

Jenny Bush rose to her feet. "Mister President, as head of the Department of Homeland Extinction, I have to side with Interior Secretary Clifton. We can't afford to start a panic right now. I just got off the phone with Dick Derringer from Titanic, and he assures me their sensors haven't picked up a thing. What's more, the last time something like this happened, Titanic was dead on. It was nothing more than a trickle."

"Oh!" said Core. "Well, in that case maybe we shouldn't be so hasty. But look at the way Blister reacted. We're going to have to do something. He's not going to be the only one to walk off the job, you know. Think about it; if they all do it the government's going to run out of money. Federal paychecks will dry up."

Chief of Staff, Madge Chainey grunted thoughtfully, then looked up. "There is a White House protocol for this sort of thing, Mister President. Perhaps we should follow procedure."

Core sat back, visibly relieved. "A protocol, thank God for that. Okay, what do I have to do?"

"Well, it's like this: after seventy two hours you'll go on TV and address the nation. If it turns out to be a false alarm, you're in the clear. Otherwise, we're screwed. At least, it'll give us some time to work a spin."

"What do you mean?" Core protested. "It can't be that bad. Can it?"

Secretary of Defense, Gladys Rumsfoiled intervened, looking as steely and decisive as ever. "Look, Al, get a grip will you? We have a frigging bunker under the back lawn. How serious can it get? Worst case, we deploy the National Guard for a few months, then we emerge all smiles and have a nice day, and we'll be treated like heroes. I mean, when we open the door either everybody will be alive and well and cheering; or alive and not too well and not cheering so much; or not alive, maybe, and not cheering at all—either way, we'll be cheering *our* little hearts out, is my thought."

"Mmm," Core said. "I see your point. Anyway, if needs be, I can always do speeches from the shelter, just in case. By the way, does anybody know where the keys are?"

"Mister President," Gladys reminded him, "you had the forehead implant, remember?"

Jenny Bush, however, was not to be denied. She held up a thick, three ringed binder. "Mister President, in addition to the White House protocols, Homeland Extinction does have plans. This is our Doomsday Response, Evacuation, And Mitigation plan for Region Three. It's what we call a *DREAM*. We have a *DREAM* for each region in the countty. The least we can do is stick to our own plan."

Core frowned. "I thought Yellowstone was in Region Nine."

"Well, it is, but for organic homeland extinction events the plans are all pretty much the same when you get down to it. Anyway, *we're* in Region Three, which is all that counts as far as I'm concerned."

Core buried his head in his hands. "Okay," he groaned, "tell me what we have to do."

Jenny leafed though the first few pages and looked up with a smile. "It's really not that bad," she said. "First off, it's right in line with the protocol. We do nothing for seventy-two hours, then you go on TV. If it's good news, you lead with a modest smile and 'This great nation, of ours.' If it's bad news, you look grim, lead with, 'My fellow Americans', and sugar the pill."

Core perked up. "That doesn't sound so difficult. What if the news is not good though? I mean, won't we actually have to do something, apart from me sugaring the pill?"

Jenny motioned impatiently. "Just a minute, I'm reading." Then she looked up, clearly relieved. "Not a problem," she said. "In the event of a confirmed extinction, you keep quiet about the full extent of the problem and declare precautionary measures. All senior homeland security staff, White House staffers, four star generals and up, house leaders, Supreme Court Justices, and well-connected citizens and clergy will be directed to serve the national interest by immediately reporting to underground bunkers. For any spots left we'll do a lottery for people on the Individual Contributor's List."

Core looked puzzled. "How come there are no lawyers, I mean, apart from the Justices?"

"Well, Mister President, if you'll recall, almost everyone on the priority list *is* a lawyer, apart from the generals and the clergy. The consensus has always been that if a lawyer isn't smart enough to run the country, or rich enough to afford to buy his or her way in, he or she doesn't belong in a bunker."

Core nodded sagely. "Yes, yes, you're absolutely right. What's an individual contributor, though? I've never heard of that before. Is it just another term for the common folk?"

"Yes it is, Mister President. You see we'll still need people to clean up and fix things, especially if we have to rebuild civilization. It's the usual suspects: personal chefs, executive assistants, speech writers, house maids, nannies, doctors, a couple of the world's most famous scientists, that sort of thing. Not to mention we'll need them to vote so you can be re-elected."

She chuckled to herself.

"What's so funny?" Core asked.

"I was just thinking," she replied. "The last thing I'd want to be right now is an air traffic controller. If this thing really hits the fan, you can kiss goodbye to Air Force One. Ain't nobody going to be flying the friendly frigging skies for a very long time."

Everybody laughed.

"So, what happens when we're all in the bunkers?" Core enquired, looking a lot more relaxed thanks to the therapeutic effect of the laughter.

"Well, Mister President," Jenny continued, turning to another section, "that's where the *DREAM* picks up and the protocol leaves off. For a confirmed homeland extinction event, you make your precautionary speech downstairs from the President's Emergency Operations Center, what we call the *PEOC*. Then when we've filled the bunkers and all the doors are locked, you break the bad news. At which time you put the civilian population on a *YOYO* footing and deploy law enforcement, first responders, and the military. You're pretty much done for the day at that point. The *PHEWH* is right next door to the *PEOC*, so all you'll have to do is kick off your shoes and go relax. There'll be champagne on ice and all the beds will be turned down with those little chocolates you like on the pillow—you know, the ones with that little mint stripe in the middle we get at the Olive Garden."

"I'm sorry," said Core, looking puzzled again, "I'm not familiar with *YOYO*. What does that mean exactly?"

Jenny sighed. "It's another one of those overworked acronyms we use all the time at *DHE*. It stands for: You're On Your Own." She leaned forward and patted Core on the shoulder. "Don't worry, Al. The good news is *YOYO* is the one thing we really know how to do."

"By the way," Core inquired, looking around the room, "I don't see Veronica."

Gladys Rumsfoiled raised her hand. "Vice President Spears is taking an enforced vacation, Mister President, after that unfortunate incident with the jackrabbit."

"Give her a call. Tell her we won't stand for that sort of thing in the bunkers, then fly her back."

"Certainly," Rumsfoiled said, rising to her feet. "Will that be all, Mister President?"

"Er, yes, I suppose so," said Core, looking confused. "But I'm not so sure. Did we actually decide anything?"

Gladys Rumsfoiled sat back down. "Gosh, Mister President, you may be right. I believe I didn't actually, um, say we had, but I know what you're thinking, and, well, I'm going to assume I may actually not have said what I didn't say. So, how about this then? Why don't we round up a bunch of scientists and send them to Yellowstone so they can check things out?"

She glanced at Chelsea Clifton. "That will be okay with Titanic won't it, Chelsea? I mean, it's not as if we'll be asking them to close the park or anything."

Chelsea nodded enthusiastically. "That's a wonderful idea. I'll get right on it. I'm sure Titanic will go along provided no one alarms the visitors. We can use the same clowns we sent to check out the birds. One of them actually used to work at Yellowstone, so at least he knows the equipment."

Core sat back, finally at ease. "Madge," he said to his chief of staff, "round up a couple of speechwriters, will you? I feel a press conference coming on. Just make it clear I won't be taking questions."

CHAPTER 46

Cocktails

Frank Chamberlain would always remember where he was and what he was doing when he heard the news. Marge was below sewing a torn sail. Hilda was stretched out on the portside cockpit cushion, deep into one of her leg twitching dreams. He was stretched out on the opposite cushion not doing much of anything—other than contemplating his recent rebuild of the aft cabin and wondering how in heck he was going to tackle what was left of the rudder.

His first inkling they had company was a frantic knocking on the hull. He sat up and peered over the side, mildly irritated that anyone could in any way be agitated on this, the slowest of days, in these the slowest of islands. Wasn't that the whole point of being here? Wasn't that why the islanders were supposed to be happy as shit: living in sunlit poverty and barely getting by on subsistence fishing? No worries. That was the secret—smiles all the time. Worrying in any way, shape, or form was taboo.

Yet, here was Jimmy-the-Fish of all people, showing evident signs of distress.

"What the heck is going on, Jimmy? Is the world coming to an end or what?"

Alfredo looked up at him, wide eyed with surprise. "How come you know that, Frank?"

"How come I know what, you dumb ass?"

"How come you know the world is ending, mate?"

"Just a lucky guess," muttered Frank. "Anyway, if the news is that bad, I want a bottle close by when I hear it. Get yourself up here and we'll share a glass of the good stuff."

Sharing beverages with Alfredo, of course, was nothing new. In fact, you might say it was something of a fast developing tradition. Shortly after Marge had introduced Alfredo to her cranberry vodka, Frank Chamberlain upped the ante. His first move was to unveil the rum and *ganja* cocktail much beloved by Caribbean Fishermen. "See, here, Jimmy," he said, "you mix water in bottle with a little bit Jamaican *ganja* or Melanesian same-same and some local hooch, like this. Just be sure you don't use kava. Then you shake it all up good, like this. Then when you fish all night and your head wants make sleep-sleep, like when you drink plenty too much kava, you take a swig. Then you be wide awake see, and you can go on fishing, and you see very much good in the dark." At the time, Frank was still under the impression, despite all evidence to the contrary, that Alfredo had a poor grasp of English. He was also still under the impression he could speak passable Pidgin. He was wrong on both counts.

Alfredo field-tested the remedy, found that Frank had spoken the truth, and in no time at all had spread the word. Frank's reward was in knowing he had in some small way improved the lot of the indigenous population; torn down yet another cultural barricade, if you will.

The next thing Frank shared with Alfredo was a bottle of Grenadian Rivers Rum. Unlike his first gesture, this was not given in gratitude for the free fish, nor was it an act of kindness. Frank had carted two cases of the rum all the way from Grenada—west by way of Colombia to the Panama Canal, across the Pacific to the Galapagos Islands, Easter Island, and Hawaii, then on to the Solomon Islands and beyond. He had graciously offered the beverage to all he encountered along the way. Without exception, he had been less than graciously refused. Marge wouldn't let him drink it and she wouldn't pour it overboard for fear of wiping out local fish populations. By the time they reached Noahu, Frank was desperate to get rid of the stuff.

Alfredo was a heaven-sent opportunity.

He did his best to explain. Above the legend "Royale Grenadian Rum," was the disclaimer, *slightly over proof*. For the River Antoine estate, which had distilled the rum since 1785, *slightly over proof,* meant twice the strength of most distilled spirits. Developed nations were unwilling to import liquor this volatile, so the Estate was obliged to seek help from fellow Grenadians, who responded enthusiastically by regularly putting away more than two thousand bottles a week.

Frank pointed to the disclaimer. "See here, Jimmy," he said, "this is the understatement of the frigging century. Make sure you put in plenty of water when you mix it."

Alfredo frowned, not because he didn't understand the exhortation; he just didn't understand why. Frank unscrewed the cap and poured a shot glass of the deceptively clear liquid.

"*Aarwarrgh, Uuuhh*!" Alfredo exclaimed when he tasted the rum. Then he wiped his eyes, shook his head vigorously, finished the drink with one swallow, and held out the shot glass for a refill. Frank obliged with a caution. "Rivers rum can be bad Juju, Jimmy. Too much Rivers, you might get very big blind. You see no good. You fish no more."

The rum caught on fast. In less than a week, one case was gone. Half the islanders begged Chamberlain to import more. The other half, namely, the womenfolk, including Marge, threatened to feed him to the crocodiles if he even handed over so much as another teaspoonful.

So to commemorate the end of all life as we know it, Frank Chamberlain called down to Marge to bring up a bottle of his good rum—the *Dominicano Columbus*—and three glasses.

"What's up now, Frank?" she asked.

"Jimmy says the world's about to end."

"Has he been at the Rivers again?"

"No, he's stone cold sober. He really means it."

"Oh, that's nice," she said. "I'll be up in a jiffy."

When Marge heard the details, she was a lot less calm. In fact, she quickly drained her *Dominicano Columbus* and commanded Frank to go fetch the Rivers.

Even Hilda perked her ears up.

"It's not as if we'll get it right away," Alfredo explained. "In fact, some experts are saying Australia and New Zealand and these parts might not be affected that much at all. Mind you, there'll still be worldwide famine and most of the oceans will die off."

"Gee, that's nice to know," Frank observed as he came up the companionway steps clutching a bottle of the infamous rum. "So I guess we may as well stay put. At least, I won't have to worry about not having a frigging rudder."

He poured three shot glasses of the Rivers.

Uncharacteristically, Marge grabbed for hers and downed it in one. After that, she seemed a lot better. "I suppose we'll be doing a lot more fishing then," she volunteered.

Alfredo looked worried. "So will a lot of people. They're already talking about restricting flights and ships out of America. Just think of it, three hundred and fifty million Yanks, all carrying castnets and spear guns, and all coming our way."

Marge beckoned for a refill. "Oh, Frank," she murmured with tears in her eyes (more from polishing off the Rivers than anything else), "this means we'll never ever be able to go back home."

"I don't think we planned to, did we, old girl," Frank observed, as tenderly as he could. "There was never much to go back to anyway—just crap coming out of the TV and a bunch of certifiable lunatics in charge. Can you imagine the bullshit they'll shovel down everybody's throats on this one?"

"Now, now Frank," Marge cautioned, fast becoming her old self, "you're being negative again. Let's look on the bright side. At least, there are much worse places we could be right now."

Alfredo raised his glass. "You can say that again, missus," he agreed.

"I'm not religious, but I'll say amen to that," said Frank.

He reached out and they touched glasses.

CHAPTER 47

Forty-Eight Hours

Dennis Floyd's lips were moving but no sound came out. Still, it wasn't hard to understand what he was saying. Jesús had said the same thing ten seconds earlier. Back then—ten seconds ago—he had said, "Oh, shit," and Wolf Blister had been saying, "… a thousand times bigger than Mount Saint Helens." After which, Jesús couldn't hear too well because he was under water. Dennis was also under water. Jesús knew this because when Dennis got up he floated gracefully to his feet and his coffee mug descended ever so slowly to the carpet. He heard Dennis the second time, though—loud and clear.

"Holy fucking Christ," Dennis yelled, "the goddamn thing is getting ready to blow."

Blister was doing something with his earpiece and walking off the set. Jesús watched with a blank stare. He didn't respond to Dennis right away. Instead, he bobbed around aimlessly in the floating Chesterfield and turned his attention to his knees, which were still submerged. He didn't even bury his head in his hands.

""Well, Dennis," he said eventually, "I guess that's it then."

"You're damn right, that's it," said Dennis, already dialing, "I'm calling Shirley. We're taking over."

Somebody must have pulled the plug because when Jesús got to his feet the water wasn't even up to his ankles. He grabbed Dennis by the elbow. "Hang on, why are you calling Shirley? You didn't tell her, did you?"

'Not yet," Dennis growled, listening to his phone, "but if she'll pick up the phone I'm going to tell her right now. If you think I'm going to spend the rest of my life fondling your ass, you can think again, pal."

"Dennis ..."

"Just a minute. Shirley, it's me, Dennis. If you're there, answer the phone. If not, call me right back on my cell."

Dennis was right about one thing: if they didn't seize the tower then-and-there, they probably wouldn't get a second chance. "No fucking way," he said, when Jesús suggested he think it over. "If we don't make our move now, come daylight this place will be crawling with uniforms and you and I will be diddling one another on the sidewalk. You'd better call Bill Gates and tell him to get his multi-billion dollar ass over here on the double. Tell him the train is leaving the fucking station as we speak. And you can also tell him to kiss his overseas friends *auf Wiedersehen,* because you just ran out of flight time, Fly-Boy."

The on-duty supervisor popped in at that moment and stayed just long enough to explain the second shift was leaving early and might not be back—ever.

Jesús buried his head in his hands.

As you can imagine, events moved swiftly thereafter. Dennis called the guard shack to tell them they no longer had a job, but no one answered the phone. After making sure the building was empty, he dropped the Kevlar shield and activated the minefield. In the meantime, Jesús manned the control tower as best he could and dealt with panicked calls from the FAA.

"No," he said, "no one has walked off the job here and we are fully operational and, no, we do not need help. No, please don't send anyone over, because they won't be able to get in. We have a self-healing minefield in the parking lot and it's switched on. If you don't believe me, talk to Roy Upstart."

Then he called Mandy Miller. Then he called Norma Flatley. Then he called Dirk Forrester. Then he called Chuck at Way-Out-West-Aviation.

Then he told Dennis Floyd the truth—well, most of it anyway.

Dennis was not amused. "Forty fucking virgins! You have got to be kidding! For Christ's sake, why didn't you tell me before I called Shirley, you numb nut?"

By then, of course, it was too late because Shirley had already packed her bags and was on her way over. Naturally, she was not the first to arrive.

When Shirley arrived, smoke and concrete dust still wafted across the parking lot, people in uniform being sometimes hard to convince, Roy Upstart notwithstanding. Not that Dennis had actually detonated a mine. Rather than waste such a valuable resource, he had simply fired a sample burst from one of the remote controlled Gatling guns.

"Yes, I know," said Dennis patiently when Shirley called to explain her problem, "I'm the one fired the fucking gun, Shirley. Here's what you do: Get back in your car. Turn on your lights full beam so I know where you are. Then dip them twice and drive like crap for the front door. I'll deactivate the mines so you can get through. Yes, I know they've put up crime scene tape. No, don't ask them to take the tape down while you drive in. Just put the pedal to the fucking metal, and don't worry about the goddamn tape. They have lots more. And, Shirley, when you get out of the car, leave the engine running and switch off the lights. Dork brain, here, has an errand he needs to run. And don't forget to unload your bags."

***

Knowing the airport helped. Jesús sped around the base building and took a back exit while Dennis sprayed a two second warning burst and reactivated the mines. The Way-Out-West Aviation hangar was no more than half a mile away—not that far really, but time enough for an entire colony of rats to clock in below. Now that the deed was done, his adrenalin rush was very definitely over. He wanted nothing more than to drive home and climb into bed—or at least crawl onto the futon—and suck his thumb. Not to mention he was suffering a sudden attack of involuntary twitching.

Chuck having mixed feelings didn't help either. When Jesús entered the office, Chuck was staring at his computer and scratching his head. On the office TV, Wolf Blister was walking off the set for the eighty-fourth time.

"What's the problem, Chuck?"

"We just got an email from the FAA. Some clowns have hijacked the control tower and won't leave. It says here all flights are suspended until they can transfer control to the ramp tower. I'm also hearing rumors they might shut the whole place down anyway to avoid a panic. The phone lines are jamming up with people screaming for flights out. Apart from that, Mister Martinez, we have another problem. I haven't been able to find pilots. The only one that called back said he was sorry, but he was fueling up his Cessna and getting the hell out. He advised me to do the same by, the way."

He shrugged helplessly. "I don't think we can accommodate you, sir. Also, you should know my wife called. She's thinking right now might be a good time to visit her sister in Florida. We've been talking about it for a long time, except she doesn't like to fly and it's a long drive."

"Tell me about it," Jesús muttered, wracking his brain furiously for a way out. Finally, he did the only thing he could do, and do well: he lied through his teeth. He had no choice. Chuck was already on his feet and reaching for his jacket.

Jesus held up a restraining hand. The twitching was gone now. In fact, all at once it was like being back underwater, except he could talk normally. "Now, just a minute, Chuck. That's why I'm here. Those rumors you heard about closing the airport are true. As we speak, the FAA is swinging into action. I wouldn't normally tell anyone this, but we have an emergency here and I have to act fast. You see, Chuck, I'm actually the special agent in charge of the FAA's Secretly Empowered Supervisory Planning and Operations Task Force for Apocalypse Mitigation—what we call *SEESPOTFOAM*"

He flashed his FAA ID badge and put on the sternest face he could muster. "I'm authorizing the flight, Chuck. We have to move fast here. My people should arrive within the half hour. By then, I want the plane fueled to the max and good to go."

Chuck shrugged helplessly again, but at least he returned his jacket to the hook. He sat down and stared blankly at his phone before looking up. "We still don't have pilots, Mister Martinez, and I've run out of people to call. I'm sorry."

Jesús didn't hesitate—even the rats stopped chewing they were that astonished at what he said next. "I'm current on the equipment. All FAA special agents are licensed pilots, so I'll fly the plane. Special agent Flatley is on her way with a co-pilot and my deputy assistant special agent for contingency support operations. She went undercover long before she signed up with Way-Out-West."

"You mean, even when she was with *TWA*?"

"I sure do, Chuck. Believe me, Norma being on that flight was no accident. We've had our eye on *SCUM* for a long time now."

Some might have said it was his finest hour.

The principal drawback was he actually had to fly the airplane.

***

Now, a full-fidelity motion-based simulator with photographic quality computer-generated imagery is one thing. Actually hurtling at a hundred-forty miles an hour down a mile and a half long runway is another, as is being at the sharp end of an airplane weighing close to a hundred fifty tons. Not to mention thirty odd thousand gallons of Jet-A fuel sloshing about and a perimeter fence that is getting taller by the second.

Jesús had often asked his instructors, "If these flight simulators are so real, what's the difference when you're actually at the controls?" The answer was always the same, "When the time comes, believe me, you'll know."

Now he knew.

When he reached a hundred sixty-five miles per hour Jesús eased back on the stick. Had he been at all emotionally detached, he might have savored the moment. Instead, he shut his eyes and prayed desperately to whatever God was on duty that night (well, you never know do you, so it's at least worth a try).

His only other awkward moment had been when Chuck recognized Dirk Forrester. "Aren't you the guy from 'Little Miss Fixit' that got the nail in his head?" was the question.

Dirk smiled vacantly and turned to Jesús for guidance.

"As a matter of fact, we count on the resemblance," said Jesús, now on a roll. "That's why we have him carry the finish-nailer, so no one will ever question his true identity."

Chuck was visibly confused.

Dennis being in the control tower helped a lot, in particular when Jesús wandered onto taxiway Tango by mistake and started to spool up, thinking he was on runway three. With all that concrete looking the same and a zillion multi-colored lights out there, it was an understandable error. Dennis, though, was not happy—forbidden pleasantries were not even in the ballpark. In fact, had Muriel been on duty, Dennis would have definitely kissed his pension goodbye.

When Jesús opened his eyes, he was airborne. He didn't bother looking down, all of that being hopefully behind him for a while. Instead, he ascended triumphantly, face uplifted to the heavens. Then a carping little voice in his head piped up and asked, "Now what do we do?" He remembered his next piece of instructor wisdom, which was: 'Hand-fly the thing to at least a thousand feet before you key in the destination code. If you key it in too soon, the equipment might freak out, and we wouldn't want to freak out two hundred feet off the fucking tarmac, now would we?'

When all was said and done, he much preferred the simulator.

A real plus, though, was when Prashant explained he had been through *SCUM* flight school. Not that he knew much, since he was only in Baltimore for a week, which is all it took for the martyrdom video and the turban fitting. Still, *SCUM* had scheduled him for a couple of sessions on their generic large-jet simulator, so at least he knew how to make turns and punch in city codes. Jesús showed him how to monitor fuel consumption and check ETA. "If I'm sleeping, and that read out shows less than twenty six hundred gallons, wake me up. This may very well be the extended range model, but when we get to Vanahu I'm not about to fly in circles for anybody. We're going straight in, and I do believe we'll arrive just in time for brunch."

Now the challenges of landing a large jet on a tiny, yet mountainous island are far too many to enumerate here. Let's just say the runway on Vanahu was some three hundred feet short of the recommended minimum because of the beaches at either end. There was also no Instrument Landing System (ILS); well there was, but it didn't work anymore and nobody understood it anyway. Because there was no ILS on the ground, the Automatic Landing System (ALS) on the aircraft was rendered useless. This came as a profound shock to Jesús since he had assumed landing would be a breeze. To wit: pick up the outer ILS marker, activate the ALS, and have Norma serve breakfast while all on board admired the rapidly approaching scenery.

It should also be pointed out that whereas closing your eyes on take-off might be excusable, landing is not like that, especially when you happen to be the pilot. This is even more true when you have the controls in a death grip and your brain just shriveled up. So, in a way, it was an automatic landing after all, since there was little or no human intervention.

Jesús did remember one thing. From out of the fog that had once been his mind he recalled a peculiarity of the ALS, namely, it always put the engines into full reverse thrust seconds before the nose wheels hit the runway—which had been disconcerting in the simulator, but suddenly seemed like something he might be well advised to try.

And, so it was.

The only upside worth mentioning is he didn't have to worry about the perimeter fence because there wasn't one.

Mandy Miller had never seen a large jet plow into a beach before. Not that it plowed very far, mind you, and it only fetched up on the beach because both engines flamed out shortly after the nose wheels touched down. She supposed the pilot must have seriously mismanaged his fuel consumption and resolved to have a word. Imagine her surprise when Prashant Nagpal waved from the cockpit. Imagine her further surprise when the chief aviator turned out to be somewhat less than fully flight-certified.

Entering the terminal building, Jesús had the demeanor and appearance of fish food making its way to the bottom of an aquarium, which is to say he moved ever so slowly and didn't look at all appetizing. "I'm sorry," he said in muffled tones from behind the aquarium glass, "but I had no choice, you see. Chuck couldn't get us any pilots."

"Who's Chuck?" Mandy enquired, not sure if she really wanted to know.

"It doesn't matter," the sinking man struggled to say, "but where are the rest of the virgins? Lookit, we flew all this way to pick up forty and all I can count is twenty-one."

"Well, this is awkward. Two of the girls, Destiny and Brianna, got a bit carried away on Outcast Island so they had to be banished.. Alfredo and George were the search mates in question and now they've sort of formed attachments."

"Formed attachments? What you are trying to tell me, I do believe, is the boys are screwing their brains out—not that that would take much, and if you'll pardon my French." Jesús had been scooped out of the aquarium by this time and thus was no longer attempting to talk through glass.

"Yes," Mandy agreed, "in all likelihood you're right. Unfortunately, they've decided to stay and so have the island girls."

"I just don't need this right now," Jesús groaned.

"Don't start that again," Mandy warned. "You should be grateful we're here at all. If we didn't believe in Jesus, the rest of us might be tempted to stay as well."

"Would you mind ever so much if I walked back to the beach and sat down for a while?" Jesús enquired. "Then perhaps when I'm feeling better, we can start over. Like, maybe you can dash across the tarmac in slow motion and I can sort of sweep you up in my arms or something?"

"Yes," she said, smiling; unexpectedly feeling weak at the knees, despite wanting to slap him upside the head, "you definitely need to start over; you're beginning to sound like Destiny."

So Jesús sat on the beach and contemplated the surf while Mandy emptied the violin case. In return for this further consideration, the prime minister's wife authorized immediate refueling and a tractor tow.

Sitting under a palm tree, watching waves come ashore doesn't ask much of a person. Which was just what Jesús wanted because he was trying to picture the immediate future. But he couldn't get beyond what he saw with his eyes. In this place, the future was pretty much the same as the present—nothing much changed and nothing more was required than what was already there—so how could a person possibly imagine the unimaginable? Eventually he stopped trying, which meant the waves continued to come ashore and the tree stayed put and the sun continued to wash the beach—even in the future. In this way, he was able to stop time for a little while. Then time kicked in again, the way it always does, and he was obliged to get back to the other future he was concerned about—you know, the one he *could* imagine.

When they took off, there was quite a turn out. The islanders were sorry to see them go, since they had never had so many virgins travel all that way. Even the prime minister made a special trip just to wave goodbye.

Needless to say, the takeoff was a blast—so to speak. Jesús directed Prashant to punch in the city code for Seattle, which impressed the heck out of Norma. All Prashant needed was one of those nice white shirts with little bars on the shoulders and you could have taken him for the real McCoy. Prashant entered the code exactly twenty-eight hours and thirteen minutes after Wolf Blister first removed his earpiece. Eighteen hours later, they would touch down in Seattle. Forty-eight hours after that, Yellowstone National Park would vanish forever—an event not entirely explainable in purely seismic, geodetic, and hydrological terms. But let's not digress; we'll get to that part soon enough.

***

Four hours out of Seattle, Jesús called Dennis using an onboard satellite phone. The news was not encouraging, but it wasn't entirely bad. Dennis did sound tired though.

"You won't believe this," he said. "The bastards gave up on the ramp tower idea because almost all the controllers walked off the job. Now, they're organizing voluntary evacuations to the east coast, and they had the audacity to ask if I could help out. What the fuck, I said, as long as my retirement's still good, I'm your man."

"Dennis, what I was calling for is could you stand by to talk me down? I'll use the ALS, but just in case something goes wrong, I'd like a second opinion. Also, when we land, how am I going to get all these virgins into the tower?"

"That's your problem. I'm here; you're there. How the hell, should I know? Hijack the fucking bus or something."

"What bus? What are you talking about?"

"When you drop out of the sky, man, all you'll get is a shuttle from the plane to the terminal. They're using the ramps for evacuation flights only. Anybody dumb enough to fly into the country right now goes straight to the bottom of the fucking totem pole."

"Oh," Jesús said, "I hadn't thought about that."

"One more thing," Dennis said, "when you get picked up in-route by TRACON, change your voice like you're a Canuck or something. If those bastards catch wind it's you flying the plane they'll drop the dime on you faster than Shirley can paint a fucking toenail."

Three hours later, Jesús acknowledged the sole remaining TRACON approach controller and foolishly ignored Dennis Floyd's advice; this being based on his assumption that no one in their right mind would think he could possibly be at the controls of a jetliner inbound from Melanesia. The next words he heard were: "Got you Way-Out-West two-nine-eight—six miles from the outer mark turn right, heading two-zero-zero and maintain six thousand feet until you're on the localizer. You're cleared ILS, runway three. Hey, is that you, Martinez?"

Jesús put his chin on his chest and came up with, "Zee-Tag, I am zo zorry, eh? Oo iz theez Marteenez, eh?" which was the best he could do given the circumstances. It must have worked, because shortly thereafter Dennis Floyd got the hand-off and lined him up for final approach.

"Whiskey-Alpha-Whiskey two nine eight, Sea-Tac tower, clear for runway three arrival, maintain one-seven-zero knots, heading one-eight-zero, straight in at three thousand feet."

"Zee-Tag, Wizkee Alva Wizkee two nine eight I am zloweeng to one-zeven-zero, eh?"

"Okay, you can cut the Canuck crap, dork brain, it's me, Dennis. Just follow the fucking Airbus in front of you and park where the ramp tower tells you. Also, tell Norma about your ground transportation problem. I think she can get you what you need." Jesús concluded from this exchange that voice protocol was no longer the issue it once had been.

"Not a problem," said Norma, when he explained about the bus. "If you're going to do a hijacking you'll need the cockpit ordnance. I'm afraid all we have is an old Glock Eighteen, but it does have rapid fire I think. Anyway, I have the key here somewhere if you'd like me to get it for you. I don't know if it's loaded, though."

"You have not to worry," interrupted Prashant eagerly, "I am taking the introduction to vehicular hijackings and the handgun basics module while at the *SCUM* academy, you see, so I know very much what I am doing in such cases."

"Great," said Jesús with a sigh of relief, "not having carried out a bus hijacking before I must confess I was a little worried. Also, can we talk about this later, as the runway seems to be coming at us a bit fast?"

"Dennis!!!!" he shrieked.

"What's your problem Fly-Boy?"

"We're going too fast. We're landing way too fast."

"Don't crap your pants, you're on ALS you fucking bird brain. It'll reverse all the way just before the nose wheels go down."

"Oh, yes, of course, I forgot," Jesús whimpered, and promptly closed his eyes.

CHAPTER 48

My Fellow Americans

The embarrassing part was explaining he couldn't get into the bunker. Mandy Miller and Dennis Floyd were especially peeved because they were under the impression he had held nothing back, told them the whole truth and nothing but, as it were. Jesus One and the Khan just rolled their eyes. Everyone else was dazed to begin with, and Shirley was still pinching herself, so they didn't change their expressions one iota at the news. Dirk, of course, had been dazed all along.

"But that's not such a big deal, actually," Jesús went on, "because we had Crony Corporation lay in a bunch of supplies and stuff anyway, and when the power goes off we'll have the standby generators and some candles."

Trinity raised her hand. "I have a question."

"Yes, Trinity, go ahead."

"When will our bags arrive? The thing is, like, seeing as how we're not doing the season finale, like, will we still be entitled to the complimentary ticket to your return destination of choice?"

"Oh Jeez," said Jesús, slapping himself on the forehead, "I'm really very sorry, but with everything happening so fast and the hijacking I clean forgot about the baggage."

This brought Shirley front and center. "Well, excuse me," she said, "but have you all been living on a desert island, or what? If you've been listening to Geraldo at the volcano site, he says it could be the end of the world. You girls should think yourselves lucky you have landed somewhere comfortable with a nice view." Shirley was not unattractive, but she had a hard mouth that rarely offered comfort. It sounded like she was talking about a person going on a free holiday and not sounding grateful.

After that, apart from Dennis putting his head in his hands, everybody settled down more or less at once. For some reason, Dennis then felt obliged to pick up where he had left off, i.e., helping with the evacuation flights. Shirley, it turned out, had taken to watching the parking lot like a bird takes to a tree. You see, Preston Pleasant had designed a spiffy console, which he had located on the observation deck in the control cab. You could observe and operate everything from this one desk—which Preston referred to as *MOM*, for Multiple Operations Monitor—including the surface-to-air missiles, landmines, and all the different Gatling guns. Shirley took Prashant and Norma upstairs and explained how they would henceforth be rotating shifts at said *MOM*—even let Norma do a test fire. The girls settled in the break room where they variously fixed lattes, glanced from *Star* magazine to Geraldo and back again, and stared hungrily at Dirk.

In the meantime, Jesús retired to the wineglass lobby with Mandy and the two previously chosen ones. By this time, it was well past dusk. On the other side of the giant window, the mountains and water were getting used to the idea of it being dark all the time, though fields of bright lights defined their edges, so you could tell where they were. Once in a rare while, a tiny fistful of lights chugged across Puget Sound. Although it was still the biggest operator in the country, Washington State Ferries was much diminished owing to recent human resource issues. To put it another way, there wasn't much ferry traffic because the summer schedule was shot all to hell.

"For starters, perhaps you might explain," Jesús began, "just what was so important that Albert had to leave in such a hurry."

The Khan put down his glass of Merlot and grinned. In the red safety lighting and with his droopy moustache he could have been the devil incarnate. "Remember when we were locked up and he wouldn't do the teleporting demo?"

"Yes, something about needing authorization wasn't it, and the previous God hitting on young virgins?"

"Exactly, well as it turns out, that previous God was exiled to the planet Gronad. He was only acting Messiah, so all he had to do was wait out his regular ten thousand year deployment. Unfortunately, he thought he could talk the Gronads out of eating their first born, so he came down from on high to mingle amongst them as a humble supplicant. Three weeks later, the Gronads ate him too. His problem in the first place was over-mingling, so in a way he had it coming."

"So, what you're trying to tell me is a Messiah getting eaten rates way higher than an exploding planet? Anyway, how come he didn't do a resurrection or something?"

Jesus One smiled mirthlessly. "Getting eaten isn't quite the same thing is it? In order to be resurrected there has to be at least something left behind, preferably all in one piece."

"*Touché*," said the Khan, "and I've still got the scars to prove it."

"Let me understand something," Mandy said right out of the blue, looking all discombobulated and talking as if she had just discovered how. "So Uncle Johnny was innocently sitting in this diner and looking to leave town, then you and Einstein showed up, just like that, on a whim?"

"Yes," said Jesús, "that would be correct, on a whim so to speak, although it's fair to say I was desperate for a cup of coffee and we didn't have much choice, seeing as how neither one of us was about to try anywhere else in town."

"He had absolutely no idea what he was getting into, did he?"

""No," said Jesús, "but nor did I for that matter. All I did was go for a bike ride on my birthday."

Mandy sized him up and nodded vaguely as if he had just mentioned it was warm out. He recognized the symptoms. She probably felt the floor was sliding backwards, so he wasn't surprised when she took a while to get her thoughts back in order. "I can see now why he was so keen to go to Baltimore," she finally observed. "All in all, I'm not so sure I shouldn't have gone with him. You did call him didn't you?"

"Yes, I called him and like I told you he was doing fine."

"Well, if you don't mind, I want to get him on a plane."

"Be my guest, and if you need money for the ticket, just say the word. I'd like to spend as much as I can before it goes out of style."

"Great," said the Khan. "In that case why not call for a bunch of Petro-Pizzas before they go out of style too."

Jesús looked out the window for a long moment and imagined it without the lights. The Khan, it seemed, was in need of clarification. "That might be difficult," he said, "on account of they probably have snipers out there by now, knowing we have a busload of virgins locked up. That would be the reason the lights are off in here."

"Oh, I see. I'm still starving though," said the Khan, casting a sly glance at Mandy. "Who's in charge of the virgins then? It's about time they made themselves useful, if you want my opinion."

Mandy returned to earth with a bump. "Don't look at me, I quit that job. We're not on the island anymore. Also, unless you're brain dead, you should know by now they're not that kind of virgin. You want food, you grab a frozen dinner and head for the microwave like everybody else."

The Khan put his head in his hands. "I've had enough," he muttered. "All the joy just went out of this frigging adventure."

"Actually," Jesús said, "I was getting to that. When Albert left, how did he leave things with you two? I mean, you're not planning to stay for the duration, are you?"

"No way," said Jesus One. "He said as soon as Gronad was sorted out, he'd bring the mother ship in close and beam us back up with the *Anti-Grav*. He also said to tell you he'd finished doing the past particle calculation while he was working on the nutty contests."

"That's nice, but he's not going to be away for another ten thousand years or so is he?"

"Nah," the Khan said, "a couple more weeks at most, maybe sooner. All they're planning to do is have him scare the crap out of the Gronads. He'll do falling frogs, crop infestations, and a big booming voice with lightning bolts. Then he'll pick on some poor bastard like me for the hard part."

"I honestly can't believe you actually conquered the known world," Mandy said, with more than a hint of sarcasm.

"Oh, really, just look at him, then," the Khan said, nodding at Jesús. "A thousand years from now he'll be remembered the same way I am: Father of us All, Lord of the Universe, Mighty Man of Steel, Warrior King, God of Gods, Protector of the Virgins, and so on. And all *he* did was go for a ride on his bike. Go figure."

"God forbid," she exclaimed.

"Jeez, thanks a lot," said Jesús. "Anyway," he continued, "I just wanted us four to get together so we can be on the same page. My understanding from Albert is there will be some kind of uprising and the president will have to flee the White House and come here. That's how we'll get into the bunker, because he has the pass code in his forehead.

So we wait until he shows up. Then all he has to do is knock on the front door and we'll let him in. I didn't want to share that with the others because it sounds ridiculous."

"News to me," said the Khan

"Me too," Jesus One agreed

Mandy buried her head in her hands. When she looked up, she seemed confused again.

"It's just the jet lag," said Jesús, "what you need to do is to lie down for a while and try to get some sleep."

While Mandy grabbed a sleeping bag and looked around for a suitable spot, Jesús returned to the break-room with Jesus One and the Khan. By this time, most of the virgins and Dirk were out for the count. He gently eased Dirk from his Chesterfield to the carpet, found the remote, and brought the volume up to where he could just hear it.

Shirley was right: Geraldo was reporting from the volcano site. Actually, he was reporting from the observatory, seeing no reason to get any closer than was necessary. Jesús had no way of knowing if he was watching a live broadcast or a rerun. He decided it didn't make any difference. He was surprised, though, to see Blister was back.

"Yes, Geraldo, it really is good to be back," Blister was saying. "I guess I was a trifle hasty. I've been in contract negotiations with Lou Dawbs and I have to say he made me an offer I couldn't refuse."

Geraldo flashed his famous jaw splitting grin. "No explanation needed, Wolf. You never say no to Lou. Last guy did that woke up next to Marlon Brando. Now we all know Marlon passed away these many years ago, but he was a well proportioned man, and I'm given to understand there was still a good bit left."

Blister sniffed and adjusted his earpiece. "Be that as it may—right now, can you bring us up to date with the situation out there? I'm told you have put together yet another team of expert opinion leaders for the nightly roundup."

The camera pulled back wide revealing Dick Derringer, Vernon Trumboy, Doctor Clump, and Giovanni Garibaldi. Whereas Geraldo was leaning casually against the balcony, his guests were sitting on lawn chairs and having to fidget, not to mention they had to look up at him when he spoke.

"Yes, Wolf, we're gathered here on the observation deck of the YVO, and it's been one heck of a nice day in the park. You can see just how peaceful it was before the sun went down."

The image cut on cue to a graceful sweep of the camera, showing vast reaches of a wilderness tinted gold and burnt ochre and deepening green by the early evening sun. Patches of vapor lingered above Yellowstone Lake like sleeping summer ghosts. Lava bubbled and glinted as it emerged lazily from the blast hole on Specimen Ridge. Far below, a heat haze shimmered over the flaming red expanse of Lava Lake.

Camera two, at the ridge get ready for a head shot of Geraldo, in tight, angle down a tad so we don't see the nose hair. Focus on the forehead then he can look up and do his crinkly eyed squinting into the sun thing and show off the Botox. Great, go with that. Cut to Geraldo camera two. Geraldo, eyes in the sun. Go on two.

"Wolf, we are definitely feeling a whole lot better about things today. I have Dick Derringer here from Global-Titanic Worldwide Entertainment and Park Ranger Vernon Trumboy (*cut to Dick, with Dirk-like grin and Vernon, blushing*), who deny absolutely that we have a problem. Also, we're privileged to have Doctor Edward Clump on hand (*cut to Clump smiling like somebody's favorite uncle*). Doctor Clump, as you know, is former head of the YVO and is here investigating for the White House. Last but not least is restaurant entrepreneur Giovanni Garibaldi (*cut to Garibaldi, looking over-prosperous and overfed*). He just opened a bunch of Shovel Houses in the park, and if that's not a vote of confidence, I don't know what is. Oh yes, Wolf, and we'll also go live to Pastureland later in the program for some stirring words from the Reverend Billy Ray Bixbee. The reverend has something to say about how his flock is dealing positively with what many are saying is an unprecedented crisis of faith."

A cut-in showed a beaming Billy Ray sitting back on a sumptuous white leather settee on the IMAX stage. Seated next to him were a radiant New Prophetess of Pastureland and a somewhat subdued Bishop Ron.

The Khan, who had been ignoring the broadcast, glanced up all ears and eyes at the mention of Billy Ray. When he saw the group on the settee, he threw down his *Star* magazine and snarled. "I owe that bastard. Remember, I told him it was war? Well I never go back on a promise. He's toast. Also, he called me a Chinaman, and nobody talks like that to Genghis Khan."

He was already rising to his feet, when Jesus One put out a restraining hand. "Calm down, will you, he's in Florida, which would be like three thousand miles away. You can't just walk outside and punch his lights out."

"I'm not so sure about that." An unsteady voice came from the doorway. It was Mandy Miller. She was clutching her cell phone and her face was as white as Erwin Schrödinger's bottom. "It's Uncle Johnny. I tried calling him and all I got was a recording. It was *SCUM*. They've kidnapped him. Billy Ray saw an interview with the bus driver after the hijacking so they know we're here. They want us to let them into the tower or they say they'll use Uncle Johnny for a mine detector. They'll be here sometime Wednesday."

"Oh, fuck," said Jesús.

"Bring it on," said the Khan, grinning like a maniac.

"Just a minute," said Jesus One, "I think we ought to watch this."

On screen, a flustered Wolf Blister was fiddling with his earpiece. "I'm sorry, Geraldo," he said, "I'm going to have to cut you off. The president wants a word."

Before he could say more, the screen dipped to black then the president appeared. There was no God Bless America, just the flag in the background and Gladys Rumsfoiled standing by his right shoulder. Rumsfoiled was removing her spectacles and smiling inscrutably. The president, on the other hand, seemed awfully grim.

"My fellow Americans..." he began.

Bummer!

Or, as the French might say, "*C'est la vie*!"

CHAPTER 49

Patriot Game

The principal reason Frank Chamberlain got involved was because Brigadier General Norman Nimegen still had it in for him—always had. Norman Nimegen was Chamberlain's personal nemesis and it went both ways, and they both knew it. To put it another way: Chamberlain despised Nimegen for being a candy assed little cock sucker, and Nimegen despised Chamberlain for being right on the money and not hiding the fact.

Of course, Nimegen didn't couch it in those terms. What he said was, "I hate to say this Secretary Rumsfoiled, but we're sort of thin on the ground right now. A good seventy five percent of our best shooters have taken off to protect their families, and I'm not sure I can vouch for the rest. The situation is getting worse by the minute."

"So what do we do, Norman? As soon as Core finishes his speech from the *PHEWH* and I make my move, I want him on a plane to Seattle double quick. So we need access to the *PHEWHW* and it's not as if we can just walk up and knock on the front door anymore, is it? There must be some way we can get past those lunatics holed up in that tower. I mean, the reason I upped you to Brigadier General is that you're supposed to be the expert on special operations. I'll tell you one thing, I'm not pussy-footing around on this one. Some crackpot has convinced Madge Chainey she can drain the magma from Yellowstone by setting off a bunch of underground atom bombs. And now she won't listen to reason. So just to be on the safe side, I'm voting for the end of the world. When those bombs go off, I want all my bases covered. I'm going to stay here and Madge has volunteered to take the president to Seattle. Before she leaves she'll want to know how she can get into that tower. So, what's it to be, hotshot?"

Nimegen stroked his moustache thoughtfully and tried not to seem confused. "Well, Madam Secretary, there is one possibility. We'll want somebody dumber than a box of rocks to bust his way into the tower and believe whatever cockamamie excuse we come up with. He'll have to be totally fearless and an expert in close combat assault; you know, kicking in doors and blowing people away, and all that stuff. Not to mention, it's vital he hasn't watched TV in a while and can do fiberglass work, which is not something we normally train for."

"What in the name of God are you talking about, General? We're not planning to fix up Mickey's Toontown Fair; this is Sea-Tac tower we're busting into."

"That's just it," said Nimegen. "You see, I spoke with Preston Pleasant. He did the defensive systems design for the tower and he tells me there is only one weak spot. Everything else is either blast proof or covered by one of his weapons systems."

This caught Rumsfoiled's attention. She removed her spectacles and polished them vigorously with a soft cloth she kept handy. Nimegen knew the signs. This one meant she sensed she was about to gain the upper hand. The polishing was a substitute for stiletto sharpening. Afterwards, when she removed her spectacles and smiled inscrutably it meant somebody just got voted off the island—stiletto pre-sharpened and just looking for the right pair of shoulder blades, as it were.

Nimegen hadn't made it to Brigadier General by gazing out the window.

"So where exactly is our weak spot?"

"It's at the top of the concrete tower beneath the control cab, where they have the big observation lobby and the break room. That whole section is made from big reinforced fiberglass panels over a steel frame, so the tower isn't top heavy. They call it the wineglass, because it sort of looks like one. According to Preston, the roof guns don't point down and the Gatling guns on top of the base building can't swivel up that far."

"So it's not blast proof?"

"No way. They figured they wouldn't need blast proof that high up, and anyway, the concrete stem takes all the stress during an earthquake."

"But isn't it rather high?"

"I'm afraid so, but we can reach it with a fire truck HLAR platform—that stands for High Level Articulated Range—it's like a giant cherry picker they use for really tall buildings. We can stand off the truck outside the parking lot and we'll do it under cover of darkness. The only problem is we can only get two men on the platform besides me. Once we're up there, though, the front man can use a heavy-duty angle grinder to cut an access hole through the fiberglass. After that, we'll have the tower secured in no time at all. That's why we need the fiberglass skills—for operating the angle grinder and patching the hole, because we wouldn't want ash or accidental nuclear fallout getting in afterwards."

"And just who might our dimwit superhero be?"

"His name is Frank Chamberlain. He retired a few years back—Army special-forces sergeant—twelve tours, three hundred twenty missions, every one a success and never lost a man. You know what they say: 'if you're gonna be dumb, you gotta be tough'? Well, believe me, Frank Chamberlain is the world champion. He's dumber and tougher than anyone I ever met. I checked pension records and he's getting mail at some Podunk south sea island in Melanesia. Best of all, he's living on a sailboat. That fact alone guarantees he almost never watches TV, spends half his time grinding fiberglass, and the other half patching it up."

"Good, pick him up and do it fast. I want this done and over with in the next forty-eight hours. By the way, what's our leverage on this idiot? He'd have to be out of his mind to head this way right now."

"*You* are, Madam Secretary."

"Please explain yourself, Nimegen, before I remove my spectacles and smile inscrutably. Don't think for one moment I haven't seen you watching me."

"Er, yes, well, the way we'll get to him is through his wife. She's very patriotic, you see, so if we convince her that the president's life is in danger and we need Frank, she'll see to it he does the right thing. That's why it helps if they haven't been watching much TV lately."

"So I make a tearful phone call?"

"Yes, we'll patch you in the minute we get a chopper to the boat."

"Go do it, General, and don't screw up, we're short on time. Oh, and there's one more thing." She took off her spectacles and smiled inscrutably. "I'm not sure if you've thought of this, Norman, but what happens when your man gets inside the tower and finds out he's been duped?"

Nimegen smiled inscrutably back, inwardly regretting having had the Lasik surgery. This is not to say he hadn't considered clear glass spectacles. He just hadn't wanted to seem overly obsequious and imitative. "Not a problem, Madam Secretary. The number two man on the platform is bought and paid for. He's a former Spetsnaz commando, name of Boris. The minute we get in, assuming Chamberlain hasn't already been shot to pieces by a reception committee, Boris will demote the good sergeant to fiberglass repair technician first class. Of course, once the hole is patched, Boris will demote him all the way down to the parking lot with the president—no stops along the way, if you see what I mean."

"Yes," murmured the secretary, vigorously polishing her spectacles, "I do believe I see exactly what you mean."

CHAPTER 50

Resurrection

As Jesus One had previously pointed out, resurrection does have its limitations. It is just not possible, as he explained, to restore and resuscitate someone after they have been totally eaten. Of course, you may still have residual DNA, but the problem with DNA is the very best you can expect is a fully functioning clone. Cloning a chosen one serves little purpose, because all you'll get is a person with a severe identity crisis, rather like Billy the Kid, only much worse. In his case, although there was significant damage, Jesus One was essentially whole when they got him down from the cross. After restorative surgery and a quick dose of post martyrdom therapy, you couldn't tell the difference—as evidenced by his brief return to tie up the loose ends.

The Khan, on the other hand, had a somewhat less uplifting experience—so to speak.

The problem with being a savior, as Jesus One well knew, is that things tend to turn out badly. For some reason—and this partly explains why the Confederation still had its doubts—humankind has never been, well, *kind* to its heroes. We could mention Joan of Arc, Sir Thomas Moore, the original forty virgins (what an exercise in vileness that was), and in more recent times, JFK, MLK, RFK, and John Lennon. The list just goes on.

Thus, it should have come as no surprise when the Khan, in his adopted persona of William Wallace, was put to death in a most gruesome fashion. The English, you see, need little instruction in such matters. Even Adolf Hitler grudgingly gave credit to the Brits for coming up with concentration camps during the Boer war. Of course, with typical Teutonic thoroughness, he did take the idea somewhat further.

The irony was the Khan should have known better. He didn't go along with God in the first place because he was smart enough to know where he might end up. Instead, he opted for delivering pretty much the same message at the pointy end of a sword. If only he hadn't listened to Jesus One—but what's a mother to do?

Week after week, month after month, cooped up in the mother ship, the Khan had to put up with a self-serving litany from Jesus One on the benefits of martyrdom. You know how it goes: how good you'll feel about yourself afterwards; how much self discipline it takes; how painful it can be, but well worth the suffering; how it sets such a wonderful example for others—kind of like the twenty-one day Oprah diet—not to mention the disciples and all those cathedrals and churches. Yet, after living to a ripe old age, and not being big on martyrdom, all the Khan left behind were lots of close family and a secret tomb stuffed full of unimaginable treasures.

What a bummer that must have been.

Not surprisingly, Jesus One felt somewhat responsible when William Wallace, a.k.a. Genghis Khan, was betrayed and taken to London, where he was hanged, drawn, and quartered and had his head chopped off. No one had thought for one moment it would go that far, least of all the Khan. So it goes without saying that when volunteers were called for to collect the remains, Jesus One was among the first to raise a hand.

The recovery squad descended via the *Anti-Grav* some four hours before dawn on the morning of the twenty fourth of August, 1305. The Khan, having been dealt with the day before, was by this time on his way to various destinations around the country. All but his head, that is, which was freshly impaled on a pike atop London Bridge.

With Jesus One were two veteran saviors who had taken to recovery work as a useful and rewarding way of passing the time. The lead recovery specialist was a fellow by the name of Bréanainn of Clonfert, otherwise known as Saint Brendan. His assistant was a minor saint, the former Marina of Antioch, who could empathize with the Khan, having lost her own head while she herself was being martyred. Jesus One, of course, was just along for the ride and to make amends as best he could.

To retrieve the Khan's head, all they had to do was follow the river Thames up from the estuary and beam down directly to the bridge. His torso and limbs had been neatly quartered and stuffed into four iron baskets. Unfortunately, the baskets were headed (no pun intended) for Wallace's old haunts, namely Newcastle, Stirling, Berwick-on-Tweed, and Aberdeen, where they were destined to adorn the city walls. Thus, having retrieved the head, the recovery squad was obliged to take a three-day break, while the baskets trundled ever so slowly northwards.

You should also know that while still alive, the Khan (a.k.a. William Wallace) was emasculated and eviscerated then compelled to watch while his bowels were burned. The other organ was fed to the palace dogs as a sort of side attraction.

Luckily, Confederation surgeons did organ replacements the way most people change watch batteries, so the missing bits were the least of the Khan's concerns. It must be said, though, he did spend some considerable time in post-dismemberment therapy. After that, he reverted to type and seemed to lose all further interest in martyrdom.

There was, nonetheless, a considerable and unexpected bonus for the Kahn in all of this. Given the state of his arms and legs after being broken in several places (to better cram them into the baskets), his surgeons opted for a procedure known as force-multiplication myoplasty—which is just a fancy way of saying they gave him bionic limbs.

So it was that three scant weeks after getting back from London, Stirling, Aberdeen, Newcastle, and Berwick-on-Tweed, the Khan was running like a racehorse and bench-pressing close to two and a half tons—attributes that would serve him well during his forthcoming encounter with the Reverend Billy Ray.

CHAPTER 51

We are Dealing with Lunatics

Naturally, Frank said no at first. He pointed out he had a real problem leaving his wife alone on a sailboat in the back of beyond with only a half-wit dog for company—notwithstanding the offer of round-the-clock protection from the Vanahu Volunteer Defense Force. "That," he explained, "would be my biggest worry. Those guys couldn't safeguard their grandmother's ass at a pot luck supper, if you'll pardon the expression, ma'am. So I'd just as soon you find somebody a bit closer to home. You also have to know I don't do that stuff anymore. The wrong people always end up getting hurt."

As you can imagine, it didn't end there. The secretary asked for a quick word with Marge, and soon drummed up the necessary support when she explained Frank was the president's only hope. "They have the president and his family held captive in a heavily fortified control tower, you see, and we can't attack with conventional forces because they have said they will kill him and the children if we try. I am further advised that because of recent force depletion there is just about no one left with the necessary skills. Not many people, Mrs. Chamberlain, can do angle grinding and successfully rescue precious cargo the way your husband can."

Then, "No, we can't give them what they want Mrs. Chamberlain. What they want, I'm afraid, are some atom bombs they can set off near Yellowstone Park and get it all over with. It appears we are dealing with lunatics."

Then, "I'm at my wit's end, Marge—may I call you Marge—I have been up half the night frantic with worry, and the people in the park have said they won't leave. If it were not for the end of the world, we could wear the kidnappers down with lies and false promises, but time is of the essence, dear, because it is ever so urgent that the president gives hope to his fellow Americans, as I am sure you will agree."

Who could say no—other than Frank Chamberlain, that is?

***

Marge was stoic, apart from her mouth turning down ever so slightly at the edges. It had been a long time since Frank had left like this, and they had both gotten used to it not happening. Now here they were revisiting the past and it wasn't the same anymore. Now, when she hugged him she didn't let go so easily; she was less controlled.

Frank was calm enough now the decision had been made. But one thing had changed: he had never told Marge, because he suspected she knew, and anyway it wasn't something you shared, but leaving had always been tinged with anticipation for him, as if he had already left in his head and was eager to be getting on with it. Not any more, though. That part of him, the part that had been eager, was now all too conscious of what was being left behind.

Even Hilda was aware.

His only conditions were that he personally supervise the refueling of a long range jet to get him back home, that the *VVDF* stay the hell away from his boat, and that he stop by Noahu to pick up some extra fiberglass matting; the heavy-duty angle grinder he already had. The other thing he did was drop off a handheld VHF radio for Alfredo with instructions to stay in constant contact with Marge.

An hour and a half after Frank left, Alfredo called Marge to inform her that the president of the United States had just been on TV—live and well from underneath his back lawn. By then, of course, it was too late. Frank Chamberlain was already out of reach and Marge knew there was not a damn thing she could do about it.

CHAPTER 52

Storm Clouds Gather

Knowing nothing of Frank Chamberlain's imminent arrival, the occupants of the tower were preoccupied with their other impending visitor, namely, the Reverend Billy Ray Bixbee.

By now all the virgins had phoned home, and without exception had been advised to stay put. The president's speech (which we will get to shortly) had made it clear that was probably good advice for the time being. In the meantime, Mandy, Shirley, and Norma had formed a sort of triumvirate that was more or less running things. Norma, it turned out, was just what the virgins needed: she was industrious, caring, and inclined to listen, but not reluctant to put her foot down when necessary. Shirley kept the wheels turning: she supervised shift changes, doled out supplies, and watched everybody like a hawk. Nothing got past Shirley. Mandy made sure the boys toed the line without realizing they didn't have a vote.

Like right now, discussing things at what amounted to a senior staff meeting, Dennis was sounding off, blissfully unaware Mandy had a rope around his neck. Ever the pragmatist, he was all set to veto any-and-all plans for a negotiated settlement with Bixbee. "Don't get me wrong, but I never met Uncle Johnny," he pointed out, "and as much as I personally cannot abide coercion in any shape or form, it's Dennis Floyd's own, private, individual ass on the line here, so I vote no, whatever it is. Call their bluff. If they poke him forward with a fucking broomstick, I'll turn off the nearest mine. Then, if anybody falls in behind him, Shirley can dispense a couple thousand rounds of attitude adjusters."

Mandy gave that idea the look of raw contempt it so richly deserved.

"If only Albert were here," Jesús said, "I'm sure he'd come up with something."

"Well, as usual, you're a big help," said Mandy, "apart from which, every single time he came up with an idea you pooh-poohed it. I'm just glad you weren't there when he was doing the nutty contests."

"I don't know what to say," said Jesus One, wisely.

"Well, I do," said the Khan. "Get me some weapons and half a barbarian horde and Bixbee is camel crap."

"As a matter of fact," said Shirley, "we do have lots of weapons that were left by Crony as a sort of closeout bonus. I keep them in a big storage locker behind *MOM*, but I'm afraid I can't be of any help to you when it comes to a barbarian horde, Mister Khan, even a half of one."

"Mmm, just a minute," said Jesús, "talking about armies, that reminds me of Albert's *HOLI CRAP*."

"I beg your pardon," said Norma.

"No, it's not like that; they were computer programs he ran. One of them predicted that seventy-two hours after word getting out about Yellowstone, three armies would rise up and duke it out. He mentioned the *NAACP*, what was left of the standing army, and the televangelists."

"Well, he was right about the televangelists," said Mandy. "If I know Billy Ray, by the time he gets here, he'll have enough people with him to storm the Bastille, let alone Sea-Tac."

"You must have missed it," interjected Norma. "I was watching reruns of 'Geraldo Live' this morning, and during that interview he just did, Mister Bixbee said he had formed a new initiative for spiritual leadership and inspiration to get us through these challenging times. He referred to it as his Adventist Army of Rapture and Perdition, which he is calling the *AARP*."

"Great," said Jesús, "so we've got the *AARP* about to go to war with the *NAACP*. All we need now is for the *ACLU* to pick up some bows and arrows and we'll have the Triple Crown."

"I just hate to say this," Dennis added, "but for once in your wasted life, Martinez, you may be on to something. Word came from airport security yesterday that the local gang bangers have signed up with the

NAACP. There's talk they might hijack one of the evacuation flights, or worse, seize the airport. Not that I personally could give a crap."

"Excuse me," the Khan said, "but where can I find this *NAACP?*"

Dennis showed all his teeth, even the molars. It wasn't so much that he was grinning, it was more his version of drop-jawed amazement. "Are you kidding? You get within a half-mile of those *cucarachas* they'll have you wrapped in a foot-long burrito before you can say Speedy fucking Gonzalez."

"So, where must I go then to be within this half mile?" the Khan enquired.

"What you do," Dennis replied, with newly found respect, realizing this was no joke, "is take a cab to Central and get dropped off on any street corner south of Madison, always assuming you can find a cabbie dumb enough to take you. Mind you, if you show up dressed like that, you won't have to find them, they'll find you. And believe me, you won't live to regret it."

"Oh, I don't know," said the Khan, "I've been through a lot worse than being wrapped in a burrito. By the way, you couldn't loan me the cab fare could you? I haven't carried money since I don't know when. Also, would you mind turning off the landmines while I cross the parking lot?"

***

They waited until midnight before raising the Kevlar door so the Khan could sneak out under cover of darkness (exfiltrate, so to speak). Not that sneaking out was the best way to describe it, since he was somewhat encumbered and not that frightened anyway of being apprehended. The reason he wasn't scared was Shirley had come up with a pair of XM214 battery powered mini Gatling guns and six thousand rounds of ammunition. Thus, when the Khan crossed the parking lot he was carrying two sixty-five pound backpacks of ammo, two linkless ammo belts, and six NiCad battery packs strapped around his waist. Total weight: two hundred seventy-five pounds, plus twenty-two ounces for a handheld radio. The six-barreled mini guns weighed in at thirty pounds each. He walked like he was carrying two water pistols and a lunch pail.

"Mister Pleasant advised me these things must only be used with gun mounts, because they are so heavy, and if you tried to fire one yourself the recoil would knock you off your feet," is what Shirley had said.

"Piss on that, Shirley," was the Khan's reply. "If only we'd had these a thousand years ago, I could have conquered China in a day and a half. Tighten this battery belt for me, will you please, I've got some recruiting to do."

Persuading a cabbie to drive him to the Central district was not a problem. Nor, was the recruiting for that matter. All it took was a three second demonstration burst that wiped out every vehicle and half the buildings in a two hundred yard radius, not to mention what was left of the street lighting.

The Lord of the Universe was back.

CHAPTER 53

Plowshare

In his precautionary speech, president Core emphasized that early reports from Doctor Clump and his task force were encouraging. That is to say, they agreed there were disturbances and tremors, but there had always been disturbances and tremors. Moreover, even though the present disturbances were severe, that didn't prove a thing, they said. Sure, the kids were right about the magnitude, they said, but lookit, everybody knows that when this thing goes off it will be a mega-colossal. Like we've known that forever. Tell us something we *don't* know dudes. The point is: no one can say for certain exactly when it will go off, not even the kids.

"Furthermore," Clump pointed out, "as far as we know, nobody that survived one of these things had either the writing skills or the inclination to document the event, so we have no way of knowing for sure how much or what kind of warning we'll get anyway. My advice," he said, "is to tell the people not to worry."

So that's what the president told the people.

President's Speech to the Nation
Monday August 23, 22:30 (Pacific Daylight Time), which would be Tuesday August 24, 01:30 (Eastern Daylight Time)

"My fellow Americans, there is no cause for alarm. Reports from the Clump task force are encouraging. Moreover, the only reason I'm broadcasting to you at this late hour from the *PHEWH* and not the *PEOC* is because Secretary Rumsfoiled suggested I try out the acoustics and for some reason she couldn't wait. Also, I must say, it's a lot more comfortable.

What I want you to do is go about your business as usual, and pretend nothing bad is happening. In the meantime, since I'm already down here, I'm told we may as well check out the rest of the bunkers, so my people and a few invited guests are doing that as I speak.

By the way, I have authorized the printing of three hundred fifty million leaflets explaining what *YOYO* means—one for each man, woman, and child in this great nation of ours. If they spell my name right this time and we don't have to print them over, you should get them by Christmas.

Oh yes, and the reason I'm looking awfully grim right now is because they moved up the timing on me, so my special order of Little Debbie's Marshmallow Supremes with the tiny presidential seal in the middle hasn't arrived yet.

Other than that, let me reiterate we really have no idea if or when Yellowstone will ever explode. So what I say is, don't give up on your day job, spend like crazy, and above all, pay your taxes on time. Remember, we're all in this together."

Now, you have to understand, we are paraphrasing here. The president's actual speech was a lot longer, and he didn't really spill the beans about his Little Debbie's cakes. He also used a lot of important sounding words like *endure*, and *heroic*, and *legacy*, and *prevail*, and *persevere,* etc, (oh, and let's not forget *peace* and *prosperity*). It was a fine speech, but it did nothing to alleviate the panic. You see, once people are convinced the end is nigh, it is hard to persuade them otherwise, regardless of how important your words might sound.

"Excellent," said Gladys Rumsfoiled when the speech was over. "I must say the acoustics were perfect. Before you get too settled, though, Mister President, there is something you should know. The girls and I got together and we decided it's time for a change. So effective immediately, you're out of a job. Given the world is about to end we thought it best you take up residence in the *PHEWHH* in Seattle while we run things from here. By the way, thanks for letting us in, the locks are being changed as we speak."

Core felt an icy hand at his throat. "You can't do that, this is a democracy. What about the Constitution?"

"We'll send you a framed copy when you get to Seattle. Also, just so you know, we did in fact keep some of the best bits when we drafted the declaration for our new alliance."

"What alliance?" He croaked.

"All in due time. You'll find out when we've got you safely settled in the *PHEWHH*. It's sort of a world peace thing. Naturally, I'll be in charge."

"Well, I'll be darned," proclaimed Core.

"Yes, doubtless you will be, but we will need to get you on a plane and off to Seattle double quick. Of course, there's still the problem of not being able to get you into Sea-Tac tower, but not to worry, I've got that covered. Unfortunately, Madge is dead set on exploding her bombs Wednesday night, so there isn't much time."

"Bombs, what bombs?"

Rumsfoiled removed her spectacles and polished them vigorously before replying. Then she skipped a step and went straight to smiling inscrutably. "Remember Project Plowshare?"

"Why, of course, they briefed me when I took over. Back when we had our first cold war with Russia it was the backbone of our *Peaceful Nuclear Explosions* program. The Russians had started what they called *Nuclear Explosions for the National Economy* and we wanted to keep up."

"Exactly, Mister President, or maybe I should be calling you, Al. Anyway, you're right, but after close to ten years and setting off dozens of underground test explosions at a cost of untold billion of dollars, some smart-ass at the Atomic Energy Commission remembered about nuclear fallout."

"Yes, well that did present a problem didn't it?"

"That depends on your point of view. They had what I have always thought was this great idea for opening up the Northwest Passage. Then the senior senator from Alaska thought it might cost him votes, so he had it killed in committee. The bottom line, is Madge found out there's a bunch of those unused peaceful atom bombs still sitting on a shelf in Nevada. Her idea is we put them all in this deep mineshaft outside Salt Lake City and light the fuse. That way, we'll get this frigging great sinkhole and the magma from Yellowstone will leak into it, and there'll be almost no nuclear fallout, and our problems will be over. Of course, we'll have to say farewell, if not adieu, to Salt Lake City, but they're done for anyway."

"What if it doesn't work?"

"You have a better idea?"

"No."

"In that case, as the venerable Richard Cheney, once said to the equally venerable Senator Patrick Leahy, 'Go fuck yourself'. Your Little Debbie's have arrived, by the way, so why don't you grab a snack and have someone tuck you in, since it is way past your bedtime. Then we can put you on the plane all nice and refreshed to get to you Seattle first thing Wednesday morning. Of course, I wouldn't be expecting Air Force One if I were you, your upgrades just expired."

CHAPTER 54

Armageddon: Part I

The Forces of Evil

The events of Wednesday August 26, 2026, would echo and resonate in the labyrinths and chambers of time for centuries and millennia to come. It truly was the end of all life on the planet as we knew it—well, more or less. Yet, it was also a new beginning. Throughout the ages that followed the miracles and mysteries of that day of days would unfold in countless retellings. Myths would multiply and abound. Reputations would be reinvented, restored, and reinvented again. Reality and reason would give way to romance and reflection. Fact would give way to fiction. Necessity would give birth to invention.

Et cetera, et cetera.

Mind you, what actually happened was definitely right up there with Nostradamus. A reincarnated Genghis Khan rounded up a fresh horde of barbarians and led them into battle. The Anti-Christ in the person of Gladys Rumsfoiled promised peace and prosperity on Earth and lied about it. A powerful prophet, accompanied by his new prophetess, came from the south to fight off the barbarian horde (and anybody else standing in his way). God made two appearances in the middle of it all. Jesus Christ ascended on high for the second time. A giant UFO shaped like a cigar was sighted hovering over Seattle. Virgins were imperiled. A lone hero (known only as Frank) came out of nowhere and vanquished the forces of evil, then mysteriously disappeared. Then to top it all, an unlikely new-world emperor and his empress emerged from the chaos and the confusion flanked by twenty-one virgins and and an odd-looking fellow clutching a nail gun. Not to mention Yellowstone National Park exploded and plunged the world into everlasting darkness—well, more or less.

Overall, it was quite the day.

***

The forces of evil made their move at four in the morning. Such people favor this time of day because it is when you are most likely to go quietly (as Adolf Hitler well knew).

The biggest downside for Frank was Norman Nimegen being present. Boris could be a handful and Nimegen was a rat, so things didn't bode well. Frank promised himself to waste no time rescuing the president and handing him over to Nimegen. After that, he would take off in his confiscated and recently refueled 767 faster than your average fruit bat could blink.

Of course, it didn't work out that way. Does it ever?

Frank barely had time to ditch the angle grinder and level his assault rifle when things went downhill fast. Boris was supposed to toss a smoke grenade the instant Frank kicked his way into the lobby. Instead, Boris kicked Frank through the opening and clubbed him savagely above the right ear with his rifle butt. Frank just had time to make out a dozen or so frightened virgins running for cover before Boris hit him again.

When Frank came to, he was in a large room full of Chesterfields and sobbing virgins—not to mention Mandy Miller, of all people, was watching over him. "I'm sorry, Frank," she whispered. "We had no idea. The rest of us were upstairs when you came in. Then the Russian burst out of the hoist firing his gun at the ceiling. But what in God's name are you doing here? You're supposed to be on your boat, and where's Marge?"

Frank struggled to sit up and decided answering would make his head hurt more. Instead, he countered with a couple of questions of his own. "So where are your Jesus friends and the Chinese guy in the bathrobe? And what the hell are you guys doing here anyway? We were expecting a bunch of terrorists."

"No you weren't, Frank, or at least *they* weren't. They tricked you. What they really wanted was to get the president in so he could open up the shelter downstairs. That's where Jesús is now, raising the Kevlar door. The funny thing is all you had to do was knock."

"Jeez," Frank muttered, shaking his head to stop the room from spinning, "*now* you tell me." He stood and gazed around the break room. Dirk Forrester was glued to CNN with the sound off. Shirley and Norma were doing their best to comfort the virgins. The room was otherwise in disarray, or decorated you might say, with a couple of day's worth of discarded virgin apparel. "Somebody needs to teach these girls to pick up after themselves," he observed, wondering, even as he spoke, why he should even care.

"Given the circumstances," Mandy said, "that's the least of our worries." Then she explained about Jesús and Dennis seizing the tower, which confused him even more. Frank quickly grasped that they were in a serious pickle, though. Boris, it seemed, was upstairs holding a gun on Jesús and Prashant Nagpal while they operated the *MOM*. Dennis and Jesus One were downstairs opening the main doors for the president while Nimegen supervised.

Of course, the door to the break room was locked and Nimegen had the key.

"Is there another key?" Frank asked.

Mandy looked to Shirley.

"There is," said Shirley. "I put all the spare keys on a peg board just outside the door here, so it should still be there unless they took that one as well."

"So," Frank observed, "we are basically screwed."

"Yes, we are," agreed Mandy, Shirley, and Norma. Even some of the virgins stopped sobbing long enough to nod. Dirk clutched his nail gun happily and continued watching CNN.

"Who's he? He looks familiar." enquired Frank.

"Oh, that's Dirk Forrester," Mandy said innocently, "he was on my show"

Frank took a small step backwards and squinted suspiciously. "I heard you put a finish nail in the poor bastard's forehead," he said. What he didn't say was, 'You pick up a nail gun around me, sister, you're dog meat.'

Mandy shook her head and sighed.

She didn't get to continue, because the door opened at that very moment and the President of the United States stumbled in. Following behind the president and his entourage were Jesús Maria Martinez, Dennis Floyd, Jesus One, and Prashant Nagpal. Norman Nimegen and Boris brought up the rear, brandishing combat assault rifles and looking stern. "I want everybody to sit down, now," Nimegen commanded importantly. "If you can't find a chair, sit on the floor. You have a visitor."

He stepped aside for Madge Chainey.

Chainey was plump and small in stature, but quick moving, like a sparrow. She fluttered into the room, eyes darting to-and-fro until they lighted on Dirk Forrester. "I know who that is," she said, "It's Dirk Forrester. You nailed him," she observed, turning sparrow-like to Mandy Miller.

Mandy sighed again. "Can we please find something else to talk about? I don't think you you came all this way to tell me I've been a bad girl."

"Quite," said Chainey, "except I was about to say how pleased I was when you did it. I never did like the way he used to show off."

"Oh," said Mandy, "well it really was an accident, you know."

"Be that as it may, my dear. The point is I want the sound on and he's hogging that remote the way he used to hog the camera."

She checked her watch. "Would you be ever so kind and get him to turn up the volume, there's something I'd like you all to see."

Blister was expecting the announcement. He smiled deferentially at the pundit sitting across from him then turned soberly to the camera. "Good morning, you are watching 'Breakfast with Blister' with me, your host, Wolf Blister. Like many of you, I am gravely concerned."

"Fucking *WIMWAC*," Dennis muttered under his breath.

Smoothing his perfectly groomed gray hair and fixing the camera with his steely blue eyes, Blister continued. "Despite assurances from the president that there is no cause for alarm, we have reports of citizens climbing on the heads of ailing seniors to get over the Canadian border fence. Not to mention the stock market collapsed yesterday and three quarters of the armed forces have quit. I cannot understand why there is all this panic. It is barely seventy-two hours since I walked off this very set and people are trampling all over one another. It is like some fool yelled "Free Hot Dogs" at Yankee Stadium. Still, I think we can rest assured our leadership will move swiftly to end the chaos. It is my pleasure and privilege to switch you now to the White House for an historic and impromptu address by our esteemed Secretary of Defense, the Honorable Gladys Rumsfoiled."

The screen dipped briefly to black and Rumsfoiled (a.k.a. the Anti-Christ) appeared. She seemed unusually cheerful given the circumstances. This time, *Hail To The Chief* opened the proceedings. Rumsfoiled carefully removed her spectacles, polished them vigorously, and put them back on. Then she took them off again and smiled inscrutably.

Secretary Rumsfoiled's Speech to the Nation Wednesday August 25, 06:00 Pacific Daylight Time, which would be 09:00 Eastern Daylight Time

"My fellow Americans, I shall not beat around the bush. I have it on good authority this great nation of ours will most likely be blown to kingdom come sometime this evening.

Mind you, reports that say something is going to happen are always interesting to me, because as you know, there are future things we know we know, and this might just be one of them. On the other hand, it may not happen, because we also know there are known unknowns in our future; that is to say we know there are some things we do not know will happen. But there are also things we don't know will not happen—unknown unknowns, if you will; you know, the things we don't know we don't know that we likely never will know we never knew.

But please forgive me for digressing. I could go on of course, it's just that sometimes when I get started, I find it hard to shut myself up. Where was I? Oh yes, when the balloon goes up, so to speak, it could well be a sad end to a great society that has *endured* and *prevailed* these many years. Unless all goes well, in which case I will emerge triumphant and take the lion's share of the credit. Yet, let me promise you all, after the ash or the dust, or whatever has settled, there will be a new world order and the *legacy* of this great nation shall never be forgotten.

Our new world order, incidentally, is effective immediately and will be known as the Alliance for Compassion, Leadership, and Unity—which we are calling the *ACLU.* The president, by the way, just resigned, and I will be in charge, ably assisted by my good friend, Madge Chainey, whose idea it was to set off the bombs.

Still, I don't want to dwell on the details of that because it might cause a panic. Whatever happens, believe me, when I say we shall continue to *persevere*, as always, on your behalf.

By the way, loyal *ACLU* forces now ring every underground shelter in the country, so don't even think about it.

Obviously, you won't be getting your *YOYO* leaflets by Christmas, because Christmas is unlikely to happen this year. Still, just in case you're wondering what *YOYO* means—it means *You're On Your Own,* but aren't you always, so what's the big deal about that anyway?

Rest assured, my friends, bombs, or no bombs, you all will be *heroes* today, and your just reward will be *peace* and *prosperity* for generations to come. Thank you my fellow Americans and have a nice day."

Since this was a relatively short speech, and historic, as Blister pointed out, we have not paraphrased a thing. It is reproduced in its entirety (with all the important sounding words italicized so you'll know which ones they are).

When the secretary was finished, the screen dipped to black and returned to the studio.

Blister was already fiddling with his earpiece and walking off the set.

"See," declared Jesús, "it's just like I said. Now, it's going to be all about the *AARP*, the *NAACP*, and the *ACLU* deciding on their own what's important and to heck with the rest of us."

"Well, sir," admonished Madge Chainey (a.k.a. the Beast), "you can grumble all you want, but that's the way the mop just flopped. Anyway, as soon as we're done here, please feel free to take your opinions with you to the parking lot. And when you get there, you can talk your little heart out forever as far as I am concerned, or at least until my bombs go off."

"Excuse me," interrupted the president, "but who is that old gentleman over there by the coffee dispensers? I could have sworn he wasn't here when we came in. Also, he's the spitting image of Albert Einstein."

Einstein turned with a mug of peppermint cream latte in hand and a merry greeting. "Please to forgive me, I was for hiding in the bathrooms," he said.

Boris and Nimegen glared accusingly at each other.

Jesús sighed with relief. "Oh, that's my granddad," he said. "I thought it would be best if he stayed here for a while."

"So what are you now," Dennis Floyd enquired, "some kind of Mexican fucking Jew?"

"And who might *you* be talking to?" Jesús retorted.

"I'm talking to you, dork brain. You didn't say anything about having a Jewish granddad."

"Dennis, will you please shut up?" Mandy said, fixing him with the Dick Derringer maggot stare—that being the end of that.

"Stop arguing and listen up,"Nimegen snarled. "You, Chamberlain, there's some fiberglass matting and pots of epoxy outside. Fix the hole and don't even think about doing Boris. He's faster, he's stronger, and he has the gun. He also has a brain, which is more than I can say for you."

"I'm not done with you, Nimegen," Frank said calmly as he made for the door.

Nimegen sniffed and stroked his moustache.

While Frank went to work mixing epoxy and wetting the fiberglass matting under the watchful eye of Boris, Nimegen locked the break room door and escorted Madge Chainey down to the *PHEWHH*.

"I guess I fell for it a second time," Core lamented. "I always was a sucker for a kind word and a pat on the head."

"Yes, Mister President, but that's what we all like about you and it's why you got my vote," said Mandy. "Anyway, all is not lost. Albert arrived in the nick-of-time. He'll think of something; he always does."

Einstein found a vacant Chesterfield and made himself comfortable. After sipping on his latte and staring at the ceiling for a while, he reached for his pipe.

"I'm sorry, sir, but smoking is not allowed anywhere in the building," Shirley advised. It was clear from the set of her mouth she was not prepared to debate the issue.

"Would you prefer Einstein with only the half of the brain, or is it that I should to smoking and you can get all of the Einstein, which is seeming to me quite the deal?" It was a simple and appealing question, and it was asked with the utmost innocence of expression, yet Shirley was unmoved.

"Maybe I can explain," Jesús intervened. "Mandy and the virgins and Jesus One will vouch for me on this. You see, Shirley, Albert really is Albert Einstein, except that he is also the being you would normally refer to as God, and I have to say his tobacco isn't half so bad in any case. You will also note he showed up out of nowhere, which has got to count for something."

Dennis Floyd put his head in his hands. Shirley started to look dangerous. The president was clearly baffled.

Convincing Shirley took a while, especially since teleportation demos were still embargoed. Dennis settled it in the end by pointing out that if the Khan said he was Genghis Khan and was clearly endowed with superhuman strength, then who was he, Dennis Floyd, to argue about Albert Einstein being God. Not to mention Jesus One radiating peace and goodwill all the time. So as far as he, Dennis Floyd, was concerned, "What is the point in denying God a simple puff of his pipe, for Christ's sake? Apart from which, what harm can it fucking do, seeing as how the world is about to end?"

"Very well, then," said Shirley, "but a rule is still a rule, even if this gentleman *is* God. And there will not be exceptions made for anyone else."

"Right then, thank you, Shirley" said Jesús. "Go ahead and fill your pipe, Albert, and I'll explain. We have some problems here."

Even allowing for God being Einstein, it still took some time to sum it all up, because a lot of water had passed beneath the bridge, so to speak.

"So thank God you made it in time," Jesús concluded, "because we thought it would be at the very least a week or so before you showed up."

"God was having nothing to do with it," Einstein chuckled, "I am getting the emergency recall when I am in orbit over Gronad beginning the seven-year crop infestations. The mother ship is intercepting this speech from Rumsfoiled, so now we know we have the big problems. Before the park is exploding, you see, I must to picking up Jesus One and the Khan with the *Anti-Grav*."

"Good luck finding the Khan," Dennis observed. "All I can do is tell you what I told him. Take a cab to Central, and ask to be dropped off south of Madison. You show up looking like Albert Einstein, they'll be on you faster than a fucking light beam, and I'm guessing he won't be far behind."

"Good, good," Einstein beamed (no pun intended), "perhaps you can then to loaning me the cab fare, only I am not for carrying the cash since I am giving my violin case to Mandy."

"Just a minute," cried Jesús. "What about us? We're locked up in this frigging room, and as soon as Frank is finished, they're going to turn us loose in the parking lot. Not to mention the maniac Russian on the other side of that door."

"This is also to being a problem," Einstein agreed. He closed his eyes and went back to puffing thoughtfully on his pipe.

"I think I'm going to scream," said Mandy, getting to her feet. "Albert, wake up, this is what I want you to do."

***

Outside, on the far side of the lobby where the hole was, Frank Chamberlain was also considering his options, which were limited to say the least, since Boris was watching him like a hawk. The way he saw it he could go slow, hoping for a miracle, or he could lay down enough matting to hold the repair in place and go for it. He decided to go for it—get it over with sooner rather than later—make the first move, and make it a kill; it was what he had been taught to do.

The problem was Boris had done most of the teaching.

He went for it anyway. "That's it," he said, when the first layer of matting was in place, "I'm finished."

"You don't turn round, Frank," said Boris. "You turn round, I blow your fucking head off."

"Sure," said Frank. "I'm just getting up, okay? My knees are killing me."

He was halfway to his feet and tensing himself when he sensed movement behind him. He knew immediately what he was in for. He grabbed for his throat and threw himself backwards, but he was too late. The thin catgut bit into his neck and Boris was underneath and heaving him onto his back. He clawed and gagged, and tried to scream but no sound came out. At first, he was only vaguely aware of the black veil of unconsciousness closing in; he was too busy fighting for his life. Then the veil was over his eyes and with it came the utter certainty he was going to die. There was no more pain; it was blotted out by the need for air. He just wanted to breathe—frantically, desperately, wanted to breathe.

Then he heard a series of quick popping sounds and Boris went down like a sack of, yes, you've guessed it, Nevsky potatoes.

"This time I meant it," said Mandy. "Also, I put it on bump fire just to be sure."

Multiple head wounds bleed a lot so Boris was not a pretty sight. He sure was dead, though. Five two-and-a-half-inch sixteen gauge finish nails through the top of the head will do that to a person.

Frank picked up the Ukrainian's weapon, still gasping for breath, and wanting to throw up because his throat was on fire and burning all the way down. "The bastard even took my gun," he whispered. "Heckler & Koch G36—finest assault rifle ever made. Kicks like a mule though." He checked the weapon, made sure it was chambered and set to rapid fire, then turned to Mandy. "I have no frigging idea how you made it out of that room, Mandy, but all I can say is I owe you one."

"Think nothing of it. All I did was ask Albert to teleport out for the key. When I peeped through the door, Boris was too busy strangling you to see me. He did take note though when I put the nail gun to his head."

"I would love to have been a fly on the wall," said Frank, still struggling to speak. "Anyway, you can leave the rest to me. I've got a bone to pick with a certain Brigadier General downstairs."

The Brigadier General saved him the trip. No sooner had Frank finished speaking than the elevator bell sounded and the doors slid open. Nimegen barely had time to look surprised before his face disappeared.

"Oh, how gross!" Madge Chainey cried.

"Out," croaked Frank, "out of the elevator, or you're next."

CHAPTER 55

Armageddon: Part II

The Final Conflict

It wasn't so much that he felt inadequate because Mandy had been the one to take charge. After all, when it came to nailing people she clearly had the edge, so he couldn't begrudge her that. No, It was more a feeling of inertia tinged with melancholy, as though his body and his brain wanted to coast for a while and mope.

He wasn't the only one. After Mandy closed the door quietly behind her, no one moved an inch or said a word. The silence clung like river mud. So when it came, the gunfire almost had to be denied—it was a quick hammering of shots, one blurring into the next—then the firing was over and nobody even blinked. It might as well have been a polite cough, or it might never have happened at all. At that point, Jesús realized he didn't much care who or what came through the door. It was done or it was not, and there wasn't a whole lot he could do or say about it.

Mandy entered first. She walked calmly over to Dirk and handed him the nail gun. Then she sat down on the floor next to Jesús, closed her eyes, and clutched his hand. Jesús wasn't so much relieved as released. What he had thought was inertia he now recognized as a debilitating fear; fear she would never make it back. Inertia gave way to elation, which in its own way was just as unwelcome.

All he wanted was to feel normal.

Frank wasn't far behind, ushering Madge Chainey ahead of him. His neck was already bruising from the garrote and criss-crossed by thin rivulets of blood. "Sit on the floor and put your hands on your head. What the hell is all this about bombs going off?" he rasped.

Chainey stumbled as she went down. Finally, she managed to drop herself awkwardly into a sitting position and reluctantly put her hands on her head. "I'm not at liberty to say."

Frank gently rested the muzzle of the HK in the nape of her neck. "I'd just as soon blow your head off your shoulders as blow smoke up your ass, ma'am. Now, you answer me or you'll get what I gave Nimegen."

"There are some nuclear devices in a mine outside of Salt Lake City. They will be set off tonight to drain the magma from Yellowstone. It will be sort of like lancing a boil."

"Good God!" Jesús exclaimed. "It sounds more like hitting it with a ten pound hammer. What happens if the whole shebang goes sky high?"

"At least we will have tried," Chainey said, showing no emotion.

"Call it off, Madge," Core urged, looking decidedly pale at the edges.

"I can't, the order can only come from Gladys, and I will tell you right now you'd be wasting your time."

"She's got that right," Core said. "That woman is a borderline lunatic. I've known it for years. That, of course is why we made her Secretary of Defense."

"Well," Jesús observed, feeling strangely calm, but still far from normal, "now at least we know the worst."

"Can I please go now?" asked Chainey. "If I can't have the *PHEWHH*, I'd best be getting back to Washington."

"Where you *can* go," said Jesús, "is down to the parking lot, madam. The sergeant will be happy to escort you, and so will I. Where you end up after that is entirely up to you."

"What about my people?"

"Your people will be right behind you."

***

There is this notion about battlefields of a neat, imaginary line with an army on each side of it. A signal is given and guns go off and eventually one of the armies decides to cross the line and have a go. The two sides knock hell out of one another for a while, then the losers run for it and the victors raise a flag. Chalk one up for the winning team. Now, those were the days. Of course, all that was before the battlefields were paved over and turned into parking lots. Life was simpler then. But it rarely happens that way anymore—as we are about to discover.

Mind you, seen from a height of two hundred and thirty five feet it could be argued Sea-Tac already was a battlefield. It looked a lot like Verdun after the smoke had cleared. The airport had been under reconstruction for close to half a century, so there was lots of dirt piled up and sand with deep holes and trenches in it; all it lacked was bodies (but not for long). Traffic was also backed up from the terminal buildings, across the relocated State Road-518 on-ramp, and as far north and south on Interstate-5 as the eye could see.

In other words, it was a day like any other.

"I can't believe I've been driving around in this shit for the past fifteen years," said Dennis.

"Me neither," Jesús agreed. "Three years was bad enough."

"You know, if it wasn't for Uncle Johnny, we'd have it made," Dennis ruminated.

"What do you mean by that?"

"Well, think about it. We've got the tower sewn up, or we will have when Norma and Prashant finish with the patch. Mandy and Jesus One are settling the president and the virgins in the bunker, we've got all the supplies we'll ever need, and it's not even lunchtime."

"Don't even go there," Jesús warned

Dennis showed his ivories. "I'm just reflecting on the situation. So what's next? Do we wait around all fucking day while Genghis Khan sits in traffic, or what?"

Jesús pointed to the north and handed Dennis the binoculars he had been looking through. "There's your answer. I don't think the traffic will be a problem."

"Holy fucking canolie," said Dennis. "How the hell did he lay his hands on all that stuff?"

Jesús took back the binoculars and scrutinized the approaching convoy. "Well, I'd say, he's either on excellent terms with the owner of Acme Construction Rentals or he's best friends with whoever climbed the fence. I count four monster front loaders and six articulated dump trucks, all bristling with armed barbarians. That was one heck of a goodwill gesture, or it was one hell of a heist."

Two miles away, southbound I-5 traffic was parting like the Red Sea. Where the traffic couldn't or wouldn't get out of the way, the Lord of the Universe made it so with an imperious wave of the hand. He could do this because he was perched atop a giant four-wheel drive front loader; the kind that could scoop up an Avis airport shuttle and not even notice.

Moses would have been green with envy.

Billy Ray Bixbee, on the other hand, wasn't that impressed—at least, not at first sight.

Ten minutes after they sighted the Khan, Billy Ray's Fanjet Falcon showed up as an incoming blip on the radar and was handed off by the sole remaining TRACON controller.

"Shirley could take the bastard out right now," Dennis growled. "All she has to do is lock on the *NASAMS*, then it's point and click and the reverend and Muriel fucking high priestess Banks will be ascending to heaven and personally greeting the Lord."

"Dream on, Dennis," said Jesús. "First of all, I couldn't live with that, and secondly Mandy would nail your ass. You saw what she did to Boris."

"Just kidding, but we need a plan, here, old buddy. There is absolutely no fucking way I am giving up this building."

"Sea-Tac Tower, Sea-Tac Tower, y'all listen up now. This here is Billy Ray and we got some talking to do."

Jesús and Dennis looked carefully at one another.

"I'm not talking to him," said Dennis. "Billy Ray is your problem, Fly-Boy. You deal with it."

Jesús sighed and acquired the approaching aircraft. "Mister Bixbee, sir, Sea-Tac Tower, you are clear runway two arrival, maintain one four five knots, heading three-six-zero, altitude two thousand feet." He couldn't help the "sir"; it was force of habit. Not to mention this was probably the last time he would talk anyone in. So he decided he might as well be professional about it.

"Is that you, dork-brain?"

"Mister Bixbee, Sea-Tac Tower, yes sir, this is the dork brain."

"Well then, y'all better take a look outside. I got me some friends gathered for a picnic. Y'all's invited, so y'all better come on down and don't be shy."

"Fuck off, Bixbee," said Jesús, deciding he was through being professional for the day. He removed the headset and walked over to where he could look down at the terminal buildings.

Dennis joined him, curious as to what Jesús had heard. "Holy shit," he cried.

The tower was about a half mile north of the main terminal building and the two terminal expansion satellites. Between the northernmost expansion satellite and the tower stood a parking lot for fuel trucks and a hold pad for arriving aircraft. Less than five minutes previously the hold pad had been practically empty. Now it was seething with a vast crowd waving banners and standards. Hundreds more were pouring from the main terminal building and across the pedestrian bridge opposite the tower.

Jesús grabbed the binoculars. "Half of those bastards are carrying weapons," he gasped. "They must have been coming here for days and stashing the guns in their cars."

The other half seemed content to carry flags and march around in circles. Two standards dominated: the blood red cross on a white background of the Knights Templar, and royal purple banners carrying the letters *AARP* embroidered in shining gold thread.

"For crying out loud," said Dennis, "what is this, a fucking Bible meet?"

"No," said Jesús, looking grim, "it's the Idiot's Crusade. This is the tower of frigging David and we're the shit-out-of-luck Saracens stuck inside. Not to mention, Richard the Lionheart just touched down on Runway Two to lay siege to the Saracens, i.e. us."

"I thought Richard gave up and went back to Cyprus."

Jesús couldn't help smiling at this unlikely flash of erudition. "Yes, Dennis, but that was then and this, as you have been heard to say, is fucking now. I think we need to get Frank and Einstein up here right away."

Einstein got things off to a poor start when he pointed out fighting other people's battles was not a part of his job description. "I must also to saying I have never liked it when the peoples are flying the flags and singing, even when it is to being a parade. I have seeing too much of this in Berlin before the war is coming." he added, less than helpfully.

"What do you think, Frank?" Jesús asked, knowing Frank had other things on his mind, but hoping for a glimmer of encouragement.

"I'll be honest with you. Right now, what I think is I need to find somebody can fly me home. If I have to, I'll hijack me a pilot. This is a goddamned airport. There has to be someone around here can fly that airplane."

Jesús gulped and shot a quick glance at Dennis, who responded with a sly grin and a wink. Then he pressed on, hoping Frank hadn't noticed the exchange. "Well at least, could you please take a look. The Khan is on his way, but he must be outnumbered ten to one by now."

Frank reached for the binoculars. He sized up the approaching barbarians and carefully scanned the airport complex. He smiled. "Your guy doesn't need me to tell him what to do. Sure, he's outnumbered, but he sure as hell isn't outgunned. He has two mini Gatlings on his lap and a bunch of light machine guns and late model RPG launchers in those dump trucks; he must have raided a fucking armory. If you look close enough, you'll also see he has scouts and snipers deployed all over the place. I figure he sent them in when it was dark. Any time now, he'll be in radio range, so you'd better start calling him and find out what he's planning. If you want Frank Chamberlain's opinion, those flag wavers down there don't have a prayer, and no pun intended."

Dennis showed all the teeth he could manage, thus putting Richard Branson to shame. Jesús almost felt like he wanted to cry with relief. Einstein fumbled for his pipe and tobacco.

Frank handed back the binoculars. "Listen," he said, "I'd be more than happy to help out, but I've got to find somebody able to fly that 767 down there. If you have any ideas, now's the time to speak up."

Jesús gazed intently out the window as though he had just spotted something of immense interest in the parking lot.

"Hey, Albert," said Dennis, coming to the rescue, "you've got a space ship. Why not help the man out."

Einstein nervously tamped tobacco. "Believe me, if it is being up to me, I should be more than happy, but after this previous God has been abducting the virgins, the Confederation is making it clear there will to being no more free rides. Also, right now, because we are to having an end of the civilizations, the apocalypse auditors are visiting, so I must to do everything on the up and up." He shrugged helplessly. "It is like this Billy Ray was to saying: they are to having me wrapped tighter than the flea's ass over the rain barrels. What is to being worse, is if I am not to beaming up the Khan and the Jesus One before the world is ending, I am in the big troubles. You have no idea what the Genghis is to being like when he is getting his hands on a barbarian horde. He will not listen, not even to God; you are to giving him an inch and he is for always to taking the mile."

Frank ran his hands through his hair and grunted unsympathetically. Jesús continued to stare out of the window, avoiding eye contact, praying Frank wouldn't think to ask who had flown the 767 to pick up the virgins. This was one occasion when he knew he couldn't lie.

Einstein eventually broke the impasse. To begin with, though, he sucked blissfully on his pipe. His eyes were closed and a little half smile played on his lips. He continued like this until Jesús leaned over and nudged him. "Albert, wake up will you? The bigger issue here is that Billy Ray is holding Johnny. If we don't give him what he wants, or if the Khan goes in guns blazing, Johnny could well be history, and we'll all be running from a crazy woman waving a nail gun. The alternative, I don't even want to think about."

Einstein opened his eyes and chuckled mischievously. "So, I can see you now, little *bubeleh,* to running for the rest of your life from this crazy womans."

Jesús sighed.

"Is not to worry, I think I can to be doing a deal for Frank if he is to helping us with Johnny. Just to be waiting here for one moment please."

Then he vanished.

Ten seconds later he was back, but he was no longer Albert Einstein; he was some other old man. He stood ramrod straight, wearing a World War II era Air Force uniform and a leather flying helmet. "Remember Einstein saying he had solved the past particle equations?" the new arrival said in a commanding voice, looking Jesús straight in the eye.

"Er, yes," said Jesús. "I believe Jesus One did mention something to that effect."

"Well, he sure did the job all right, yes sir. As soon as he got back, he reprogrammed the ionizer, so now I can pretty much show up as any old fart I please. All I have to do is stick my head in the thing for a couple of seconds while they key in the new DNA algorithms and I'm good to go. How do you do, son, my name is Doolittle, Lieutenant General James Harold Doolittle, United States Army Air Force, retired, but you can call me, Jimmy. I'll fly your plane."

"Of course," said Jesús, shaking God's hand vigorously, "I did a term paper on you once—Doolittle's Raiders it was—you led the bombing raid over Tokyo in World War II. But you set out knowing you wouldn't have enough fuel to get back so you kept going to China and ditched the planes."

"Had to bail out, son, seeing as how there weren't too many airfields in China back then. I came down in a dung heap outside of Chuchow; softest landing I ever made. Chinese held their noses for a while though. You want somebody to fly halfway across the world and not come back, I'm your man."

"Well, I'll be a son of a fucking gun," said Dennis.

Frank eyed Doolittle suspiciously. "I'll be honest with you, General, I don't hold much with promises from senior brass like yourself, but if you'll fly me back to Marge, I'll help out. Just don't screw with me, is all. You do, and you'll end up like Nimegen."

"Son," said Doolittle, "what I do is fly planes. I never asked to be a goddamned general, and that's a fact. If I say I'm flying you home, you can take it to the bank. Now, let's get on with it."

Frank nodded thoughtfully, then turned to Jesús.

"Is there a back way out of here?"

"Yes, there's a loading bay with another Kevlar door over it. We can operate that from here, then there's a roll up door you can lift by yourself."

Frank seemed to lose all further interest in the doors. "So what's the deal with this guy, Johnny?"

"He's Mandy's uncle," Jesús explained. "Bixbee had him kidnapped. If we don't let Bixbee and his gang into the tower, Uncle Johnny is toast."

"Mmm," Frank considered, "well this could be your lucky day. I thought I'd kissed goodbye to all that, but it seems I haven't. It just so happens, rescuing precious cargo is what I used to do best."

"Yes, Frank, we know. That would be why we're asking, now, wouldn't it?"

"First things first," said Frank, seemingly unaware of the sarcasm. He turned to Dennis. "You. Get on the VHF and keep trying until you raise the Khan, then get me a handheld. I'll want to talk to him."

"Yes, sir," said Dennis, "I'm on it."

"And you," Frank said, turning back to Jesús, "just watch your fucking lip. No more sarcasm, *capiche*?"

"I've raised him," said Dennis, and passed a handheld radio to Frank.

"What channel are we on?"

"Sixteen."

Frank switched on the radio and thumbed the channel selector. "Listen up, Khan, this is Frank Chamberlain. First off, we'll switch channels. Go to seventy-one."

"Going to seventy-one," said the Khan, "Goddamn it, Frank, if we'd had handheld radios when we invaded Persia, I could have done it with half a horde or less."

"Never mind about that, just switch to seventy-one, will you."

"Khan on seventy-one, here."

"Okay, now can you have your guys spot the flag wavers to see if they're using radios? I don't see any, but you never know. We don't want anybody listening in."

"Roger, Wilco," the Khan responded smartly.

"Where in hell did he learn about Roger fucking Wilco?" Dennis exclaimed as Frank hit the callback button.

"I heard that," the Khan came back. "Just for your information, we watch World War II movies all the time on the mother ship. My favorites are the ones about the Battle of Britain where they always fly home on a wing and a prayer."

"Yes, sir, I can testify to that," Doolittle broke in enthusiastically. "Why, there was this one time I was waiting on the *Hornet* for some of the boys to get back from practice, when they got jumped by Zeroes."

"For God's sake, will you let them get on with it," Jesús cried. "You're turning out to be worse than Einstein."

Doolittle sniffed. "Actually," he said, "being Einstein wasn't half bad if you really want to know."

Jesús put his head in his hands.

"No radios, just lots of bullhorns." the Khan reported back, after a few minutes of silence.

"What's the plan? But listen, no details, just in case."

"My barbarians want the airport. I want Billy Ray. First we blow Billy Ray off the face of the planet, then we seize all the planes so my guys can leave."

"Correction, pal. One of those planes is mine. What about Uncle Johnny?"

"I'll give Bixbee one chance to hand him over. If he says no Uncle Johnny could end up being toast, and I do mean toast."

"I'll take care of Uncle Johnny, just give me time to get close."

"You better not get too close, Frank. You see the big parking lot just north of the terminal on your side of the street?"

Frank peered out the window. "Yeah."

"Need I say more?"

"No, you sure as hell don't. I'm on my way."

"Roger, Wilco, and out, standing by on seventy-one," concluded the Khan, sounding ever so professional.

"For God's sake," cried Jesús, "he's planning to blow up the fuel trucks."

"Damn right," said Frank. "The Army of the Righteous is in for one hell of a surprise. Anyway, I need to get out of this combat gear and into some street clothes and yours will do, so take em off, dork brain."

"How the heck did you know to call me that?"

Frank grinned. "You weren't the only one talked to the virgins at Mama Lu's, so stop talking and start stripping."

When they were done, Frank put his sheathed combat knife into his right trouser pocket; everything else, including his pistol, grenades, radio, and the HK, he left with Jesús.

"I'll need these later," he warned, "so keep em handy."

Jesús made to hand back the pistol. "At least take this. They're not kidding down there."

"Nah, I'm betting Uncle Johnny's going to have muscle on all sides, and believe me, those bastards can smell a gun at fifty paces. I need to blend in and get real close. I'm heading down there and I'm going to grab me a banner, and I'm going to make like I'm Sister Anna."

As he was making for the elevator, Frank turned, looking puzzled. "Hey, only thing I forgot is how the hell do I recognize Uncle Johnny"

"No problem," Jesús replied, "He's got ears like storm shutters and he'll be surrounded by muscle."

Frank grinned. "I told *you* to watch your lip, dork brain. Now, open up that back door and if anybody's waiting, shoo em away with the Gatlings. Also, don't forget to turn off the claymores. When I get back, I'll be in a hurry so don't wait for me to knock, *capiche*?"

***

Once in a while, ghosts came to call on Frank Chamberlain. Today was one of those days. Few of the children of the righteous had stayed home, you see, so there they were: these flag-waving children who would soon be ghosts. To Frank's way of thinking, the wrong people usually ended up getting hurt, and too many times the wrong people were just kids; this being one of the reasons he had quit hurting people for a living. On this day, though, Frank's reluctance to see the kids get hurt would almost cost him his life. He should have known better than to believe in ghosts. Wasn't that what he had always preached? "The day you put yourself in the middle is the day you get killed."

No one was waiting for him out back. The Adventist Army of Rapture and Perdition wasn't enraged at this stage, so it wasn't focused enough to post lookouts. It didn't have an obvious enemy, or a leader telling it what to do, or a clear plan of action like a real army. Despite carrying weapons, the Seattle chapter of the *AARP* wasn't seriously out for blood yet. It was just a hastily organized get together of impassioned believers. Bu we all know what that can lead to, don't we?

Frank made his way around the base building to the front parking lot, skirting the crime scene tape, which had been left as a handy reminder by the recently departed forces of law and order. The *AARP* filled the holding pad and spilled all the way into the fuel truck lot, singing "Oh, Christ how we adore Thee." Banners and flags waved and fluttered majestically. New arrivals poured across the pedestrian bridge and teemed out of the main terminal building. Naturally, this being the end of all life as we know it, no one tried to stop them. Apart from which, airport security was otherwise engaged in bidding for seats on the last flights out.

Frank was choosy about his banner. He looked for something with a brass ferrule and preferably a spike on top. He didn't want anything unwieldy, because he might have to put it to good use. It wasn't long before he spotted what he wanted. When the previous owner woke up, his banner was lost in a waving forest of flags.

In danger of being engulfed by the adoring crowd, Billy Ray and Muriel made the fatal mistake of climbing onto the hood of a fuel truck to be better seen and heard. Of course, the last person they were expecting was Genghis Khan, so it was an understandable error. Even when the front loaders and the dump trucks circled the base of the tower, they still didn't get it. They were more concerned with working the crowd, more focused on performing their special miracle of the day—the one where they turned adoration into blind rage with nothing more than a bullhorn and a few well-chosen words.

Billy Ray was dressed for the occasion in a pure white western-themed suit, accented with a crimson Stetson, a crimson silk-twill handkerchief poking out of his breast pocket, and hand-tooled crimson leather boots. Muriel had kept to the same blood-red color she had worn at the wedding, except now she was clad in a sheer-silk pants suit that shimmered and glinted with every movement. She brandished a large white cross (made from Styrofoam painted to look like wood).

Billy Ray grabbed a bullhorn and opened the proceedings forthwith.

By this time, Frank Chamberlain had worked his way to within a few feet of Uncle Johnny and his escort. They were standing close to the cab, and it was clear to Frank that Uncle Johnny would soon be hoisted up for all the world to see. The three guardians were already looking up at Billy Ray, waiting for a cue.

"In the name of God, we are all soldiers of Christ today," Billy Ray began.

"Hallelujah, Hallelujah," Muriel prompted, waving the cross vigorously over her head.

"Hallelujah, Hallelujah," the crowd responded.

Frank reached into his pocket and unsheathed the knife.

"Y'all hear me when I tell y'all I done took solemn vows before the Lord to rid the Earth of pagans and heretics on this day of days," Billy Ray boomed, in his best voice from heaven. "Today is the day of the Rapture of the Faithful, my friends, and them as bears False Witness will be left behind. And they will face the Tribulation. And they will be damned to Eternal Perdition."

"Hallelujah, Hallelujah," Muriel called.

"Hallelujah, Hallelujah," the crowd cried.

"Hallelujah," Frank murmured, holding the knife down at his side.

Billy Ray swapped his bullhorn for Muriel's cross, and she took up the harangue. "God has proclaimed this is the day foretold," she called out, hardly needing the bullhorn. "Today, He has sent me, your New Prophetess of Pastureland, and the Reverend Billy Ray Bixbee, to vanquish the Saracens of the city of Antioch and the tower of David, which is before ye. For ye, my children, shall wreak vengeance on the Saracens in the name of the Lord. For they are not the children of the Lord. For they are the offspring of the Beast."

"Hallelujah, Hallelujah, Oh Christ how we adore Thee," chanted the crowd, no longer needing a prompt from Muriel, or from on high, or from anywhere else for that matter.

Frank's personal preference for close work was a razor-sharp, two-edged British commando knife, gunmetal black, with a cross-grooved steel hilt, circa 1942. The seven-and-a-half-inch blade was to all intents and purposes a stiletto, although broader in proportion and thicker at the center to give it extra strength. It didn't have a serrated edge and it wasn't curved, so it went in smoothly and offered no resistance when you pulled it out. You just had to know where to cut and shove it in—which was one of the reasons Boris had been hired.

Muriel gestured to the upper reaches of the tower as if she were beckoning the very gates of heaven. "Behold, the good Lord sayeth unto me 'With death shall come Resurrection, and the Remission of all Sins, and I the One God, sayeth unto thee, my prophetess, ye and all that walk with thee shall be Redeemed, and ye shall pay no more for thy Earthly Sins, for ye shall take to the Tower of the Lord, which is the Tower of David. And I shall be thy Savior and thy Rapture, and thy Sacrifice for Evermore.'"

"Hallelujah, Hallelujah. Oh, Christ how we adore Thee," from the crowd.

Muriel handed the bullhorn to Billy Ray and went back to waving the cross.

Frank handed his banner to a non flag-waving neighbor and went to work.

There were three of them and not one of them made a sound as he went down. They were big men, however, so they didn't drop without a commotion of sorts. Billy Ray, who had finely tuned instincts when it came to crowd behavior, caught on fast, despite being in mid tirade.

Frank was already moving, pushing Johnny Chittenden ahead of him like a startled animal. "Run like fuck for the tower and don't stop," Frank shouted, pressing the knife into Johnny's hand, "and if anybody gets in your way use this." He turned to head-butt a startled bystander, kneed a second one in the groin, yelled, "They did it!" and plunged into the crowd.

"Y'all will die in the name of the Lord," Billy Ray screamed from his vantage point on the truck, pointing an accusing finger at the fleeing Frank Chamberlain—but the *AARP* thought this was part of the sermon and he was beckoning them to a glorious end.

"Hallelujah, Hallelujah. Oh, Christ how we adore Thee," they rejoiced.

Knowing all hell was about to break loose, Frank hunched his shoulders, put his head down, stuck out his elbows, and charged.

The Khan, who had been closely observing matters, noted Frank's quick dispatch of Johnny's guards, dropped his binoculars and reached for his own bullhorn. "You, sir, have chosen war," he bellowed. "I am the Genghis Khan and I have returned, and today I shall not leave a single eye open to weep for the dead." He gave Frank and Johnny a three count to get out of the way, then unleashed the barbarians. "Fire!" yelled the Khan.

Billy Ray and Muriel may or may not have seen or heard the Khan, and they may or may not have registered the rocket-propelled grenades heading their way.

We shall never know.

***

Remember what we said about battles not being as simple as they used to be? For example, Frank's day was ruined, as was his exit strategy, when the white supremacists showed up. He saw the oncoming flags first because a panic-stricken mob was seriously impeding the rest of his view. The flags were in pairs. One was the Stars and Stripes. The other was black and decorated with a gray wolf's head dripping blood. Underneath the dripping wolf head was the acronym *WOLF* in bright yellow. Underneath *WOLF*, in startling white, were the words *White Oppression Liberation Front.*

A hundred or more of the twin flags raced towards the barbarians. Between the ear-splitting thuds of exploding fire trucks, Frank heard the unmistakable and equally ear-splitting suck-squeeze-bangs and blows of massed Harley Davidson's. So much for Einstein's theory of three emergent armies: now there were four.

He snatched a Holy Cross pennant from a passing supplicant and used it as a prod to gather human shields in front of him.

Not all was pandemonium, however. A goodly number of the *AARP* faithful, taking heart from the sudden appearance of the bikers from hell, regrouped and charged the dump trucks, firing as they ran. Like Frank, they used their panicked brethren for cover.

Frank didn't want to get too close. Cutting through the noise of the Harley's and the exploding fire trucks was the intermittent burp of Gatlings and the steady chatter of light machine guns. He recognized the slower rhythm of the latest drum-fed squad automatic weapons, mixed in with the faster hammering of older belt-fed M249s—the Khan had chosen well. By contrast, the weaponry of the advancing *WOLF* brigade and *AARP* irregulars was a mixed bag of combat shotguns, modified AR-15s, AK-47s, and M-16 assault rifles—with the occasional hand grenade thrown in for good measure (so to speak).

It was quite the symphony, but knowing what he was listening to didn't help much, not to mention he was in no mood to appreciate it. Even a dork brain could see it was time to stay low, run like hell, and find cover. Frank had a problem with this because he had nowhere to run, let alone hide. Behind him, the fire trucks were a blazing inferno; ahead of him, the barbarians were laying down a lethal crossfire; on each side, the Khan's snipers were systematically trimming the outer edges of the faithful, the confused, and the supreme.

Now, this is where we would like to say, "and with one bound, he was free." Unfortunately, having gotten himself into the situation, Frank was now obliged to get himself out—and one bound wasn't going to come close.

For starters, the arrival of the *WOLF* brigade was a serious complication. Frank's intention had been to thread a path through the fleeing faithful to where he could safely reveal himself to the Khan. This was what he had thought of as plan *A*. It was based on his assumption the Khan would not fire into a panicking mob, unless he was fired upon, thus preserving his firepower for a subsequent assault on the terminal buildings.

The arrival of the bikeborn attackers had radically changed the goalposts. Now, the Khan and his barbarian horde were letting fly at everything and everyone in sight, namely: bikes, bikers, standards, standard bearers, panicking faithful, enraged and charging faithful, unexploded fuel trucks, exploding fuel trucks, parking signs, fire hydrants, flower beds, whatever.

Plan *A* was no longer a go.

There was no plan *B*.

Frank quickly realized he had two immediate and less than compelling choices: he could stay on his feet and be shot to pieces, or he could hit the deck and be trampled to death. He dropped the pennant and grabbed for someone to pull down on top of him.

As he was going down, he saw the kids. The two of them were slightly ahead of him, a boy, and a girl, not more than twelve years old, heads down and running like frightened jackrabbits, and directly in the path of an out-of-control Fat Bob Special. The rider still clutched the handlebars with one hand, but otherwise flopped to one side as if he were broken in the middle. Frank had the impression his head was missing.

Frank pushed the children out of the way no more than a second before the bike hit him.

When he came to, he was underneath the bike. What was left of the machine was still sucking, squeezing, banging, and blowing. There was no sign of the children.

He supposed it was all over. The shooting was sporadic now, mostly single shots and the occasional burst of rapid fire. He felt as though he had been hit by a dump truck. From past experience, he suspected at least one of his ribs was busted. The top of his right leg hurt like hell and he couldn't feel anything where his left leg was supposed to be. He drifted in and out and vaguely worried his spleen might be ruptured. Still, he had always worried about rupturing his spleen, so at least that part was normal.Eventually, all the gas leaked out and the Harley stopped farting and banging.

Frank was lucky he hadn't been burnt to a crisp, and he knew it.

***

From Shirley's perspective, firing on God-fearing citizens was definitely out of bounds. "Also," she pointed out, "there are children down there."

"Yes, Shirley," agreed Dennis, "I'm not arguing with you, but we could shoot up in the air as a warning or something. What I'm saying is the Khan might appreciate a show of fucking support right now."

Shirley pointed to the *MOM* monitors displaying the view from the base-building roof. "Dennis, does it look to you as if he needs a show of support? Hardly a single one of those men on bikes down there is on his feet anymore. They keep falling off, but they never get up."

Jesús put down the binoculars. "She's right, Dennis, it's a massacre. Apart from which, Frank is still out there. I had him sighted until the fire trucks went up then I lost him in the crowd. If he's still alive, he'll have enough problems without Shirley dropping bullets on his head."

He went to the window and surveyed the parking lot. It looked like a bomb had gone off in a Harley Davidson chop shop. Assorted bike parts were everywhere, some intact—front wheels and handlebars mostly—the remainder nothing more than charred lumps of metal.

These were the unlucky ones: the ones that had made it past the dump trucks and plowed into Preston Pleasant's field of leaping munchkins.

Then he saw Uncle Johnny, curled face down in the giant scoop of the Khan's front loader, arms over his head, knees up to his chest, and not moving, and clearly not about to any time soon. Above Johnny, the Khan straddled the roof of the cab, legs wide apart, both Gatlings still spitting fire in short bursts. In the articulated dump trucks, the barbarian horde, a.k.a. the Klick Clack Gang, the Brown Pride Locos, the Sons of Samoa, the East Union Street Hustlers, El Monte Flores, and the United Latinos, were winding down the crossfire, thus saving ammo to purchase tickets east. What was left of Billy Ray's army was running for the airport entrance led by the remnants of white supremacy. There was no shortage of discarded banners, the dead, the dying, the confused, and the wounded.

Jesús buried his head in his hands.

"Maybe you can understand now why the Confederation is as picky as it is," Doolittle said. "Anyway, I'm going downstairs to see if I can find Frank. Dennis, will you please get the Khan on the radio and tell him I'm coming, and please point out I'll be an old geezer wearing a leather flying helmet, just so he doesn't get the wrong idea and think I'm a biker. Also, if Shirley can lift the door and turn off the minefield I would appreciate it."

"Hang on," said Jesús, "I'll come with you."

Mandy was waiting in the elevator lobby, arms folded, distraught, but dry-eyed, and forcing a smile. "I couldn't bear to come up and watch," she said. "All I want is for Uncle Johnny to be alright."

Jesús took her by the arm and led her back to the *PHEWHH* doors. "I don't recommend you go outside, sweetheart. As I said on the phone, Johnny is just fine. He's with the Khan. We'll send him in, then we'll go look for Frank. By the way, this is the gentleman I told you about. He was Albert, but now he is General Jimmy Doolittle."

She held out her hand, looking confused. "I'm so pleased to meet you, sir," she said, "maybe one of these days, you could come back down and explain all of this." She nodded at Jesús. "As much as I'd like to believe this one, and I know he's harmless, he can't even manage two honest words side by side in the same sentence."

"Gee, thanks a lot," said Jesús. "I'll take that as a compliment."

Her smile widened. "I'll wait here," she said. "Just be careful."

When they emerged, the acrid smell and taste of burning fuel made

Jesús wanted to gag. He wiped his eyes and peered through the haze. The Khan was helping Uncle Johnny climb from the scoop. Less than half a mile away, a towering mass of thick black smoke engulfed the terminal buildings and mushroomed skywards.

"Good God," he muttered, "there'll be no more flights today."

"Oh, yes, there will," growled Doolittle. "Pull yourself together, man. I made a promise and I intend to keep it. You," he barked, pointing at the Khan who was now gingerly picking his way across the parking lot with Uncle Johnny in tow, "get yourself inside and find Jesus. As soon as I get back, I'm beaming you both up, and don't even think about arguing."

"Do I look like I'm arguing?" protested the Khan, wiping soot from his eyes. "Jeez, a word of thanks might not be out of place. I've been up since midnight rounding up barbarians and half the ordnance in Seattle. Not to mention fighting World War frigging three. Give a guy a break can't you?"

"Inside, now!" Doolittle commanded, with zero sympathy.

Jesús climbed to where the Khan had been perched and surveyed the battlefield. The binoculars didn't help much; there was too much smoke. "I can't see anything," he called down to Doolittle, "there's smoke everywhere."

"Give it a few minutes," Doolittle called back. "What we were trained to do in the Air Corps was try not to stare too hard. Just move your head from side to side very slowly. If anything at all moves, your peripheral vision should pick-up on it first."

Doolittle was right. After a few passes, Jesús thought he noticed one of the downed bikes move. When he focused on it, though, the bike was still—but it was lying at an odd angle. "There's a bike on its side over there. I thought I saw it move. I think somebody might be under it," he called down.

"If you thought you saw it, son, you saw it. Now get yourself down from there on the double and we'll go take a look."

***

Frank thought he recognized Jesús, but he wasn't sure. The older man reminded him of Dwight Eisenhower, except he was wearing a leather-flying helmet.

Which was odd, to say the least.

CHAPTER 56

Black Rain

Frank was fully conscious by the time they reached the tower, or he thought he was. Then he looked up and saw a giant space ship shaped like a super robusto cigar, and he wasn't so sure anymore. The craft hovered silently, silhouetted by the late morning sun and no more than a few hundred feet above the burning airport complex. Its shadow covered the length and breadth of the three runways.

"Can you stand by yourself?" Doolittle asked.

"Sure," Frank answered, "but what in God's name is that? I'm not seeing things, am I?"

"It must be the mother ship," Jesús whispered.

Doolittle took a small device from his pocket, rather like a miniature cell-phone, and spoke into it. "*Roñon da œ wœlspaέr aṇdi aṇdi waχenfώrd, ή́aret mar, ή́aret mar*," he said, slowly and distinctly.

Frank leaned against Jesús for support. He didn't feel groggy, but he suddenly had the impression the ground was slipping away from him. "What's he saying?" he whispered.

"I've no idea," Jesús whispered back.

Doolittle returned the tiny communicator to his pocket. "I heard that," he said, "it's the mother tongue, actually. Normally, we wouldn't use it in planetary-surface mode, and I wouldn't be using this galactofone either, but under the circumstances, it hardly matters. I was just fine-tuning our position for a pickup."

Sure enough, the mother ship floated sideways until it was parked directly overhead.

"Excuse me," said Doolittle to Jesús, "could you get Jesus One and the Khan on the radio? It's time they left. Also, we'll need to move over by the doors if you don't mind. When they turn on the *Anti-Grav* it's not too fussy about who or what it picks up. That's how come we get so many alien abductions; it's those silly sods up there not watching out."

Five minutes later, the Khan and Jesus One emerged. Jesus One was teary-eyed. "I always hate it so when it comes time to ascend," he murmured with a sad smile, shaking Jesús' hand. "Anyway, I hope we were able to be of some help. We try to do our best, you know, even if sometimes we seem to be a bit off target."

"No, no, not at all," Jesús said, with a lump in his throat. "Really, there's no way we could have done it without you. Just take care and try not to get martyred any time soon."

The Khan pumped his hand vigorously. "See you around, Jesús," he said, grinning broadly. "Man, I had a blast."

"What do you mean, see you around? I thought you were finished here."

The Khan raised an eyebrow. "You're a chosen one, dork brain, don't you ever listen? When the time comes, you get to choose everlasting life on the mother ship, or you can go for the regular three score and ten down here."

"Mmm, I did wonder about that," said Jesús, "but Albert never said anything, and I didn't want to seem pushy. Which reminds me, how come Albert never sent down Noah? Not to say you weren't a big help or anything, but to my way of thinking he may have had a bit more to offer."

The Khan shrugged. "Never ran into him. You'll have to ask the boss. All I know is the everlasting life benefit didn't kick in until around three thousand years ago, so my guess is he never got the offer. Anyway, I gotta go, man. You take good care of Doris now, she's a bonnie lass."

Then the Khan and Jesus One walked towards a large red laser dot that had appeared in the middle of the parking lot and gracefully ascended to the mother ship.

"I feel quite sad," Jesús said, almost wanting to cry.

"You'll get over it," replied Frank impatiently. "Listen, Jesús, I can't say it's not been nice knowing you, pal. but now it's my turn to skedaddle."

***

He was hurting when he jumped, and he knew he would hurt a hell of a lot more when he landed. Frank Chamberlain was a poster boy for the walking wounded: badly bruised head, a hairline skull fracture, lacerated and bruised throat, four cracked ribs, a deep gouge in his right thigh, a severely twisted left knee, a second degree burn across his back from the Harley exhaust pipe, and what felt like a broken nose. Not to mention lingering symptoms of concussion.

Prashant had patched him up as best he could, given him two large containers of an amoxicillin antibiotic and ibuprofen, and told him to get lots of bed rest (thus becoming a shoo-in as the first great healer of the new age). Jesús presented him with a box of carbon-filter smog masks, and a thirty-second lecture on Marie's disease.

Eight handshakes later, Frank was on his way.

Eighteen hours after that, Doolittle came in at a safe jump height from the south, overshot the island and put the aircraft in a low banking turn. He reached over and shook Frank's hand. "Time to do it Frank. Do a ten count when I say go, then jump. That should put you somewhere on the south side of the island. It's the best I can do in the dark. I'll ditch her in the drink then teleport up to the mother ship. Good luck. Now go."

Frank made it to the exit on seven, counted two more, wrenched the door open, and tumbled out.

What had worried him most was not so much the jump, but not being able to contact Marge. Before and after take-off, he had tried the cell and the satellite phones repeatedly, but the phone system was log-jammed. Then, seven hours out of Seattle the GPS had shut down, which meant there was no more autopilot. Shortly thereafter they lost satellite radios and phone communication completely. Even Doolittle's galactofone stopped working, and they both knew what that meant. Someone, somewhere had pressed a little red button and Madge Chainey's bombs had gone off, and her magma leak theory had evidently been a non-starter. High in the upper atmosphere above Yellowstone, countless billions of tiny sulfuric acid droplets were wreaking havoc with global communications—not to mention Direct TV.

After the loss of the GPS, Doolittle was obliged to hand fly the aircraft and use the on-board inertial navigation system to stay on course. Ever the sailor, Frank found a bag of backup aeronautical charts and mimicked the inertial navigator, using dead reckoning, his eyeballs, and the standby magnetic compass—shaky as it was. When the sun went down, Doolittle flew low and Frank looked for lights. Approaching Noahu, Frank and the inertial navigator were within six nautical miles of each other. "Dang, I'm good," said Frank, " I used paper charts and a sextant all the way from Florida and never missed an island. Take her in, General."

The only downside was Noahu had no lights, other than the one sitting on top of the cell-phone tower. "Look for a flashing red light at about two thousand feet," Frank instructed, "then circle round it from the south and head back over it. If we don't see the frigging thing when we get there, just take her south over the water and I'll swim for it." He felt like Doolittle was Amelia Earhart and he was Fred Noonan, except Fred and Amelia didn't get to jump; so at least he had that going for him.

The light showed up a full minute ahead of schedule.

Frank was right. After plowing through the forest canopy, amputating a bunch of tree branches, and ending up in a dank pool of stagnant forest water, he couldn't move, the pain was too great. So he decided to stay where he was, take a handful of ibuprofen, and get some bed rest. At least, the water was warm. He slept like a half-submerged log.

***

When Frank woke, there were no new pains so he assumed he must have landed okay. He unbuckled the chute and crawled out of his waterbed. He was on a steep hillside, but he had no idea how high he was; he could be near the summit, or a hop, skip and a jump from the beach. All he could see were very tall trees. Since one-legged tree climbing was not appealing, he left the chute hanging as a marker and hobbled uphill, hoping to get above the tree line, or at least find a vantage point. Half an hour later, he found an open area with a small outcropping. It wasn't much. The height of the rock wasn't sufficient to see over the trees below, but it was far enough out for him to make out the summit. The top of the cell-phone tower was just visible.

Frank took a compass bearing and moved out in the direction of the tower. If he remembered anything at all about survival training, it was this: if you don't know where you are or where you're headed, you're lost, and if you're lost, you likely won't make it. Only in the movies do you stumble blindly through the jungle and emerge not ten feet from the chief and his lovely daughter. It took him almost two hours of hobbling and scrambling before he made it to the summit. The ocean view to the south was magnificent. As he expected, all he could see to the north was more jungle and an impassable barrier of high, tree-covered hills. The fully provisioned cavern, complete with candleholders and a large earthenware pot, however, came as a total surprise.

Insofar as Frank Chamberlain was not inquisitive by nature, and had spent the better part of the previous three weeks rebuilding his back cabin, the various goings on of the virgins had passed him by. Not to mention, Marge had made it clear she didn't want him knocking back kava with Barry and his cohorts while a bunch of maidens frolicked about in plain sight wearing next to nothing—although, he did remember the occasional helicopter flying to-and-fro.

"So, this is where they were going, the sly bastards," he chuckled, when he came across the cavern. "I guess somebody decided to take the virgins out of Virgin Beach."

He made his way to the south-facing overlook beyond the entrance to the cave and looked down. Far below, he sighted the lagoon. *Mary Rose* lay peacefully at anchor. A column of black smoke rose lazily from the village. At the sight of the smoke, he grabbed urgently for his binoculars and trained them on the sailboat. There was no dinghy, there was no sign of Hilda, and there was no sign of Marge.

He panned the binoculars across the water to the island.

The village was a blackened ruin shrouded in smoke. He made out four large outrigger canoes dragged in close to Barry's table, which was lying on its side under the collapsed umbrella. The fishing canoes were beached in their usual spot. Pulled up on the beach, several yards from the canoes, was his dinghy, or at least what was left of it. The outboard motor was missing and one of the pontoons was torn to shreds.

Not far from the dinghy were four smoking mounds littered with banana leaves.

Other than that, the beach was deserted.

He put the binoculars away and reached for the VHF handheld. "Mary Rose, Mary Rose, Jimmy the Fish, Jimmy the Fish, this is Frank. Anybody, come back please." He tried twice more then dropped his backpack and fished out the disassembled HK assault rifle.

It took Frank the rest of the morning to make it down from the mountain. There were still no signs of life on the beach, but he could hear faint sounds of chanting from the village. He thought about that for a few moments, then looked across the water to where his boat was anchored. 'It doesn't much matter what's going on in the village, Frank,' he told himself. 'Right now, you've got two choices: you can check out the boat or you can check out the choir, but either way you're going to check out the frigging choir, so they can wait.'

He stashed the backpack and the HK close to the chain-link fence, took off his boots, and waded into the surf armed only with the commando knife, wondering about the crocodiles, but not in a mood to give a damn.

***

The *Mary Rose* was a shambles.

He paused at the foot of the companionway and let the rage wash over him until it was gone and he could think straight. Charts and the rest of his papers from the chart drawer were crumpled and strewn across the cabin floor. Clothes were piled on the dining table. Closet doors hung open. The single sideband radio had been smashed, along with the radar display and the chart plotter. There were holes and wires hanging out where the stereo unit and the VHF radio had been. Books and magazines were acattered everywhere. The galley cupboards had been emptied, apart from a few cans of dog food and Marge's spice collection. The refrigerator and freezer compartment hatches stood open.

Frank climbed the companionway steps back to the cockpit and sat down. His mind was empty—devoid of emotion, devoid of intent. His chest hurt, though, deep down under his ribs, as if a knife had been shoved in and left there. He supposed he should feel grief-stricken, or berserk with rage, or something, but he didn't. Apart from the knife buried in his chest, he didn't feel much of anything. So he sat for a time and looked at his feet, and thought about things. More accurately, he let his mind wander, because that's what it wanted to do.

Then he went downstairs and checked the refrigerator. All the fresh food was gone, but some used items were still there. Among them was the old pot of Grenadian nutmeg jelly, which neither of them had tried a second time, although Marge had not been willing to come right out and say she didn't like it, which was why it was still sitting there, waiting patiently for her to come clean. Frank would have ditched the jelly months ago, but he had learned a thing or two about women and refrigerators, and what he had learned was this: never make disparaging remarks about aging leftovers, never get rid of half empty jars or other like containers, and never, ever throw out a Ziploc bag with purply gray stuff in it.

Thus it was that the unloved nutmeg jelly was still there, and Frank had gotten around to thinking about that in the cockpit, and he had recalled the last time he had observed the pot. Sitting next to it had been the black pearl in its tiny Ziploc bag. If Marge had wanted to hide the pearl, the purply gray nutmeg jelly would have been the perfect hiding place; and that is also where she would have concealed a note—he thought.

So it was. The note was there, tightly folded around the black pearl in the tiny plastic bag. Frank wasn't squeamish, but even he had hesitated when it came to putting his hand in the jelly. He unfolded the note, but it didn't say much. Not that he was expecting a memoir, given the circumstances.

> *Frank*
>
> *There is no time. Don't worry about Hilda and me. Some canoes came and they have attacked the village. It must be because of the bombs and the volcano going off, which we have heard about on the radio before it went dead. Everybody on the islands is panicking. Alfredo got me on the VHF and is coming for us in the show tender. The canoes are not far behind. Frank, I don't know where you are. I hope you find this. I will take the handheld. I must go.*
>
> *I love you Frank, please come back*
>
> *Marge*

Frank carefully refolded the note and put it in his breast pocket along with the pearl. Then he returned to the cockpit and studied the four war-canoes for a while. After that, he swam back to the beach, deliberately emptying his mind, leaving only the one thing to think about. When he had put his boots back on and strapped on the backpack, he chambered the HK and set it to single shot. Then, Frank made his way quietly through the trees toward the village. By this time, the usual mid-afternoon rain clouds were gathering from the southeast. Today, though, there was an extra layer of clouds, much higher and coming from the west. The higher clouds were darker and denser than the rain clouds, and they were moving in fast, spreading across the sky.

He thought he knew what that might mean, but he wasn't sure—until it spotted rain, and he saw black streaks on the backs of his hands.

For some reason, the rain seemed to take the urgency out of things, so Frank slowed his approach to the village and he took his time doing what had to be done. When it was done, he shouldered the still warm HK, and stared up at the wooded heights of the old volcano for a long time. He didn't mind that he was soaked from the rain and the swim. He avoided the beach though. He didn't want to think about what might be buried there and still smoking, despite the rain. He didn't want to find out. A debt had been paid and there would be no more digging.

He reached the cavern six hours later. By then, it was dark and the black rain was a steady downpour. It was dark because the ash-filled clouds now covered half the sky, and the sun was no longer where it should have been. He supposed the experts must have gotten it wrong again—as usual. He also supposed he wouldn't be going anywhere for a while.

The knife in his chest didn't seem to be going anywhere, either.

CHAPTER 57

Ringside

The Atomic Energy Commission foresaw some problems with this program…

Department of Energy report on Project Plowshare

This will be a short chapter because the defining event didn't take that long—less than half a second, as a matter of fact.

Picture a quiet scene, if you will, out on the observation deck of the YVO. It is another heart-breaking sunset. The vast and magical mountainous domain seems to go on forever. There is, however, an absence of birds, wolves, bears, jackrabbits, and badgers, but we know why that is and we wish them well in their new habitats. Above all, everywhere is strangely calm. Even the trees seem to be holding their breath; they are that still. Somewhere in the servants quarters a TV murmurs. But it is outside we want to be on a night like tonight.

We were up at dawn because Vernon had finally agreed to give us that tour of the park he's been promising. It was an all-day affair, pretty much like a safari without the guns, according to Giovanni, who has shot a lot of animals in Africa, although he didn't seem to think much of what we saw by way of big game—just a few elk wandering about, and even they didn't seem at all well. The servants were not here when we got back, and if the ungrateful bastards know what's good for them, they'd better not be here in the morning.

So we are pleasantly tired now, and looking forward to beverages, which Dick Derringer is kindly preparing, and we have all convinced ourselves there is no cause for alarm. Dick and Vernon, you see, never thought there was a problem in the first place. Steve, recently arrived from his groundbreaking ceremony for Garbage World in New Orleans, is a firm believer in prognostications coming out of Pingyang. Doctor Clump, back from counting birds in Botswana, is steadfastly unconcerned for reasons he has already stated and with which we are familiar. Giovanni Garibaldi, eagerly awaiting the first week's tally from his recently opened Shovel Houses, also thinks Edward Clump has hit the nail on the head.

In short, it is time to open a fresh bottle of Balvenie, or in Dick and Vernon's case, break out a six-pack of Michelob, and consider the possibilities. The possibilities, according to Garibaldi, are endless, starting with the Villas at Lava Lake, which are now going for a song. Apart from which, there is always the nuclear hardened safe room in the event something untoward should ever happen (and always assuming one can get to it in time).

If you prefer, we can be detached about what happens next—like the proverbial fly on the wall, so to speak.

***

First, the abandoned coal mine outside of Salt Lake City was stuffed full of atom bombs (a.k.a. nuclear devices, which is such a neat expression—atom bombs not sounding at all appropriate, ever since that unfortunate business in Japan). Then, all *nonevent-related personnel* were *evacuated; this being done mostly for reasons of personal safety*. You should know the italicized bits in the foregoing sentence were lifted verbatim from an official document explaining how to set off atom bombs underground. Reading it, leads one to wonder what reasons *other* than personal safety might persuade you it was time to get the fuck out. Also, if you were a *nonevent-related person*, what in the name of creation would you be doing down there in the first place?

After all *nonevent-related personnel* had departed, a four-man *event-related* team armed the weaponry. Then the four-man team also left, carrying the detonator switch ever so carefully to a nearby government-owned Fanjet Falcon. Two hours later, at precisely 22:00 Central Daylight Time, flying over Fort Smith, Arkansas, an *event-related person* got the go-ahead from Gladys Rumsfoiled, pressed the little red button, and was heard to say, "Hey, y'all, watch this."

Coincidentally, this was not the first time such a phrase had been uttered in the vicinity of Fort Smith.

As Einstein's famous equation predicted, within milliseconds the bombs vaporized, along with billions of tons of adjacent rock. Think of a gigantic underground cavern suddenly opening up in the shape of a sphere big enough to fit Baltimore several hundred times over. Think of gasses inside the cavern cooling instantly to form a puddle of molten rock the size of Lake Michigan. Think of the outer edges of that cavern breaking through to the ocean of magma lying beneath Yellowstone National Park. Think of the shock wave and the pressure from all those expanding gasses hitting that ocean of magma.

An hour or so later, when the gasses had cooled some more and there wasn't enough pressure to support it, the cavern roof collapsed. Thus it was that the biggest sinkhole in the entire history of the Universe was formed, and into it slid what was left of Salt Lake City. Not to mention what was left of the ocean of magma formerly situated beneath Yellowstone National Park—which wasn't that much. Most of it, you see, had rocketed skywards.

As you might imagine, nobody made it to the safe room.

What Vernon found astonishing was the way Dick Derringer vaporized in advance of his beer can. Thus, for the briefest possible instant in time, Vernon Trumboy was astonished and a can of recently chilled Michelob hung tilted in mid air, as if the invisible man himself were taking a swig. Then there was no beer can, no fly, no wall, and, of course, no Vernon.

CHAPTER 58

A Happy Ending

Well, More or Less

Jesús and Mandy are in the control cab watching a fiery crimson glow cover half the sky. The other half of the sky, where the sunset used to be, is black and all used up like charcoal. Soon, the crimson turns to a brooding purple haze then gradually fades to utter darkness—for what promises to be a very long time. Far beneath, the earth still kicks and trembles, but the booming outside is muffled now and smoothed by the thick glass. Jesús is convinced he can smell toast burning. Samuel Barber's *Adagio for Strings* plays softly in the background. The red emergency lighting casts a lambent pall of irrevocable doom over the assembled survivors.

Mandy turns to him, eyes welling with tears. "It really is the end of all life as we know it, isn't it? I'm scared, Jesús. How could this happen? Why were we chosen to survive? What does it all mean? I'm so confused."

Jesús gently squeezed her shoulders.

"I'm not so sure it *has* to mean anything, my love. You know, some idiot once said 'We are naught but products of our very own curious and peculiar circumstances.'"

Mandy seemed puzzled.

Undaunted, Jesús pressed on. "For some reason, that just came back to me. When I first read it, I thought it was stupid too. Now, I'm not so sure." He looked skywards; rather like Einstein contemplating Jupiter. "Maybe that's it. Maybe that's all we are, really—just little random happenings. I was a History major, you know, so useless stuff tends to stick in my head. Peter the Great summed it up nicely on his deathbed. 'Nothing matters' he said. Those were his final words." Jesús was warming to his topic now. He paused, searching for the right thing to say. When he turned to Mandy, he had the look of a man on the brink of some divine truth. He weighed each phrase carefully, speaking with calm deliberation. "Look at this way. Just for starters, being born is like a zillion to one shot; after which, genes pretty much take care of the rest. Family is luck of the draw. Then teachers we didn't ask for tell us about stuff we don't want to know. Then we get jobs where certifiable lunatics make us do crazy shit that makes no sense. On top of that, the government grabs all it can from us and spends it on even crazier shit. Not to mention normal shit happens all the time. So, where, for Pete's sake, is the meaning in all of that?" He shrugged despondently. "Life, my sweet, if you want my opinion, is just one long frigging crawl to the grave."

It was like feeding strawberries to a donkey. She went for it. She didn't even hesitate for a second. "Oh, you're always so negative!" Mandy cried on cue. "There's always hope; there's always something to be done, Jesús. Think of the serenity prayer. I do. Whenever things get bad, it really helps keep me going." Mandy gazed up to where the heavens used to be and prayed softly. "'God, give us grace to accept with serenity, the things that cannot be changed, courage to change the things that must be changed, and the wisdom to distinguish the one from the other.'"

Jesús gave her another squeeze. "Personally," he said, "I prefer Mother Goose."

She turned to him in bewilderment. "Mother Goose? What, in God's name, are you talking about now?"

"It goes like this," he said. "'For every ailment under the sun, there is a remedy, or there is none. If there be one, try to find it; if there be none, never mind it.'"

"But that's just the same thing," she protested.

"I know," he said, "but Mother Goose said it first, and anyway, it rhymes."

EPILOGUE

One Year Later

He had often wondered who would drink the last bottle of wine on Earth. Where would they drink it? Would they be alone? When would it happen? Would they even know it was the last bottle? What kind of wine would it be? You know, the sort of deep searching questions we all ask ourselves from time to time.

Well, as far as he could tell, he was about to be Mister Lucky and he was going to finish the bottle right here and right now in this goddamned piece-of-shit cave. As for when: he didn't know when. He had thrown away his watch shortly after settling in. He had been checking it obsessively—so much so the damn thing had been driving him crazy. He soon discovered that knowing what day it was slowed time to a crawl, and *that* he definitely didn't need. Now he had no idea what month it was, let alone what day of the week. He hadn't given a monkey's toss what day it was since he pitched the watch. When didn't matter anymore.

There was no when.

"All that bullshit about counting off the days and scratching useless marks on a wall—what good did that ever do? Who was it? Gertrude Stein? She was famous for saying *when you get there, there is no there*. Well, I have news for you, Gertrude: when you get there, not only is there no there, there is no fucking when, either."

What really mattered was that he was down to his last bottle. *Maybe the very last bottle of wine on Planet Earth!* Whereas this was a momentous event in the history of the world, it was bad news for Frank Chamberlain personally. The good news was that it was a large bottle—a liter and a half. He also had a cup, a corkscrew, and a boulder to sit on. He even had a pot to piss in, well, the vote-counting pot, actually.

"Why not go outside, you might ask?" he demanded of the earthenware pot. "'Why bother dumping in me? Why not go out there and do it in what's left of the goddamn wilderness?' Well, I'll tell you why, Percy the Pot, old son. Bears get to crap where they please because they own the place, that's why. You crap in their backyard they'll come looking for you. So I fill you up, my boy, then I take you to the nearest cliff and empty you out, because you never know, do you?" He grinned mirthlessly. "Mind you, I haven't seen a bear since the Lord knows when, this being the wrong part of the frigging world. Still, something big lives out there, Percy, old chap. I've heard it shuffling about in the dark. You can even smell where it's been. It grunts and growls too—shits wherever and whenever it wants to." The grin vanished. "Why the hell am I talking to a cheap earthenware pot? Because no one else will listen, that's why. What am I saying? There is no one else. I don't even have a dog anymore, for Christ's sake."

Frank sat down on a boulder and carefully removed the composite cork from the bottle of wine: a 2025 Yellow Tail Australian Shiraz. He reached for his penlight so he could read the label, the candles having run out after the first few months of darkness. "How's that for a game of soldiers? Would you look at that? Does this get the coincidence award or what? Our final toast will therefore be: a Yellow Tail, for Yellowstone, without the sudden disappearance of which, we would not be celebrating this momentous occasion."

He removed his smog mask, poured the violet liquid into a green plastic cup, and raised the cup reverently before drinking. He drank eagerly and silently until the cup was emptied.

Then he poured himself another.

Midway through the third cup, Frank Chamberlain started to weep. Grief rose from a deep well to fill his chest. Tears flowed until they dripped from his chin. After which, he continued grieving, and drinking, and weeping until the wine, the grief and the tears were all gone. It had gotten to be a habit. Soon, he fell asleep, drugged by the wine and exhausted by emotion, but it didn't last. He woke early, still dulled from the wine, then he slept fitfully until daybreak, except the days didn't break anymore. He didn't eat. What was the point? He took an empty Percy the Pot for the walk, though, through force of habit, and carried the pot to the cliff edge. He felt his way through the trees towards the sound of the river, conserving the flashlight batteries as usual, not wanting to be noticed by whatever it was that was out there, then reminding himself he no longer gave a damn, and why had he even bothered to bring Percy in the first place, and realizing he had arrived anyway.

***

Ever since the darkness came there had been constant downpours. The river was easy to find because it was in permanent flood, roaring and cascading into the remnants of jungle below. He avoided the downpours, and he sure as hell didn't drink the water without boiling it twice over; it made the old acid rain seem like Seven-Up.

The chasm was deep. He knew that. Just to be sure, he threw Percy as high and as wide as he could. Then he closed his eyes to listen. He counted off the seconds until he heard a faint splash from far below. Now it was his turn. He raised his face to the heavens one last time. Then he felt a hint of warmth and opened his eyes. A thin sliver of amber light shone through a growing tear in the blackness. What had been utter darkness was fast turning to mere gloom.

"For Christ's sake," Frank muttered. "It's breaking through. The fucking sun is back."

He smiled for the first time in at least a year. "Hey, Percy," he yelled. "Sorry about that, pal, I guess I won't be joining you after all."

***

Now, when you set out to jump from a cliff, you aren't likely to take much of anything with you, least of all a Heckler & Koch G36 assault rifle, or a British commando knife, circa 1942. In Frank Chamberlain's case, this understandable lack of foresight turned out to be a serious mistake.

He heard it first, before he saw—a deep, coughing grunt—somewhere between a pouncing tiger and a charging rhinoceros. When he turned, the biggest wild boar he could imagine was not five paces away. Its enormous head heaved up and down. The tusks gouged great clods of dirt. Even in the gloom he could make out two tiny eyes, glowing like coals. Worst of all, he could smell the beast. It had the stench of death on its breath. Blood came out of its mouth and nostrils, congealing on the tusks and spraying outwards with each shake of the head. In the monochromatic half-light, the blood glistened like hot tar.

Over time, Frank Chamberlain had developed a battery of protective instincts and reflexes. Now, none of them kicked in. He was paralyzed. His mind bloomed with one final, all absorbing thought: 'The poor fucker's dying; it's got Marie's disease. This is it. I'm so sorry, Marge.' Marie's disease or not, all at once the boar shook its head in a frenzy and charged.

A gray blur came out of nowhere. Then the boar wasn't there anymore. The impact carried the boar and the dog all the way to the cliff edge. Frank snapped out of it. He grabbed for the boar's thrashing hind legs, wrestled them apart, and hauled the animals back from the drop. Something or someone screamed. It must have been him. It certainly wasn't Hilda. Her massive jaws were buried deep in the boar's throat. One of her front legs had caught in the tusks and flopped uselessly. She embraced the boar with her other leg, pulling and holding the flailing beast close like a jealous lover. Blood poured from Hilda's shoulder and gouted from the boar's neck.

Frank screamed again.

Alfredo finished it with his machete.

"So what took you so long, Jimmy?" asked Frank when he got his breath back.

"Marge is right behind with George and Barry. We've all been holed up with the girls in the Empire State Building,"Alfredo answered with a huge grin. "She's been sick with worry, Frank. Barry's been doing mind melds for almost a year now, but it's been so bleeding dark he had no idea where you were, mate. Trouble is, we didn't know if you'd even made it back to the island. All Barry knew was you were still alive and pissed as a fart all the time."

Frank gaped. "What do you mean, the Empire frigging State Building? What the hell are you talking about?"

"We had it built for the show, Frank. It's on the other side of the island."

"Well, nobody told *me* about it."

"You never asked," Alfredo responded patiently, "you were too busy fixing that back cabin of yours."

"Anyway, what in God's name is a mind meld?"

"Don't even go there," cautioned Alfredo, his patience wearing thin, "you wouldn't have a clue. Anyway, not long ago Barry tried again, and he could just make you out on this cliff, getting ready to jump. We knew it had to be some time in the future because it was still black as coal where we were. So Barry said, what the fuck, we'd better get going. Of course, he actually said it in Pidgin. So here we are."

Frank Chamberlain let out a deep, prolonged sigh and sank to his knees. Suddenly, he felt weak. He looked down at his hands. They were shaking. Then he looked at Hilda. She was struggling to sit up, watching him all the while with intense, sad eyes.

"Hilda," he said, "I take back everything I ever said about you. Now listen, girl, just you lie back down and hang in there. Your mom is the best combat nurse that ever was. She'll fix you up in no time." He unbuttoned his breast pocket and fished out the black pearl with trembling fingers. "And when she gets here, we'll give her the best frigging present she could ever ask for."

FIN

A BRIEF AFTERWORD

Which Also Contains Cosmic Thoughts

Let me remind you that *Yellowstone Four* is a work of fiction and therefore prone to exaggeration. Would a fourth Yellowstone eruption really be a global extinction event? I don't know for sure, but others better qualified than I believe so. Would it trigger the next ice age? Probably. When will it happen? I have no idea. Will praying help? What do you think? Will nice people be raptured? No comment.

But consider this: as recently as seventy-three thousand years ago, Lake Toba erupted on the island we now know as Sumatra. Toba was a mega-colossal event that reduced *Homo-sapiens* to less than ten thousand mating pairs, possibly as few as one thousand. Evidently, if some divine being had a Cosmic Protected Species List back then we were not on it, and I'm willing to bet we still aren't, *pre-trib-rap* notwithstanding.

Go figure.

As to acknowledgments: my everlasting gratitude goes to my wife, Marty, for her dedication and diligence in combing through the first gestations of the manuscript, to Kathryn Lynn Davis for a thoroughly professional read, an unflinching critique, and extraordinary words of encouragement, and to William Sudah for taking a chance.